MONIKA CARLESS

THE
WILDERNESS
YEARS

BOOK 3 OF THE DARK POOL TRILOGY

STONE'S THROW
PUBLICATIONS

Cover design by Sue Reynolds, Stone's Throw Publication Services
Cover images: bigstockphoto.com
Interior Layout and Design: James Dewar

ISBN: 978-1-987813-26-5 (book)
ISBN: 978-1-987813-27-2 (e-book)

Published by Stone's Throw Publications
Port Perry, Ontario, Canada
www.stonesthrowps.ca

1 2 3 4 5 6 7 8 9 10

We were together. I forget the rest

~ Walt Whitman

Dedication

For Aiden
You believed I could

Acknowledgements

Sue and James at Stone's Throw Publications; such gratitude for your beautiful cover art and the process of publication. I've loved the journey.

Brenda Jackson-Mead, thank you for your keen editing eye and constant love. You've been my encouragement since the beginning and have understood me. It's everything.

To my daughters, Elizabeth and Jessika - the earth beneath my feet. Sorry, not sorry I wrote erotica!

To my devoted readers; thank you for your heartfelt messages. Pure gold.

Steve, my rock. There are no words for the belief you have poured into me. Eternal gratitude and love.

Before There Was You, There was a Space in My Heart That Waited

For Kate

I want to feel it all today—with you.

The fire of our beginning and the burn of our ending.

I find myself counting up the years we could have together and wishing that we had met a century or two ago so I could look into the future and not see a horizon.

Centuries with you don't scare me but horizons do, even if it is bathed in the sweetest sunset I have ever seen. You are the sun that spreads itself across the sky in brilliant hues of amber and vermilion, filling my eyes with impossible dreams.

You are the inconceivable made real, the rise of a flock of sparrows into a cerulean sky.

In the beauty of your love, there has been an awakening of my soul. That which has been born within me now feeds the moments of each day we share. It is the manna for the hungry, an artesian well hidden in the dusty Sahara.

I want to feel it all today, the ache of being apart, the searing anticipation of being together, the insecurities that haunt me—the fire that singes the corners of my being.

I want to feel what it would be like to watch you walk away. It's not the ranting of madness, it's the allowing space for whatever will be, and loving you through every motion of the wheel that spins us together.

I would like to know what it would be like to hold your hand when it is wrinkled and soft because we've grown into wise old souls, and to know that your hand would still be in mine while I draw my last breath.

I would like to drown in the youth of your body as it is now and offer you mine and for what are just seconds in the face of eternity. I want to draw every ounce of passion from your skin. I would like to paint the essence of my rawness onto you like a tattoo. I would like to wear you also.

Today I feel the intensity of when we were not yet, and what is now, and ours no more. It is all beautiful in its own way. It is all a part of what makes us real.

If you were a painting you would be a Monet, a garden made of my own inspiration, my own impressions, a symphony of colors that translated onto canvas was only a shadow of the depth of my feelings—because those I could not share wholly with the world—some things are only for you and me.

I want to feel it all today, what makes us and what unmakes us, what is real and what is soaked in fear, the shadow lands and the fullness of the moon on our faces.

Our love appeared as an approaching wave, a mirage of aquamarine and frothy whites. It threatened to drown me, then, cocooning me in the sanctuary of its belly, offered respite from the years of searching for you.

"And then there was you," is how I begin the stories that I recount to myself at night when I want to remember how we started. You found me. Today I want to feel again what it was like before there was you—it's becoming difficult to remember that me.

Before there was you there was a space in my heart that waited.

When there was you, I unfolded my wings and testing their strength, leapt from the edge of what was known into the abyss. I'm still on the wing—flying an uncharted course. But, that is all I ever really wanted—to be free even as I was the taken.

I want to feel it all today. Your kiss, your smile, your words as they caress me.

On this journey, I would like to know you as a wolf knows the call of its pack, to be embraced, to be lonely, to be the huntress and the hunted—to be consumed.

Today, we are the dawn, one day we will be the dusk.

I want to feel it all. With you.

Original publication @ elephant journal.

Foreword

Myths, fairy tales, our personal stories - create culture and help us to understand each other and our environment.

Once upon a time, I set out to write a trilogy. Conversations with Spirit led to a connection with Aiden, my intra-dimensional guide. This book is for him. He knew what lay inside my soul, and the story that required breathing into life. He continues to be available to me and many others who seek inspiration from the outer realms.

The Dark Pool trilogy became the portal through which I stepped into my work as an intuitive coach. We rarely know what lies ahead of us when we begin a project. I barely recognize the woman who began this one. But that is the magic of dancing with possibility.

Blessed be, Wild Ones. May this erotic fairy tale be a portal for you as well.

THE WILDERNESS YEARS

"You were born together, and together you shall be forevermore.
You shall be together when the white wings of death scatter your days.
Ay, you shall be together even in the silent memory of God.
But let there be spaces in your togetherness,
And let the winds of the heavens dance between you.
Love one another, but make not a bond of love:
Let it rather be a moving sea between the shores of your souls.
Fill each other's cup but drink not from one cup.
Give one another of your bread but eat not from the same loaf.
Sing and dance together and be joyous, but let each one of you be alone,
Even as the strings of a lute are alone
though they quiver with the same music.
Give your hearts, but not into each other's keeping.
For only the hand of Life can contain your hearts.
And stand together yet not too near together:
For the pillars of the temple stand apart,
And the oak tree and the cypress grow not in each other's shadow."

~ Kahlil Gibran

CHAPTER 1

Follow her down the silent path
Past willowy trees and the shadows they cast
Follow her though you know you'll be lost
Past streams and marshes, tripping over rocks
Follow her quickly, she knows the way
Soon the moon—she says with a sway
Of her hips and a smile on her lips
A smile so secret that there's no key to unlock
what she means when she leads you
On and on, deeper and deeper
Yes! I know the way!
She says when your grip tightens on her sleeve
Don't worry my love, soon the moon
Soon the light will come your way
And then you'll know why I've brought you here
Follow me there is nothing to fear
Follow me the way is clear
And you follow like a child though you've lived a century or more
Luna your mistress
Like a moth to a flame

Dagr rode toward the sunrise on the horizon. He had urged his horse into a dangerous gallop, face ripped raw from the wind, as was his heart with the anguished sobs escaping from Brigida's mouth. She was held securely in his tight grip, her own hands clenched into fists through the horse's thick, black mane. Her head hung low. Her body shook with grief.

He hardened himself against what he had done; against the impulse to simply lie on the ground weeping. The hand he kept on the reins was numb with cold. He wished he had the courage to turn around and reverse his decision, but he did not.

Quite unsuccessfully, he attempted to push away the images which forced their way into his brain; Arinn at his feet begging forgiveness, Richard's astonished and pained face, Brigida's horror. All these things were like poison to his soul, reminding him that he had chosen to leave his beloved behind.

Only Brigida's constant wails of grief brought him back to the task at hand; getting them safely to the coast and on a boat to Calais.

But how could he leave his beloved country without Arinn at his side? How could he continue a life without her? How could he ever entertain happiness knowing she was forever wounded by his anger and his lack of trust in her? Knowing that she was forsaken to Richard's care?

They did not stop until the sun was firmly settled into the morning sky. No one had followed them and Dagr felt reasonably safe. He slowed to a canter then a walk, the great war-horse he sat upon frothing at the mouth and slathered in sweat. The beast was too old for such exertions now.

Dismounting under the cover of a coppice of trees, Dagr lifted the forlorn Brigida into his arms and held her against his heart. He had no words of comfort, nothing but his body heat and his lips pressed to her forehead.

"Drink!" He handed her a flask of mead. "We will ride until dark. I know of a place we can stay for the night."

When she did not answer, he lifted her chin to meet his gaze. He was shocked at the emptiness in her eyes. His heart broke all over again.

Brigida took the flask and drank obediently. Then, she left his side and finding a spot in the woods, relieved herself. Dagr kept guard until she was done then opened the satchel of goods Richard had given him. Quickly, he helped Brigida into warmer men's clothing. He tucked her hair into a cap and observed her transformation into a rather skinny, bedraggled impression of a farm boy. In spite of himself, he smiled. Her lips were too full, her cheeks a bit too high, but with a bit more dirt on her face perhaps they could make a go of the disguise.

"I will need your help with something, my lady."

Dagr fished deeper into the bag.

Brigida looked up, curious. "What is it my lord?" she asked, voice courteous but flat.

Dagr winced, feeling the distance between them.

"Take these scissors and cut my hair," he said. Finally, some spirit in her eyes!

"No!" She shook her head and retreated.

"My lady?"

"Are we to cut everything from us? Will you not leave me this one joy?"

"I must," he replied, voice hard with regret. "It will grow again."

She seemed to measure his resolve silently then took the scissors from his hand.

"Careful, they are very sharp!" Dagr admonished, lowering to his knees to come within her reach.

Brigida nodded.

They were both caught in the memory of how he had once acquiesced to a similar request from her, not so long ago. Dagr's waist-long hair fell to the ground, and with it years of their journey together. She cut it to his shoulders, the length it had been when she had first become his lady.

Eyes brimming with tears, Brigida dropped the scissors at his feet and turned away. She stood despondent while he prepared for the road, whispering against the horse's neck, stroking his flank. Dagr watched and hungered for the moment when he could become her solace again. If she let him. If she loved him still. There was no hiding his tears from her now.

Placing her behind him, Dagr steered out of the coppice and broke into a brisk canter. He wanted to save his horse a little, because he could not bear the idea of trading him along the journey if he became overtired or lame. They would have to adjust to the great beast's needs. If all went well, and they did not meet trouble along the way, they could sleep by a fire tonight. He touched his sword out of habit. Brigida's arms tightened around his waist. It was the smallest of gestures, but it gave him hope.

"May we not stop my lord?" Brigida shouted, her body aching to be on solid ground.

"Not much further now!"

The light was waning and the landscape had changed dramatically after a whole day in the saddle. Dagr was fairly sure that he could find comfortable accommodations for them in the village they approached. Only one thing worried him—the nagging feeling of a pair of eyes at his back. Sometime around high noon, he had begun to sense someone tracking them. Whoever was behind them was an expert at staying in the shadows. He thought about the hoof prints he had discovered at his and Richard's meeting place by the Oracle Wood. If it was the same man, then he would have to change his plans for staying in the village. He hoped not, because he feared Brigida's succumbing to road weariness. Perhaps it was a lone robber. There were many hidden in the woods waiting for travelers. It was not a group, of this he was sure. Either way, Dagr knew that he would have to keep his warrior instincts sharp.

Brigida looked up hopefully as a small cluster of stone houses appeared in the distance.

"There!" she pointed.

They rode in silence approaching the village from the hills behind it. The wind was fiercer here, the valley dotted with sheep and slippery footings as the rain began to fall in great, pelting sheets.

"My lord let us stop!" Brigida insisted.

Dagr steered them into a dark alley then pulled up smartly at the only light visible. They had been abandoned as they had left the edge of the tree line. *He will wait until we are on the open road once more,* Dagr thought. He knew this land well, having ridden it many times on his way to the coast when leaving on the King's business. He made a plan for the morning ride.

Grateful for the purse Richard had left him, Dagr tossed a coin at the stable boy and gave his instructions. He knocked on the public house door, Brigida standing behind him, shivering in her wet clothes.

He shoved his hand through the door showing a coin that was sure to buy a night's sleep, some food and maybe even a tub of hot water for Brigida. He was inspected suspiciously but the coin left his hand in a hurry.

"A room and some supper, kind lady?"

"Yea, we have that. Will you be wanting a fire... that costs more."

"A room with a fire and a hot bath."

"Ah, that will be our finest room, m'lord."

Dagr nodded and placed another coin in the grubby hand. The woman's eyes were kind. He smiled and received a gap-toothed grin in return.

"Will your lad be needin' a place in the stable?"

"No, he will sleep at my door."

Dagr felt Brigida's instant distress. It was common for the servant boy to sleep at the foot of his master's door.

"We will take our supper in the room."

He spoke with authority and expected no argument. None was given.

"And what about the mornin'?" the woman asked hopefully.

"We will take our leave early. No need to tend to us."

The old woman nodded. "I will be grateful for that, m'lord. Go there to the top of the stairs. I will send the lad to light the fire and fill the bath."

Dagr bowed politely, noticing from a quick glance around the room that they were most likely the only travelers. He expected the bedding to be filthy and the fire to be meager. He was right. The best room faced the street and as he placed the candle given him on the rickety desk by the window, he noticed the crumpled sheets on the tiny bed. The hearth looked as if it had been abandoned for months. Brigida began to cry from exhaustion and nerves.

Dagr was about to take her in his arms when there was a knock at the door; the stable lad appeared with a bundle of firewood. He took it from him, ordered more and the hot water for the bath.

"I will light the fire first, m'lord?" The bewildered boy craned his neck upward to look Dagr in the eye.

"I will light the fire, lad, go fetch the water."

The boy stood dumbfounded.

"Now, lad!" Dagr insisted and laughed under his breath as the lad scurried off.

"My lady, do not worry, soon there will be a hot bath for you and supper." He set to making a fire, hoping the chimney was not stuffed full of bird nests.

"Will I have to sleep at your door, my lord?" Brigida whispered.

He caught her in his arms. "You will sleep against me, my lady!"

She looked at him with grateful eyes. She had nothing left. She was spent from grief and worry. They melted into each other, savoring the moment.

Soon the fire was making a smoky effort. Brigida sat huddled before it. Dagr sent the boy for more wood once the tiny bathtub had been filled. Clearly, he would not be able to fit in it once Brigida had had her turn. Perhaps he could warm his feet. He shuddered thinking about when it had last been cleaned.

"We may not have this kind of luxury each night," he warned.

They burst into quiet laughter in spite of themselves. Brigida was stripped bare and standing in the tub as he scrubbed her briskly, not daring to sit her down fully, fearing the dirt at the bottom. She was back in her riding clothes as the boy appeared with two bowls of greasy soup.

"M'lady says this is her best lamb stew. If ye wants bread..."

"...It will cost more." Dagr tossed a coin at the boy and sent him back to the kitchen.

"Lamb, my foot," he muttered to Brigida as they tasted the swill in the bowl. "Five-year-old mutton more likely."

But they ate quickly. It was warm and coated their stomachs against the coming cold. The fire would not last the night. He looked forward to the body heat they could share.

5

"Tell me a story, my lord. About the sun," Brigida asked as they lay curled up in the lumpy bed wrapped in their cloaks avoiding the pillows stuffed with stinky straw.

"Ah, the sun, my lady," Dagr began. "Where we are going, the sun is much warmer than you have ever felt. So warm, in fact, that you will hide from it in the afternoon, seeking shelter in the shade of the trees."

"No! It cannot be. This place we are going to... is it far from the Great Sea you told us about?" Fresh tears appeared as Brigida thought of Arinn.

Dagr held her tighter. "Not far, my lady. Two days ride. I give my word to take you there."

"The water?" Brigida prompted.

"The water is clear to the bottom near the shore, and warm like the warmest bath, full of beautiful pebbles and shells that we will gather. We shall play in the waves, my lady, and make a fire by moonlight and look up at the stars."

"Tell me about the sun when it sets, and the warm nights, my lord."

And he told her all the stories he had told her before, until she lay sleeping soundly. Only then he allowed himself some rest.

CHAPTER 2

They woke up while dark still surrounded them, in the smothering, fetid confines of the room.

They tore at the dry husk of bread they had saved from their supper and shared the flask of bitter ale left at their door by the stable boy who stood half-asleep in the street, horse at ready.

Dagr led them through the village knowing full well he did not have the luxury of confronting his follower alone, he would have to do so with Brigida in tow. This worried him, but he had few choices, as leaving her in the scrub while he looked for the man was not an option. He had done that once before and lost her. So now he hoped that his idea of quickly looping back into the woods and employing surprise would work. Common robbers were often quite daft, making avoidable mistakes in judgement. Perhaps this one was too.

He had said nothing to Brigida. He wanted to afford her as much time ignorant of the follower as possible. They rounded the corner toward the village square, the mist heavy and wet. Visibility was worse than he had expected—good cover for them but also for anyone else. His arm tightened around Brigida. She pushed back against him. He smiled, then stiffened as he heard the snort of a horse directly to his right. The flank of that invisible creature brushed his foot next and in that instant he had drawn his sword and jumped off, slapping his horse on the rump in their trusted signal for his mount to take cover. He had to hope Brigida would stay in the saddle, ignoring her cry of bewilderment.

Ready for battle, Dagr pulled the rider from his horse and had him pinned to the ground in seconds. Somehow, he had hoped that his killing days were over. He felt a rush of nausea at the idea of more violence when a familiar voice and the sharp recognition that followed caught him completely off guard. He lowered his arm and pulled the man to his feet, then tore at the hood which covered his head.

They stared at each other for long seconds, Dagr reeling with shock. Their embrace was quick but fervent.

"Mark!"

"My lord!" Dagr's bailiff from days past, Brigida's brother, bowed his head.

Dagr whistled for his horse while shaking Mark by his shoulders. "I thought you long dead! Brigida is with me!"

"I know. I have been shadowing you for all the time you were in hiding... keeping watch over the Earl as well. I was just waiting for the right time to make myself known.

"How have you survived? Where have you lived? Did you speak to Richard?"

"Yes. I met him on the road away from the Oracle Wood and vowed to serve you." Mark looked down, embarrassed. "My lord, I am sorry for your troubles."

"We will talk later. We must make haste now... here is Brigida! My lady, look!"

Dagr's horse with Brigida clinging to his mane had appeared out of the mist, and there she sat with surprise on her face when she saw the brother she had thought lost to her for good. She slid off the horse and landed at his feet.

"My darling! I thought you dead!"

"So, everyone keeps saying! But I am here now, and you will not be rid of me again!"

"But I may not be able to find passage for you on the ferry," Dagr said, mounting and turning his horse for the road. "Come, let us away."

"I will find my own passage." Mark moved his cloak aside and Dagr noticed the hefty purse at his side. He understood then that Mark had made his way by relieving unlucky sojourners of their resources. They exchanged glances. Survival did not always guarantee keeping one's honor.

Brigida's spirits rose significantly, taking long and wistful looks in her brother's direction as they settled in for another long day's ride. Dagr too, let some of the worry about the trip fall from his shoulders and began to dream about the chateau and the land that awaited his stewardship. Seeing Brigida with a smile on her face almost made his heart escape from his chest. As long as he kept down all other thoughts, he was sure he could survive the next few days.

Just one day at a time, that is what he planned. Dagr looked over at the young man riding at their side, with his swarthy, dark face, worn too much by the wind and the sun, and was grateful for this gift in their lives. Brigida would have her family once more, and he would have a trusted companion.

He knew Mark had not approved of the arrangement Brigida had come into with him and Arinn, he had said so, angry and concerned for Brigida's future. But he had been a loyal bailiff, strong willed and dependable, always keeping his word, always one eye out for his sister's well-being. Dagr respected him. He wondered what he thought of his leaving Arinn behind. This thought brought back a twisting ache and he shut down—a grimace on his face, hands tighter on the reins. Brigida, attuned to his energy, leaned back, offering comfort. But her love only made the pain worse. Arinn!

<hr />

Mark motioned that they stop by a stream winding its way down a rocky hillside. The horses would need watering, and it had been six hard hours in the saddle with hardly a break.

"My lord, may I ask your plan? There are two villages, one within two hours ride and the other, not far beyond. A good inn at the first one, a better inn at the second."

Dagr let his horse to graze and bent down to untie Brigida's boots so she could dip her feet in the stream. He noticed Mark observing with a curious grin. When Brigida had been just growing into womanhood, Mark had tried to discourage her from spending too much time skulking around the barn, spying on the lord of the manor. She had been a wild one, too much for Mark's care at times.

"I remember," Dagr replied. "We will stay at the first. The second is near the home of a man I know very well and cannot say without any doubt it would be safe. I just do not know anymore whom I can trust."

"You can trust me, my lord."

Dagr took Mark by the arm. "Do you know anything about the time Richard had a... erm... run-in with a traveler?" he whispered.

"Yes. I was already following him then. My contact at the castle told me Brigida had run away and that there had been trouble with a certain servant. I swear, my lord, I looked for her in every place she would have had to walk but never found her!"

"Never mind that now. What about the man servant?"

"I found him on the road, speared through. The Earl Dumont had been there just before. I ceased following him to dispose of the body—erase the evidence as it were."

"So, there is nothing which could lead that incident back to the Earl?"

"Nothing. I was thorough, my lord."

Dagr nodded, a little more at ease. "Thank you." He looked at Mark intently. "He has Arinn in his care now. It is important he is not discovered as the one who..."

Mark interrupted. "Nothing will be discovered, my lord. I assure you. And as far as Arinn is concerned, Hannah will see to her care just as she took care of Brigida. Not much gets past her keen knowing. You can find some peace in that."

"Oh, do you know her?" Dagr asked, puzzled.

Mark looked sheepishly at the ground. "I came to the castle here and there, on a ruse to sell goods. I got to know Hannah."

"I am forever in your debt," Dagr replied.

They rode in silence the rest of the day, a certain security having fallen over them all, taking comfort in each other's company. The next few days would bring them to the shore and a new life none of them could completely envision. They could not know if they would ever see England's green beauty again, or what each day would look like without the one they loved.

Mark's dark eyes had never betrayed the desire he had once harbored for the fair Arinn while he had managed Dagr's estate. For all these years he had bitten his tongue and never spoken of his dashed hopes when Arinn had been betrothed to the old warrior whom Dagr later supplanted. He had never even fully admitted to himself how much he had cared for her until he saw her on Richard's horse, broken in spirit. She had looked at him with a surprise and joy that had made his heart leap, but seconds later she had lowered her head and looked away. He did not understand all that had happened, but he knew Dagr would never have left her unless it was a very serious matter. He would find out what. And maybe, after a while, he could find a way for them all to be reunited. Surely, Dagr would not be able to stand her absence. He had many a time seen the raw emotion on Dagr's face as he had followed Arinn around the stable yard with hungry intent. Men like Dagr loved completely. One day, Mark agreed to himself, all would be set right.

He looked quickly in Dagr's direction and returned the kind smile from his one-time lord. His respect and love for Dagr was unconditional. Still, he wondered how one man could have more than his fair share of lovers? But he checked his heart and admonished himself of disloyalty. If he had anything to do with it, he would see the return of Arinn to his sister, who had already suffered far too much. Yes, he would speak of this to Dagr when opportunity arose. There was always hope.

CHAPTER 3

"I need to be silent for a while, worlds are forming in my heart."
~ Meister Eckhart

While the scent of pine receded from the room, while the candles sputtered their dying glow, Aiden opened his eyes to a pained silence. His heart beat with an agonizing slowness, denying what he had just witnessed during the past-life regression with Sahara, Richard and Iona.

Returning to a full awareness of his surroundings, he glanced around the room and seeing Holly still sound asleep, focused his intensity on Iona. She, like a wounded animal, growled and backed away from his reach.

"Iona! Please, come to me," Aiden beckoned, his voice firm, insistent.

"You abandoned me! To a man I barely knew." Iona didn't even glance in Richard's direction. Fully immersed in the pain from her ancient past, she missed the shocked look on her lover's face or that Sahara had taken Richard's hand protectively in hers.

"Forgive me, my lady! Dagr acted too quickly out of fear. It was thoughtless and callous." Still Aiden beckoned, body tense with the need to reconnect with Arinn.

"I deserved it anyhow," Iona hissed, shaking.

"Nobody deserves to be abandoned."

"I caused such harm, such irreparable harm!"

Iona slid into Aiden's arms and succumbed to violent tears. He held her in silence, his own tears in her hair, kissing her forehead and as she turned up her face, fully on the lips. Her mouth opened, she invited him in, climbing into his lap like a child seeking solace or a cat who's been left home alone far too long. Aiden gave up trying to resist her. Memories clashed with the present. He was sure he would regret it later but in this moment; he needed to remember the love he had once thrown away.

From the shadows of the room, Holly found her way to Sahara, and nestled between her beloved and Richard's hard, virile body. She sat wide eyed, teary eyed, watching her man as he begged Iona's forgiveness. He seemed to be in another world, oblivious to her awakening.

"What has happened?" she whispered, her skin tingling with foreboding.

Sahara embraced her. "Darling, there's so much to tell, but the short of it is, this regression has revealed that Dagr went to France without Arinn. In the last moments as they were departing, he sent her away to Richard's care. We don't know yet if they saw each other again, but in any case, it was a brutal parting. Iona has carried her pain for so long, and our man is just realizing Dagr's part in it."

Sahara wiped her eyes as she remembered those moments. Her childless womb made perfect sense now and the love she had felt for Arinn returned full force. She fell into the moment of Brigida and Arinn's parting once more, her breath short and labored.

"Oh, my love! How terrible! I can't imagine..." Holly whispered.

It was as if a spell had been cast over their lives and now in the early morning light with Aiden's house bathed by a few tendrils of searching sun, there was nothing she could do to undo it. Holly turned to Richard, shy as his eyes bored into hers, making sense of the woman before him.

"Are you alright? I mean..." And here the two of them spent a long moment observing the sight of Aiden's hand fisted in Iona's hair, whispering words of comfort, while she clung to him for dear life.

"Thank you, yes, I understand. Perhaps this is not natural in relationships, but I have been with Iona long enough to know convention won't be our style. I suppose these things no longer matter. I wonder..." Richard broke off and furrowed his brow.

"Yes?" Holly let her fingers drift across Richard's jaw. It was a familiar gesture, and it threw him, but he softened under her touch.

"I wonder what happened later. Dagr's story, our story. It's been haunting me."

Richard made room for Holly in the crook of his arm. He looked down at her and marveled at her innocent incarnation as a striking resemblance of Arinn.

"Somehow, although I was not part of your lives then, I am joined with you all in this mystery. I often wonder why. What is the purpose?"

Keenly aware of Holly's shifting energy, Richard, a man well versed in women's subtle emotions, kept his eyes well-guarded. "I suppose to awaken us, to help us find the deeper meaning between this life and that. I don't know. But I have a feeling we'll find out as time goes on."

He thought Holly would like to say more, because he felt her fear, but didn't prod as she fell silent. *'Confusing'* was an understatement, he thought wryly, as his body responded to Holly's close proximity and he longed to comfort a golden-haired maiden who had ridden to his castle in a watershed of tears.

He remembered the ache now, of knowing it might very well be years before Richard saw Dagr and Brigida again. He remembered the apprehension of not knowing how to care for Arinn as the days unfolded before them. All these emotions made Richard's countenance dark and foreboding. Catching Sahara's eye, he felt the rush of sexual energy that had passed between them during both lifetimes. Brigida had been his beloved, but fate had pushed Arinn into his life, and since then, their lives had been nothing short of complicated.

Aiden and Iona were still now, eyes closed and breathing in unison. They were finding their center. Maybe this would bring the healing Iona needed, Richard pondered, hopeful.

Sahara got up to stoke the fire and open a window. They would all stifle in the heaviness that surrounded them! She found comfort in the ritual of grinding coffee beans. She filled two bodums and made enough for five small cupfuls. She also made a mental note to suggest Aiden acquire a coffee maker for such gatherings. It would take forever to make enough coffee for them all this way! She preheated the oven and rummaged in the freezer for croissants, then took the eggs and green onions from the fridge for omelets.

She was a bundle of nerves as she glanced at Iona still in Aiden's arms. She could share him, that wasn't what was unsettling. It was the look on Holly's face. Try as she might to remain fully open to the situation, Holly was scared. More than a little. The fact that she sat tightly in Richard's arms was another clue of her fear. She would otherwise never, at this stage in her and Aiden's relationship, be comfortable enough to be that forward with another man. But perhaps these thoughts were out of place, as really, what was normal in their lives? She touched her belly in a subconscious act of mourning for the children that were once lost to Brigida. She glanced at Iona again... a hint of bile rose to her throat, but she pushed it away out of loyalty for her teacher and friend.

Motioning to Richard, she pointed at the coffee being brewed and held her hands out to Holly who came gratefully.

⁕

Aiden looked up. Suddenly, he was alert to his betrothed's distress.

Leaving Iona to Richard, he joined Holly in the kitchen.

"My darling, there is so much to say."

He stared into Holly's deep blue eyes. She was shaking, a little unsteady on her feet. The ring on her finger shone iridescent between them, reminding them of their love and commitment.

"Sweetness, I won't lie to you, there has been so much lately. I'm adjusting as quickly as I can, but I do think I need a break from all this. Maybe I'll go to work, and leave you four to work things out?"

He could tell she needed him to fight for her presence.

"If you need to be alone, of course, but... I would like you to stay. Please stay."

"I want to be alone with you tonight."

"I want this also."

"Unless you think Sahara..."

"Sahara will understand. It's ok to think of yourself first my darling."

He watched her drink. She looked very young. Too young and too un-initiated into the life of witches and sorcerers to be quite comfortable with their complicated lives. And so much like the young Arinn. It broke his heart... what Dagr had done back then. But he had to remember it was *Dagr*, not really him. And yet, it felt so familiar.

"I don't remember falling asleep. The last thing I remember we were doing ceremony and closing the circle after Sahara did her magic and then—oh yes." Holly blushed as she remembered her kiss with Richard.

Aiden grinned. "You looked beautiful, you know I couldn't possibly hold that against you. What we do inside the circle is sacred. But I'll be pleased to hear your impressions about it later?"

"You're a beast!" Holly laughed and blushed deeper. The mood lightened somewhat, Holly squeezed Aiden's hand. "Let's join the others. I promised you once that I was willing to learn from you and Sahara and wanted to be part of your magical world. I still mean that. I might sometimes need to adjust to what's happening, but so long as I know that you love me, I can handle it. I know I can."

"We need to discuss boundaries. Things become blurred rather quickly, especially as we discover the past more."

"Remember when you were courting me, and I told you I was scared of a man like you?"

"Yes."

"And that I wasn't in your league?"

"You know that's not true!"

14

"Well, as we go deeper, and I discover more about Dagr and see you through that lens and witness your magic work, I'm realizing that we're from such different worlds... and you become ever more intense."

"What are you saying *exactly*?" Aiden's eyes darkened as he held her tighter.

"I'm saying I find you incredibly interesting and beautiful—I don't want to lose you."

"No hope of that, my love! You can't get rid of me. I'm yours. No matter the mire we get into as a result of this life's journey, you are the center of my world."

"You mean *Sahara* and I are the center of your world," Holly corrected.

An instant telepathic re-assurance arrived from Sahara. Aiden sent one back. They were on the same page. Richard and Iona were speaking softly by the fire. Sahara was weaving healing magic to cover the house. He had a few moments more to speak to Holly freely.

"There are not two relationships alike, sweetness, and as you know, Sahara is a free spirit, she bows to no man." He smiled. "Well, only in the bedroom."

Holly nodded.

"What she and I have is very different from what you and she have, and what you and I need. She doesn't want to be the center of my world. On the other hand, she does need to be yours completely, and I know you'll always need *her* sexually more than *me*."

Holly began to protest but Aiden caught her hands and kissed them.

"Darling, I know this to be true and understand it completely, it neither hurts me nor offends me. I am in deep smit with who you are, and yes, you are my grounding, and I wish to be yours. But with Sahara..." Aiden paused and looked into the distant past. "Well, we are as together as we can be without stepping over her boundaries. She knows you're my undoing. I can't explain the intricate differences in how I love you in comparison to her, and it's not about degrees of love. It's more about honoring the uniqueness of each love and leaving it as it is instead of molding it into something it was never meant to be. You're my center in a way Sahara will never be. Doesn't want to be."

"I see," Holly whispered, longing for the heat of Aiden's mouth again. "I'm learning about this kind of love. It's nothing like what I have ever heard of or read about, but it is so liberating and at the same time so encompassing. Who would believe us anyway?"

"This is the way forward, I think. Love should be free to explore itself in its many forms. For centuries there have been so many rules which frankly have made a mess of how we relate to each other as human beings. Perhaps as we learn, we will teach as well, not so much with our words, but how we live amongst each other."

"We shouldn't be comparing our separate loves should we? Just accept each other's emotions and boundaries as they are."

"Uhuh. It's a process and we're all learning as we go along. I know it's been overwhelming to say the least."

"Yes, but I feel invigorated and heightened as well. Aiden, when you kissed Iona..."

Aiden grimaced. "Yes, I know. You must know this is not how I operate, if our situation wasn't embroiled in past lives and this strange reality—Holly, I am yours, I am yours!" His eyes reflected his deep commitment.

"I get scared when you kiss her, she's so attractive and such a powerful woman."

"Honesty. Holly, I need that from you! You're powerful and stunning and you know what you do to me. I want to grow old with you, have a family. Iona, no matter how beguiling, and I won't lie to you and say I don't notice, is Richard's love through and through. She and he belong together."

"But don't you wonder about the love Dagr once had with Arinn? From all accounts, she was the love of his life, and then suddenly they were separated, and she obviously became Richard's. I mean, where does the love go?"

"I know what you're saying. You're comparing us to Dagr and Arinn. All I can say is that they were caught in very difficult times when women had few choices and Dagr made a decision, out of his fear for Brigida. I know he didn't stop loving Arinn, how could he have? But the reality does seem to be that Arinn and Richard fell in love, which we still have to explore. There's no chance of me falling out of love with you darling, it's a different century and very different situations; we really shouldn't compare." Aiden's hand drifted through Holly's hair. She sighed and leaned into him.

"But lover, we will always be the five of us now, won't we? We'll never have something safe and regular, even as the three?"

Aiden's lifted her chin and scanned her eyes. "No, my love, we won't be regular or maybe not even safe. But we're not usual people, and if I can give my word that I will always honor the truth between us, will you love me as I am?" Heart pounding, Aiden fought tears.

16

"To be truthful I don't want anything but what we have. I can't imagine my life without you and Sahara, and even Richard and Iona now feel like a part of me. I can't know how I will feel as things unfold, but I, too, promise to honor the truth between us."

"This is all we can promise and give; our truth. It's the best kind of love, one that finds the spaces between circumstances and fills them. I love you Holly."

CHAPTER 4

"What shall we do today? We need to integrate what we've experienced."

Sahara settled in among the others by the fire. She sat at Aiden's feet and immediately warmed to the hand he placed on her shoulder. She needed his touch and looked up at him, appreciative. He gave her a wink. It sent a rush of excitement up her spine. She loved his handsome face and the look of mischief in his eyes.

"A group yoga?" Holly suggested, laughing.

"What's so funny?" Aiden asked.

"I can't imagine you doing yoga, somehow... nor Richard. And what would you wear?"

"For your information I'm not new to yoga. How do you think I keep so limber?"

Sahara and Holly looked at each other. This was something about Aiden they knew nothing about.

"You've not done yoga!" Sahara said. "You've never once mentioned it."

"I have done, with a private instructor in Aspen. I'd be pretty beat up doing all that heavy work without any stretching."

"Whaaaat? I don't believe you!" Sahara challenged. Show me a pose, any pose. And I want to know who your yoga instructor is!"

"Ok... but only if Richard joins me." Aiden shot a look of doubt at the man who was quickly becoming an unexpected friend.

"I think you'll be surprised," Iona purred. "Richard's been doing yoga for years. You don't get those long, lean muscles from lifting weights. And he's no stranger to meditation either."

"Truly?" Sahara eyed the two men with open admiration. "Ok, let's do some yoga, then walk to my place. We need air and I have to see to the cat. We have some work to do later—we can do it at my place."

"What work?" Iona perked up. "And what about mats?"

"You'll see," Sahara got up. "Right, mats. I've got two at my place, I'll go get them. After that, I don't know."

"I've the one that's always in my car," Richard said.

"I have one in my truck," Aiden stretched his legs and yawned. "Has anyone given any thought to napping? And that leaves us still one mat short."

"I have one at home," Holly said.

18

"Too far!" Everyone chimed in at once to uproarious laughter.

"I'll lead," Iona said, "I can sit on the rug and do my own yoga later."

"That settles it then," Richard said. "Would you like me to drive you to your place to get the mats, Sahara?"

The tension that rose with the question surprised them all. Iona quickly shot through Richard scanning his intentions. Holly looked up with curious eyes. Aiden tensed and stood.

"I can take her," he said, voice rougher than he intended.

"As you wish, my lord," Richard agreed and they stood in stunned silence at Richard's slip into another era so comfortably, the words he could have spoken to Dagr right on the tip of his tongue. "Right. That was unexpected," he muttered.

"This is what I mean about integrating. We need to seal some portals and cut some cords," Sahara sighed.

"Not again!" Iona whispered, just loud enough for them all to hear. Wild-eyed, she stood and faced the fire.

The air in the room charged uncomfortably with unsaid words.

"Richard, I will accept that ride," Sahara said and offered Aiden a soothing smile.

Holly took Iona's hand and gave a gentle squeeze. "Come to the kitchen with me? I'm going to make us some lemon/lime water for our yoga and maybe you could light some incense and prepare the yoga space for us? I'll show you where Aiden keeps his music." She opened her arms into which Iona eagerly entered.

Holly's hands ran over Iona's unruly, red hair, soothing and cooing under her breath. "One moment at a time, one moment at a time," she reassured. "We're all safe here with each other, no matter what, we are friends first."

And everyone understood at once that Holly's innocence and wisdom would be their healing, just as long ago, Arinn's pure heart had been the solace for a rugged warrior.

<hr />

They didn't share any words while they drove to Sahara's. Richard kept his emotions to himself, but the intensity of them filled the car. Sahara stared straight ahead, following her breath, in and out, in and out—it calmed her heart reasonably well.

Finally, at her homestead, she turned to him, one hand on the car door handle.

"Richard?"

He turned toward her, all of whom he had once been evident on his face.

"There's so much to absorb."

"I understand. You feel Richard betrayed Brigida, don't you?"

Shocked, Richard nodded. "How do you know?"

"He fell in love with her, and when Dagr left Arinn with him, he most likely fell for her. You think you were disloyal to all of them... and to me?" Sahara nodded, eliciting his agreement.

"Yes! Neither Brigida nor Arinn were his to begin with, then he had the ill manners to fall for them both. I could feel Richard's agony over Brigida's leaving during the regression. When I look at you, Sahara all that love comes rushing back. I betrayed everyone." Bristling with the dark heat so inherent to him, Richard reached for Sahara's hand.

"Do you remember the previous regression during which Dagr and Richard made love to Brigida and Arinn... in the old woman's cabin?"

"I do." Sahara's hand closed over his, tiny against his olive-skinned, elegant fingers. Her body shuddered involuntarily with memories and her heart began to beat wildly once more.

"That scene has entered my dreams repeatedly. I can feel the essence of those days, the way their skin felt against mine, how you looked at me when I had you near orgasm, trusting—full of love, surrendered."

"Darling, not me, Brigida."

"I can hardly tell the difference some days."

"We're in deep waters here Richard, and we must find our way out. We can't forever be lost to another lifetime. Knowing our past is only good if we learn from it."

Richard traced a spiral on Sahara's palm. He lingered over the pulse on her wrist.

She could feel his immensity, the male fragrance of his being.

"Do you remember when Brigida fell in love with Richard back then? Do you know the moment?"

"Yes. The moment he opened his chamber door to her, the night they shared his supper, right after he had given her the book about herbs and healing."

"Yes, that was the spark. The moment she let her guard down and he allowed himself to be softened by a woman he could respect. Richard had never respected women before that. He'd used them, adored them, even felt a strong fondness, but never respected them."

"I agree, but what is your point?"

"I remember that man. In some ways it's who I used to be in my younger years, before Iona's love taught me about women. When I went to England this last time, I visited the ruins of Richard's castle. They're still alive there, the pain and the beauty of it all. It's in the soil and the stones. I met myself there, in layers, who I once was and all my progress since then. But the essence of you, I mean, of Brigida, Arinn and even Dagr is still etched on my heart. If it's true time is not linear and that all lifetimes are happening at once, not in the past, present and future as we perceive, then we're all living that love still. We're never really separated by time. It's all existing now in separate dimensions."

"Yes." Sahara's eyes reflected her wisdom.

"So, how will we, knowing and understanding this thing about time, live separate relationships while this immense love beats between us?"

"That's our challenge, Richard, the work we must do to establish how we want to experience this lifetime. Remember, we are viewing this through the eyes of society and what is considered acceptable. If we drop those perceptions, I think we'll have an easier time of knowing who we are and how we want to live."

"There are two challenges. One is Holly, who is obviously incarnated as a part of this puzzle, otherwise the synchronicities of her appearance and that she found herself in your and Aiden's path wouldn't have materialized. The other is the alchemy work you, Aiden and Iona do. The rules of The Society, as Iona tells me, is that no outside influence must disturb the sacred energy of the work; but Holly already has been allowed knowledge of the group... more knowledge than would be sanctioned if the others knew."

Sahara let go of Richard's hand. "Holly's not an outsider. But this is something the others don't know. The Aspen King... the King of the Fey, has already initiated Holly into his court. Most of it she doesn't remember consciously. It was with her consent, there are things she came here to do and this is part of her walk."

"Why ever don't you tell Aiden and Iona! Aiden can't be ok with this, you know how he protects her!"

"I do know, and this is what he will learn, that no matter how much he loves her and is afraid of letting her into our world, it's not his call. He'll find out more in time. I am not at liberty to instruct him."

"But you told *me*." Richard shifted in his seat. "Why?"

"Because, my darling, you will be directly charged with her safety as events unfold. I do not know why exactly, but I do know that when Aiden, Iona and I are away, you will be the one left here to tend to Holly."

"Sahara! For the love of God, that's the most terrifying thing I've ever been asked to do. One, what if something happened; what the hell would I tell Aiden? He would fucking kill me! You can't leave me in charge of her while she possibly tromps to the Underworld! That's insanity. I won't be able to follow, in any case. And then, I know nothing of the workings of the Fey. I'm an art dealer for Christ's sake, not a magician!"

"Richard, you know more than you think. I am surmising from bits and pieces of what my and Iona's life has been so far, that she as Arinn, became schooled in the sacred arts, the mysteries, and you, as her master, were part of it. I think this because Iona would never trust her life now to someone who could not understand her on an elemental level. So, you must know more than you have awoken to thus far."

Sahara reached and ran her hand along Richard's arm. He tensed, and she fell into his electric energy. The intensity of his mood shone as a dangerous glint in his eyes. Her clit fluttered. Her nipples perked. Richard was alert at once to the change in her scent.

"Let's get the mats." Leaving the car, he held the door open for her and took her hand as she stepped out. She lowered her eyes. Richard could not have been more appealing to her in that moment, more of the dark horse she remembered from so long ago.

"My sweet," he whispered in her ear as he pulled her close, "I won't be played with. I will ask you to tell me everything you know when you know it, I hate being at a disadvantage, and right now I feel as though I am a pawn in some kind of chess game. Promise you won't leave me vulnerable. There's too much at stake here. I consider Aiden my friend."

Richard's warm breath along with the faint scent of his cologne made a mess of Sahara's equilibrium. He was holding her one hand at her lower back, the other at the back of her neck. She could tell he was deadly serious.

"I promise, as much as I am able, I won't leave you vulnerable," she mouthed the words softly, trembling in his grasp.

She led the way into the cabin as his eyes bored into her back, her pussy wet and throbbing. This was entirely a matter of keeping control of oneself, she thought. She squared her shoulders and took a deep breath.

Richard waited at the door, observing silently as she cuddled the cat then ran upstairs to get the yoga mats.

"Brigida. Did I ever see you again?"

CHAPTER 5

"The very thought of you
has my legs spread apart
like an easel with a canvas
begging for art."
~ Rupi Kaur

Moments. That was what life was made of. Each day comprised of moment after moment, some running into each other, while some stood out as painful reminders of life's brutality. Brigida settled deeper against Dagr as they approached a quick, swollen river with a questionable bridge for a crossing.

Dagr's arm tightened. He leaned down to reassure her.

"My lady, there is no danger. We can make this crossing safely."

She nodded, weak from the feel of his mouth on her neck and the tedious days of riding. She lifted her face to his, eyes begging a kiss.

Dagr, obliging, pressed his mouth to hers. His lips were warm and salty. She licked hers, savoring his taste. She had missed their intimacy but had felt it wrong to ask for pleasure while Arinn was suffering. Indeed, they were all suffering. Still, she longed for his weight upon her.

For the first time in days, she could feel his manhood erect against her back. Her breath quickened flooding her spine with a surge of heat. Color bloomed on her face. She closed her hands over Dagr's where they held the reins. She heard the rumble in his chest as he responded to her touch. He leaned in once more.

"Do you desire me, my lady, or am I mistaken?"

Brigida looked to where her brother rode in front of them, out of earshot.

"I do, my lord. Is it improper of us?"

"No, my lady, it is fitting of our love. But I will not press you, if you wish for more time?" Dagr's hand belied his words, as it made its way around towards her breast.

Breath suspended, Brigida imagined his fingers tangled around her nipples. She begged another kiss with a look that tore a groan from Dagr's lips.

"My lady, you torture me with your eyes. I will be at your service this night!" His mouth burned hot in her hair, and her clit fluttered, pussy throbbing with expectation. She lowered her head, consenting to his words.

Mark circled around as they came to the foot of the bridge.

"My lord! The water is fast, the bridge quite old, perhaps we should find a better crossing?"

Dagr handed him control of the reins and jumped down to inspect the bridge. Brigida watched hungrily as he strode along the bank of the river. His back had always been a source of lust for her —the back of a warrior. Her mouth watered. How she loved his strength and sense of purpose. From the time she had come of age and noticed him as a woman would, Dagr had been the tallest and broadest man she had ever seen, the knight she had coveted.

He paced back and forth then lay down on the ground to inspect the under-girding of the stone structure. Seemingly satisfied, he smiled at Brigida and gave her a wink. Her heart melted. She had missed his smile these days, and that confident square to his shoulders.

"My lady, give me your hand, I will carry you across."

"Carry me? I can certainly walk it myself!"

"I will carry you." His tone was final.

He helped her down and picked her up handily. To her surprise, Dagr made his way across running, but with soft feet, in an effort to not jostle the stonework. With her safely on the other side, he ran back employing that same light-footed swiftness. She had never seen someone of such imposing size move so effortlessly.

Mark was next, leading his horse gingerly. Was it her imagination or had the river risen to the top of the bridge? Nervous, she watched as Dagr whispered to his horse, who nodded his great head and stepped to the edge of the river then in one quick effort, cantered across. The bridge groaned, and the river rose once more. She was sure now her eyes were seeing correctly.

She called with a frantic wave of her hand, "Come, my lord! The river rises!"

Dagr took one last look back. *What was he waiting for?* Brigida worried her hands in her trouser pockets. *Come, my lord!*

But then he was beside her and the bridge gone in a rush with the angry river.

"My lord, I was ever so frightened."

They both stared at where the river had torn the bridge from its moorings.

"We are like that bridge, my lord, torn from her homeland." Brigida's eyes filled with tears.

Dagr cupped her chin in his muscled hand. He stared long into her pale and drawn face.

"My lady, I beg your forgiveness. This is my doing."

"No. I will not hear it!"

Mark broke in on their grief. "We must go on."

With a nod of his head, Dagr lifted Brigida into the saddle and jumped on behind her. They rode with only one purpose in mind—to find solace in each other's arms.

The room they had secured was warm and clean, and a hot supper lay before them.

It was almost too much, and they looked at their surroundings with some suspicion. After so many nights of filthy beds and dingy bath water, the sparkling clean tub was a surreal reality.

"What is this place?" Brigida sipped her hot soup and stuffed a large piece of crusty bread into her mouth.

Dagr laughed out loud. "You will regret eating so quickly tomorrow!" He tore a piece off for himself. "Mark tells me the inn is newly owned. I have been here before and it was in a sorry state, I can tell you."

"Must be the King is coming." Brigida joked then recanted. "I mean, he will not be coming?"

Dagr's smile disappeared. "If he was, he would not be welcomed by me."

"I beg forgiveness, my lord, I did not remember."

Dagr scowled. "After all my years of service..." He stared out the window.

"But you do not hate him, my lord, you still foster a fondness?"

"What do you know of this my lady? Do you pretend to understand my heart in this matter?"

Brigida shrank from Dagr's harsh tone, so unlike his usual manner, but spoke back bravely. "Sometimes, one cannot put away all the love they once felt, no matter how much it seems they should." She guiltily thought of Richard's face at their parting.

Dagr took her hand. "My lady, your wisdom cuts me. Aye, I should hate the man, but some part of me remains loyal."

"You are his knight."

"Was his knight, before he cut away my family and my life."

"No truer words have been spoken my lord, and he did destroy us; but you are trained to his service and at one time was as a favorite son to him. I know this because Hannah told me many things, as did Richard. Both spoke of your bravery."

"Is it bravery to kill men?"

"It is bravery to serve with an honest heart."

"I wish to serve you," Dagr steered the conversation.

Brigida blushed and lowered her head. "As you wish my lord."

"You wish it as well?"

"I do, my lord. Very much."

"This is our last night on English soil. Tomorrow we sail."

"Yes, my lord. And we will make love to remember it by."

"I will call for a bath." Dagr stood, towering over Brigida.

She warmed under his shadow, her stare fixed to that place she adored and licked her lips.

Dagr groaned and wrapped his hand in her hair, tugging a little harder than he meant to. He bent one knee before her and brought his mouth close to hers. Her breath rushed out as she closed her eyes.

"My lord," she whispered.

Later that night, while moon shadows danced along the walls, Brigida found Dagr sitting in the chair by the desk, staring at their bed.

Propping herself up on her elbow, she offered a shy smile. She was sore and wet with his seed still having found deep sleep after their lovemaking, which was sure to have woken the dead. Dagr had not muffled her cries as she thought he would have, nor had he spared her his strength. Her breasts felt deliciously bruised.

"Will you not sleep my love?"

"I have slept," his voice rasped with desire.

"My lord?"

"Come to me!" he commanded.

Brigida luxuriated under the force of his will. She slipped out of bed and padded on silent feet to his side. He raked her over so indecently with his gaze that she shivered.

"Are you sore, my lady?"

She nodded.

"Too sore?"

She shook her head and smiled.

He offered his hand and she let herself be led astride his lap.

"Kiss me."

She dropped a timid kiss on his forehead, then his cheek, then, when she heard frustration growling in his throat, she pressed her mouth to his.

"Spread your legs further."

Her head dropped back when she felt his hand cupping her sex; gentle, hot.

"You are ever in need of my touch."

"Yes, my lord. You are my constant craving."

Dagr kissed her neck and tugged with his teeth against her ear. His tongue made lazy contact. Brigida began to tremble under his attention. She pressed her quim into his hand.

"What a hungry cunt you have, my love."

Brigida moaned and pressed harder still. He released her and settled her on his leg. She began to ride it, swollen clit rubbing against the rough of his hair, as he tensed his muscles to offer more resistance.

"Have I told you, my lady, how much I love the feel of your wet cunt?" He cut off her reply with a deep, hard kiss. His tongue lashed hers and demanded her surrender.

"Yes, my lord."

Dagr leaned her back, sucking on her taut nipples; tugging until she cried out.

"My lord, please take me!" She slid off and immediately lay herself across his lap, raising her hips and begging his hand on her bottom. He complied without hesitation, the sound of the slap he administered loud against the silence of the night.

"Harder, my lord!" She raised up again. She reached down and teased her clit, moaning as Dagr spanked rhythmically.

Suddenly, she was in his arms as he stood and positioned himself with one hand against the wall, while he mounted her on his thick, throbbing manhood.

"Aaaaah!" they said in unison and rocked together as he fucked against her cervix, reaching her deepest source of ecstasy. She was helpless in his grip, mouth open as she gasped for breath, his teeth in her neck and the smell of his lust filling her nostrils.

"You will come for me my lady?" he whispered in a dangerous tone.

"I will..." Brigida shuddered as she looked into his eyes. "Will you fill me with your seed once more, my lord? I want to feel the heat of your love."

Dagr groaned and pumped his hips. Balls at her entrance, he allowed himself release. Brigida cried out as his cock throbbed inside her. Waves of orgasm washed over her, covering her in a shroud of sensations while her ecstasy gushed down Dagr's legs.

Broken open by their love, they curled up in bed and slept until Mark's knock awoke them a few short hours later.

CHAPTER 6

"A half day's ride and we shall be at the coast, my lord." Mark pointed ahead.

Dagr nodded, chest tight with worry. They could cross the channel without any altercations, it was utterly possible. But something in his gut churned violently. He could already smell the ocean. The wind brought the taste of salt to his memory. Brigida sat blurry eyed before him. Her tears at leaving everything... and everyone behind, made the journey so much worse. But if he was honest with himself, his own tears sat urgent as well. He swallowed the lump in his throat and thought of Arinn's sweet face as she had once sat at his feet in their old manor home.

My darling, my darling! The bitterness of the memory brought a rush of bile.

"Best to ride in separately," Dagr suggested to his companion. "We will reunite on the other side."

"Are there lodgings on the way inland?" Mark shouted above the wind.

"In Calais, yes, but not where we shall be riding. We will find sleep in the woods."

"Hmmm," Mark worried.

Dagr knew he was, ironically, thinking of robbers, and there were plenty. But they would have to find shelter in the wilderness tonight. There was no other way.

"Do you speak the language?" he queried Brigida's brother. How grateful he was to have him at their side!

"I do not, my lord."

"You will learn quickly, I will teach you what I can, but once we adjust to the new life, the language will come."

"As you say, my lord," Mark looked dubious.

"You do not like the French?"

"The ones I have met were pompous rogues all," Mark's mouth turned down in distaste.

"They think us quite uncivilized."

"Hmff! I should think them uncivilized."

"Will the people be unfriendly then, my lord?" Brigida sat straight and tried looking ahead as far as the heavy fog would allow. She shivered under the cool, moist air.

"Do not worry, my lady, in the cities, yes, the people can be distant, but in the country, they are warm. Farmers. People who love the soil can be trusted."

"I do hope so, my lord, it would be unbearable to come to a new land and find all its inhabitants disagreeable. I wonder about our new home... do you think..."

"Hush, my love. I do not imagine the Earl to have found us unsuitable lodgings, do you?"

Brigida wiped her eyes and the never-ending stream of tears. "I suppose you are right, my lord. If I know my... er, the Earl, he would have provided handsomely."

Dagr stiffened. "Yes, Richard is ever generous when it comes to his favorite lovers." He hadn't meant to be cruel, but the stress of the last two years spilled out with his words. Immediately contrite, he begged Brigida's forgiveness. Anger clouded his eyes. *Damn the whole world!* He squeezed Brigida's hand.

"The sea is ahead. Can you smell it my love?"

"Yes! Is it like the sea I know?"

"Perhaps not as pretty, it is a harsh water."

"The crossing...?"

"The weather willing, it will only take a half-day."

And they fell into silence, each with their own fears tucked against their hearts.

⁂

The closer they got to the coast, the heavier the rain fell and the stronger the wind. It pulled at their wet cloaks, determined to have them. Dagr did his best to keep tight against Brigida. She was soaked to the bone. The last time he had pulled her face to his for a hurried kiss, her eyes had been bright with fever. She was taking sick. There would be no way to boil fever herbs until they reached their camp for the night. Dagr feared the worst for the crossing. His nostrils flared as he remembered the stench of the lower hold where Brigida would have to wait out the sailing journey. That alone was enough to make anyone ill.

They rode quickly over the cobblestone streets of Dover towards the harbor where the ferry would be waiting. Mark waved impatiently for them to hurry ever faster, feeling the same sense of urgency Dagr did. Something did not feel right. Dagr nodded and gave his horse a nudge with his heel. The hair on the back of his neck rose, and he pressed his legs tight around his lover.

"I see the ferry, my lord!"

Brigida's fevered cheeks glowed red, sweat stood out on her forehead, but her voice carried the hint of excitement. No doubt, Dagr thought, she imagines the vessel will bring respite, having no experience with the filthiness of the more common carriers. They could not find passage on what the lord of a manor would be accustomed to, they were not dressed appropriately and would invite suspicion with a hefty purse. As well, this port was too often the launching point of the King's army. He pulled his hood lower over his face.

"There!" Mark gestured. "She's moored and waiting."

"You go ahead. We will be along shortly."

Mark nodded at his sister. She gave him a falsely brave smile.

"My lord, I think it best if I go to the lower hold with my lady sister, and you stayed... I beg your pardon, I do not mean to tell you how best protect her."

Dagr understood. She could not be left alone, and he was best to stay on deck.

"Your plan is wise. We shall do as you suggest."

Finally, at the foot of the water, Brigida slid off the horse and arranging her clothes around herself, allowed Dagr to hang a few of their belongings around her shoulders. It would have to seem, after all, she was his servant, and not some weakling either! Her back sagged under the weight and she noted the anger in Dagr's eyes at having to burden her.

He growled and shoved her along the plank as he led his horse behind him. The great beast and his lover would be lodged in the same area, strong with horse piss and chicken shit. Altogether, they looked the picture of bedraggled master and miserable stable boy. When they reached the steward of the ferry, Dagr extended his hand with the customary passage cost plus a little more.

The man, drenched and scowling dangerously, shook his head.

"More," was all he said, and stood blocking the way.

"More?" Dagr barked. "I offer more than is usual."

"More, or ye do not sail. It is extra for the boy and the horse."

Dagr bristled and reached into his pocket again.

For a moment he thought the idiot man would keep pressing, but with a grunt, he moved aside and let them board.

"Stand here," Dagr hissed and pulled Brigida by the shoulder, wedging her between the horse and himself.

"Do you see anyone you know, my lord?" she whispered.

"No. There is no one here I recognize," he lied. In fact, he had already seen several soldiers in the King's employ who would know him immediately. Three had boarded and were standing in a huddle nearby.

"Then we are safe my lord!" Brigida's face brightened.

"We are safe." Dagr pressed her hand with his, hoping the heat of his skin would be reassuring and healing in some small way. How he hated himself for putting her in this dangerous position. Mark was leading his mount below and pushed past them as a stranger would. Only a quick glance between the two men acknowledged their combined intent to keep Brigida safe.

"Take Anam Cara down below," Dagr ordered, handing the reins of his great war-horse to Brigida. He had never used his mount's name aloud before, always referring to him as 'the beast' because of his size. The name was sacred to him, from his mother's language. She had taught him that Anam Cara was a teacher, a companion, a spirit guide. Brigida's eyes widened some from fear, he imagined, to be down in the hold away from him and because she had once asked him about his horse's name and he had left it unsaid. She would want to know the meaning, and he would tell her when they were alone again. He looked forward to sharing this story of his mother and her beliefs. The thought brought him great comfort.

"Shall I stay down there, my lord?"

"Yes, keep to Mark's side."

He winked at her, hiding his sorrow at sending her away. She would suffer down there, as the boat lurched in the stormy waters, he knew that well. He would not be there to hold her as she wretched, nor would he be able to help the fever that had her shoulders shaking violently already. The air in the hold was toxic to the lungs of both man and beast. Dagr gritted his teeth, anticipating Brigida would be in far worse health when they arrived on the shores of France.

"When do we leave?"

"At low tide. Not long now."

"How long will the voyage be?"

"Six hours, at best, but may be longer, as the sea dictates." He did not say that once, he had crossed at an agonizing pace of more than seventeen hours under a brutal sky.

"Will you come down, my lord?"

"I will not."

"Then I will pass the time dreaming of our new home," Brigida whispered.

He nodded. "Go!"

She left his side, and he felt the tear in his heart. *My love forgive me!* It seemed he said that quite often these days.

Mark came up once, in the hours that followed, green under the gills and swearing under his breath. Dagr stood nearby as the man threw the contents of his entrails over the rail.

"Not long now!" Dagr hissed from beneath his hood. "Perhaps a half-hour. How is my lady?"

Mark looked up briefly. Dagr gathered the worst from his expression.

"We will ride southeast, on the only road in that direction out of Calais. You will see a monastery a hard ride away, quite modest, and beyond that, a wood. We should be able to reach it by nightfall. We will meet there."

He did not need to give Mark instructions on how to travel inconspicuously, that he was already well-versed in. If all went well, they would sleep by a fire tonight, and he could brew some tea for his lady love. He knew those woods well. There were caves to hide in, and the monastery could provide added medicine if necessary. The monks would not turn Brigida away. Himself... that was a different story. He would be remembered as the enemy. Dagr scowled. He was grateful those years were behind him.

The boat lurched as it moored, and immediately a noisy commotion arose, with every man for himself rushing to depart. Dagr stood back as the deck cleared. The men he had recognized left quickly, disappearing into the mist. No doubt headed for the nearest whorehouse, Dagr surmised. He was happy to see the back of them. Everyone had been too ill to pay him any attention. In any case, he had kept disguised sitting by a troop of travelling gypsies. He looked properly disheveled and not of any interest to anyone, aside from his exceptional height.

Impatient, he watched for the first sign of Brigida. What the hell was keeping Mark? It seemed impossible there could be anyone else left down there after the long trail of travelers with their drawn faces, their horses and pens of domestic fowl. The air coming from the hold reeked of feces.

Finally, just as he had made his mind up to charge down the rickety ramp, his horse trotted up unattended, then Mark's, and Brigida, in her brother's arms. She lay limp and grey, her breath shallow.

34

Dagr ripped her from Mark, no longer cognizant of his surroundings, and clutching her desperately to him, begged her to open her eyes. She did. Dagr gasped at their low light, black shadows beneath them.

"My lady, it will not be long now, I will secure you a warm bed and medicine."

"You will take to her to the monastery? But how...?"

"You will take her... I cannot. Let us make haste!"

They left the boat, each considerably taken up with their own thoughts, and neither of them spying a lone man who stood in the shadows of the dock, a dangerously satisfied smirk on his face.

This was France. A country for life's exuberances, a place of hope for those who needed to hide, but not so far from the English King's reach that his brand of justice could not be enacted.

CHAPTER 7

*"Being deeply loved by someone gives you strength, while loving
someone deeply gives you courage."*
~ Lao Tzu

The scent of snuffed candles and incense wafted up the stairs to Aiden's bedroom. The house rested in silence, absorbing the magic which had been made that evening. To those who could see, a blue-grey light surrounded the cabin; the mark of the Fey.

"I'm so exhausted," Holly piled her luxurious blond hair atop her head and stuck two pencils she found in Aiden's bedside drawer into her bun.

Aiden stood leaning in the doorway of his bathroom, a towel hung around his hips. He was fresh out of the shower, wet hair clinging to his shoulders. A soft smile played on his lips.

"Is it too cool up here for you? I forgot I had the windows open, the bed must be freezing!"

Holly smoothed the crisp white sheets and patted a spot beside her.

"Get in, lover. You can warm me!" Her eyes twinkled and her nipples perked as Aiden pulled the towel off and turned back to dry his hair.

"I will, give me a minute," Aiden promised, fully aware what the sight of his perfect ass and broad back was doing to her. "Are you too tired for a drink?"

"I'd love one, what'll you have?"

"Scotch, please."

"K."

When she returned, Aiden had turned down all the lights, and lit the floor candelabra standing in the corner by the bed. He was sitting in his chair, a blanket draped over hips.

"Oh, won't you join me in bed now?" Holly handed him his drink.

"You get in." He looked up at her, grinning.

"I don't know what you have up your sleeve, mister, but you look positively devilish!"

Aiden sipped his scotch slowly, watching her take a sip of her wine.

"You asked to share my bed tonight?"

"I did."

"What did you think that would mean?"

"I thought we would sleep together. After all that's happened today, I figured we'd be bone-tired." She laughed as the blanket began to move in Aiden's lap.

"Interesting choice of words, darling." He took another sip. "This scotch Richard gifted me is fucking good." Aiden caught the rush of color in Holly's cheeks at the mention of Richard. "Would you like a taste?"

"No," Holly shook her head. "I'll stick with this." She raised her glass of wine.

"You're lying," Aiden observed.

"Am I?" Holly put her hands to her face.

Aiden stood, the blanket dropped to the floor and Holly let out an appreciative breath.

He crawled over the bed toward her. "Here," he said and offered her his glass.

She took a small sip and handed it back.

"Do you like it?"

"No."

"Are you going to lie all night?"

"It's... too much."

"Let me try," Aiden kissed her, ripping her hair down from its perch, bruising her mouth with his. "Mmmm, it tastes different on your tongue."

"Aiden..."

"I saw you staring at Richard with that look in your eyes."

"What look?" Holly asked, startled.

"It's ok, sweetness, I'm only intrigued. The look of curiosity. Awakened sexuality. I know that look well, so don't bother pretending I may be mistaken. You had that same look the first time at your apartment. Remember?"

"I remember that night, yes."

"Your first taste of a man. I think you're curious about Richard." He took Holly's glass of wine and put it down on the nightstand. "Lie on your belly," he instructed.

She slid down and turned over. Aiden's hand caressed her ass. She lifted by instinct, already wet. He moved behind her.

"Close your eyes."

"Do you think...?"

"I don't want to think right now. It's been a long couple of days and we've been to hell and back. Close your eyes. Trust me?"

"Yes, mmmm," Holly purred as Aiden's mouth brushed along her back, the heat of his body and erection close against her skin. He smelled good, like her favorite soap that he used. She loved how it mixed with his natural scent.

"I'll only take you places you want to go. If you don't want something, just tell me. I'm here to serve you."

The word serve lit a fire in Holly's body. She moaned and spread a little as Aiden approached her ass. "Yes please."

It was Aiden's turn to growl. "Your cunt smells divine. Like candy. Wider, wench!"

She spread and waited. His mouth moved excruciatingly slowly along her skin, his breath teasing her into a throbbing desire.

"Are your eyes closed my love?"

"They're closed. Please!"

The first tender lick drew a cry.

"Earlier, when we were sitting by the fire and I caught you staring at Richard, were you thinking of this?"

"Yes. Why are you doing this?" Holly whispered, her hands gripping the sheets, her hips pumping back to feel that sinful tongue once more.

"Ssshhh, I want to give you this. It's ok to be curious. I want to give you everything you need. I don't want to own you." He lowered his mouth. Actually, he was *working* on not wanting to own her. He had made a commitment to himself to give their love more room.

Holly moved to the rhythm of his tongue. "Darling! I love you! I just feel so wild lately, I don't know why really!"

Aiden turned her over. Hovering just inches above her, he smiled as she spread to receive him. "You're a woman. You're opening to a freedom you didn't know before. I love you so damn much." He thrust inside her, fucking with practiced strokes while stealing hard kisses.

"Harder!"

Aiden obliged, his eyes dark and moody.

She passed her hands over his belly, hard and chiseled. She loved the way his hips moved, how his hands possessed her and yet... she was curious. She wanted to imagine them both. She looked up into Aiden's eyes and found his soul naked.

"I told you to close your eyes." He flipped her over again and pulled her ass in the air.

She closed them and let herself imagine, pussy gushing as Aiden

38

pumped hard, his hand tangled in her hair pulling her head back, the other firmly gripping her hip. This was rough and raw, her lover's moans having receded somewhere into the background as she thought of Richard's steely, raven eyes. He was a man only Iona could tame, but it was that hint of danger in his smile which had Holly scream out her orgasm.

Aiden came inside her with a groan, love words sweet like honey on the air.

They collapsed together on the bed. Aiden drew her in.

"I could feel every spasm of your orgasm, every ripple inside your pussy, you get so tight when you come." He ran light fingers over her belly and tits, then grasped her cunt with a firm hand, grounding her energy.

"How do you know how to do that? That it feels nice to have it held hard after coming?"

"I had this lover, she was very, let's say, hands on. She loved to play with herself in front of me, it was a thing with her. After an orgasm she would hold herself tight like that. She told me how settling it felt. Her orgasms were very full on, loud, she really let herself experience it. There was nothing shy about that woman. I learned a lot from her."

Holly traced softly around Aiden's chin.

"I like hearing about this. I get to know you better."

"I'm glad. I prefer love this way. Why should we pretend we've never slept with anyone else? It's a denial of our journey."

"Mmm, yes. I agree. But, as you know, I have nothing to share, as I was practically a virgin when I met you!" Holly giggled.

"Well, I don't know, you had your adventures in France. Tell me something?"

Holly sighed. "I tried blocking it out for a while, before I met you all, because I seriously thought I'd never find anyone again... especially in this corner of the world. It's not like Riverbend is lesbian central!"

Aiden laughed out loud. "You're the worst lesbian I've ever met!"

Holly joined in on his laughter. "God, you made a mess of that!"

"Ok, tell me something about Julie."

"Right. Well, she was completely un-inhibited. She would laugh at me because I would scan the street whenever she wanted to kiss in public. She said people would stare if we *didn't* kiss. Anyway, she never wore underwear! The first time I noticed she was sitting on a swing, I was pushing her from the front and gave her a kiss on each return.

She spread her legs and I almost came right then and there. She laughed her head off! After that, she would make me touch her in all kinds of public situations."

"Did she convert you into not wearing knickers?" Aiden snuggled down under the covers and pulled Holly in as well. Laying on his side, he dropped lazy kisses on her forehead, palm teasing her nipples.

"Sometimes. At the movies, where she fingered me. And she liked having her nipples sucked until she came. But to come, she had to have her legs spread really wide, and she would open her pussy just as wide using her hands, and that was how she got off. She had a really pretty cunt. Before I could suck her nipples, she made me look at it and comment on how pretty it was and tell her she was a slut—*la fille salope*. That's how she got off." Holly turned bright red.

"La fille salope!" Aiden tried the phrase on his tongue. He adjusted the fresh erection which rose between them. "I have a feeling you have more to share... one of your fetishes, perhaps?" He grinned, the devil in his eyes. "Here, finish your wine."

"Do you think Sahara is sleeping already?" Holly stalled.

"Oh no, you can't distract me with her. But yes, I do think she is. Now, out with it. I want to hear something about my own wench!"

"I'm pretty boring, I don't know really anything you could find interesting. You've done it all."

"Ummm, I'm not that easily played. Tell me. I don't know if you've noticed, but I'm very interested in you."

Holly sipped the very last of her wine. She thought of getting more. The look on Aiden's face reminded her of when she'd first been at his house, he'd always been a shade more man than she was comfortable with.

"I think I've told you all of them by now."

"I'm sure you haven't," Aiden grinned and tweaked a nipple.

"Ow! Ok, ok fine, I can see you'll torture me if I don't!"

"Darling, that's one thing I will not do. Here, I'll turn off all the lights, and just leave these candles on, if it helps?"

"How about if you blow out the candles too?"

Aiden got up to please her. "I'll still be able to see you in the moonlight, darling."

They lay facing each other, Holly's hand against Aiden's chest. It was a rock under her fingers, unrelenting, like his love.

"Are you afraid it'll turn me off?" Aiden whispered, pressing his fingers through Holly's hair, illuminated now by the moon.

"You'll think I'm strange."

"Never! I love every one of your secrets." He kissed her, lash up-on lash of delicious tongue on tongue.

Unable to stop herself, Holly reached down, a moan escaping her mouth as her fingers found her clit.

Aiden's eyebrow shot up. She was letting herself go. He craved this woman who constantly surprised him!

"She used to ask me to sit on the edge of the bath, legs spread, and pee."

Aiden growled. His hand tightened in her hair. "Was this her fantasy or yours? I asked for yours."

"Mine. But she took it a bit further. She would ask to lick me dry. Oh God! Are you going to run a mile?" Holly hid in Aiden's arms.

"Tell me more." That rumble in Aiden's chest was a sure sign he wasn't going anywhere.

"She had a way of spreading her tongue wide, and she'd lick me with loud, smacking noises as she pulled my lips into her mouth then let them go." Holly looked up then hid once more, whispering against Aiden's neck. "She's start at my ass, end at my clit. I had to keep my eyes open, watch her. There was a lot of talk in French, telling me how good I tasted, what a good girl I was, that she loved my wet cunt."

"What else?"

"How do you know there was more?"

"Because a girl like that is not ashamed of her desire, so I imagine she had more than that in her repertoire." Aiden pulled Holly on top of himself, hands resting on her ass, pulling it open as her legs surrounded him. She let herself sink, resting her cheek against his heart, listening to the comforting sound of it beating; steady, strong.

"Do you like being opened like that?"

Holly nodded. She sank deeper into his being.

"Tell me what she did to you when she had you spread like that."

"You know, the thing you like to do. Explore, with fingers and tongue, kissing it, licking, talking into it, tongue right in... everywhere." Holly listened to the heartbeat beneath her ear, the sound of Aiden's life. Nothing existed but the sound of their breathing and the hum of their emotions.

Aiden's hands on her ass, kneading, caressing, and the flick of air on her exposed pussy was an elixir that normally would have had her begging for penetration. But her lover's quiet embrace, the way he kissed her forehead and lips took her to another place.

"Aiden?"

"Hmmm?" Aiden sighed, content.

"What do you think happened when Dagr and Brigida got to France? I'm so interested to know what their life would have been like, away from Arinn. Do you think they ever got over it... having to leave her? Or maybe they saw her again? Sometimes when I look at Sahara, I catch something in her eye, and I can almost see the other girl she used to be."

Aiden looked at her, curious. "You do? That's something, to be able to catch a nuance like that."

"Since I've been with you... well, really, since we became engaged," Holly looked at the unusual ring on her finger, "I've felt somehow more part of your world."

"Yes," Aiden agreed, "I gathered."

"You're not happy about that, are you?"

"I simply wish to keep you safe, that's all." His hands traveled up her back and held her tight. "I think they probably had chances to see Arinn again. But it would have been difficult."

"Do you think of her when you look at me?"

"Yes, sometimes, only because of the resemblance, but you don't feel like her obviously, your energy is very distinct."

"I can't imagine what it was like for Brigida to have to leave her love behind. I couldn't... not that she had a choice."

"I know," Aiden let out a deep sigh.

"I don't blame Dagr!" Holly explained. "I mean, he had no choice really."

"He did. But that was the one he made. I think about it too, what happened, how they made the crossing, travel was very dangerous then especially for fugitives, or enemies of the crown. People often got quite ill from the sail across, those boats were filthy, and the air in the hold vile. And remember, they were travelling under disguise so Brigida wouldn't have had any comforts along the way, as in any special treatment a lady might receive."

Aiden closed his eyes. Holly moved to the space he made in the crook on his arm.

"Sometimes I'm able to dream bits of memories," he murmured.

"I'm so glad we have tonight. I needed this. It's been a crazy couple of weeks. And we never did have your parents over like we planned."

But he was already asleep, his handsome face marred by a frown.

CHAPTER 8

Fog was a friend when one needed its cover but a foe when that cover hid one's enemies.

Dagr hurried along the sodden road before him, Calais behind them. Brigida was wrapped in a blanket and his cloak, tight in his grasp; but he could not stop her shivering. Beads of cold sweat rose on her forehead, her lips dry, and cheeks ashen.

He had only a couple hours ride before he reached the fork in the road where he would meet Mark. From there, Brigida would be out of his hands, and hopefully into the care of the French monks with their vast knowledge of healing herbs and tonics. He scowled, thinking of the separation and his total lack of control over what would happen to his lady love.

But thankfully, there had been no interceptions in the streets of Calais. One could be grateful for the fact that all his imagined fears about the journey had never materialized. He thought he could hear the sound of Mark's horse ahead, but then, he had left immediately upon disembarking. Dagr reached for his sword, safe against his leg. His hand closed over the hilt, soothing his worries, sure of his skill as a swordsman.

He slowed his horse, listening intently. The sword was out of its scabbard in the same moment the hair on his neck rose and his body reacted to his horse's pinned ears. The fog denied any visibility of who was against him.

Anam Cara screamed in pain as a tendon was slashed on his hind leg and hobbled to a full stop while Dagr slid off. Scrambling to keep Brigida safe, Dagr roared at his invisible assailant.

"Come forth coward, so I may kill you!"

Rage filled his chest and numbed his mind. "Show yourself, you bastard." Spinning in what seemed like slow motion, Dagr was desperate to get his horse and his lady away to safety.

A low, guttural voice intercepted his thoughts, and out of the mist rose the face of a man Dagr knew well, ever his enemy, ever the one who had envied his connection and favor with the King.

"Ah, it is you!" Dagr spat. "On the King's business, are you?" Weapon poised, Dagr had no intention of waiting for the explanation, his resolve was to kill and kill immediately. He dropped Brigida to the ground and pushed his way forward sword first, knocking the man back on his heels.

Perhaps another day he would have sparred, or maimed only, or heard the bastard out, but today he had to be ruthless, as he had been many times before during acts of war. There was not time to think about how his spirit reviled the taking of life.

It was the gurgle of blood spilling from a man's mouth when his throat was cut that marked his memory. Was killing never to leave him?

Stepping over the dead man, Dagr first found Brigida, sitting up and clutching at her blankets, eyes wide with fear.

"Forgive me," Dagr's voiced rasped as he choked on her distress. He lifted her and moving towards the sound of his horse's wheezing breath, found a sight so revolting he fell to his knees before it. Anam Cara's life was slowly ebbing, his chest slashed and blood pouring into the muddy ground.

The sound which escaped Dagr was for the ears of demons only.

Brigida draped herself over the body of their faithful companion whose eyes now showed white; his tongue lolling out his mouth. Dagr broke into violent sobs, witnessing the beast's last labored breaths.

He would not be able to honor him with ceremony or burial. He would have to leave him in this way, indecently splayed on the road, to rot and be ravaged by vultures. The ache in his heart yelled obscenities, suggesting this was the price of leaving Arinn behind. Dagr did not hide from the voices, sinking into his pain.

"My lord," came the weakened voice of Brigida. "He is no longer."

Dagr looked up, awareness slapping him in the face like a cold, wet cloth. He nodded and stood; offered his hand. They would have to walk. He hoisted her up in his arms and with her hands clasped around his neck and her head against his chest, they carried on without any further tears, only the balm of shock to cushion them.

Along the way, Dagr called out to Pan. Brigida was too ill to walk and he could not carry her fast enough to safety and warmth.

Send intuition to Mark, bring him back to me!

Pan appeared, a shadow in the woods beside him, then disappeared into the mist. Dagr sighed with relief. He was tired and distraught. If only... but thoughts of life having turned out differently were pointless.

Finding a small stream, Dagr stopped to rest and cupped his hands to scoop some water for himself and his lady. Brigida drank gratefully and asked to have her face washed. Dagr's hands on her cheeks soothed her soul. In his arms, she had sanctuary.

"Will we carry on?" she asked, her voice hardly above a whisper.

"We shall wait. Your brother will surely come in search when we do not arrive as planned."

"Ah yes!" Brigida's face lit up. Any form of hope was a boon to the spirit.

She fell asleep, too exhausted and broken hearted to fight it. Dagr sat with all senses on alert. He had moved them to a thicket of bushes where they could wait unnoticed. The sound of barreling hooves came two hours later as the sun dipped below the horizon. Dagr called out, "Ho!" when he recognized Mark's mount.

"Where is your ride, my lord? What has happened?" Mark looked around, puzzled. They secured Brigida in the saddle. The eerie sound of a vixen reverberated through the woods.

"Dead. One of the King's men followed us here."

"I see," Mark, grim-faced, considered his friend. He did not need to ask what had happened to the man. In such a situation, he would not like to be the one meeting Dagr's wrath. "I am sorry to hear this, my lord."

Dagr nodded but offered no reply. They left with Mark on foot, trudging resolutely onward.

She had to be starving, Dagr thought when Brigida smiled at him attempting to bring him solace. How he loved her for her kind heart!

The forest rustled with grunts unfamiliar to her ears and she wondered what they could be.

"Wild boar, my lady" Dagr informed her, but waved away her fear. "They want nothing with us."

"They would make for a fine supper," Mark grumbled under his breath.

"We must be close now to the fork in the road," Dagr observed. The fields to their left shone silver in the moonlight. There had been fields like this by the fork, he remembered.

"We are but a half-hour walk from there. How far to the Monastery after that, my lord?"

"Very close, a quarter hour perhaps. Beyond the fork runs a river and a path leads close to its banks. You can follow it all the way to a break in the trees. Turn towards the break. The path runs out there but walking towards the moon, you will see the monastery ahead. There is no mistaking it. It is the only building, and quite sturdy."

"Do you mean to part from us, my lord?" Brigida sat straight, alarmed.

"Yes, my love, I cannot follow you there."

"I will know the reason, my lord! I do not wish to be parted from you." Brigida's voice rose, anxious on the still night air.

Mark and Dagr exchanged glances. Dagr shrugged his shoulders in defeat. There was no reason to avoid the truth.

"I was once an enemy in these parts," he confessed but offered no further details.

Brigida stared at him, then looked away. "I am not one to judge you, my lord. But, feel my brow, my fever has receded. I am able to travel on."

"No, my lady," Dagr insisted, his tone final. "You will find board at the monastery until the monks deem you well. You need a bed and a hot meal and the medicines they grow."

"But we have our own medicine! If you would only make a fire, I could brew a tisane for the illness."

"I cannot make a fire, my lady, for safety's sake," Dagr growled, "and you will do as I say. We will be reunited in a few short days and soon we will make our new home." The last part was to appease the hurt in Brigida's eyes.

"Yes, my lord." Brigida lay against the horse's neck, tears flowing into his mane.

Dagr kept from holding her hand as he wanted to. Touching her now would only make his regret worse. He was not like most men, who raised their voices and hands to the women they married. He wished for this night to end. Indeed, he wished to lie down and close his eyes and forget everything.

When they reached the wide divide in the road, Dagr lifted Brigida to the ground and held her so tight that she fought to push him away. He searched her face for blame but found none. Her heart shone clear through tear-stained eyes.

"All shall be well," she said now, and stood on tiptoe to kiss him. He found her lips too warm and her body too thin as she pressed against him.

"I will find you," Mark promised. He meant to bring food and drink as soon as he was able. But he knew that on his own, Dagr would find sustenance of some sort; he had been a warrior for too long to not know how to survive.

They embraced quickly. Then, Dagr turned on his heel and disappeared into the woods.

CHAPTER 9

I was knit together of bones and skin
Of dreams and sins
Of whispers and promises
I was made of quiet tears
Destined for silence
And solitude

Sahara stood at the door of her cabin, nose lifted to the air. The cold was penetrating, and she pulled her shawl tighter around her shoulders. A brisk wind brought the scent of evergreens marked by the freshness of snow. The landscape before her stretched for miles in deep shadows of white and grey. Dark was settling in even though the hour was barely five in the afternoon.

She was happy to find solitude again. Her soul greeted the land, gathering signals from the Fey and the spirits of the nearby forest. Touching the witch's plaque Aiden had made for her, Sahara smiled and turned in, closing the door behind her with a firm push. A simple whispered spell left her lips. There was always reason to thank Goddess for her blessings and ask for protection.

From wicked winds and fiery sprites, I ask protection for this house.

Tugging her hair, she let out a sigh. Here, in this sanctuary, Sahara was most comfortable. With Ulfred at her feet and Willow in a basket by the hearth, she could, at last, sit peacefully with her thoughts. So much had happened in the last two weeks that she was fairly starving for a chance to process her emotions.

She would make tea. Days after the wild ceremony she had led within these walls setting boundaries for them all, she could still feel the energy they had raised. The hearth stones and the old logs had absorbed much of that evening. She sighed, picturing the scene of the shadows the candles had cast and the closeness of the air when she had invoked her magic. It had felt as if, at any moment, the cabin would disappear, and they would find themselves in another century. The sexual tension between them had fired her spell casting, unrequited passion singing in their souls. And yet, they had managed to agree on a way forward. To find peace with the past and wisdom about the present, was their highest goal.

Soon, in the New Year, she would be leaving for a week-long trip with Aiden and Iona to the secret meeting of The Society. She had to prepare in every way possible in order to be of utmost service to The Society's purpose—to create a successful joining of mankind with the Fey on the planet. Such endeavors were met with solemnity. The location would be a secret they would have to keep from Holly, and indeed, even her and Aiden would travel separately. Each member practiced complete autonomy in their travels, no two would share a plane, or a taxi to where they were going.

This was Aiden's first time attending, and auspiciously, he would be the newly appointed, long-awaited leader. She anticipated seeing him in this role. No longer would he only be her lover, but her teacher. To his wisdom she would be called to surrender, as would everyone, even Iona, who had for so long been their most skilled alchemist.

While there, she would have to lay aside their love and their physical relationship and bow to his governance. But this, she would do with pleasure. Complete surrender was natural to her. She was curious as to how he would approach his new status, but if she knew him at all, it would be in his usual way of quiet strength and irreproachable integrity, ego set aside for the good of their work. And to step into their midst, to lead, without previous conscious knowledge of their projects would take considerable courage. But he would rise, as he always did to the task before him. A warrior still, only now employing magic, having laid down his sword so many years ago.

These thoughts brought her to another question, one that had been on her mind of late... she wondered how Dagr's life had ended. This question had come upon her during a fitful sleep... a dream had percolated just beneath the surface of her awareness. She woke up in a dreadful sweat, panting with fear, but without any knowledge of what it was about. Still, she had seen Dagr in the misty distance of her shrouded reverie, slipping away from her outstretched hand. No matter how much she tried to retrieve the dream, she could not, and felt a sickening in her stomach when she thought of it.

Sahara stirred the fire. The cabin was warm and cozy, fairy lights on the mantle and along the kitchen beams gave her just enough light to put the kettle on to boil and search her cupboards for her favorite blend of tea. She loved the smell of the tea cupboard. In it were, not only the herbs she had dried and crushed into precious jarfuls, but also her witch's apothecary. She had been a skilled healer once, she remembered that much, and her knowledge had come back to her with ease in this lifetime.

Next spring, she would plant an herb garden with Aiden and Holly's help and create a better store of medicinal simples. She longed to marry her love of plants with the creative effort of making tonics and salves. As soon as spring warmed the land, she would take her basket and trowel and search the fields and forest for native plants to add to her larder.

She had seen yarrow, mint, wild roses for vitamin-rich hips, chicory and wild carrot, immortal and beebalm, shepherd's purse and dandelion, mallow and St. John's wort.

She would grow comfrey and mugwort, loosestrife and the more common herbs such as parsley, sage and thyme. From these she would make savory dishes for her lovers. Oh, how she loved the country life. She would search the woods for nuts and elderberries. Holly had promised to forage with her. This was all she wanted, to live in communion with the land and the two people who made her heart sing.

The kettle whistled. Sahara poured her tea. The scent of rooibos, rose petals and lavender filled the air. Lavender that she would grow in a protected sunny corner for tea and to supply Holly with flower buds for her scones. She smiled. There was no better thing than being nature's child. She had kept to herself the last few days and tonight she ached a little for the touch of a woman. Glancing at the old wind-up clock in the kitchen, she realized Holly and Aiden were most likely settling down to supper.

She lifted the small clock from its resting place and began her nightly ritual of winding. The sound of the clockworks turning; the imminent ticking of the hands; the pleasure of the repetitive motions summarized how Sahara liked to live her life—according to the seasons, a continual cycle of honoring the wheel of the year.

Her plans for the next year included creating a sacred space among a grove of trees to the left of her cabin, on the far side of her home. Aiden had such a sacred circle among some quaking aspens and Douglas fir—a naturally formed circle which was a portal to the Underworld, where magic and Druidic ritual could be performed during special times of the year, used to observe the eight sabbats and the cycles of the moon.

She had already spoken to Iona and Richard about attending such celebrations and her idea had been met with enthusiasm. With four or more participants, they could invoke the Four Directions, and place a Gatekeeper at each compass point. The Gatekeepers would perform the important task of greeting the spiritual gatekeepers of the four directions, as they came to join the ritual. The Shining Ones, as they are called in Druidic tradition, would protect the circle energy as it was raised with whatever purpose was at hand. Sahara wanted to incorporate Druidic tradition into her magic. There were some variations to how Wiccan magic was performed, but the work of The Society was steeped in Druid roots which had long honored the spirits of the land and the Fey.

Already, this fall, she had discovered her grove. Among the aspens and fir were also several Gambel oaks—a very special find in this area where the weather was not suited to their more sensitive nature. This winter, she would erect a cauldron in the center of the grove and light the first fire to open the gateway for ancestors to pass through. She would initiate the circle and absorb the energy of her magic instead of releasing it to the vast Oneness as would be done within Wiccan tradition. She had a basketful of offerings to leave for Mother Earth once the initiation was complete.

She and Aiden could alternate Sabbats to make ceremony at his or her place. In this way, the land could partake in both their invocations and spellcasting—the presence of the Fey called in by two very different voices. She was sure this would be pleasing to the inhabitants of the unseen dimensions.

How long had she waited to have such a safe space to work her magic? She thought back to the ad she had seen in the paper for the cabin's sale. There had been no way of knowing what this place would mean or what it would bring in lovers or awakening to past lives.

Heat rose along her spine and released through her crown as Sahara remembered the first time she had laid eyes on Aiden. He had turned toward her, all force and gentleness combined, a man who was a feast for her eyes as well as her heart.

Aiden had come with this land. There were no coincidences, and no doubt they had made an agreement to meet once more in this lifetime. The convergence of events that led to their meeting was mind-boggling. How many choices and decisions had they both made, in their lives, to bring them to this corner of wilderness? Sahara thanked Goddess for the day she had opened the newspaper and casually browsed the want ads and that purchasing a property sight unseen had been a totally sane act, from her point of view.

Her clit tingled thinking about Aiden's hands. They had been one of her earliest fascinations with him, strong, yet capable of the softest touch. They symbolized his commitment to function and form as it related to his building style, and the deft way he tied her when

50

aroused into dominant fervor. They were keepers of her love; decadent reminders of his consummate passion.

In a few short months he had become her master and her liberator, her path into authenticity, her seducer, her keeper of secrets. To him she would bow, as her respect for his character was great. It was as if he was made of Dagr's steel and a modern man's evolved sense of being in the world. Both aspects of him raised a hot desire, and while she relished this time alone, she also counted the hours until she could be in his arms once more.

Sahara stretched her feet toward the fire and took a sip of tea, noticing the fragrant scent of the brew. A notification on her phone brought her sharply back to present reality. Holly.

"You're so close and yet so far, my darling. What are you doing?"

Sahara smiled, picturing the blond-haired woman who had equally as magically appeared in her life.

"Sitting quietly doing nothing... well, having tea by the fire. Thinking up magic for this winter. What are you doing, Beautiful?"

"We're just finishing making supper. I'd like to feed you... miss you."

"Ah, you're so sweet. Miss you. I'm long overdue for some solitude, we've been knee-deep in crazy for a couple of weeks, haven't we?"

"Yes, too much, and yet, all necessary. Our unfolding."

"I love how your intuition has grown over the last little while. My magical fairy girl!"

A pile of emojis exploded over the screen as Holly responded... *"Heart explosions over here! I love you!"*

"What is our man up to?"

"He's pretending to be busy in the kitchen while wondering what I'm saying to you. He's pretty transparent. Haha, he's coming over!"

Sahara laughed out loud. She imagined the tumble Aiden and Holly were having over her phone. Being this close and yet having time to herself suit Sahara very well. Tomorrow Holly would be back to her regular schedule, and Aiden to renovating his office space. Their lives would gain a new equilibrium and for a couple of months they would be in each other's lives on a daily basis.

Once early spring came, Aiden would be off on more distant projects and she would be gone on a tour of ten cities to promote her book. She didn't relish the idea, she didn't need the money, but she did write with a purpose, so getting the books out into the world was the goal. She wondered how this latest work would be received. Her readership was used to illicit content and magic, but this time, she had taken things to a new level.

What she really wanted was for people to awaken to their ancient heritage of Earth wisdom. She hated the disconnect between the Feminine and Masculine, the lack of understanding of what sexuality was all about by society at large; the severing of mankind's relationship with the Unseen.

This is what she was here for; to shift consciousness in her own way. She wanted to tell whomever would listen that the force of creation was within each person, beautifully cradled within the spinal cord, the Kundalini serpent that rose when called upon. She wanted to teach that orgasm was nothing to be chased or feared, it was, when met unconditionally, a release of the divine creative force—a moment of healing and transformation. This healing, transformative force, which dwelled within each human being, had been twisted into something dirty and forbidden. This was, in Sahara's opinion, one of the biggest lies ever perpetrated upon human-kind. For centuries, this self-empowering and divine wisdom had been hidden and lost from the conscious mind. Now, she was sure, was the time to break open the memories of those who were ready to listen.

The Divine Masculine and Sacred Feminine would once more join in ecstasy, finding truth in their embrace. They would know sexual expression was a direct portal to the One, and all people had access to the Tree of Life through it, no priestly intermediary required.

Such was the power of intimacy; those engaged in it were indeed participating in a sacred dance of spiritual connection to all wisdom and the source of all beginnings. But sadly, the world had been indoctrinated into believing woman was the bearer of all ills, sins, and of man's separation from his God. What a travesty!

Well, she would be a voice, as much as she could be, no matter if she was called mad or grossly mistaken. Kathryn, her agent, had already received requests for speaking engagements on this very subject. Women everywhere were waking up to their inner wisdom and were exploring their re-wilding.

Tonight, she would eat a simple meal and read by the fire. If she wanted to, she could call on her lovers and they would come as quickly as she beckoned. Knowing they were near was enough right now. Having time to engage her mind with some favorite books would be her solace tonight. Having a love that allowed for her complete freedom was a gift she had not expected in this lifetime. She had not known that people like Aiden and Holly existed outside of her books and ancient memories. But now she'd met them—she wouldn't stifle their love. She would breathe space into their togetherness, as one of her favorite quotes read.

Sahara was poignantly aware how rare her situation was.

She grabbed her phone again.

"In a couple of weeks, we should have our evening of seed ordering... want to do it still?"

"Yes! Let's! Remember when we talked about this first? We hardly knew each other."

"I know. And yet..."

"And yet..." Holly finished Sahara's thought... *"we have always been."*

"Yes darling. We have always been. I love you so much."

"Aiden says hello."

"What are you two doing?"

"Making plans for his parents to come over. Do you mind if it's during New Year's week?"

"Anytime that's good for you and Aiden is good for me. Yikes! So much initiating of parents!"

"Right? It does feel as if we're initiating them. Good word. Aiden thinks it'll be ok. That they'll take it well."

"I have a good feeling about it too. Hugs to you and Aiden."

She imagined Holly as she probably was in this moment, lying in Aiden's arms, against his hard core, typing contentedly. She could picture Aiden's lazy smile as dropped tender kisses in Holly's hair, his heart full.

"Kisses for you too! Aiden sends his love."

They ended with their usual slew of emojis. Sahara smiled at the silly things they sent each other, funny little love stickers.

Turning back to focus on the fire, her thoughts drifted back to Dagr. She wondered what her dream had meant. That intense little ache returned to her chest when she thought of Dagr fading away from her. Adjusting the pillow in the corner of the sofa, Sahara lied down. The fire danced and spit sparks of embers, rising to the invocation on the witch's lips. She called to the past.

"Show me! I would meet Dagr again. Take me to his love."

CHAPTER 10

Mark banged thrice on the heavy wooden door of the monastery. They waited for a good long while until they heard a faint shuffling on the other side. A jingling of keys came next. The door opened with a rusty creak and they stood facing a small man in monk's garb, holding a candle high to see Mark's face.

All they could express was their tired greeting, and a few words Brigida knew, offering their names.

The monk took a seasoned evaluation of the people before him then waived them in. He spoke in his language, but all they understood was his question—*Anglais?*

"Oui... Anglais" Mark replied. *"My sister is sick, she needs your care."*

"Soeur? Yes. Veins avec moi."

The man shuffled along a long, dark, endless hallway. Finally, they came to a large kitchen, where he sat them both on stools by the hearth and ladled two steaming cupsful of a minty herbal brew.

With more conversation they had no hope of understanding, the monk, who introduced himself as *Estienne*, laid out a wooden platter of dark, crusty bread and a fragrant cheese. Mark tore in ravenously, while Brigida took to shredding tiny bites of bread with trembling hands. After a few moments of watching her carefully, the monk returned to the fire to heat some clear broth.

Another cup was filled and while Brigida drank, he laid his palm to her forehead. Muttering to himself, Estienne prepared a large basin of hot water and sprinkled in a powder from a jar of crushed flowers and herbs. Unlacing Brigida's boots, he lowered her feet in slowly to acclimatize her to the heat.

She shivered and pulled her wrap tighter. From what she knew of healing, she anticipated the herbs in the foot bath would release bad humors. The broth would supply nourishment but not upset her stomach. It would be readily absorbed, rich with minerals, and bring on a sweat. The remedies warmed her to her very bones.

Mark was given a tumbler full of red wine, which by his expression, she judged to be very good. When Mark seemed satisfied, they were led, once more, down another hallway to a small room with several cots. The beds were fitted with pillows stuffed with straw; a sheet whiter than snow; and a generous woolen blanket. Brigida fell in and almost cried with gratitude. They were left alone, a chamber pot to share between them. The sound of the key in the lock to remind them that while they would be taken care of, they would have to prove their trustworthiness.

———————————⟶∗∗∗⟵———————————

Brigida woke when the sun shone hot on her face through the small window. She looked around—she was alone. Panic set in quickly. The room was chilly, the stone walls thick and impenetrable. The window was too small for escape.

She was wearing a heavy sleeping gown of roughly woven flax. Who had changed her? Where was Mark? Her heart called to Dagr. She thought she had done so silently, but what her mind did not register was... she had yelled at the top of her lungs.

In moments, Estienne was in the room, Mark not far behind.

"Who... who?" Was all she could get out, clutching at the gown and looking wildly about for her clothes.

Holding her close, Mark cooed to calm her.

"It was I, dear sister. Etienne has washed your clothes, they are here, look!"

"But when was there time?" Brigida blushed knowing her brother had seen her unclothed. Her undergarments were missing as well.

"You have been sleeping for three days and nights."

Brigida tore away. "But Dagr? Three days and nights! He must be wondering about our safety?"

"He does not expect us back until you are healed, or at least until I can leave you safely. Do not worry about him."

"But he must be hungry!"

"Darling, he will not! He knows how to survive. Please sister, save your energy for getting well."

"When can we leave here?"

"Soon. Estienne will know."

Mark smiled at the monk who was quite animated to see her awake and had come back with a tray of food and a tiny cup of wine.

They left her alone to use the chamber pot and dress. She ate quickly and was more hungry than she could ever remember being; warmed by the wine in her belly and the thick slice of bread slathered in golden honey.

What she didn't expect was that her legs would be so weak. Estienne took them back to the kitchen to sit by the fire. Mark set to telling her about the monastery, whom he had met, and about the garden he was about to take her to.

"You have never seen a garden like this! Not even on Dagr's old estate. This is a healer's garden and supplies most of their food."

"Oh! I would be most interested to see. Perhaps I could learn some. Where is everyone? There must be others?"

"They have a strange schedule, mainly prayers and more prayers. A lot of chanting in Latin. Everyone seems to have allotted responsibilities. Some work in the garden, some in the kitchen, some are scholars. All very kind. Estienne is the only one who speaks some English."

At the mention of his name, Estienne came forward and revealed a smile that breathed strongly of garlic.

"You are well. No fever," he said with a twinkle in his eye and a slurry accent.

"Merci!" Brigida took his hands in hers and kissed his fingers. Her eyes shone with tears. "I am well."

"Ah, bien!" Estienne gestured that she get up. *"Au jardin"* he said, and led them to the outdoors.

It was true, Brigida had never seen such a garden! Her exclamation of joy was so genuine that Estienne clapped his hands and began speaking very quickly, waving his hands to show off the different areas. Women were not a usual visitor to the garden, indeed, the work within its walls was considered a sacred occupation for the men cloistered within the monastery. Several other monks walking along a path scowled at Estienne for allowing the intrusion.

Estienne waved his hand to dismiss their displeasure. He barked something, and they scurried along at a much faster gait than they were normally used to.

"Women... Ils ne sont pas habitues aux femmes ici," he said. Brigida nodded. She understood, but wild horses could not have dragged her from this place.

Every corner of the garden was laid out with an eye for structure, organized beautifully, fruit trees espaliered against stone walls, fruiting shrubs in another corner, beds and beds of leeks—a staple in French potagers, garlic, herbs, calendula flowers for salves, lavender, mint and roses for tisanes.

Brigida was most attracted to the healing herb garden laid out in a geometric pattern with a statue of a monk at its center. "How lovely!" she uttered, sitting down on a nearby stone bench. This was heaven. She allowed herself to dream of having such a garden at their new home.

"St. Francis d'Assise," Estienne whispered reverently, pointing at the statue.

Brigida made a note to ask Dagr about this St. Francis. He and these monks were of the religion that had broken their family, but if she were to judge by Estienne and this garden, there seemed to be men among them who also revered nature? Only it was strange to not see women among them. What a lonely life it would be, she pondered. Basking in the warm sun and the fragrance of the garden, Brigida could feel herself gaining strength.

"Mark, we must tell Dagr of this garden." A further tour had revealed an apiary, with its charming willow bee-skeps, a chicken yard and further still, an enclosure for pigs. "There is everything here for keeping one in supplies. I suppose they get their flour from local farmers, I must ask the recipe for the hearty bread."

Remembering Hannah from her stay in Richard's care, Brigida could almost taste the bread they had baked with cracked seeds sprinkled over the top crust.

My, she was excited to again have a home where she could bake and dig in the soil. She only realized now the ache inside for the life she used to have at the manor, with a stillroom and a garden... her heart ached even more for the woman with whom she had shared those places.

"Come, my lady," Mark said. "You must not get over-tired."

"I am well already, see?" With a last fond look over her shoulder at the garden, Brigida stepped into the cool interior of the monastery. "Perhaps tomorrow, we can find Dagr and journey on?"

"Perhaps. We will ask Estienne."

"You can trust I know my own body!"

Mark smiled. *She must be better*, he thought, her stubborn spirit was back. "Yes, my lady. But I must answer to your beloved, and I am more afraid of him than you."

Brigida laughed. "Indeed. But you would be wise to be more afraid of me."

CHAPTER 11

"Mother," Aiden grinned into the phone. "How are you little mama?"

"Oh, darling! You know what I'm doing right now?"

"No idea, but I'm sure you'll tell me."

"Your father and I are packing up for a trip to Alaska. You know I've always wanted to go."

"I remember Dad saying he would take you one day. When is it?"

"Not for months but I'm so excited!"

"Ah, I see. You're always well prepared. I'm so pleased for you. Anyway, I'm calling with a request. Actually, I wanted to apologize again about not having you out for Christmas, I did mean to."

"Oh, that's ok. We understand."

Aiden furrowed his brow at the hint of hurt he heard in his mother's voice, thought she hid it well. He hated being the one who had put it there.

"In any case, I'd like to invite you and Dad out for a few days New Year's week. I've been busy, but that's not a good excuse really. To be honest, I've been... well, there's someone I'd like you to meet."

There it was out.

Bronwyn's hoot of surprise had Aiden laughing out loud.

"We were wondering if you were ever going to find someone... err, more permanent."

Aiden knew this was his mother's way of saying she hadn't approved of his younger day exploits.

"Who is she? Someone local?

"Um, yes, a neighbor," he answered. *Or two*, he thought.

"Well, what does she look like? I never could get a read on a type with you," Bronwyn chuckled.

"Listen, instead of all these questions, why not come up and see for yourself? Should I speak to Dad or will you give him the news?"

"Oh, I'll tell him. When exactly do you want us?"

How about January second and stay till the fifth? There's plenty of room, of course, and no need to bring anything."

"Sounds good. Have you told this young lady anything about us... I mean..."

Aiden's heart pounded hard. He loved this woman and how brave she was. He couldn't imagine her pain at losing a daughter.

"Yes, Mama, she knows. And I've told her you're the best mother in the world. So now you have to live up to that... but no pressure." He laughed, eager to distract his mother from thoughts of his beloved sister.

"Ok. I'll try, but it's your Dad you really have to worry about. I can behave."

"He's over my not going to university and moving away, isn't he?"

"Oh yeah. He's proud of you, he just doesn't like to tell you. He thinks it'll spoil you."

"Love you, Mom. It's been much too long."

His mother had always been the intermediary, ever looking to his happiness, always the peacemaker and strength in the family.

"Well, I love you too darling. You're a good man, and that's all I need to know."

"See you soon."

"Soon."

"Mom?"

"Yes, my boy?"

"I miss her every single day."

"I know. I know."

Aiden hung up with tears stinging his eyes but relieved the arrangements had been made. He sat down with his schedule book to review the week's projects; but all he could do was stare blankly into space.

Something about his dreams the last few nights was prickling his memory. Most of it escaped him now, but one thing stood out—he thought he had seen a foreshadowing from their lifetime together to this one. In the dream, Brigida, standing on the edge of a cliff, pointed toward the horizon, which Aiden understood had meant the future. She had named him something... what was it? He shook his head as if to rid himself of invisible cobwebs.

Brigida. She was haunting him still since the last regression. His heart ached for the woman who had lost two of Dagr's children. Lately, he'd been harboring a hope of being a father. How had they dealt with it... the loss? Maybe tonight he would connect with Brigida again. He hoped he would. That world was dragging him in, little by little, to places which held clues to who he was now.

CHAPTER 12

"Synchronicity is an ever-present reality for those who have eyes to see."
~ Carl Jung

Among the supplies Estienne had packed for their departure, Brigida found several tiny packets of seeds. Among them were lavender, calendula, leek and leafy greens Estienne called *salade*—purslane, dandelion, cress and borage. There was a vial of bitter tonic for digestion with a recipe for making her own. A very special package of poppy seeds was marked *maladie grave, papaver setigeum*—Estienne explained several processes by which the seeds were used in baking or tea and other ways to control pain and disease. A resin could be made from the milky sap of the poppy stalks and smoked, or a tincture made for adding to one's wine... but this Estienne cautioned against. It was for someone who suffered from seizures or had such severe melancholy as it to be life threatening.

Brigida was grateful for all the advice, especially as she knew women were not trusted with such healing work by the new religion. In the herbal book given to her by Richard, she had read about the magical poppy; referred to as *God's Medicine*, but had not seen one until she had stepped into the mystical world of the monastery's garden.

Mark handed Estienne a generous handful of coins in return for his kind care.

Estienne blushed red with gratitude, bowed his head, made a few weak protests and then the coins disappeared within the folds of his woolen garb.

After that several loaves of bread, cheese and dried fruit was thrown into a sack. A jug of wine accompanied it. They left in high spirits, Mark anxious for their travel days to be over, and Brigida almost bursting with excitement to see Dagr once more.

By the light of the rising sun, they made their way into the woods where they hoped Dagr would be waiting for them. Before Mark could use the whistle signal they had agreed upon, Dagr materialized from the mist in the trees.

"My lord!" Brigida shouted, then jumped into her lover's arms.

"Are you quite well, my lady?" Dagr held her away to see for himself.

"I am well," Brigida answered, then, seeing the twinkle in Dagr's eye, blushed, hiding her face in his cloak.

"Come, let me kiss you!" Dagr's joy spilled into his smile.

Mark turned away to give them privacy, pretending to tend to the horse and tie their supplies to the saddle.

"Ho, Mark!" Dagr called out. "While the two of you have been languishing in the lap of luxury, I've explored the road that will take us home."

"Languishing, say you? It has been nothing but torture drinking that vinegar those monks call wine."

"Oh really, let me have a taste then!"

Mark passed the jug. "I am warning you, only a taste, it is vile."

Dagr raised an eyebrow. He had been to that monastery once, and drunk of their wine, although it had not been offered. He remembered a sweet concoction very different to the mead he was used to. Back then, it had been a very delicious surprise. Maybe the monks served the worst batches to those they took in.

One sip led to another. This was the best he had ever drunk, even compared to Richard's privately imported stock.

"Should we save this for when we find home?"

Mark nodded in agreement.

"How long will it take, my lord?" Brigida, asked, fearing the worst. She was so very weary of traveling.

"No more than two weeks' time, my lady."

"Will any of it be by boat?"

"Yes, but a gentle ride along a river. The worst is behind us."

"I am pleased, my lord. I have full hope that when we make our home everything will return to normal."

Dagr stared into Brigida's dark, moody eyes. He knew what she hoped, and he could not promise the one thing they both craved above all—to be reunited as a family, with Arinn.

A pained look marring their present happiness, Dagr could only lift her onto horseback and kiss her hand.

"We shall see, my lady. We shall see."

Their first concern was to find a horse capable of a hard ride for the fourteen-day journey ahead. But finding one in good condition could be difficult, as they were in farm country where horses were used for plowing or short distance journeys to the local village. To find the kind of horse they were looking for would have been easier in Calais. Dagr had not anticipated the horror of losing his steed.

"I have had a chance to scout out some farms in your absence," Dagr confided to Mark.

"You have spoken to someone?" Mark asked, a little alarmed.

"Not yet, but I did spy a gelding in a field not far away."

"Will it be possible to convince someone to part with their best horse, my lord?" Brigida wondered.

"A good price will usually sway even the most stubborn owner. I will venture a guess we will be successful." Dagr led the way to the farm in question. "See, yonder? That one!" he pointed at a handsome, grazing chestnut.

"He's huge!" Brigida exclaimed.

"As befits a man of your size," Mark observed.

"Ah, yes, he is a fine boy," Dagr's voice softened.

No one spoke of the great beast who had devoted himself to Dagr for years of service, but he was on everyone's mind. No horse could replace him.

"Wait here while I make the inquiries."

They were at the edge of the woods, with the road toward home stretching before them.

"Hurry, my lord!" Brigida pleaded.

A scant twenty minutes later, Mark and Brigida saw Dagr and a hobbling farmer wandering toward the edge of the field. A sharp whistle, the horse's head shot up, and he cantered to the field gate.

There was much waving of arms on the farmer's part and then Dagr was riding bareback across the expanse of the field. Closest to where they were hiding, rider and steed stopped along the fence line. Dagr's smooth strokes along the gelding's neck were met with a whinny and a toss of the head. His coat shone as if brushed diligently, even from a distance. This was a well-cared-for animal. Soon, Dagr stood before them, beaming, the horse saddled and snorting a greeting.

"Would you look at him? As fine a beast as any I have ever seen. Well-trained and used to exercise. The fellow will never ride again, poor sod. Broken leg. He cost a pretty sum but look at his coat and how solid he is! Let me see you upon him."

And with that, Brigida was in the saddle.

"Aye, you look like a proper lady."

If the beginning of the trip had been fraught with sickness and a frightful interception, the next two and a half weeks could not have been any more of a stark contrast. Each day brought pleasant spring weather, decent enough roads and plenty of opportunity for hunting small game or eating simple but tasty meals at inns scattered throughout picturesque villages.

They spent many a night under the stars, Brigida tucked warmly against her lover, her prayers to the spirits full of gratitude for the beauty of the countryside and the kind people they had met along the way. There had not been one time they had felt danger or had been greeted by an unwelcoming stranger. Dagr's proficiency at the language was truly admirable and an obvious asset. A few nights along the way, they paid for accommodation, a hot bath and wine.

Brigida smiled secretly at the looks Dagr garnered from pretty French maids. And on one occasion, a young man, whose forward nature was duly noted by Mark and scowled upon.

France was welcoming them in a way she had not expected—both the land and its inhabitants. It was not the cool, vibrant green of England, but there were ancient oaks and forests rich in mushrooms and healing plants she readily recognized. The further south they rode, the more she fell in love. The houses of honey colored stone, brightly colored doors and window shutters and the music of this foreign land gladdened her heart. And oh how she needed this respite for her soul.

A fortnight of travel behind them, they stood at the edge of a wide river, Dagr negotiating passage on a stocky boat captained by a swarthy Frenchman of few teeth, but a boisterous laugh.

"What does he say, my lord?" Brigida tugged on Dagr's sleeve.

"We board shortly. Apparently, our destination is not as far as I imagined. I have a surprise my darling! By day's end, we should be at the village nearest the chateau. What do you say to that, my sweet?"

Brigida's teary sob turned the captain's head and brought on a sudden song.

Dagr lifted his beloved into the air swinging her around as she whooped and hollered. It was so gratifying to see the light in her eyes. It was their first full moment of joy not over-shadowed by Arinn's absence. Both of them craved safety and the comfort of home. Being unsettled these last few years had taken its toll.

The boat drifted smoothly on the river, revealing stunning views of the Perigord Valley past lush forest, rocky escarpments and rich meadows.

"My lord, I am grateful for this land. Look, everywhere orchards and sun... I do not remember ever feeling it so hot on my face, and this only late spring!"

Dagr kissed her hand, one arm around her waist. "It pleases me so to see you smile. Were my stories of France true then? Do you find it as I described it?"

"Better! Yes." Brigida stopped mid-thought to stare with a gaping mouth at a chateau sitting squarely facing the riverbank, surrounded by formal gardens, an oak forest behind it.

"Ohhhh!" was all she could say.

"What do you call that sort of home, a manor?"

"A chateau," Dagr answered. "Can be compared to a manor home, the home of a nobleman most likely, or an important man of state."

"Richard said he was finding us a chateau... surely he did not mean something like that?"

"I most certainly hope not, my lady. Whatever would we do in a home of such grandeur?"

"Have a very large family?" Brigida blurted out before thinking. They held hands as they sank into their own thoughts and did not speak any more until the captain of the boat announced that around the next bend, they would see the village where they would leave his company.

Suddenly, their hearts were overcome with the enormity of the situation. Home, at last. Home in a new country, perhaps never to return to England again. Home away from Arinn, away from Richard. Years ahead of them to make new friendships and alliances. Would they ever smell the fresh sea air and mist that rolled in over the moors... would they hear the voices and accent of their countrymen?

Stepping over the plank to the shore, Brigida allowed her emotions to wash over her. This was her family, these two men. But Arinn! Sweet Arinn. In this instant she mourned the loss of her lover, the scent of her skin, the touch of her mouth.

She refused the ride Dagr offered her, choosing to walk alone with her tears. Tears of grief mixed with tears of relief.

Following the well-trod path across a field to the village ahead, all she could think of was getting in a clean bed and sleeping for as long as she were allowed. Would she ever get enough sleep to wear off this ache in her heart?

CHAPTER 13

"Hey lover!"

"Hey sweet thing!" Aiden wiped the sweat from his brow and put down his tools.

"You're making a very big racket. My customers are wondering what you're up to."

"Sorry, I'll stop now. I didn't realize you had opened already. Just lost track of time," he grinned.

"You've been ripping walls apart and running that saw since we got here at four in the morning. Everything ok, babe? You were restless in your sleep last night, I think you were having a bad dream?"

"Yeah, just something I'm grappling with."

"Hmm, Brigida?"

"How do you know? Was I talking in my sleep?" Aiden pulled Holly in by her waist.

"Mmm, you smell good. Reminds me of our first kiss—you're wearing the same perfume."

Holly giggled and tried squirming away.

"Nope. I'm not finished." Aiden's grip tightened.

"I have to go. I only came up to get you to stop hammering."

"If you want me to let you go, why are you offering me your neck to ravage? I don't think you know what you're saying."

Holly pushed at his chest but gave up as Aiden sought her mouth.

"Will you be here all day? I'll bring you some lunch," she breathed between kisses.

"I will, but I'll come down, you don't need to serve me."

"I want to... oh, you have that look in your eye. You're impossible!"

Aiden let her go and took a step back to look at her.

"You look properly disheveled. You might want to fix your hair before you go down."

"Or I might not," Holly teased.

"Have it your way. But don't blame me when people stare."

"I want them to stare. I want them to know I'm yours."

"Ok, go, before I bend you over this table."

"I'm wet," Holly said, turning away and heading for the door. She looked back to blow Aiden a kiss and almost fell to her knees at the look of lust on his face.

"I love you woman. Go!"

Aiden turned back to his work. He didn't really need to do this demo on his own, but he was hungry for physical work and anxious to have his new office remodeled. The staircase to the upstairs had been replaced with a handsome new structure, along with a custom door of solid maple stained a pickled grey. This was a thing for him, he couldn't abide for the back of a building to look any less welcoming than the front. Once this space was finished, he could move in the assistant who would take over his accounting, phone correspondence as well as a myriad of other business details he had been tending to himself for far too long. As much as he had avoided this progress, he was now looking forward to the help. Having Sahara assist him the last two months had really opened his eyes to how much he needed help.

In the next two weeks, this outdated area would house an elegant new reception area plus a private office for his use. That would clear the clutter at home where he'd been storing building plans and bookwork. He was excited to see what furniture Sahara had picked out to furnish the two rooms. He had asked for a large desk, and a generous sized sofa with a pull-out bed, and of course, the men he had hired to do the finishing work would make built-in book shelves and storage to span one wall. A full bathroom with a stunning natural stone shower rounded out the renovation. Always practical, Aiden looked to the future and outfitting the building in a way which would increase its value. If he was gone, Holly could always convert this office into a rental suite by adding a small kitchen set-up to the rooms.

Now, why, after his dreams last night, was he still thinking about something foreboding? That same vision of Brigida pointing to the future ruffled his equilibrium.

The smell of coffee and pastries wafting up from the bakery convinced him to break early. Suddenly he missed Holly's presence. Yes, he would break now and take a later lunch. That way he would still be here when Holly was finished, and they could decide on dinner.

Just as he rummaged through those thoughts, the door opened, and Sahara stepped into the dusty room carrying a tray of coffee and Portuguese custard tarts.

"Well, aren't you a lovely surprise?" Aiden reached to take the tray from her so she could remove her coat.

"Hello handsome. Fancy a break with me?"

"I was just this minute thinking of coming downstairs. I didn't know you'd be in town today... or are you working in the bakery?"

"Nooo. Not in the bakery. Was picking up some groceries and wine. You're both coming to my place for supper tonight."

"We are? I like this idea. Miss me?"

"I *fucking* miss you, to be honest. All work and no play make Sahara... well, horny."

They burst out laughing. Aiden made space on the work table for the tray.

"I think you should kiss me now," he said.

"Didn't you just get a kiss from Holly?"

"Is nothing secret? Come here. I don't have time for this counting-kisses game." He pulled her roughly towards him.

Did I tell you I like it when you tell me what to do?"

Aiden growled. "Stop talking." His mouth seared onto hers as her hand brushed along the growing erection in his jeans.

"You're so fucking hot, darling."

"You're still talking."

"Rip my shirt open."

"No." Aiden's insistent kisses drew a moan.

"I want you to fuck me here!" Sahara spit out.

She expected another protest from him and cried out when suddenly his hands were in her shirt, buttons popping like spilled candy along the floor, bra roughly shrugged over her breasts, and then she was turned around, face down on the table covered in coffee-soaked sawdust.

"Aiden!"

"You asked to be fucked and so you shall be." Ripping her jeans down in one swift move, Aiden pressed against her.

Sahara felt the warmth of his legs against hers, his hands hard on her ass opening her up, and before she could answer, his cock thrust inside her.

His hand over her mouth kept her scream from reaching the rest of the building, and he smiled as she collapsed her face to the table top, eyes closed, orgasm gushing over his very thick cock. With a last push deep inside her, Aiden allowed himself release. Sahara's pussy tight around him. He moaned against her back.

"I'll never get tired of this. Of you."

"Hold me."

If fucking made Sahara open like a flower at sunrise, being in Aiden's arms sealed her into utter contentedness.

She tried to put her blouse together but gave up and instead offered Aiden the only sip of coffee left in his cup. Hands shaking a little adjusting to the throbbing of her clit and the love which poured from her heart for the remarkable man before her, she smiled coquettishly.

"Now that we have that out of the way, darling, want to tell me about the dreams you've been having lately?"

CHAPTER 14

Today I see you
As the magic beneath your skin
As the shadows behind the moon
As the depths of the Seven Seas
I travel your heart...
Whose landscape has bewitched me

The village was like so many they had passed along the way, charming, familiar in that it was arranged in a cluster of dwellings like the villages at home, with the addition of a tantalizing aroma of bread wafting from the baker's shop. Children ran amok; a rooster crowed in someone's back garden and a herd of goats ran before an old man waving a crooked walking stick.

Altogether it was a very pleasant sight, if not a little unnerving that, quite quickly, the houses emptied of their inhabitants and a circle of ogling town folk gathered around them.

In the flurry of conversation which followed, they found that everyone in town had been anticipating their arrival. The cook Richard had hired for the chateau had spread the news a new Vicomte would be arriving with his family. But they had been told two women... now who was this other man and where was the missing woman?

The cook, Hermine, had been going out of her mind worrying about the day they would arrive, as the Earl had very strongly advised her to not be caught unprepared.

A young lad was dispatched to make the trek up the hill with a basket of bread and two squawking chickens clutched upside down by their feet. He ran off at top speed, the baker yelling after him.

Everyone seemed very excited that Vicomte Montagne and his English wife *Brigitte* would be reviving the old estate. Where was he from exactly? Would he be employing anyone for the gardens and household? And could he advise on the usage of the common lands surrounding the chateau, as there had been much dispute over who could hunt what in those woods? Of course, everyone had been hunting whatever they wanted in the absence of the chateau's owner which, normally, would have garnered an unpleasant punishment.

Dagr did his best to translate for Brigida and Mark here and there, as both stood quite overwhelmed by the barrage of inquiries. Finally, he waved them all into silence and explained they had been travelling for days and that once they were settled, he would look to all their concerns.

A young girl offered Brigida a posy of wild flowers. Another woman shoved her daughter forward for the role of lady's maid, while yet another said she had experience as a chatelaine. The guffaws from her neighbors did not seem to faze her one bit.

All in good time, Dagr assured, and then, placing Brigida in the saddle, broke away from the crowd.

"What a rabble of peasants!" Mark commented.

"Altogether, it was much better than I had expected. They were friendly if curious—prepared for a new owner of the estate. Whatever information Richard told the cook to gossip into the village was strategic to keeping us safe."

"Vicomte Montagne?" Mountain?" Brigida asked.

"I assume it is a testament to Richard's sense of humor... playing off my height."

"What about Dagr? Will you change your name fully?" Mark wondered.

"I have been thinking about it. Dagr is not recognizably an English name, and the French do use the name Dag... perhaps Dagr will not be so very strange after all? What say you, my lady?"

"I say we keep your name. There have been enough changes of late."

"As you wish, *Brigitte*," Dagr grinned.

They kept on, marveling at the rich fields closest to the river before following a winding cart track up the hill and into the woods.

"What beautiful trees, my lord!" Brigida exclaimed. "Ancient, that's what!" A litter of fallen leaves decorated the forest floor. These were not scrubby woods, these were ancient groves of oak and mountain pine, chestnut and beech. Everywhere she looked she saw food to forage. This was indeed a land of plenty.

Dagr and Mark exchanged glances, grateful that Brigida's earlier sadness was dissipating.

When finally they came out from the protection of the trees, they stopped to gape at the view unfolding before them. To the south, on an open slope, an old vineyard. They would have to see to its restoration... but even so, it was impressive.

To their left, the chateau. It was massive! Bigger than Dagr's old manor, perhaps three times the size. Built of the golden limestone native to the area, it stood proud and sturdy, perfectly symmetrical in architecture, approached by an avenue of fragrant olive trees and a large courtyard.

"Oh my!" Brigida breathed, eyes filling with tears. "I thought..."

"Good Lord!" Mark exclaimed.

You never listen, Dagr thought of Richard's promise to acquire something modest. He should have known, Richard was incapable of anything less than what he would be happy to live in.

"Where do we start?" Brigida asked.

"Inside. Let us greet our new home, and later we will explore the grounds."

Within minutes the cook was flying from the around the side of the house, hands wiping in her apron, smiling and performing a comical half-bow, half-curtsy. She gestured toward the front door, ushering them in. Dagr assured her it was perfectly fine to follow them in but she rolled her eyes at him and disappeared to the back of the building once more.

Before they could explore even one room, arrested by the stone fireplace dominating the foyer, she had returned with a tray of bread and cheeses, a flagon of wine and some sweet biscuits. The young boy who had run up ahead of them swung open the doors to the front reception room.

"What does she say, my lord?" Brigida asked as the cook continued to chatter, quite apparently distressed.

"She's apologizing for the meager tray," Dagr tried very hard to not burst out laughing as the corners of Brigida's mouth twitched in amusement.

"Meager? Oh, tell her..."

"No! We must pretend we have been eating like royalty, my lady, it would not do to divulge our troubles. Will you remember? And we cannot go around awed by every room in the house, even though we obviously are."

Dagr settled into a comfortable chair, crossing his long legs elegantly. The room they were in could easily have been found in Richard's castle.

"Yes, my lord. Would you ask Hermine for water as well? Tell her that whenever she brings wine, she should also bring water. And tell her I will come to inspect the kitchen once we have had a bath and rest."

"You do understand!"

"I do. Remember, my mother was your chatelaine, and she taught me to serve your lady."

Brigida blushed as she recalled the arrangement she and Dagr had entered into for the good of her and Arinn's love. It seemed so very long ago now. She had been young and a servant's daughter.

Mark shuffled his feet, not sure of where he should stand or sit. Dagr waved his hand at him reassuringly.

"For the love of God, Mark, sit beside us. You are my bailiff, as before. I will need your counsel to revive this demesne, and you have a place at our table."

Mark nodded and sat. He was, though, uncomfortable.

"Perhaps we will have to re-think this situation," Dagr said between mouthfuls of bread and cheese, some of the best he had ever tasted. "You and Brigida look very much alike, and now that I think of it, perhaps 'bailiff' is not the right title for you."

Mark looked shocked, as did Brigida.

"But this is what I know, it is my honor to serve you in this capacity!"

"I do not mean that you should take a lower position, man! I think for the sake of your and Brigida's relationship we should assign you a nobleman's title, as the brother of my lady, and you can oversee a steward, let's say, in his duties of running the estate. This way, we remain family and you can continue on with what you are good at; being my right hand. The less pretending we do the better. I have no desire to treat you as a servant."

"I am used to that, my lord. It is no offense, I was born to it." Mark replied, color rising to his cheeks.

"It is decided," Dagr insisted. "Brothers by law. Now, *Lord* Gregory, would you have more wine?"

"Thank you, my lord," Brigida, grateful for this new turn of events, poured wine for both men.

"By the way, do you know what your surname means?" Dagr grinned as Mark bristled under the strange address. "Oh, you will get used to it, just give it time. It means *watchful*. How very fitting you were born with this. You have always been the watchful one as long as you have been with me."

"I am deeply honored, my lord."

Hermine returned to inform them of supper plans. They had four hours to bathe, rest and take a quick tour of the chateau. But who would fill their baths? Mark offered. He was quickly denied. Hermine set the errand boy—who was hoping for a place in the scheme of things—to boil water for three baths, one in the master's and lady's chambers, and one in a room appropriate for the Lord Gregory.

"How many bedrooms have been made ready?" Dagr asked.

"Four, with linens, hearths ready for lighting, and clothes for the Lord and Lady," Hermine advised. She begged forgiveness, but there were no clothing provisions for the Lady's brother. A good tailor could be found in the next town... where were their trunks of personal goods?

"We were robbed along the way," Dagr explained.

Hermine bobbed up and down expressing her distress at such news. But the Earl Dumont had promised a shipment of 'necessities', word only had to be sent to the Comte de Beauchene. Surely, they had seen his estate earlier along the river?

Dagr recognized the name of his trusted French ally, and secretly thanking the Gods for their favor, led his lady up the expansive staircase to their rooms. But nothing could have prepared them for what Richard had spent a small fortune on when they flung open the master's chamber door.

The room was dominated by a large oak four-poster bed, a deep red velvet canopy and curtains decorating its expanse. Crisp white linens dressed it, a goose-down duvet and an assortment of furs were piled on top. Wide balcony doors opened to reveal a stunning view of the gardens and valley below. A warm breeze caressed them as they stood hand in hand absorbing the sudden change in their circumstances. Staring with disbelief at each other, they spoke no words but felt the immensity of the moment.

Brigida tried the door leading to the adjoining room. Here, the lady's quarters, as sumptuously outfitted with an identical oak bed. Carved oak wardrobes were stuffed full with dresses for every occasion. A trunk opened, revealed layers of undergarments and hose. There were slippers to match each dress.

She looked up at Dagr, tears stinging her eyes. "These were meant for Arinn," she whispered.

"For both of you," Dagr wiped her cheek with a tender hand.

"There must have been a room prepared for the lady's maid..."

"You are my lady, the one for whom this is for."

"No. I cannot. It is ever so disrespectful to her... oh Dagr!"

"You must, it is as it should be. The Fates have decided."

"But when Arinn comes, what then?"

Dagr hung his head. "It will be as it has to be. One of you had to assume the role of lady and the other the role of lady's maid or pretended to be blood. Arinn offered to be your lady in waiting, remember? We will make sense of it when..."

"Yes, when?" Brigida interrupted. "When can our beloved come to us? My lord, I am not afraid that she would repeat her—her mistakes! She has learned her lesson, of this I am convinced!"

A knock on the door interrupted their conversation. The boy and another he had brought from the village carried two buckets of hot water each.

"Fill the lady's bath first," Dagr gestured.

Two more trips with clattering buckets and Dagr ordered the lady's brother be attended to next.

* * *

"Allow me to help you my lady."

Undressing Brigida, Dagr noticed how thin she had become, how fragile and how utterly despondent she was to be enjoying his company while Arinn suffered far away.

"It will become easier, my lady, with time. I promise."

She nodded and stepped gingerly into the steaming bath.

Dagr closed the door to his chamber and sat down beside her; wetting her hair, pouring lavender scented oil into the bath.

"I know that you blame me, and I accept the responsibility of what has happened. I hope you can forgive me for my decision. I give you my word as your beloved that when the time is right, I will find a way for us all to be reunited. But you must trust me on the timing."

"Yes, my lord," Brigida whispered, lulled into a deep state of relaxation by the hot water and scent of the oil.

He washed her hair and body, gently scrubbing her back and massaging her shoulders. She moaned, a deep sound from the core of her being, allowing herself to melt into the complete luxury of the experience. The last time she had sat in a tub like this, it had been in Richard's rooms, with his hands where Dagr's hands were now. She blushed, finding Dagr knew what she was thinking. He only rubbed harder, smoothing knots in her muscles.

He combed her hair with a silver set found on her dressing table.

"This comb... is it like the one Richard gifted you once?" Dagr's voice soothed further.

"Not like, this is the set."

"Stunning. I should tell you, Richard was not prone to lavish gifts for the women he courted. This one speaks of his devotion to you."

"We barely knew each other when he brought me these. In fact, I

74

hated him still then, and he only cared for me because he cared for you."

"I know Richard, and if he was moved to give you such a thing, his heart was already open to you my lady."

"Does it bother you? There will be these constant reminders... cruel reminders perhaps?"

"No. I love Richard and I love you. However complicated this is, I welcome it. I do not care for society's rules. I prefer we chart our own course."

"I do love that about you, my lord. You are like no other."

Brigida stood obediently as Dagr toweled her dry and slipped a hand-embroidered nightdress over her head. He examined the fabric between his fingers.

"I cannot imagine what outfitting our life like this must have cost," he muttered. A thought stole into his mind about the business Richard had mentioned running along the river... it must supply his official income handsomely, was his conclusion.

Looking at Brigida flushed at his side, her hand gentle on his shoulder, he realized she was beyond the measures of exhaustion and carried her to her bed.

"I think it best you should sleep a while, my love."

Brigida nodded. "Will you join me my lord?"

Dagr kissed her forehead. "I will bathe first, but yes, I will join you in your bed. Although we may never get out once we are in. It has been a while since we slept in..." he stopped mid-sentence, Brigida already snoring softly. His heart melted with gratitude. At least physically, she would no longer suffer. It pleased him to see her snuggled into the downy softness of her bed.

No more hunger, or hiding, or struggling to survive in the damp woods. The boys could be heard in his room, filling his bath. He suddenly felt every ache in his body, or perhaps it was his spirit that ached so? Nonetheless, he looked forward to the hot water and scented soap, and indeed, a clean set of finely tailored clothes.

"I will repay you, Richard, somehow, someday," he vowed.

For now, it was enough to ease himself into the copper tub.

He was happy for the sound of Brigida's slumber, for it covered the whisper of his tears. Arinn's perfect slender face rose before him in memory. Could enough time pass to erase his pain at leaving her behind? Would he ever forgive himself? Would she?

CHAPTER 15

He awoke to the slightest movement in the bed, deep in the night with the moon streaming into the room, reflecting bright and eerie against the white sheets and the woman sitting naked on her knees beside him.

Dagr rose on his elbow, surveying his new and strange surroundings.

"What is it, my lady?"

"I had a dream."

"Do you remember it?"

He reached for her, but she maintained her position.

"Yes, but first, a drink? How long have I been sleeping?"

Dagr rose to fetch a cup of wine. He handed it to her and watched amused as she drank the full contents at once.

"You have slept through the dinner hour, and through a whole evening of Mark and me walking the grounds, then a few hours in the garden making plans."

"What time do you suppose it is, my darling?"

"Judging by the position of the moon—four in the morning or so."

"I am hungry, my lord!"

"I do not doubt it. Shall I fetch something from the kitchen?"

"Later. First, I will tell you my dream."

"Will you not come to me? It would be my pleasure to hold you."

"No, my lord, I will not come to you, but I will bow to you."

Dagr's puzzlement grew as Brigida lowered into submissive pose before him.

"What is this about, my lady?" Dagr questioned once more, squaring his shoulders and running his hands through his hair. He was momentarily distracted by how scented and untangled it was for once. An encouraging smile lit his face, but his eyes grew dark at the sight of his woman in supplication before him. She rose once more and pointed out the window.

"I saw you... in the future, another time, another land. You looked much like you do now, but softer, you were a warrior, but not like this—as you are now. You were surrounded by people, a group of many, who listened as you spoke of making a new way. There was magic, a magic I do not recognize. The room was smoky and dark, candles burned in a hundred iron sconces. There were people chanting a strange song in the background and the wind was inside the room!"

Brigida spoke in a heavy whisper, shivering in the cool night air.

"Let me cover you, you are cold, Sweet Dove!"

But Brigida stretched out her hand to stop him. Her hair spilled wild over her shoulders, her nipples pursed into tight peaks. She continued.

"You are a Lightbearer my lord, an Earthkeeper! You carry the wisdom of the Ancient Ones to future generations. You are the protector of those the world cannot see, the small folk. Beside you stood two women. One, with long, red hair, a wild woman with a forked tongue, a wise woman, one who carries fire in her breast. The other woman was a gentle soul, a healer, she carried the moon in her hands. The moon and the Woman of Fire bow to her, and both women bow to you."

Brigida's voice rose into a plaintive howl. She turned to face the moon. Dagr's heart pounded with a deep knowing. The heat rose in his loins watching his lover engage in a conversation with the sky. She was wondrously beautiful to his eye. She was his strength.

"I also had a vision of Arinn. She stood with you in another place, a wood much like the one we have known, she was iridescent with the light of the Fey. She wore a ring, and a crown, both fashioned by a King... the King of the Aspen trees. But Arinn had a new name and it was not truly her and her crown was braided from holly, like the one that our Arinn wore the night you discovered her, her..."

Tears spilled down Brigida's face, but still she wore off Dagr's advances to comfort her.

"In this life, this land, you found solace in all three women, but the one who looked like Arinn, she was your healing. The Woman of Fire wove strongest magic with you for the protection of the land and the Fey, the Lady of the Moon was your safe harbor and the priestess of your body. The new Arinn, the one fashioned from the best of all three of you, she was the wisest. Her wisdom came from a purity long gone from the Earth. It was she you needed the most protection from."

"Why would I need protection from a woman so pure?" Dagr asked, falling powerfully into the energy surrounding them now, surging, leaping waves of tension and need.

"Because when you are with her, you forget who you are. You fall under her spell and come back to the past. You cannot live here, where you cannot find forgiveness for yourself."

Dagr broke with those words. His tears and angst spilled like torrents of rain. His great body shook with emotion.

Brigida slipped into his lap, straddling his hips. His arms flew around her, holding her hard against his chest. The warmth of her sex roused his.

"My lord, let me worship you with my love."

"You have seen the future, my lady, but it is only this moment which matters to me now. I so love your heart and your wisdom... Lady of the Moon."

Brigida stared into his eyes, her body responding to the hardness rising between them.

"Will we remember each other, my lord, when we meet again in that future time?"

"I swear upon the grave of my Lady Mother, we will, my love. We will!"

Blinded by their tears, by the bond of their love and the promise of the future, they stretched out to their passion on a bed bought by guilt. Dagr lay surrendered as Brigida made love to his exquisite body, forbidding him reciprocation until she allowed it. Under her skilled mouth, hands and cunt, he found a pleasure he had long denied himself—one of complete abandon to his own needs. She kissed him with tenderness and fucked him with fury. And when she wanted to be taken, she presented in the way men have always found irresistible—on hands and knees—spread open for his eyes to ravage her beauty.

He lay atop her in the end, spent of tears and energy, lighter of heart. Bidding him to move his weight, Brigida lay satisfied in his arms.

"We have made a child," she said, drifting off to sleep as the sun rose pink and orange over the valley.

CHAPTER 16

"And so, you see how we made a pact, my darling? We consciously created our meeting, and to remember each other," Aiden stretched his legs out, recalling his dream to Sahara, as requested.

She, shaken, could only nod her head.

"Are you alright?"

"Yes, only... I remember! I remember something of that place, the chateau and this conversation seems so familiar."

"I, as well. As the dream came and went each night, it became less dream and more memory. You are the Lady of the Moon, my darling, and Iona, the Woman of Fire. Holly is the incarnation of all that was best of us—like a hologram of energy reminding us of our love and what once made us honorable. She is forgiveness made manifest into a physical being. How incredible is that?"

"We have been coming together for centuries."

Sahara kissed Aiden tenderly. "Do you think the child they made that night... I mean, I wonder who she or he was. That would have been their third child, had all of them lived."

"I have an ache to know about this child. To know what happened in the months that followed."

"I believe we will know more, as time goes on. We'll have more dreams, perhaps more regressions, or even time-travel. Now that we know more of our connections, we can pursue the past with more confidence. I'm not afraid anymore. The worst of what happened is known to us."

"Or at least we can hope."

"Why, do you think there were other dark times?"

"Who knows, it was the Middle Ages, and even though they should have been relatively safe in their new life, it was still the time of witch hunts. There were ways they could have been discovered in their true identity."

"They had already been through so much! I hope that was all there was to it. I want to ask Iona about Arinn's time with Richard but know better now. She won't reveal anything that hurts her heart and we'll have to dig it up for ourselves."

"What do you think Brigida meant when she said all three women would be my solace?" Aiden asked. "Do you think she meant physically or in the esoteric sense? If she meant the latter, it casts a foreboding shadow on our lives now, because to be my solace physically would mean, well... I can imagine that would be a complication none of us want."

"You mean, a complication only Iona would want."

"Right."

"Let's not jump to conclusions. Speaking of which, I have to move on, or you won't be having any kind of supper at my place."

"Ok. I have to keep going here too. Let's de-brief Holly tonight?"

"Let's. Love you."

"Come here. One more kiss."

Sahara tucked Aiden's kiss into her memory.

"Hey lady! Before you take off, let me show you the finished design for the café expansion. The architect sent the files and they're beautiful. He used the furniture pieces you selected in the illustration, and—wow!"

Holly pulled her laptop from under the counter and waved Sahara onto a stool.

"Ok, or you can show me tonight? I've still got some stuff to pick up. Mmm, actually, show me now and pour me a coffee?"

"Didn't you just have coffee upstairs? You'll be up all night!"

"Something happened to the coffee. It spilled," Sahara winked.

"Ugh. I see. A flagrant waste of good java. Unacceptable."

"Just pour, no judgment. I'll explain later."

"Here, look!" Holly turned the screen to face Sahara.

"Oooh! It feels Old World with the stone fireplace surround—very comfortable but elegant. You're going to attract a crowd with this. I can see Aiden's stamp on it; in the beams and leaded glass for the back window."

"I know. I think that's one of the things I love best about it, having his energy with mine, and the pieces you picked remind me of your earthy style. Everybody's been asking when it'll be ready, and I can't wait. I'll need another server for the extra seating."

Sahara sipped her coffee and nibbled on a lemon tart Holly had shoved in front of her.

"Remember the first day I walked in here and crashed into you?"

"Yup. Like it was yesterday. Why?"

"How long ago was that?"

"Five years ago? No, wait, four months ago! But it does feel like years, I don't even know the girl I was back then. Doesn't even feel possible it was such a short time ago."

"It's as if time stopped so we could discover each other."

"You're leading up to something, I know you."

Sahara lowered her voice a little, the cafe crowd were beginning to listen in. "We've been talking about Aiden's dreams upstairs. We'll update you tonight. It's more information to help us understand our meeting and virtually instant connection."

"Oh, is that what you were doing up there?" Holly teased. "Ok, tell me later. What're you feeding us, by the way?"

"You know, frog's legs and eye of newt." Sahara picked up her bag and leaned over the counter to give Holly a kiss.

"My favorite!"

"Bring some of those cheese things you once wooed me with for breakfast."

"I'm staying for breakfast?"

"Of course. Frog legs and eye of newt are powerful magic. You'll be under my spell until morning."

"Why do I feel like you and Aiden are planning to sacrifice me on some kind of hedonistic altar after you've indoctrinated me with this new information?"

"Because we are." And with that, Sahara slipped away, a sparkling laugh on her lips.

CHAPTER 17

Once there was, and once there was not
Is how stories begin
When things are not as they seem
Once upon a time, in a land far away
Is how we are taken
Far beyond our senses
It is the alchemy of storytelling
Where portals open
And reality shifts

"Once there was and once there was not, a girl who lived in the woods. She was young and naïve and did not see the terrible creatures who walked behind her as she frolicked along. They were most silent and skilled at not making the dry leaves crunch beneath their feet, their long, eager fingers almost tugging at her hair, hissing their delight at the thought of catching her when she least expected it..."

Holly lay against Aiden in bed, sprawled in the light of the winter sun where it warmed the sheets. Naked and satiated from an afternoon of lovemaking. She purred as he caressed her neck and shoulders, reciting a story she had begged him for.

"Why do you want a story about the dark forest? Let me tell you something more cheerful?" Aiden wrapped his legs around her, a subconsciously protective move. He kissed her forehead when she turned her face up to look at him.

"Because. You always tell me stories to make me laugh or some such thing. I want to go deeper... to know you... know the dark stories inside you."

"Oh, how do you know that?"

"I know who you are, and if all you and Sahara told me the other night is true..."

"Which it is..." Aiden confirmed.

"Right. Then, since it is, you know things the rest of us rarely tap into... you know fairy tales, and that they're real."

Aiden laughed. "Ok, Miss Smarty Pants, since you have answered correctly, I will continue."

"Were you raised on fairy tales? I wasn't. I was told they were gibberish and best to concentrate on reality."

"Let me guess, your mother?"

"Uhuh." Holly moved so she could fit into the crook of his arm. "*Mmmm...* I love how you smell after we make love." She sniffed in his hair.

"I love the smell of you always."

"So anyway, fairy tales?"

"Yes. I *was* raised on fairy tales. My mom read them to me every night until I was reading on my own and then I begged for every fairy tale book in the store. There was one for each birthday and Christmas under the tree. My Dad thought that by sixteen I should give them up, but I never saw them as children's stories really. I wondered why anyone would write such things for children when those things would clearly scare any little one out of their right mind."

"And...?"

"And stop fidgeting!"

"I'm not fidgeting. I'm kissing your nipples."

"Exactly. No stories if you can't keep still. I can't concentrate."

"Sorry," Holly cuddled back in. "So, what did you come up with about them not being children's stories?"

"I figured they were read to children to plant a seed about wisdom. Like a puzzle or an allegory for our inner world. We then carry those stories and they unfold as we unfold. Or not. Sometimes we would discover the bit of truth in them and apply it to our life. Sometimes we did so consciously and sometimes subconsciously. Either way, fairy tales are meant to teach. I think people read them to their kids hoping to scare them out of being reckless or 'bad'. But beneath the top layers of each story is a journey into the deepest, darkest parts of the human psyche. My theory has good company. You'll find it in the books downstairs by Jung and others."

"And that's exactly why I want these stories from you. You're always protecting me. I do love it in a way, don't get me wrong, it's very romantic and all, but I want to grow like you grow. I want to understand these mysteries you and Sahara are always muttering about."

"Muttering?" Aiden objected.

"Yes, muttering. The two of you mutter under your breath as you go about your day. Sahara told me that it's constant prayers, blessings—invocations of some sort. I want to learn about that."

The door downstairs opened and Sahara hollered up. "Is anybody here doing anything to prepare for tonight?"

"Yes!" Aiden replied.

"No!" Holly laughed.

Sahara appeared in the doorway of the bedroom.

"Oh my God! What are the two of you *doooing*?" She disappeared into the closet to hang her clothes. Coming back, she looked at them pointedly. "What sort of lollygagging is this? Don't we have to leave in a couple of hours for New Year's dinner?"

Aiden sat up. "There's plenty of time. And everything's set up at your place for the evening ceremony anyway. Come sit down, I'm telling a story."

"Well what about appies and drinks before dinner?"

"All ready and... oh my gosh Sahara, have you looked in the mirror lately?" Holly asked.

"What?" Sahara went back to the closet to look in the mirror. "Ha-ha! I'm wearing my shirt inside out! Well, at least I'm *wearing* clothes."

"Ok, listen, take off that silly shirt and get in here with us. Let's have a quick nap. We'll be up all hours of the night," Aiden advised.

"What are we, ninety?" Sahara laughed as she stripped naked and they all got under the covers, giggling and jockeying for position.

"No, but New Year's is exhausting. All those drunken people celebrating at the resort. I don't know how I let you wenches talk me into going out on the craziest night of the year."

"Cause... the views over the mountains, and it's fun!" Holly said, sliding her legs between Sahara's, undulating her hips gently. "Is it still story time?"

"I guess I'll tell you the story tonight by the bonfire when we initiate Sahara's grove."

"Will it be a scary story still, darling?" Holly moaned as Sahara rose up over her, scissoring clit against clit.

"The scariest I can come up with, I promise. Who can tell stories with this going on?"

"Here, nibble on these. And I poured us some champagne... just a little tipple!" Holly laid the tray on the bathroom counter, appetizers and three champagne flutes intact.

"How'd you not spill these coming up the stairs?" Aiden tucked his shirt into his pants, and pulled a belt from its hanger.

"Gosh, you look handsome! Your shirts fit you so well." Holly handed him his drink.

"You're blushing."

"Well..."

"Let's make a toast," Sahara suggested. "Is there any way to keep you two on track here?"

"Probably not," Aiden grinned. "That's a very elegant outfit, darling. I beg you not to burn it this time."

"Not even because you hate that my nipples are impertinent, and that I refuse to wear a bra?"

Sahara turned to show off what she was wearing; black, wide-legged, high-waisted pants, in a classic forty's style, and a cream-colored silk shirt, the neckline cut in a low V, accentuating her small, high breasts. Her nipples poked the fabric, just so.

"Not even. I agree completely that a woman's nipples are her own domain and she shouldn't have to hide them to band-aid a man's behavior. I reacted from an archaic state of emotions that other time when I objected to your dress... I'm glad you stood your ground. Just no more burnings!" Aiden pulled Sahara in. "Your hair is growing I noticed. Are you going to get rid of this pixie style? I'm rather fond of it."

"I think I *am* growing it. I used to have long hair... I'll show you a photo."

"I'd like that. What do you think Holly?"

Holly had drunk her champagne and was struggling into her stilettos. She stood and drew a gasp from them both.

"What's wrong with the two of you?"

"Umm, you look incredible. Your legs are a mile long!" It was Sahara's turn to blush, eyes travelling to the hem of Holly's little black dress, perfectly fit to her curves.

Holly giggled. "These old things? And yes, Sahara with long hair... yum! Although I, too, love the pixie."

"I have a strange urge for long hair suddenly." Sahara popped an appy into her mouth. "Oooh, these are good! Mushroom phylo, my fave."

"Francois made them. He's really skilled with phylo and all kinds of pastry, really. And you know what?"

"What?" Aiden and Sahara asked in unison.

"I think he has a crush on Lilith. He's been kinda mooning over her but she's completely oblivious. I think it's because she thinks no boy will like her with her limp."

"That's ridiculous," Aiden commented. "As is this tiny amount of champagne you've brought us. Anyone can see she's bright and lovely; and she's fit as a fiddle despite her injury."

"Oh, you've noticed?" Holly teased. "You know she used to have a crush on you?"

"Don't even start, little girl. I'm twice her age practically."

"Yeah, and that has nothin' to do with nothin'. I've seen sixty-year-old women ogling you and sixteen-year-olds as well."

"Pffft. Someone should get more champagne. If you still want me to dance with you tonight, I'll need more courage."

"Why Aiden Halloran! Are you too shy to show your dance moves? We can teach you!"

"I can dance very well, thank you very much. I just don't enjoy crowds or displaying myself on a dance floor."

"Well I'm afraid you'll be plenty on display tonight. You'll be the only man there with two dates." Holly yelled as she ran down the stairs to find the bubbly.

Aiden sighed. Sahara embraced him, searching his eyes.

"Relax darling. We've been through this before, and we don't care what anyone thinks, remember?"

"I know. I don't care about that. I'm just private."

"Everybody will be drunk anyway."

"Except us. And when people are drunk they say stupid things."

"Ok. I know now what you're worried about. Holly and I already talked this over. She's not going to be hurt by some idiot's comments. We must be able to live normally, like everyone else. Being in a poly relationship will be as normal as we make it out to be. If we don't make a big deal of it, others will follow suit."

Holly was back with a small bottle of prosecco. "No more of the other. Let's try this. What are you two in a huddle about?"

"I won't have any more, I'm driving," Sahara replied. "I'm just letting Aiden know you and I have talked about what people might say tonight, being drunk and all, and that you're not in the least worried."

"Oh sweetie!" Holly brushed her lips against Aiden's. "You know me, I hate confrontation and I wouldn't want some uptight person in our faces, but I'm not going to fall apart if they do. We're together, we're going to have fun and that's all there is to it! Anyway, who's going to change the world if not us?"

"See. What did I tell you?" Sahara glanced at Aiden sitting on the edge of the bathroom counter in his perfectly pressed slacks and shirt, tie hanging around his neck, watching her apply her make-up. He looked so fucking handsome. She wondered how she was able to stand it.

"Do you really know how to dance?" Holly asked, shoving Sahara over at the mirror.

86

"I do," Aiden grinned. "It was another one of those things I had to do with my sister. Mom made us learn, so we could grow up to be 'civilized', as she called it. No children of hers were going to stomp around at weddings and what not. I somehow took to it like a duck to water. Not sure where that came from. But you took dance, too, so I'll be curious to see your moves." He stood up behind Holly and wrapped his arms around her, nibbling her neck.

"We'll see. Sahara and I will rate you at the end of the evening." She smiled at him in the mirror. Aiden's strong, hard body against her back felt like home.

"Fine, just remember, we're not staying till midnight. We'll be by the fire in Sahara's woods when the clock strikes twelve."

"Yes, yes! But that doesn't mean I won't want kisses on the dance floor just because it's not midnight. I know how you think!"

"No more time people! Let's go!" Sahara smacked her lips over her red lipstick and fluffed her hair. "Happy New Year, darlings! I can't think of anyone else I'd rather spend this evening with."

CHAPTER 18

Richard stood as they approached a table in a private corner with a view of the lights on the mountainside.

Sahara and Holly beamed into broad smiles and stared up at Aiden, who was already turning heads.

"You sneak!" Sahara exclaimed. "I didn't know you had invited Richard and Iona!"

The five exchanged hugs and kisses, European style, cheeks well adorned with greetings.

"Seems like we just saw you! Did you even go home between Solstice and now?" Sahara asked Iona, who glowed with health and happiness.

"No. We stayed here. Aiden and Richard concocted this plan before we came up last week. If all went well, we would stay on and meet up again for New Year. It's much more fun with friends, wouldn't you say?"

"Yes! You look incredible," Sahara said, admiring Iona's floor length gown, the same green velvet one Aiden had described from their meeting. Iona's red hair was coiled atop her head, giving her a very regal appearance. A long gold chain with a clear quartz point hung between her breasts.

"I'm feeling especially good. Must be the mountain air."

"You're always very beautiful," Holly said, "but yes, tonight especially so."

Iona squeezed Holly's hand and they seated themselves. She caught Aiden's curious glance at her cleavage. A tiny sigh escaped her. Only she noticed the thought that crossed his face.

"We're already attracting plenty of stares," Holly whispered. "I say we make it worth their while tonight."

"Why, Holly, you're quite brave!" Richard motioned for the waiter who hustled over with a wine menu.

"We're not going to need that," Richard said. "We'll have a bottle of the Domaine de la Romanee-Conti Grand Cru 1961." He smiled at the young man's stare.

"Ummm," the waiter stuttered with a half bow. "I'll speak with the sommelier."

"I've already spoken with him," Richard advised.

Aiden cocked an eyebrow as the waiter scuttled away. "That

young man has probably never touched a bottle of that vintage before."

"Well, we have something to celebrate besides New Year tonight, so I say, why not?"

Iona and Aiden's eyes met. She smiled, an easy smile wrapped in joy.

"What is it?" Sahara clapped her hands. "Oh, I love news! Do tell!"

Aiden sat straighter in his chair. He took Sahara's hand and held it under the table, rubbing her fingers gently.

"Let's wait for the wine, shall we?" Richard said. "That way we can have a toast."

"What is the matter?" Sahara sent a telepathic message to Aiden.

"I love you, that is all." Aiden leaned in to kiss her on the cheek.

"Oh! Here it is!" Holly exclaimed. "This is fun!"

After the usual theatrics by the waiter to do with sniffing and tasting, the wine was poured and Richard asked them to raise their glasses.

"Iona and I are pleased to share that we have all the final roadblocks cleared for building our new home, the design images are here, and Aiden has sealed our good fortune by giving his firm consent to be our builder... which I asked him to not tell until all the permits had been issued." He smiled at Sahara and Holly. "Sorry to have him keeping secrets from you, but I just wanted to have all my ducks in a row first."

The three women were beaming, Richard was shaking Aiden's hand and thanking him for his commitment; it meant everything to him. This home needed Aiden's touch. Hugs and kisses were dispensed all around once more.

Richard mistook the steely glint in Aiden's eyes as a bit of leftover reservation. "I promise you will be rewarded far beyond your fee, my man, and I have other benefits coming your way that I know you'll appreciate."

Aiden's hand over his, Richard was once again reminded of his new friend's intensity and strength. "I really mean it when I say there is no one else who could build this."

"I am pleased as well, thank you." From the corner of his eye he noticed Iona had placed her wine down without taking a sip.

Seated again, Richard took his phone from his jacket. "Ok to show some images now? We can also look tomorrow, if you prefer?" He scanned the faces of the women flanking him.

"I want to see!" Holly piped up. "You know Aiden is remodeling my café as well. I can relate to how you feel, Richard, I couldn't imagine anyone else taking care of my dream."

"Exactly," Richard agreed. "He's got the sensitivity for the plans."

He passed the phone to Aiden. Holly and Sahara leaned over to see. The first image was an artist's rendering of the grounds, the position of the house and surrounding structures.

"Oh. My. Goodness!" Holly exclaimed. "That is... a... a castle!" She looked up at Iona. "How beautiful! And are those stables?"

"Yes, stables and you'll see the trails through the forest mapped out." Richard confirmed. "There's a small lake on the property and the trails will lead to it. We wanted it to be reminiscent of England, stately, of course, but not pretentious, with a sense of an earlier time."

"Well, I'd say you've accomplished that," Sahara said. "How far is it from here? What view is from the hill you're building on?"

"A view of the surrounding countryside, the lake of course, and towards the bigger mountains beyond. It's halfway between here and Denver," Iona said, color blooming on her face. "And something you'll appreciate, Sahara, Richard has agreed to build me a stillroom! For my work."

"A stillroom?" Sahara breathed. She locked eyes with Iona, remembering. She shivered, uncovering something she could not place her finger on behind those captivating yellow/green orbs.

"I hope you will join me there, Sahara, when you can, Holly, you too. We could continue your studies there if you're still interested?"

"Interested?" Holly smiled from ear to ear. "Yes please!"

"There's too much to look at right now," Richard proposed. "Why not join us tomorrow in our suite for lunch and we can see it on a bigger screen. I hope you know we'd like you to visit us often and share in our happiness there? We certainly have enough bedrooms!"

"Yeah," Holly said. "Enough for a large brood of tiny Richards and Ionas!"

"Wouldn't that be something?" Richard smiled at his lover. Iona turned her face to his and took his hand. Aiden once more took Sahara's.

"Well, my love," Iona began. "I do have another surprise, one I should have told you earlier, but I also wanted to be sure."

Richard turned his full attention to her. "What is it darling?"

"You're going to be a father, Richard. We're going to have a baby!"

90

Aiden's hand squeezed hard over Sahara's. Her almost inaudible gasp cut his heart. Tears surfaced in Richard's eyes. Holly, one hand to her heart, smiled her delight at Richard and Iona's good fortune. Her other hand slipped around Sahara's waist, while she ignored the pang of longing in her own heart.

Richard was clearly in shock. Suddenly, everyone was congratulating Iona, Aiden first. He kissed her on the cheek. Memories of their past life collided between them, the love, the misery, the children lost to Brigida.

Fate was adept at irony.

Sahara was next, the two women embraced, holding on to each other, tears hot on each other's cheeks.

"Darling, no wonder you are glowing! I am so very happy for the two of you. You will be wonderful parents, to whomever this little one is."

They stood in an embrace for so long that Richard had time to come to his senses. He was warmly hugged by Holly who kissed him joyously on the lips. He shook Aiden's hand vigorously, grinning from ear to ear. Aiden decided on a full embrace, and laughing, told Richard that now he would have to give up his wild man ways.

"Oh, I have been tamed a long time ago, my friend," Richard replied. He shook his head. "I just never..."

Iona was by his side. He took her hands and kissed them. "Darling, this is the best surprise of my life. Sit down, for heaven's sake!"

Everyone burst out laughing, even the father-to-be. The idea of Iona needing any kind of coddling was indeed hilarious.

"You are pleased, darling?" Iona sat just to make Richard happy.

He moved her glass of wine away and everyone laughed once more. "I have never been happier my love! Well! What a way to end one year and begin another." He sighed contentedly. Sahara's eyes met his. He remembered, too, and together, they all acknowledged silently how life moved on with lessons for the soul.

They ate with gusto, Richard never more handsome, his jacket off, shirt sleeves rolled up; the dashing pirate who spun his lady love around the dance floor when the music began. They were electric, hot. Sahara and Holly drew many glances when they took to the floor together. Iona accepted their urges to dance with Aiden, whose graceful waltz had the rest of them mesmerized at the table. "How does someone so tall and rugged dance like that?" Richard wondered.

But it was Holly who took the house down. Accepting Aiden's invitation to dance, she wound her way around him, all long legs and hair spilling down her back, perfection swathed in a sinful dress. Aiden supposed everyone hadn't intended to stare, but she danced with such abandon, so seductively, that they did. He was too mesmerized to realize that the patrons, some known to him, some not, had witnessed a peck on the cheek between Sahara and Iona turn into a quick but sensuous taste of each other's mouth, which Richard stared down without shame, while pouring himself another glass of wine.

This was really more intriguing than paying attention to their own dinners as far as the resort crowd was concerned. Over the evening, as food came and went and music continued to draw people to their feet, five insanely attractive people switched places at their table, taking turns conversing and laughing together, a kiss here, an embrace there; they were the most elegant, yet most irreverent people ever seen within the confines of these walls!

And just when the room's curiosity about the fivesome's dynamic had reached a fever pitch, Aiden and Richard stood to escort their lovers to the door. They were leaving before midnight! And that left quite the speculation as to where they were going, to do what and with whom?

Ever since that author had moved to town, nothing had been quite the same. It was is if she had cast a spell over them all. Suddenly, Riverbend had taken on an air of something special, something they couldn't describe. Something magical almost, even if they might not use those exact words.

CHAPTER 19

"I don't know, but my life has changed so much since September, since I met Sahara, really! It's quite surreal." Holly slipped out of her heels and dress.

Aiden hung it up and bent down to pick up her shoes.

"We're all in a tail spin, you, me, Richard, the whole bloody town. Nothing will ever be the same again."

"You omitted Iona."

"Well, she's in a league of her own. And she was already floating in Sahara's atmosphere."

"Are you happy for them darling? I mean about the baby? I am. I just think that child will, for one, be wildly beautiful, and obviously adored. Did you see Richard tonight? He was completely overwhelmed with emotion!"

"Ah, yes! He was. He told me he hadn't been holding out hope for a child because they had had unprotected sex since their beginning and never once had there been any chance Iona might have become pregnant. One doesn't really expect a man like Richard to be too attached to the idea of a child. But he's always surprising me with his sensitivity."

"But *are* you happy for them?" Holly pressed. "Because you were so busy worrying about how Sahara and I would react..."

"Yes, I am. Very much so. The irony of the situation, because of what happened between Arinn and Brigida, wasn't lost on me, nor Sahara. And I wasn't sure how it would touch you. I've never wanted to have a child with anyone before the two of you, so I'm not used to the nuances of it all, but I imagine once a woman sets her heart on a child, it becomes a sensitive matter." Aiden dressed in jeans and a plaid shirt. He smiled. "You like this shirt, don't you?"

"I like this James Bond to carpenter transformation going on here!" Holly slipped into her leggings and sweater. "But to continue, Richard and Iona, yeah, I love them, you know?"

Aiden raised an eyebrow.

"Are you raising your eyebrow at what I said or how my ass looks in these leggings?" Holly laughed and turned to give him a better view.

"Both."

"I was worried for Sahara, as well, because she's still processing all that stuff from before, and she's a lot more tenderhearted than she shows. But imagine the life this child will have! And we'll get to love it as well."

Aiden took Holly in his arms. "Darling, you are the sweetest soul!"

Holly stood on tiptoe to receive his kiss. "Mmmm. Do you think Richard, back then, had any children?"

"I don't know, but if he did, it would have been with Arinn, I suppose. Somehow, I think not. We'd better hurry up. Sahara will be anxious to start."

"Why do you think she didn't invite Iona and Richard to attend the ceremony tonight?"

They turned the lights off and let themselves out the side door.

"Because Sahara is, and always will be, a solitary witch, even though she has work with The Society. This is her home, her initiation. Some things just run so deep for her. And they needed time alone to celebrate baby news anyway."

"Well, I'm just going to sit quietly and observe. I have no idea what to expect and will be soaking everything up!"

"You're wearing your ring?" Aiden asked.

"I am. Don't forget, you promised me that story!"

"I haven't forgotten." He opened the truck door for her. "Hey," Aiden leaned in as Holly reached for her seatbelt.

"What?"

"I love you, that's all."

Sahara was waiting with a box of her things on the front porch. Driving up to the cabin, Holly commented that it had the appearance of something from a storybook.

"It's like one of those huts from Eastern European Baba Yaga stories."

"Oh, have you read those?"

"Yup," Holly giggled. "Found one book on Eastern European mythology in your library."

"Ah, I see. I always wanted a woman who would read my books."

Aiden turned the ignition off. "I told you she'd be waiting out here," he said to Holly. He pulled a box from the back seat.

"What's in there?" Sahara asked

"Just some of my magic tools. Have you been standing here long?

I'll carry these, lover." Aiden put Sahara's box on top of his.

"Just a few minutes. The stars are so inspiring I had to come out here and stare. I'm so excited for tonight!"

"Thank you for inviting us. I know you like to do these things alone... but I really wouldn't want to miss it." Aiden winked.

"I need you both here. We're all living here now, and we'll all be consecrated to the land."

Holly lagged behind, head turned to the heavens. The indigo sky was festooned with the twinkle of constellations. Their feet crunched the sparkling snow where Aiden had cleared a trail to the grove.

"Wooooow," Holly exclaimed. "This is sooooo beautiful! We have to come out late at night more often. Wait for me darlings!"

Sahara held out her hand. "Come! I know, right? And so much easier to see the stars when the moon isn't full!"

"Maybe we should have waited for the dark moon?"

"No. The dark moon... I don't usually do magic on the dark moon. It would have to be a very special circumstance."

"Another thing I didn't know!" Holly squeezed Sahara's hand. "I'm all goose-bumpy with anticipation for tonight."

Sahara squeezed back. "Remember you're safe with me and my magic but if there is anything you prefer to just watch, that's fine too, or even not watch. I mean, it's not anything that unusual, but you have to trust your energy and intuition."

"Oh, I trust you completely! And I thought I was only watching anyway?"

"We'll see... as you wish."

Sahara stopped just before a natural opening to the sacred circle.

"Let's put on our cloaks," she whispered. "Everyone's waiting."

"Cloaks?" Holly whispered back. "I don't..."

"Here's yours. I had one made for you," Sahara smiled and pulled a fawn colored winter cloak lined with velvet from her box.

"Thank you! How pretty."

Aiden's cloak, black with a rich amethyst lining, echoed the Druid styling of Holly's. Sahara's, also black but with carmine velvet softening the hood and body. Dressed so, Sahara spoke to the trees and spirits with hands folded in prayer at her third eye.

"Spirits of this place, we come in love and peace, to share in your wisdom and to join ourselves to the land."

Touching the pendant she had received from Aiden upon his return from The Aspen King, she waited until it warmed. The wind rose in a sudden flourish around the grove.

Receiving the invitation to enter, Sahara led the others to the inner sanctum where a large fire pit had been dug by Aiden, lined with river rocks and in its middle, hung from a tall metal tripod, a black, cast iron cauldron.

The witch, the wizard and their maiden stood reverently until the wind died down. Lighting a smudge stick of cedar, sage and meadowsweet, Sahara offered a prayer to Goddess before clearing her energy with the sweet-smelling smoke. Beginning at her heart center and moving to her crown chakra, she prepared herself first, then turned to smudge Aiden.

She spoke words over him, blessing his presence in the grove and sending away any negativity that might be clinging to him. The energy moving between them spiraled into a visible coil of light.

Handing the stick to Aiden, Sahara stood with palms up welcoming the smoke of the sacred plants. Aiden's powerful essence enveloped her, and she warmed with gratitude for his magic. Circling her, a prayer on his lips, he left her wide open to the intention for the night.

Next, Aiden smudged Holly, who with tear-stained eyes followed his every move. This was the Aiden she had been afraid of, but in this moment, she understood she was not to fear any of his magnitude. He was not a man who used any of his powers to elevate or distinguish himself; and he certainly hadn't used his beliefs to win her over. What she had picked up on had been honestly and humbly shared as his chosen life path. It had never been a way to bamboozle her feminine instincts. And Holly knew that Riverbend had its share of those who might use spirituality to poach hearts.

The smoke of the smudge hung on the winter air with grace. Sahara began with a Sanskrit chant, her voice lifting the wind again.

"Ong Namo Guru Dev Namo I Bow to the creative power... divine energy... force which created this entire universe, this cosmos. I bow to the great divine teacher that is within me."

Aiden joined her while lighting the fire, lifting away the cauldron to be used later in the ceremony. A carefully arranged pile of cedar, oak, aspen and wild apple wood made up the majority of the fuel, with a bundle of dried rosemary branches on top to invite the Fey. As Sahara and Aiden spoke agreed-upon words over the fire, it leapt and hissed, coming alive with fire sprites. In the sacred triple circle they would cast, fire would be the unifying force for the three realms of Earth, Sea and Sky.

"We invite and thank the forces of illumination, balance, creativity, intuition, transformation, courage, lust, energy and radiance.

96

We surrender to the wisdom of the Goddess and seek to co-create with Her through the element of fire, for the good of the Collective Consciousness. May our words spoken, and our actions taken serve the reunion of mankind and Fey upon the sacred land beneath our feet and everywhere."

Representing Earth, the first circle was cast clockwise beginning in the North, with Aiden, sprinkling sea salt surrounding the area of the fire. He chanted— *"May this circle of Earth and protection remain unbroken in our hearts, this realm and others. Blessed be."*

Representing Sea, the second circle was cast clockwise just outside the first by Sahara, sprinkling moon water scattered with a bundle of twigs, beginning in the East. She spoke— *"May this circle of love and sacred Waters remain unbroken in our hearts, this realm and others. Blessed be."*

Representing Air, the third circle was cast just outside the second by Holly. Moving clockwise East to West, a lit smudge stick of sage, cedar and pine, her witch's tool, she uttered these words— *"May this circle of Sky and power remain unbroken in our hearts, this realm and others. Blessed be."*

The Four Directions were now represented, Earth to the North, Air to the East, Fire to the South and Water to the West. It was time to begin communing with the Fey.

"We shall drink some of this tea, to improve our *sight*," Sahara picked three tiny glass cups from her box, and a small insulated canteen. She poured the steaming liquid and handed a cup to Holly. "It's thyme, clary sage and violet flowers. With this, you will be able to see the Fey, should they wish to be seen. It is always up to them. Perhaps we will see other energies as well."

"Alright darling?" Sahara asked as Holly sipped her tea.

"Yes. I feel a strange sensation in my... right here..." Holly touched along her breast bone.

"Your heart space opening. That's wonderful! It means you can honestly partake in the magic here. Your heart chakra opening will allow your higher chakras to open as we proceed."

Aiden agreed and smiled to encourage her.

Holly nodded, shy with Aiden's attention upon her. He was not entirely human in this space, his aura visible to her now she had drunk the tea. Radiating in waves of green, purple and white, it was immense! So, this is what she felt when she was near him.

"All you need do is stay as you are right now. Your integrity will lead the way," Sahara said and poured more tea.

The ground seemed less solid after that for everyone, while music emanating from the forest enchanted them into a state of awakened wisdom. Fey of every variety poured into their midst. They carried instruments and wore bells on their feet. Every movement brought a new sound, and while one would think it would be a clamorous, riotous noise, the music produced rivaled all human compositions. Dancing in a circle around them, the Fey, shimmering in their colorful costumes, invited them to join in the merriment. Only they didn't use words, Holly noticed. She heard everything in her head!

Don't think so hard, it won't be so overwhelming, Holly heard telepathically but wasn't sure who'd said it.

Stepping into the Fey's midst, she no longer wore her own clothes, but a gossamer gown that quite surprisingly, she wasn't cold in, considering the season. And while they twirled around and around, the tree spirits slipped from their stationary homes and formed an outer circle. Encased so, a rumble rose from the ground and from it appeared a most sacred and looming figure—The Aspen King!

Holly would have fainted had she the presence to do so, but having her hands in Sahara's and Aiden's she was filled with courage and wonder. Oh, how handsome he was, sometimes even resembling Aiden, or what she imagined Dagr had looked like. His blond mane was the longest hair she had ever seen on a man, falling in rivulets down his back. Shaking the majestic rack of horns on his head, he bowed low before her. Dressed in the splendor reserved for such a creature, he was impossible to refuse when he asked for her company in a dance. Sahara let go her hand, Aiden clung on a second longer. But then, she was close to the fire, so close to the fire, in his arms, the ring on her finger pulsed with light. Next to them, Aiden and Sahara, illuminated by their love for each other. On and on they spun. On and on the music played—the forest lit for miles.

A hundred and one times they circled the fire, with sometimes Sahara or Holly in The Aspen King's arms. With amazing fluidity, they changed partners, Aiden, light of step, wooed at every point by damsel fairies but never wavering from his two loves, keeping a keen eye on his beloveds. When they had spun the hundredth and first time, the music shifted and the dancing began in the opposite direction. The energy was out of control, spiraling towards the heavens and reaching from somewhere very deep beneath the Earth.

The fire kept roaring, though no one added to it. At a hundred and one turns counterclockwise, the King raised his hand, stomped his foot and bellowed into the night air as a stag would do during a mating call. All Fey dropped to the ground, the dancing ceased as quickly as it had begun. With foreheads plastered to the ground, silence surrounding them, all inhabitants of the Underworld waited.

Sahara, Aiden and Holly waited too. Sahara's heart beat wildly, anticipation raising sweat on her upper lip. Aiden at her right, Holly trembling at her left. A strong scent of cedar and pine permeated the forest. In the outer circle, the Standing-Still Ones began to sway. A hum rose from the Fey... a soft, reverent sound. The wind returned and the flames rose higher.

Pan appeared in their midst, the most terrifying creature Holly had ever seen, and she gasped for air, thinking her lungs might collapse. Two horns sprouting from his forehead were adorned with dead branches and rotting snakes. His eyes shone red and ghoulish. His tongue was forked and his breath, foul.

He reached dirty, greedy fingers to touch Holly's hair. She wanted to run but Aiden's hand gripped hers and there was no escape. She screamed... this was the devil incarnate and she was terrified. But as she screamed, fear leaving her body with the vibration of the sound, the devil transformed into a stunning creature, half man half goat, his eyes soft, his manner gentle, fragrant ferns and ivy decorating his crown. The Fey surrounded him, adoring, bowing and singing his praises. He led them in a new dance and a song for the healing of the planet.

Sahara's eyes streamed with tears when Holly stepped away from them and joined the circle. She comforted Aiden who was visibly unnerved.

"All is as it should be. This has always been. She was meant to awaken."

"I wished to keep her from this world of shifting realities. I didn't want her to face that image."

"She is safer here than anywhere in the Middle World. You know that."

"Yes, but into this world—she can disappear."

"As in the other. In the spirit world at least, we are forever. In the other, we are mere seconds in time."

"You are right as always, wise woman. I bow to you."

Aiden and Sahara returned their attention to the fire, the song and the dance winding down. A plaintive voice rose from their midst, a clear, bell-like voice. It came from nowhere and everywhere, the words in an ancient language, the language of witches. The Aspen

King fell to one knee. The Fey sat down on the ground in little groups, hands clasped in front of them. Aiden, Sahara and Holly waited. Pan held out his hand and when he did, out of the deep woods stepped an effervescent vision. Iona.

"Oooooh!" Holly whispered.

Aiden bowed his head, Sahara met Iona's eyes.

Standing at The Aspen King's side, Iona lifted him to his feet.

"My lord, you have called me, and I have come. How may I be of service?"

"My lady, I would hear a legend from you. The legend of a time long ago when your kind and mine walked the Earth in harmony. Would you remind us of the great tragedy when man forgot his true nature, and brought harm to the natural world? Would you tell us the story of Pan and how he was disguised as something fearful? Would you then remind us of the vision we have seen of a new man and woman who would remember us... remember to honor the Earth?"

"Aaaahh, the story of the Garden."

"The garden, the garden, the garden," the Fey chanted softly, eyes bright with anticipation.

"I will, but this story has to be told by man and woman, it is the story of how both were tricked into believing their intuition was *EVIL!"* Iona swept her arm over the sitting Fey, and they were blown flat onto their backs with the rush of wind.

"Evil, evil, evil," they chanted in hushed voices.

Iona beckoned Aiden to step beside her.

"This is my lord Aiden! The new leader of all those who do the Work. You know him, you remember him, as the one who was once called 'A New Day'."

"A new day, a new day," the Fey repeated.

"He will tell the story with me. He is returned to care for the Earth, and no better man in Middle Earth than he for this calling."

Aiden lowered his hood, his aura blinding the lot of them.

"I am only a man, in service to *Her—Come my Lady Mother!"*

Aiden's voice raised the sound of fiddles. From the forest came The Aspen King's lover; his strength, his Queen.

"Here stands before us, the embodiment of the Earth Mother. We bow to her because she sustains us. She is everything we must aspire to be—kindness, generosity, love, peace and wisdom." Aiden kissed his Lady Mother's hands and bowed his head for her blessing.

"We are all one here, no one is above another in this gathering," the Fairy Queen's voice smoothed over them in lilting tones. She sat on the ground beside her King. "Tell us your story then, we shall listen and be blessed by the knowledge of what the world has become will not persist forever."

Aiden began;

"Once, a long time ago, in a land far away, there was a garden. This garden was filled with every kind of plant, flower, healing herb, and fruiting tree. It was and it was not.

The garden was tended by a man and a woman, who lived in great harmony with the beasts of the land and able to speak with everything in the Animal Kingdom and everything in the Plant Kingdom... everyone spoke the Universal Language. They were in harmony with the Crystal Kingdom, also, it was the crystals and gemstones that held ancient knowledge. The man and the woman made amulets, rings and necklaces from the crystals which were brought to them by the dwarves who lived beneath the mountains.

Every now and then, the man and the woman made a long journey to the sea, which was at the edge of the garden, and of their known world. There, they would swim and play with the fish in the water and listen to stories from the mermaids who brought them shell necklaces from the bottom of the sea. Their bodies would become like ebony when they played by the sea, and ivory when they lived in the garden under the canopy of the trees.

'We are two kinds, the dark and the light, sometimes we are children of the sun, and sometimes we are children of the moon,' they would say to each other, and wonder at their transformation. 'We are always the same on the inside, but our skin is like that of the chameleon.' And they would laugh and run along the beach, naked, free; grateful for the bodies the Goddess had given to them while they lived on Earth.

At night, they would make a big fire on the beach, and wait for the great sea turtle to come ashore. The sea turtle was a very old Turtle Mother, who laid eggs while the man and woman sang songs and played their flute and drum. She once told them she had laid the egg which birthed the Earth.

Sometimes the turtle would come as a mermaid. She loved to shapeshift. Sometimes she came as the wind. Always, she brought them a gift. The gift was Intuition. They could not hold it in their hands but received it through a secret portal to the Inner Being who lived in their heart. The turtle told them their heart and the sound of the drum vibrated to the same song as that of Mother Earth.

The best way for the man and the woman to open the secret

portal which was a mysterious eye hidden in their forehead, was to stand upon the ground with bare feet, and to feel the heartbeat of Mother Earth within their body—hands on their own heart, thump, thump!

After a few moments, their energy would align with Mother Earth and be filled with her abundance and joy. Their Inner Being would speak to them reminding them that before they were in the garden, they had been part of the stars. One day they would return to the stars, when they had learned everything there was to learn in the garden.

Inner Being also told them that the gift of Intuition was their way of knowing which path to take, should they ever become lost or meet someone who would try to make them forget the turtle's stories.

But the man and the woman were not afraid of losing their stories, because they had been woven into their hearts, and one could not lose their heart.

But there did come a day when a stranger came to the garden, and he carried a bagful of tricks. They invited him to their fire. While they shared their simple meal of roots and berries; the stranger told them they had been naïve to believe stories told by a turtle. He said their Inner Being was nothing more than a slippery snake who had possessed them and was not to be trusted. He offered them a tea of his own making, and after they drank it, they could feel Intuition coiling at the base of their spine and falling into a very deep sleep.

They called to Intuition, but Intuition remained silent.

Now they did not know which story was which; but the stranger was very convincing, so they decided they would listen to him. After all, what did an old turtle know? They did feel a sadness; but sadness was foreign to them, so they did not know to trust its prompting.

The stranger told them that all their crystals, wind chants and silly carvings of the Goddess were superstitions and if they really wanted to live a happy life and one day return to the stars, they would have to change a few things.

First of all, they would have to stop running around naked; they should be ashamed of being like the animals. They should stop enjoying their bodies so much; it wasn't right for them to be wild. For the first time, the man and the woman saw each other with embarrassment. This was another new feeling they wished to ask Intuition about.

Next, they were told that the man should take away the wom-

an's say at the fire. The woman's place would forever be in tending the man's desires. When the man saw tears on the woman's face he was greatly confused because he had never seen such a thing as water flowing from his lover's eyes. It pained him to see her without her smile. Once more he called to Intuition, but the stranger bade him drink more tea, and Intuition remained asleep.

'What is this tea we drink, stranger?' the man asked.

'Oh, it is made from the leaves of piety, godliness, and fear,' the stranger said, knowing full well the man had never known fear in the garden before, nor piety, nor did he understand how God could be separated from Goddess.

'I have never encountered these herbs, and I should know, all the plants here have told me their names!'

'Nonsense! Plants do not speak, and if they do, then you have been possessed again by that Inner Being! This tea is from my garden; that is why you have not seen these herbs before.'

The man and woman were surprised to hear there was another garden, and the woman wanted to ask where it was but she remembered that she did not have a say at the fire any longer.

'Could we visit your garden perhaps?' the man inquired. 'We have never left here except to swim in the sea.'

The stranger smiled and said, of course, they would be welcome in his garden, but first they would have to weave some clothes from the palm leaves nearby, and swear they would not speak of the Goddess, but bow to his God. And further, the woman must not look at the man in a lustful way for it would cloud his wisdom and perhaps even impede his return to the stars.'

The woman did not want to dishonor the man, for she loved him greatly—he was her Soul Twin; so, she agreed to all the conditions. But she ached to think she could not be lustful for this was one way they communicated soul to soul. Since she could remember, they had enjoyed each other's bodies with abandon; and always it had felt as if they travelled to the stars together.

And so, because Intuition slept, and by now they had been possessed by the stranger's tea brewed with Fear; they did as he said.

The next day they set out to visit the stranger's garden. They took a path they did not recognize. It was not like the paths in their garden. It was full of stones that tripped them and cut their feet. When they bled upon the path, the road back to where they lived sprang up in thistles and thorns so big no man or woman could have found their return. Along the way, they became very familiar with

Fear, who whispered to them the way the Inner Being used to do.

But when the garden came into sight, they were delighted once more, for it looked much like their garden, bathed in sunlight, full of creatures great and small and fragrant with the scent of flowers. The stranger told them this would be their new home. They were, also, forgetting their stories, so they were not distressed by this. In the middle of the garden, stood a tree they had never seen before. It was magnificent!

'Oooh, what is this tree?' the man asked. 'The fruit looks delicious!'

The stranger threw his arms in the air and cried out, 'You must never, ever, touch this tree! You will surely die if you do!'

'What is to die?' the man asked, shocked at the stranger's vehemence.

'To die, is to never return to the stars and more than that it is to burn in a never-ending fire!'

When the stranger said that, Intuition rose up as best as it could and fought to restore the turtle's stories in the hearts of the man and woman. They almost woke up from the spell of Fear, but alas, it was too late.

'What is this tree called?' the man asked.

'It is the Tree of Life,' the stranger said. 'If you eat the fruit, you will know everything God knows; but this is forbidden, and you will never, ever return to the stars.'

'But,' said the woman, forgetting her place, 'We already know everything the Goddess knows, because she lives inside us, and she shares all her wisdom. Why does God separate himself from you? Where does he live if not as part of you? How will you know your path?'

'Silence! Woman!' the stranger roared. 'You are not to speak of such things, and you are not to think about your old ways. God lives above you, and evil lives below you. God is always watching you. If you touch this tree, you will die.'

And he went away.

Leaving them bewildered and lost; forlorn and not quite as much in love as they had once been. The man lay by himself and the woman, too. For the first time, they felt the space between them. They wondered each to themselves, how uncomfortable they were with God above them and Evil below them. They longed for the familiar joy they had felt in their own garden.

The man slept, overcome with fatigue from all he had heard.

The woman could not sleep. Her Intuition had always been stronger, and she lay awake all night calling to something she did not quite remember, but knew existed. She tossed and turned, thinking and thinking, and by morning she had decided to touch the forbidden tree. She did not truly know what death was, but the fruit seemed to call to her. She had ached all night for the touch of the man. She knew she would be disobeying the stranger, but the fruit called to her, it seemed to know something she should know.

Before the sun rose, the woman slipped away and plucked the forbidden fruit from the tree. She bit into it. Oh, it was sweet, tender and luscious; it reminded her of the magical place between her legs. Now she remembered! This fruit was like the fruit of their lovemaking. It was a pathway to the stars, to Goddess! When one ate the fruit, they would remember the sacred pathway of Love. Instantly, Intuition woke and uncoiled itself from the base of the woman's spine, travelling up, left and right, left and right, in a spiraling figure eight; electrifying her wisdom; waking Inner Being and opening her mysterious hidden eye.

Suddenly she saw the truth. The stranger had stolen their connection to Goddess with his Fear tea, he had hidden their true path, and had shamed their connection to each other by declaring their nakedness vile.

Taking a handful of fruit from the tree, she determined to waken the man. She was very hungry for his love and was convinced if he ate of the fruit, he, too, would remember turtle's stories.

Waking him gently with a kiss, she waited for his eyes to adjust.

'Why, you're naked!' he cried. 'Quick, hide yourself, or we will lose our way to the stars.'

Stung by his words, the woman refused to hide herself. 'If you will only eat this fruit, you will see why I should not cover my true self! You will remember turtle's stories and your Inner Being will once more speak to you.'

But the man was afraid, and was so sleepy with forgotten memories, Fear immediately took over his words.

'You will be the death of us!'

'But see, look at this fruit...' the woman bit into the sweet fig and showed the man the tender inner flesh.

Seeing that the fruit was as enticing as the woman's sacred place and wondering at how beautiful the woman looked awoken; he bit into it. He, too, instantly remembered. The path before him was so clear!

He took the woman by the hand and spoke urgently... 'We must leave this garden and return to our own. We must return to Goddess. I have missed you woman, lying by my side. When you are gone from me, I no longer understand myself.'

'It cannot be right to cover our vulnerability and our true nature,' the woman replied. To reach the stars, we must be as Goddess made us, free to Love. In this garden, we lose our sight.

They called to Intuition. Intuition shapeshifted into a beautiful snake. Coiling herself around the tree, she declared the fruit an agent of healing. She invited them to eat more, so they would never again forget their true selves.

Before they could eat, the sound of thunder broke over the garden, and the stranger returned in a powerful rage.

Ignoring the woman, he bellowed at the man, 'Why have you eaten of the tree?'

The man trembled and looked to the woman. His memories were still weak. He should have eaten more fruit, sated himself on more wisdom!

The stranger sensed the man's weak memories. He turned to the woman. 'YOU! You gave him the fruit to eat. You have caused the man to forget his way back to the stars!' And he waved his staff, which held a very strong magic. Intuition fell from the tree unable to show them that the true Tree of Life was alive within them all along."

A loud gasp escaped the Fey as they listened to the story. They had heard it many times before but it always terrified them.

Aiden walked among them, touching a head here, a head there, reassuring them there wasn't any danger. Iona stepped forward to continue.

"So, you see, this is how the man and the woman were tricked into forgetting the Goddess, the Tree of Life, Intuition, and that they could not truly ever lose their way back to the stars.

From that day forward, all the old stories were buried deep inside them, to be remembered again when the time was right. God became the new ruler of the tribes, and Goddess wisdom was banished.

Woman continued to be silent at the fire, and man, forgetting that the Feminine was part of his Masculine, unbalanced in his sensibilities, began to fear the woman's blood and her womb, which created life. He was jealous that she was capable of such magic, and also wanted to participate in the magic of blood shedding... But the only way he could do so, was to kill.

And so, for many years to come, he covered the Earth with blood, but was never able to create life the way woman could. He grew mistrustful of her body, and the way she made him feel peaceful inside when she lay with him.

He found new ways to take away woman's power, and while he needed her to heal him from his war wounds, he was also afraid that she could return life to him with her chants and potions. The woman loved the Earth, so he began to pillage it. The more he wished he could recreate the woman's magic, the further he got from being able to do so.

Intuition was feared as never before. The stories and connection to the Fey were buried with the last of the tribes who had clung to the Old Ways.

Pan, god of the green earth, was replaced in their memories with stories of a monster who led them away from God.

Everyone forgot that to make love was to open the mysterious third eye and return to the stars while in the holy temple of one's body. To eat of the fruit, was to eat of each other's passion. It was to awaken.

Woman became the pathway to evil, and to be erotic became shameful—shrouded in dark, ugly notions—the transformative magic of pure sensuality was hidden for ages to come.

Woman—compassionate, nurturing by nature, in whom unguarded Intuition blooms, when she remembers her wildness, still longs for man's awakening. She senses his desire for fullness and prepares strong magic to help him come back to his own Intuition and compassion.

With love in her heart and the magic of her sacred fruit, she opens the door for his enlightenment. Sometimes, her magic is what the man needs, and sometimes she is lost in his territory, giving so much she keeps no magic for herself.

Our work, between humanity and you, the Fey, is to help all women and all men remember the garden, the path to the stars, Intuition, Inner Being, and to remove the veil from sacred sexuality. We must lift shame and guilt from the woman's shoulders and return her to her magic, her wildness.

We must remind ourselves that when Intuition rises along the spine, our internal Tree of Life, it is the Kundalini wisdom which nourishes our actions upon the Earth. To 'remember' is to understand ourselves as Beings of Light, made of stardust, tending the garden, our Earth.

Shall we rise up together, united in this cause?

Shall we dance like wild ones, taking hands with Pan, god of the green earth?

Shall we remember what beauty there is in joining bodies in ecstasy, eating of the fruit of sacred sexuality?

We open to the greatest mysteries of the universe when our pleasure rises, a journey between dimensions!"

With this, the iridescent Iona clapped her hands and all the Fey rose, The Aspen King took the hand of his Queen, Aiden joined hands with Sahara and Holly. Music filled the forest. Iona began to dance. Her shimmering gown cast down, she stood naked before them. The music guided her body into a sensual gypsy dance, bangles on her wrists, bells on her toes; a glittering gold belt around her waist. Tapping the cymbals on her fingers, a wild cry rose from her lips.

Ayayayayayayayayay!

The crowd leapt into movement, snaking their way around the fire, slowly, then faster and faster yet. The Aspen King and Fairy Queen danced with grace, eyes fastened on each other. Never had Aiden seen his Lady Mother of old so rapturously happy.

His heart exploded with the great pressure of love, his beloveds on either side of him, his body burning with desire. He knew Holly was now fully initiated into her connection to the Fey—privy to some of the greatest misconceptions about the magic of women and the alchemy of sex.

Sahara's hand squeezed his. How grateful he was for the wisdom and tenacity of this woman who had loved him into awakening. How fortunate he was to know the magic of two women, to be part of their love for each other. If only the world could accept such things. It would be his life's work to be part of the *remembering*.

Thinking deeply thus, Aiden was surprised to suddenly find the forest quiet except for the rustling of the trees, all the Fey gone, Iona disappeared from sight. If he was someone else, he might think he had imagined it all, but he knew they had slipped dimensions to experience the last few hours. Looking up at him, Holly and Sahara threw off their capes. They helped him with his. They laid out their blankets in the fire's glow, on a patch of bare moss.

"My darling," Sahara purred, "I am so in love with you. I am in love with who you are, with your strength of purpose, with the way you love us both." Her kisses landed soft on his lips.

Aiden was truly lost for words. He had absorbed so much this night, been cast fully into his place upon the planet and with the Fey, delved so deeply into ancient memories from the beginning of humanity, that he was now too spent to speak. But he was not too spent to honor them with his body and his love.

He returned Sahara's kiss with passion, lustful mouth taking hers. Her moans were met with the crackling of the fire. Sahara and Holly stood obediently as he stripped them of their garments. Unable to resist each other any longer, the two women fell to the ground in their nakedness, tangled limbs, skin on skin.

"Teach me about making magic with our love, darling," Holly whispered. "Teach me how to make a spell with our orgasm, how to move energy in this way."

Sahara responded with hungry bites on Holly's neck. Writhing against each other, their mouths explored and sucked, nipples worried pink, wet pussy rubbing wet pussy.

"Let me taste," Aiden said, stepping out of his jeans. His cock sprang out, handsome, erect.

"Let us taste first," Holly suggested.

Aiden could hardly deny her. On his knees, and the girls on theirs, they met for a torrid kiss. An electric surge of pleasure sprang up between them. Here, in their forest hideaway, by the fire blessed in magic, they could indulge their wildness. The sensual pleasure of being naked in the elements and the sensation of Aiden's hands gently cupping their sex while he roamed their necks created a delicious tension.

Their pussies quivered, wet and tight with need. Exchanging dirty kisses with the man they adored, they could close their eyes and allow his slow caresses to open their emotions. He was ever so patient, ever so dedicated to creating their assent into ecstasy. They knew him well enough by now to expect his excellence. There was nothing selfish about Aiden's love.

"Lie down," he commanded with an adulterous grin.

They did. Sahara's gaze gripped Aiden's. Illicit and soaked in centuries, their love couldn't be contained. Her cunt was swollen and soaking wet. He noticed, eyes burning her flesh. He didn't have to ask, she spread for him, legs wide, hands pulling her lips apart.

"Here, darling!" Sahara's voice was urgent.

He bent his face to her, allowing his breath to wash warm over her clit. Sahara moaned. Waiting was unbearable. Holly's hand in hers, she lifted her hips a little.

"Please!"

His mouth found all the tender places between her legs, inside her thighs and soothing across her belly, along her hip bones and back to her pubic bone, just a millimeter from where flesh parted towards her clit. Holly supplied Sahara with kiss after kiss, moaning into her mouth, raising the energy between them, until Aiden asked her to lie down, because he wanted a taste of her lips too.

Sahara groaned, because she now understood he was going to torture them with pleasure, and she could hardly stand the pressure building at her sex. He was doing what he was supposed to be doing, allowing pleasure to penetrate her lower chakras fully, before he unleashed his purpose. Having two of them to concentrate on would only make the waiting practically unbearable.

But she found great satisfaction in watching him kiss Holly, allowing her to feel his weight and intention. Holly pushed up towards him, trying to wedge him inside her. She was fully ready for his cock. She wanted him inside her, thrusting against her cervix, calling down her orgasm. But he wouldn't, that much was clear.

And so, they were at his mercy while he took his time, mouth engaging their every sense, nibbling their ears, speaking filthy words that brought them dangerously close to coming but never laying his tongue where they begged; and then he pulled back, allowing a bit of mercy. They fell into each other's arms while he watched, assuming their favorite position, legs scissored, letting the motion of their hips, the wetness of their cunts, the heat built up in their bodies release in a gushing, echoing orgasm. Seeing Aiden with his cock in his hand edging dangerously close to orgasm while they came only made the release so much better.

Presenting on their hands and knees, Holly and Sahara finally received the tongue lashing they'd been waiting for. Hungry like a wolf, Aiden devoured them. They begged for his tongue inside, but he refused. No, this was going to be a masterful union, unhurried, deliberate.

They returned his gift with one of their own, mouths wet, tongues rolling his cock from base to tip, deftly sharing the velvety hardness, hands working the length while lips sucked loudly. Sahara licked his tight balls until he groaned and pushed her away.

"Not yet," he breathed, chest heavy with emotion. He surrendered them down to the ground again, on their bellies. Kisses landed on the backs of their necks. Hips raised but he ordered stillness. Lips moved down their backs, taking turns to roll each of them over so he could suck erect nipples, then back on their bellies, anticipating his arrival at their bottoms. There he lingered.

"Mmmm, fucking delicious," he murmured, between tender smacks and love bites. "I have something for you Holly," he added.

"What is it?" she turned, chest heaving, dying for penetration. He had forbidden her to use her fingers inside herself, and now her cunt dripped liberally down her leg. She spread to show him. Aiden's groan had her clit jumping in response.

He reached inside the box of magic tools and showed a large, smooth, rose quartz yoni wand. It lay enticingly inside the palm of his muscular hand.

"Oooh, yes please!" Holly spread wider.

"It will be cold, here, hold it in your hand first, feel it, feel the smoothness, anticipate its energy inside you." He waited while Holly felt the wand first in her hands, then against her face, then licking the length. Sahara sat up, she began a chant, tugging her nipples. Against the fire, she was illuminated like a goddess.

"I'm ready darling," Holly spread herself once more, unashamed, a woman whose desires were never taboo with the people she loved.

Aiden ran the wand between her breasts, he let her feel its heaviness on her belly, resting it there while he put his hands under her hips and gripped her clit with his mouth. She cried out, there was so much pleasure in how he rolled it with his tongue. Sucking it into his mouth, pulling it tight, he sent her flying to the edge... then he let it go. She gasped, pleaded, but orgasm was not his goal yet.

"I absolutely adore your pussy," he said, opening her with warm fingers, taking his time to explore with his eyes.

"Yes! Open me wider, look, she wants you!"

This time he let his fingers circle her opening, then slid along her perineum, then pressed against her bud.

"Oh!"

Sahara was now dancing, swaying around the fire, raising energy for their lust.

Softly, Aiden pressed the yoni wand against Holly's pussy. She jumped from the cold. "I want it inside me, please Aiden!"

He slipped it in, waited the seconds required while Holly's pussy clamped down against it; then he began the agonizing exploration of her inner sanctuary. Here and there he asked her to lick the wand, then kissed her, then sucked her nipples so hard she arched her back and asked for mercy.

When she was bucking her hips against the wand, and pulling his hand toward her hoping for release, he pulled it out and told her to get on her hands and knees.

"Will you fuck me now?" Holly was almost in tears.

"Not yet, darling. First I will give you something you've asked for many times."

"What?" Holly turned her head, face in a blush, hopeful.

"This," Aiden presented a whip. "I've not had the courage for this, and don't bother asking me for what I give Sahara, this is just to tease you."

"But!" Holly's pussy dripped again, heat covering her, anticipation so great she welled up in tears.

"Hush woman! Tell me, where do you feel your passion right now? Is it at heart center, or higher?"

"Higher. Here," Holly touched her throat.

"Perfect. Present, whore."

Aiden's words, greedy lust-laced with intoxicating love sent Holly spinning towards release. But he forbade it once more.

Before he touched her with the whip, he let his tongue swipe from clit to ass, thrusting his tongue deep.

"Please may I come?"

"No! Lift your ass."

The whip caressed with tenderness, tickling. Holly's moans filled the forest. Sahara danced.

The first hit was so light she almost missed it. He built on each strike, until her ass bloomed pink. His cock was dripping with anticipation, his mind a little blurred, his hand itching to strike harder. Holly begged for more. He allowed one crack that fell her to the ground. She had wanted it but hadn't expected it. He had said...

Tears burst forth. Aiden grabbed her by the throat and squeezed with just the right amount of pressure.

"More!" she gasped.

"No more. Do you still feel your lust here?" He gripped her throat a little harder.

She nodded, pumped her hips back.

"Face down."

Holly did as she was bid. She felt his hands spreading her open, his muttered curse, his cock filling her fully and then... the pounding thrusts evoked a scream from her throat, the force of her orgasm spilled upward toward her crown and filled her body with hot waves. Energy rushed from her cervix to her heart then filled every crevice of her being. Aiden roared as he came inside her, hot cum searing her sanctuary, and they collapsed by the fire at Sahara's feet.

She had stopped singing, her body glistening with the dew raised while she'd danced. She was ready. She'd watched them from the corner of her eye as she'd held space for their lovemaking. Now she wanted that deep ache in her pussy to be satisfied. Aiden pulled her close and closed his mouth over hers, lashing her tongue, a kiss so forceful and evoking such fire in her belly that he had to hold her up. In his strong embrace, Sahara felt the explosion of sexual energy that she'd been waiting for. She came as he kissed her, dripping wet to the ground. He laid her down. Gently, gently, he touched her there... a whisper of a caress.

"Please, my darling. Have mercy."

Eyes closed, legs spread, nipples poking the cold air, Sahara waited. It seemed like centuries, Aiden's kiss on her clit, his nuzzle against the wet folds, his long and languid lick between her lips, then fingers, first a slow circle of her opening, then barely inside her, in and out, brushing the edges, until she was begging in no uncertain terms.

She opened her eyes. "Let's make magic, Aiden."

She had made a clear intention for her orgasm, had opened the space for intention to manifest, she had a dream seed placed upon her third eye and would release it when they joined together.

He didn't ask her what she was manifesting, he trusted her magic. If she'd wanted to share she would have. Aligning himself with her wishes, calling down his own magic, Aiden determined to bring her to her highest expression of lust.

Her cries echoed against his body while he plunged his fingers inside her, fucking hard. She arched, he desisted. When her breathing had slowed a little, he licked her with a wide and hard tongue, each stroke ending at a play of her clit. Holly sat on splayed knees, accepting Aiden's kisses here and there, rocking to her own climbing energy, seducing the others with her wild eyes. It was impossible to stay unengaged with their play. She crawled over to Sahara, positioning herself so that her breasts grazed Sahara's mouth, first one, then the other, dipping her nipples in her mouth.

"Will you come with me again, sweetness?" Sahara bit a nipple evoking a yelp from Holly.

Aiden pulled a bottle of blood red wine from his crate. He unwrapped three crystal goblets. Next, he produced a tiny bowl into which he added ashes from around the sacred fire. It burned lower now, and the winter air began to nip at their skin. He knew that the Fey were winding down the magic they had been weaving over them for the last few hours.

With the pointer finger of his dominant hand, he drew a sigil for the Goddess Aphrodite on their foreheads and Sahara drew one on his. He poured their wine, then took his hunting knife and cut a quick nick into the tips of their ring fingers. He had expected Holly to protest but she absorbed solemnly. They each pressed a drop of blood out and let it fall into their wine.

"Blood magic is very powerful, darling," he said. "I'm sure that you and Sahara will be doing other blood magic together, when your moon time comes. This magic is to declare our connection as lovers, to consecrate our feelings for each other and we'll all add our own wishes to it. You can speak your intention out loud or we can all agree to silent manifestation."

They drank from their own cups, then passed the goblets around until all had drunk from each other's. A kiss sealed the blood bond further. Holly swam in the headwaters of their energy. Was she still here? Her body swayed... this was what it felt like to be enchanted!

Sahara continued, "I wish to manifest in silence." The others nodded agreement. "As our energy rises, and our orgasm nears, place your intention on your third eye, visualize it there and the moment you climax, release it to the universe. Any sound you make at the time will carry your intention further."

Aiden asked for the blessing of the Feminine. They each laid their hands on his crown.

Sahara spoke a prayer from the Tantric tradition. *"Obeisance to Her, who is pure Being, Consciousness, Bliss. As power, who exists in the forms of time and space, and all that is therein, who is the Divine Illuminatrix in all beings."*

By now Holly thought that if she allowed it she could float out of her body. She finished her wine, as it burned down her throat and all the way to her sex. She was on fire once more.

From a distance she knew they were chanting the sound which birthed the universe over and over like a rolling wave escaping their throats. They were part of the fire, and part of the air, and part of the earth and part of spirit. Naked, ecstatic, they joined in steamy kisses. Sahara and Aiden were at once part of her and separate; at times wearing clothes and at times not, adorned like the Fey had been with forest gifts of ferns and ivy.

They ate from a bowl of pomegranate seeds and oranges, feeding each other; Aiden rubbing the scarlet fruit over his lover's breasts then sucking their achingly taut nipples. Sahara abandoned herself to his hands around her waist, bending back for the kisses he bestowed,

114

lower, lower, lower, until she was lying on the ground and he parted her legs for a deep, salacious kiss of her sex. He made love to it, an animal in heat, coaxing her with wicked words, demanding she surrender to pleasure. Turning her over, he began his assault of her skin once more, bites on her back, slick fingers inside her, tongue exploring her darkest secrets. She allowed. Allowing was the sweet spot of lovemaking... dissolving all expectations and accepting being pleasured without thinking, without anticipating anything but what was in the moment.

When Sahara was spread before him like a glittering treasure on the beach, he turned his attention to Holly, her breasts full in his hands, her naked need lighting up her eyes.

"Darling, I have waited for you for so long, years of longing and imaging you like this, wild and uncensored."

Holly's hands roamed his body. Her mouth salivated.

"I've been waiting for you my whole life too," she admitted. "I've wanted this. This irreverent fucking, this absolute freedom."

She dropped to her knees and worshipped his cock. This was where his power lay, the way he penetrated the world was represented by this delicious part of his body. His relationship with it and the way he shared it with her and Sahara was part of his spiritual journey. With all her love she devoured him, encouraged by his fierce moans and the way he gripped her hair when she brought him close. She was amazed by how fine-tuned they were to each other's signals. She read his body language like a favorite book, the tensing of his abdomen, thighs and ass. But even more than that, she sensed the shift in his energy when orgasm neared, they were two, but they were one. They were God and Goddess, Shakti and Shiva, an erotic union of opposites.

Holly's body filled with a surging light. Aiden lifted her to her feet. His mouth stole hers, jaw hard with desire. Turning her gently, he pushed her to the ground on all fours.

He bent over her, whispering in her ear. "I love you."

Locking eyes with Sahara, he nodded. She didn't need to speak. Love was theirs, the sweetest love of all; the kind that poured from their pores and filled the spaces between them.

Sahara lifted her hips a little, offering herself to Holly and it was Holly's pleas that set everything in motion. Aiden's cock grazed her pussy, she bucked her hips back, anticipating his first thrust. He slid in deep, filled her fully and savored the undulations of her hips. Sahara pulled hard on Holly's hair, bringing lips to lips, hungrily anticipating the burn of Holly's tongue.

Engaged thus, cock to pussy, mouth to a divinely soaking cunt, they began their dance. Fucking hard responding to his lover's cries, Aiden drove them into a delicious frenzy. Sahara was held fast by Holly's hands around her hips, Holly held by Aiden's around hers. After all these hours of magic and eroticism, they were ready. There was little time to prepare for the pleasure that would visit them. Wild-eyed and lost to everything around them, they moved like waves on an ocean, each one of Aiden's thrusts coursing through Holly to Sahara's core. Heat spreading from her cervix to her heart, she panted the words they were waiting for.

"Now!" Sahara's voice set sparks flying from the fire into the night sky. They set their intentions, opened their third eye, activated their throat chakra and with a collective howl, gushed their release.

"So mote it be!" Aiden cried out, cock soaked with Holly's cum, Sahara's body arcing in orgasm.

"So mote it be," his lovers repeated. They fell into each other, laughing, crying, enraptured by a feeling so complete, it overtook all thought and erased the boundaries of skin between them. Stillness, solace and sanctuary... the other names for Love. Each of them had sent powerful magic with their orgasm, and each of them lay spent but very aware of the impact their intentions could have.

Aiden lay in the arms of the Feminine. He was complete. He was infused with Shakti as they were with Shiva. Neither was above the other but benefited from the gifts of opposites. Lying so, their auras mingled. Searching beneath the illusion of separate bodies, they breathed the essence of their devotion. Tender kisses brought them back to where the fire had died and with it, the door to the Underworld had closed.

Aiden stood and offered his hands to them.

"Come, darlings! We are finished here."

He smiled at Holly, who was entirely changed, a woman bathed in the mysteries of the universe. She would never see the world in the same way again. Now there was a depth to these woods and to life that would guide her in her every day.

They walked in silence to Sahara's cabin, night ebbing, exhausted but elated. Ulfred barked his greeting. Coffee was made, and a bath run. Aiden revived the fire. A baguette was crisped in the oven; butter, blackberry preserves, and boiled eggs set out. This was heaven, they agreed, moving about the cabin with grateful hearts. This simple pleasure of eating together, of homemade sustenance, of earthy grounding, of fire to keep them warm was worth more than any other treasures. And that they were free to love each other and practice their spirituality in peace... a gift they had been denied in centuries past.

"I don't feel like the one on the outside any longer," Holly said, breaking the bread with her hands and passing pieces around.

A flash of regret in Aiden's eyes was met by her explanation, "No, you never made me feel this way darling, it was only because I hadn't been initiated into the magic world you both live in. I was new, and actually am happy that I am. I can have a perspective on things the rest of you don't; because I'm not carrying the memories you do. Perhaps new blood was needed in this story? Like a fresh sacrifice to sanctify an old agreement? Do you know what I mean?"

Sahara and Aiden stared at her. Of course, they knew what she meant. The shedding of blood had always been a symbol of birth, of renewal—of washing old energy clean. Women did this every month, transformed the universe with their blood. A woman could bleed and not die, something a man couldn't do; it was how woman created. When Holly had come into their lives, their ancient story had begun to shift, a new container was being created for their love and the past. She was the holder of strong magic. The magic of dissolving karma.

They talked this over at great length, and would have kept on so, but not even the coffee had the power to keep their eyes open. They climbed the stairs to Sahara's loft and got in bed just as the first rays of sunlight hit the winter snow. Snuggled into each other's arms, they fell into a deep sleep.

The only thing that was strange, was that when they dreamed, they dreamed as one. Holly woke in fits and starts, startled by her travels, then fell asleep once more, slipping effortlessly into the damp coolness of a room high up in a castle tower, where she saw herself bending over a table of unfamiliar objects.

CHAPTER 20

"You must be ready to burn yourself in your own flame.
How could you become new if you had not first become ashes?"
~ Nietzsche

Arinn jumped, startled by the sudden opening of the door. She turned quickly, like an animal caught unawares.

"Oh!" she said, relaxing, if cool in her tone. "It is you."

Richard stood in the doorway, as always, arrested by the vision of her, so unusual was she to these surroundings.

"Apologies, my lady," he bowed curtly. Despite his best efforts, Arinn had pushed him away, refusing to allow the comfort he sought to provide for her. It didn't bring out his best side.

"Is it time I came down for my meal?" Arinn questioned, her mind rebelling against her lot in life. No matter how much she wanted to, she couldn't reconcile the events which had brought her here, nor forgive the man who held her captive. She understood it wasn't his fault, and yet...

"I came to propose we take a picnic and eat by the river. There are things we need to discuss and that is best done away from prying ears."

"As you wish, my lord," Arinn acquiesced.

Richard watched the play of emotions on her face.

"You need not be so cold toward me, Arinn. I am not the enemy. I am simply carrying out Dagr's wishes, and you cannot blame me for the events which led to *that* decision."

Arinn's eyes shot fire. Richard felt the familiar stir in his loins. He wished it was not so and took hold of the door.

"I will have the cook make up the basket. Meet me by the garden gate. And make sure you lock this door."

"Yes, my lord," Arinn's anger receded. She felt sorry for him. He was caught in a terrible quandary, and she was the reason. His life would certainly be less complicated was she right now in France.

The thought of France brought on instant tears. They slipped hot down her face. She brushed them away quickly, then made a neat pile of the papers on the table. The other objects she touched with a reverent hand. At least she had this... the studies Richard had agreed to allow her to pursue.

Not long after they had arrived at the castle, ensconced in the room once occupied by Brigida, Arinn had discovered loose bricks in the wall behind her bed. They led to a secret compartment filled with mysterious writings and tools Richard explained as belonging to a long dead hermetic and astrologer once employed by his father. The writings, alchemy, were those of Dagr's mother, Lara.

Arinn had immediately clung to these as an avenue of connection to Dagr, her soul stirred by the strange words that were at once familiar and indecipherable.

Arinn was explained as the new herbalist to take over poor dead Hannah's role. She had free reign over the healer's garden, her own apartment as it were, and the room upstairs was where she took up her studies. It was a great danger to play with the tools on the table, or to know what the books on alchemy taught. She took the heavy iron key from her pocket and locked the door. This small bit of danger and hope was her only solace.

Richard was where he said he would be, waiting by the garden gate. He gave her his hand, leaning down from his mount to help her up behind him. For an instant, she pressed herself hard against his back, starved for the touch of her beloveds. He didn't flinch, as if he'd been expecting it. With her hands around his waist, they rode down the hill into a small stretch of forest. They stopped by a river winding its way north.

"We have been very fortunate this year. There is a surplus of game."

Richard waited until Arinn had spread the wool blanket on the ground then handed her the basket. She unloaded bread and meat, a jar of wild berry preserves and some sweet meats.

Richard settled beside her, rakish good looks unchecked, white shirt stark against his olive skin. Arinn lingered over the cut of his hunting leathers, then looked away, aware of his stare.

"I really cannot wait until you have baked some of Hannah's bread. Cook's is fine, but nothing compares to what Hannah made. And I miss the activity in that kitchen... well, to be able to escape to it." Richard shook his head. "I miss her."

Arinn nodded. "I know. You said once before that she was your one confidant."

"Besides Dagr," Richard added, not thinking.

Arinn lowered her eyes. Richard growled with regret.

"I suppose we will have to talk about this sooner or later," Arinn sighed. She looked up and fell into his dark eyes. Compassion reigned there.

"I was just as surprised as you were. I think he will soon tire of being angry and send for you. I very much do, my lady. And then I will deliver you to France, and we shall forget all this."

"It is not from anger he has left me behind. It is because he could not trust me. And I have no way of building that trust again. I do not believe he will ever send for me," Arinn wiped at her tears.

"Rubbish! He will. I know him and he has a very soft heart."

"You miss him too," Arinn observed.

Richard kicked a stray stone. "I have no right to miss him."

"But you do. There is no point in pretending, you miss them both. You love them both."

"Can you forgive me that?" Richard leaned closer on the pretense of reaching for a sweetmeat.

Arinn caught her breath. He smelled of Dagr's familiar scent.

"Why do you smell like that? Where did you get that fragrance?" she demanded.

"Brigida made it. There was some left over."

"Did you wear it to distress me? Are you playing with me Richard?" It was the first time since she had arrived that she had used his name.

Richard denied it. Hotly. "I wear it sometimes to remind me of him. It was a mistake. Forgive me." The last part was more of a demand than a plea.

Arinn lay her face against the ground, sobbing; beating the blanket with her fists.

"I cannot live this! I cannot and will not! I would rather be dead than miss them like this. It is cruel to remind me, Richard. Cruel!"

Richard, suddenly scared she would take her own life to suppress the grief that consumed her, gathered her up into his arms and cradled her there, rocking her, his lips in her hair.

"No, sweetness, it will not be a lifetime, I promise. You will see, he will relent." He dropped kisses on her head, ignoring the passion she evoked, and his desire to comfort her like he had once comforted Brigida. Oh, this was cruelty indeed.

"And what if he does not, my lord?" Arinn looked up into his eyes, her body awakening at the touch of a man, her nipples aching against the press of her kirtle. She felt like a traitor and wondered if this is what Brigida had felt.

Richard faced her query like the warrior he was. "Then I will love you."

Arinn laughed, mocking his promise. "Love a servant girl? Love

120

me when you already love them? You are deluded, my lord. You are just as broken as I am." She slid away.

He poured them some wine. They drank in silence. After a while, sensing that Arinn had gathered herself, he spoke, "Yes, my lady. I am broken as well. But I will not live my life pining for something that tortures me. If we cannot have what we want, we must want what we have. And until I hear otherwise, I plan on making my days with you count for something. If nothing else, we will have a pleasant life of meeting like this and when you say the word, I will expand your studies. Would that please you, to learn more? I actually have a surprise for you, and which is why I brought you here."

Arinn sat up, curious. "What kind of a surprise?"

Richard poured more wine in their cups. "I know a man who would be able to tutor you in your studies. I have already spoken to him and he is willing to come live at the castle."

"A tutor!" Arinn's eyes lit up. "Can you trust him? How is it he knows such things?"

"I can trust him. He was a young man who studied under the one whose tools you've discovered, Lara's tutor—my father's astrologer. He is part of a Society that carries on this work. He is quite old now himself."

"What would you say of him... the reason he would be in your service?" It was always a tricky situation what with not knowing who in Richard's employ could betray him.

"I will say he was hired to help you in the garden. Hannah's old gardener was let go and has passed since. It will not seem strange for you to have an old man helping with your work."

"Aaaah. I see. Why yes, I would be grateful for such an opportunity. Thank you, my lord," Arinn observed Richard over her cup. He smiled, flashing his perfect white teeth.

"I can sense you have a question on your mind. Out with it."

Arinn could not deny it. She did. "Why would you go to so much trouble to find me a tutor, and risk having a heretic in your household?"

"I do so because I think you are a natural for these studies, as was Brigida, and it will take your mind off your troubles. And I do not like to see a gifted mind go to waste," he grinned.

Arinn smiled too, in spite of herself.

"And...?"

Richard laughed. "And, I would like you to teach me, once you have learned. I have long been curious about such things. Brigida re-ignited my curiosity."

"An ulterior motive. I should have known," Arinn teased.

"I give this to you with a clear heart, Arinn," Richard turned serious. "I do care for you and I have made a promise to Dagr. But please do not mistake me for a gentleman. I am not one who forgets about his own needs. I do not intend to go through my whole life without anything to stimulate my mind." He picked up her hand and grazed his lips over it.

"Is it your mind you wish to stimulate, my lord?" Arinn shot back.

He looked up sharply. She was ever so bold. "Like I said, I am no gentleman."

"I do not believe you. Do you know why?"

He shook his head.

"Because neither Dagr nor Brigida would love a man who was lacking in character."

Richard stood and turned away. He was the picture of a ruthless man, and if he had been anyone else, Arinn would have shrunk from him. His body language spoke of something Arinn was sure had made many a person frightened. But she had tasted his lips once, and more. And behind the fierceness, she had discovered something else. Something quite gentle.

"You lie, my lord. And not very well. You are a gentleman. You cannot fool me." She stood and took his hand. It closed suddenly and with a hard grip over hers. "I will be an ambitious student. You will see."

He looked down at her. For the first time in months she was not directing her anger at him. In fact, she looked as tender as she had the first time he had met her. He longed to kiss her, remind her that all was not lost. He wanted to offer solace, but could not take advantage of his position and her vulnerability.

"We must get back. I have work to do and you have yours."

They bent to the task of packing their wares.

CHAPTER 21

Sahara found Holly in the kitchen. She wrapped herself around her back.

"You're up."

"Couldn't sleep. Had a dream."

"What about?" Sahara settled on the stool at the counter.

"It was very strange. I was in Richard's castle. I saw Arinn, but in my dream, it seemed to be me. She and Richard were talking about a tutor, someone who would teach her astronomy and alchemy."

Sahara's eyes opened wide. "I had the same dream! So, did Aiden! We were just talking about it!"

"You're kidding! How does *that* happen?"

"It happens," Aiden said, coming down the stairs, "when we are joined in one mind. A state of consciousness where more than one person shares an energy wave length." He kissed them both and sat down beside Sahara.

"I'm able to do this?" Holly stopped what she was doing. "I really thought I was watching myself. I *felt* the room and could feel my hand on the table. How is that possible if I've never been there? Can you explain this?" A shiver ran up her back, like a cold finger from that dim, damp, room.

"Well," Sahara drawled, searching for the right words. "It's like this. Your cellular memory carries the imprint of everything that has ever happened to every human being on the planet since the beginning of time. It contains a recollection of the moment the Earth was created, and as part of the One consciousness, we can, in the right circumstances, experience anything anywhere, anytime."

"Ok," Holly mused, watching Sahara fidget in her chair. "So, what would another circumstance be?"

Sahara offered a wry look. Holly smiled. "I know you, lover," she said.

"If some magic was made to invite you to the past, to live alongside the person who had lived it, that would be another scenario."

"I see," Holly made herself busy steeping herbal tea for their morning drink. She stayed silent for a few moments. Aiden and Sahara held hands, watching her process the information. Telepathically, they agreed to help her gently with the journey she was on. On the surface, it seemed as if Holly was an accidental replica of Arinn, but of course, there were no accidents or coincidences as such, and Holly had incarnated as part of their soul group, intentionally agreeing to join them in this mystical exploration of past lives.

"As you've both said before," Holly spoke up at last, "time's not linear. The past, present and future happen simultaneously. I believe that." She set out the teapot for them and three glass cups. She poured the brew, a pretty hue of red hibiscus and rose petals, scented with lavender and mint. "Whatever Iona's purpose is in this, I intend to trust her. There's no quicker way for me to understand your past and dynamic than to be thrown directly into the fire."

Those last words seared through Sahara. Her fingers tightened over Aiden's. A flash of memory rose upon her third eye with precise clarity. She cried out. "No! My love, no!"

"What is it? Sahara, speak to me," Aiden commanded. He held her fast, pressing her head against his chest. When her breathing slowed, Sahara sat by the fire.

"It was Arinn... I... I thought I saw her being taken to a pyre." She laid her head in Holly's lap, unable to look at her, hoping to chase the image away.

"You may be recalling a collective memory, darling," Aiden soothed. "We don't even know whether Brigida and Arinn saw each other again."

"You're right," Sahara said, sitting up. "That's probably what it is. I'm sorry I scared you."

"Not at all, sweetness," Holly reassured. "We share everything, whatever comes to us, we are safe to share."

"I think it would be good for us to take a break from the esoteric," Aiden suggested. "Let's eat and get dressed. I'm going to clear the paths around the cabin again. Why don't you two come out and get some air as well? My parents will be here tomorrow. There's lots to do." He stood and stretched. It broke them out of their introspective mood.

"Let's stack some wood in the alcove," Holly said. "I could use some exercise."

"After all that dancing and sex last night?" Sahara laughed. "I'm tired."

"Ok, I'll stack wood, you stay in here and tidy up... and maybe make us breakfast? I'm starving again. Then we'll all go to Aiden's and get organized there."

"Right. We're sorted then." Aiden slapped both their bums with his t-shirt, grinning at their appreciation of his rock-hard body, then ran upstairs for his clothes. He knew Sahara better than to think she was over her frightening vision. She wanted time alone, in her own space. Glancing out the bedroom window at the great expanse of white toward the mountains beyond, he was distracted by a dot of black on a tree outside.

She was, as he had thought, near.

CHAPTER 22

"Who wants to come to town with me?" Aiden rolled over onto his side. His bedroom was soaking up the earliest rays of morning sun. It was one of his favorite moments, watching the sun enter his space, tentative at first, then boldly stretching its rays across the floor.

"Too early!" Sahara complained.

"I do! I have to pick something up from the café."

Holly had closed the patisserie for three days. It was a veritable holiday and she had been glad to offer Lilith and Francois some time off.

"Ok, you come with me, little lady. We'll leave sleeping beauty here to her own devices."

"Thank you!" Sahara groaned. "I promise I'll be up and ready by the time you come back. Just leave me some coffee in the pot?"

Aiden nibbled her neck. "You don't need to rush. They won't be here until late afternoon."

"Are you ready for this?" Sahara asked, opening her eyes and staring into the gorgeous blue of his.

He smiled gently. "No. But it's going down."

She touched his face. "I love you."

From where he stood on the front porch of his home, Aiden could observe the peaceful scene inside. He had always loved the aesthetics of the building, and the way it interacted so organically with nature. It had never looked out of place in its surroundings. And now, watching Sahara and Holly moving about inside with the soft lighting of table lamps and candles, the warm cast of shadows from the fireplace, he felt a deep gratitude for his life. His dreams of a life with two women he adored had come true. Even as he'd been unaware of the steps he'd taken towards it, his soul had guided him to this magical place of being.

The wind blew fresh through the forest, bringing a crisp scent of evergreens. The Solstice tree had been replenished with fresh treats for the birds and squirrels. It was lit now, to welcome the arrival of his parents. They would be driving up shortly, according to their plans, and Aiden was awash with mixed emotions.

Always, he felt the pleasure of seeing them again, they were his foundation. But it also brought up the memory of his sister, and all

126

the pain that accompanied it. Tonight, it heralded another step into his authenticity. It wasn't so much that he needed their approval, although that was something Aiden relished when given; but more than anything he wished to not be a source of any anguish for them.

They'd had enough of that. But here he was, once again at the center of unexpected news. This time, he hoped they would find joy in his happiness. He hoped that it was his, Sahara and Holly's delight at having found each other which would be at the center of his parent's discoveries.

He sighed, heart pounding. He realized he had been standing there with arms folded, hands clenched. He relaxed and opened himself to a more free flow of energy.

By the time the light from their headlights rounded the corner of his driveway, he was once again centered.

"Well, well! That was quite the drive," his father said, getting out and stretching his tall, lanky frame. His son was reminded of how much he had looked up to him as a child, a bit stern but also strong of character.

Aiden opened the passenger car door.

"Mama!" He kissed her heartily on both cheeks and swung her around.

"Put me down! Oh, you're silly!" Bronwyn laughed and straightened herself. "Look at that tree, hon, we should do something like that!"

"Sure thing. We could do..." Liam winked at his son. "More jobs for me."

"As if you mind," Aiden joked. His parents adored each other, and his father would drop anything to please his wife.

"Oh, I do love your house, sweetheart!" Bronwyn surveyed the cabin. "It couldn't be more you if it tried."

"I'm glad you like it, Mom. Let me grab your bags."

"Your mother's been wondering the whole trip about your new young lady. If you don't introduce her soon, she'll burst!"

Aiden sobered momentarily. He looked to the front door where Holly stood smiling and waving. His heart exploded with love.

"Aaahh, there she is!" Bronwyn waved back. "I'm going in, you boys hurry up."

"Wait Mama! I'm coming with you." Aiden took her arm as she hurried to the front step.

"Ok, ok. I understand."

Holly greeted Bronwyn, taking her coat and accepting Liam's rather hearty handshake.

Aiden looked around for Sahara, who was just coming forward from the kitchen. She was wearing a peaceful smile. Apparently, introductions and confessions were to happen immediately. Surprisingly, he was ready.

"Mom, Dad, this is Holly. Holly, Bronwyn and Liam."

Hugs and kisses were exchanged. Aiden stood proudly by. Liam caught his eye and Aiden could see his Dad was impressed by Holly straight away. She had chosen to wear black pencil jeans, a periwinkle angora sweater that hugged her curves, and a short string of pearls. Elegantly sexy, which was her signature look, with black heels to finish.

"And who is this?" Bronwyn didn't see any reason to not hug the petite woman hanging back. Perhaps Holly's sister? But no, their coloring was entirely different.

Aiden took Sahara's hand and pulled her close. "And this is Sahara."

Liam shook her hand, confused by the closeness his son exhibited toward the mysterious looking creature. He exchanged looks with Bronwyn, shrugging his shoulders.

Color rose on Holly's cheeks. The moment was here.

"Mom, Dad, I should probably sit you down and hand you a drink first... but... Holly *and* Sahara are who I wished to introduce you to. They are my loves, both." He waited.

Bronwyn and Liam looked from one to the other. They took stock of the situation in their usual manner, straightforward and polite. Liam took his wife's hand. His intense grey-blue eyes surveyed them top to bottom. Finally, after an agonizing few moments, he spoke.

"Sahara and Holly, we are *delighted* to make your acquaintance! My son is an incorrigible rogue, but you look up to the challenge, my dears." He broke into a broad grin. Bronwyn gaped with surprise at her husband, then took to hugging the girls all over again.

With much laughter and happy tears from Holly, they opened champagne and toasted to the unconventional news.

The entire evening was consumed with questions and more questions, a few words of advice from the gob-smacked parents and finally, an intimate dinner by candlelight.

Bronwyn took great interest in what inspired the girls. She listened attentively to Holly's excitement about the patisserie and didn't bat an eye when Sahara said she wrote about magic. In fact, Aiden hadn't seen his mother's eyes so lit up with joy in a very long time.

They admired Holly's ring. Aiden and Sahara, holding hands, confessed they had already had a commitment ceremony and were married as far as they were concerned. Holly made strong coffee and served dessert. Bronwyn and Liam weathered all news gracefully, but everyone knew it was a lot to take in and that they would need time to process. Sitting by the fire, the evening wound down to a quiet, reflective mood.

"You know, Aiden," Bronwyn said, tears clouding her eyes, "I've been sad for a very long time." She acknowledged the alarm in Aiden's eyes with a kind smile. "And I thought I might never get out of it again. Now, your father has done all he could to make my life as wonderful as possible."

Liam cleared his throat to stave off the mist in his eyes but to no avail.

Bronwyn continued, "Coming here today, gave me something to look forward to, and I thought your news would be just the thing to wake me up again. We haven't seen each other much since Lorelei passed away, and I know that part of your moving here was to get away from the memories. Now, you haven't exactly been too conventional to begin with, but this really takes the cake, sweetheart. I just want to say I'll need a bit of time to get used to all this; but Aiden, you have made my heart feel joy again. You have chosen two adorable, strong, kind women, and I aim to love them as hard as I can."

By now, Aiden had his face in his hands and was openly weeping. Holly and Sahara made no attempt at hiding their emotions. Liam spoke next.

"I see I'll have to be the voice of reason here."

Everyone laughed through their tears.

"Listen, son. You'd better not be playing at anything funny, these are live women here." He winked but Aiden knew he was deadly serious. "You'll tell us if there's anything you need from us, or how you'd like us to handle things if our friends ask. And for God's sake, try to make some grandchildren before we're both dead. And don't stay away so long next time."

"Will there be a wedding we can attend, or will you be doing another one of those secret ceremonies?" Bronwyn wanted to know.

"There will be a wedding, Mama," Aiden promised, "... and grandchildren."

Liam groaned. "Boulder will never be the same again. We'll have to move."

"Closer to here, maybe?" Bronwyn dreamed out loud.

CHAPTER 23

"We do not "come into" this world; we come out of it, as leaves from a tree. As the ocean "waves," the universe "peoples." Every individual is an expression of the whole realm of nature, a unique action of the total universe."
~ Alan Wilson Watts

"I'll be away quite a bit this year," Aiden put on a blue dress shirt and tucked it into his slacks. "But we knew that when I took on Richard's house."

Sahara sat on the floor of his closet, arms wrapped around knees. "There's no way around it, I suppose."

"I don't like the idea of it, but it is what it is."

Sahara's eyes twinkled. "Where do you get such perfectly fitting shirts, anyway?" She admired the way Aiden's back stretched into the fabric, his shoulders and arms well accentuated by the luxurious material.

Aiden grinned. "I have them made for me. The tailor in Denver has my measurements and when I need one, I order it. I know I know, somewhat elitist of me." He checked himself in the mirror then grabbed his watch from the dresser.

"I love your style. I don't mind elitism when it comes with a kind heart."

Aiden offered his hand. "Come, woman, I have to leave shortly."

"Why do you dress up to meet with the architect? Surely he'll be more casual than you?"

"He won't be. He's old school, and I like to meet him where's he's at."

"I'm glad we'll have a few more weeks together. Soon the madness will begin, and we need to stock up on each other."

Aiden led the way downstairs. Sahara fed on his powerful build, the fluid way he moved.

"I promise I'll be as available as possible. We'll have to be organized. With you helping Holly until April managing the café expansion and my office reno, I'll be able to concentrate on the bigger projects. I've got the crews set up for my other two house-builds, but now I need to concentrate on gathering craftsmen for Richard's place. He's exacting in his vision, as you know. I'd love to take Drew with me but he's managing work I already had booked. Anyway, Richard's foundation pour will take a while."

"Well, now you'll have an office manager and an accountant, so you can let go of all those responsibilities."

"Mmm. That's going to take some getting used to."

"You've no choice," Sahara smiled and stood on tiptoe to kiss him goodbye. "By the way, I've found someone to clean your house."

"What?" Aiden growled, displeased. "I don't want anyone in here! You know that, darling."

Sahara stood firm. "I do know that, no need to bark at me. I've done my research, and I'll be here the first time she comes. I'll put away your magic tools. Trust my intuition, darling. I wouldn't have taken anyone on that I wasn't sure about. We simply will need help with some things if we're going to run two businesses plus my writing. Besides, I'll be expanding my homestead."

Aiden relented. "Ok. I'm sorry, I know I can trust your instincts. But you could have asked me first?"

They smiled at each other, knowing he would never have agreed to it if asked.

"You don't have to be the knight anymore, my love," Sahara purred. "You've got two women capable of taking care of themselves and you're not required to be everything to everyone. Our past lives are much too big an influence on us still. We'll have to work through that." Sahara pulled her scarf tighter around her neck as Aiden closed the front door behind them.

"I agree, but the more I find out the more I need to know. I don't think we're anywhere close to moving through it all yet. Every time I look at that painting Richard brought back for me from France, I feel more and more pulled back."

Sahara nodded. "Me too. My dreams are full of bits and pieces. It could have been such a magical time for them had Arinn come along."

"So..." Aiden took her by the chin and kissed her. "You'll forgive me if I slip back now and then?"

"As long as you come back, my lord," Sahara melted into his arms.

CHAPTER 24

Brigida wiped the sweat from her brow, bending low over an overgrown bed of herbs. She was working in the potager, the kitchen garden long forgotten and left to grow wild. She was feeling the morning sickness quite strongly this time. Dagr had cautioned her to take a rest when she needed it, but she was so excited to have the garden ready for planting, she often worked right through her nausea.

The garden help had done most of the difficult work, cutting down miles of vines and pulling up mountains of weeds. Now, she could plan the layout of the garden. She had asked Dagr about building something similar to what Estienne had shown her at the monastery. They would mix practicality with beauty. After all, beauty healed as much as any of the simples she had set to making.

She thought back to their first weeks at the chateau. It had taken them days and days to explore every nook and cranny of the house, which was far too big for them even with the staff they had hired. There had been much to do as well. Each room had need of airing and freshening. Many rooms stood empty, but the ones they used had already been furnished by Richard to a high standard. Brigida's main work was in creating the stillroom where she planned to make simple medicines and continue her herbalist practice. Already, she had found her knowledge was useful in the village. She visited the sick and the bedridden, helping in any way she could. She had taught the midwife to wash her hands when helping with birthing; although this was met with much protestation. Whenever she felt it safe, she brought a brew to young mothers fearful of subsequent pregnancies. Where she could, she made herself useful in the way of the wise woman she had once known in the Oracle Wood. The only thing was, all of it reminded her of Arinn, for whom she ached every second of the day.

Dagr, too, had that yearning in his eyes, but he had thrown himself into the running of the estate as she had.

The land and its uses had been organized; who would run their pigs where and when, the orchard made stock of and new plans drawn, fields plowed, and farmers set to work. There was no need for thievery, Dagr had stated to a cluster of men, there would be common areas allotted for grazing and certain days in each month when the villagers could forage in the woods for their larders. He was fair, if strict. He would not see anyone go hungry, but those who could do, must work for their sustenance. Those who could not, Dagr made sure were found a helping hand. From the beginning, he was respected, if challenged. He soon made it clear he was to be obeyed. If he was to be Vicomte, then he was to take his position with strength. But nobody could have accused him of lacking in humility or a willingness to throw his back into bringing prosperity to the area.

Next to the kitchen garden was Brigida's private chicken yard, where she kept a brood of hens and a rooster. No one had ever seen such an extravagant effort put to making a chicken's life so pleasant. A treed area already half fenced with a stone wall was further fortified to keep the foxes at bay. There was plenty of shade for their protection from the afternoon heat, and a sunny area for dusting themselves in the sand. Kitchen scraps made up for their otherwise foraged diet, when they were let out to roam the herb garden and beyond. The rooster led them back home dutifully each evening, to be shut up in a coop designed by the village carpenter. It was the talk of the village.

Dagr had organized a small row boat for her to use on the river and took her out each Sunday afternoon to escape the hustle of the week past. Brigida most adored those moments when they floated lazily together. He would strip to his waist, teasing her terribly with his good looks and tell her stories he'd made up on the spot.

Every night he would visit her in her room where he would make love to her or lay in her arms, as she wished. She was full of passion these months. Brigida touched her belly where it swelled into a now noticeable bump. She wondered if all women's desire grew when with child. She wondered too, if this child was to be hers, as now she had a fear of losing every one of her babies. But she had to stop thinking this way, nothing would happen, or at least that is what she prayed to the fairies in the woods.

She had found it very easy to connect with the local Fey. They understood her and came out to play when she went out in the mornings to gather wild plants for healing and helped her find treasures she would have had difficulty discovering on her own. Dagr laughed when she had told him she had thought French fairies only spoke the language of their countrymen.

"Well, of course they understand you. Like the dog that has adopted you!"

Brigida looked to where the mutt lay under a tree, watching her with heavy-lidded eyes. He had appeared one day, full of mange, starving and growling at everyone but her. She had nursed him back to health and he never left, but had assigned himself her guardian. She also had a basketful of kittens tucked up in a corner of the stable.

"Mousers... that's what," she had told Dagr, who rolled his eyes with affection.

"I am beginning to wonder if you are not assembling some kind of a menagerie," he had said. "And where did you get that peacock?"

The peacock belonged to no one in particular. It had come up from the woods; the villagers said there had been a few of them, at one point, at the chateau. It shrieked at all times of the day, scaring the wits out of the kitchen girl, Agnes, whom Brigida had decided she liked very much. She was quick of wit, sunny, and ever so helpful. And besides, there was no one else close to her age at the chateau with whom she could chatter.

Agnes sometimes sat on a low stool in the stillroom, which was formerly a summer kitchen the cook found too primitive for her uses. It faced the potager and was filled with the scent of herbs Brigida loved so well. She would ask a hundred and one questions, gossip stories from town, helping the afternoons roll pleasantly by until Cook reminded her she had work to do. But Brigida never scolded her. There was something too innocent and sweet about her, and she couldn't bear to chase her away.

Early mornings and evenings Brigida spent loitering in the barn with its smell of horse, hay and leather—another thing which reminded her of the lover so far away. Dagr would often meet her, and hand in hand, they would stand at the stable door, words unspoken, tears unshed, hearts joined in mourning.

A flurry of hooves and shouts from the courtyard snapped Brigida from her daydreams. She wondered what new visitor had come now, because there seemed to be a never-ending array of strangers coming to make their acquaintance. From Dagr's old confidant, the Comte, to men curious who had taken over the chateau and lands. Already, word had spread that Dagr was employing modern methods of farming, and even had gone so far as to organizing the peasants into some kind of a cooperative.

Dagr came up on her quite suddenly. He waved a letter in his hand. His eyes shone with anticipation.

"A letter!"

"Yes, my lord?" Brigida replied, puzzled.

"From Richard!"

Brigida almost fainted. She sat down unceremoniously on the stump by her feet.

"Open it my lord!"

Dagr tore the seal and knelt beside her. She could feel his excitement and his angst. Finally, he read.

My friend,

Please accept my apologies for not writing earlier. As you can imagine, the events following your departure left me somewhat perplexed and scrambling for a smooth transition at the castle.

You can rest assured a way has been made for the new addition to my household. She has taken over the work of Hannah and is quite entrenched with the work that was done before her, in years long past. She is proving quite useful and is in good health, if not pining for her old villagers.

I hope that you and yours are well, and finding the chateau to your liking? I have some business, as mentioned before, in import and export along the river, and around the time this letter should reach you, the captain of my boat will be visiting your home with some supplies for the house. It would please me greatly if you could show him your hospitality for the few days he will be stationary.

If you are lacking in anything, he would be the man to speak to, he will provide whatever you require and is bound to my service. I trust his ability to source anything which might be needed in the running of the estate.

Please extend my greetings to your lady love and advise me immediately should you require my travel to France. I am, in fact, planning a trip next spring. What treasures should I bring you from fair England? Just say the word.

Kind regards,

Earl Richard Dumont

Brigida looked up. "That is all? Is there no more?"

"That is all."

"But surely, he would have sent us something more personal, something more about the first few days, how Arinn is fairing now, besides that she is *useful*?" Anger bloomed in Brigida's eyes.

Dagr sought to comfort her. "This is the first correspondence. He cannot know who to trust yet, and so he has given us a very proper letter. Here, in the first sentence, he means that it was difficult at first, they probably spoke very little and she probably blamed him for his role in her life."

"How could you know this?"

"We have had occasion to write in code before. I can decipher his style of communication."

"Oh. What else?"

"In the next few sentences, he is telling us that she has relented somewhat, but misses us terribly, and then... she is doing the work which was done in years long past... I think he may be allowing her to do the work my mother did... the study of alchemy and the stars... if I understand correctly."

"Really?" Brigida's eyes grew round. "Would that not be dangerous?"

"Truly, it would, but if we think about it, Arinn would be a natural for such work and it would distract her. He has probably found the perfect work for her, and if she has taken over Hannah's practice, then she would fit quite naturally into life at the castle, and her presence will not raise any concerns."

"I see," Brigida shook her head. "But do you not think she would have wanted to include a few words of her own, my lord?"

"Perhaps, but more likely she is hurting too much to do so, and as I mentioned, it would not be safe yet. Now here, where he mentions a visitor, someone he trusts, he may be saying a more personal correspondence will arrive. And most likely, he will require me to engage in some of this river business he has been running."

"You do not sound too impressed by the possibility?"

Dagr grimaced. "I am not partial to river dealings, and secondly, I plan on being quite busy with estate business."

Brigida observed him silently for a few moments. "You mean that you might have to go on the river sometime and you do not wish to leave me?"

Dagr laughed. "Now who is being a clever sleuth?"

"I can care for myself... I would never stand in your way like a simpering maiden, my lord."

"I know very well how capable you are my darling, but nonetheless, leaving you is the last thing I wish to do."

"Is Richard asking whether he can bring Arinn next spring, when he mentions treasures?"

"Yes," Dagr looked away.

"Please, my lord, can we not forgive her? The babe will be here by then... imagine our joy if we were all reunited once more?"

136

"We shall see," Dagr stood and folded the letter into his pocket. "I will join you at supper, my lady." He bent over her hand, her fingernails full of garden dirt, and pressed his lips to her skin.

Brigida burned at his touch and immediately felt his sorrow as he walked away, shoulders squared.

———————————❖———————————

As foretold by the letter and anticipated by Dagr, three days' time brought a visitor. He was short and eagle-eyed, a river pirate with a curt manner. He bent over Brigida's hand with his whiskey breath, muttering something unintelligible. She would have been resistant to his touch, but behind the rough exterior, was a genuinely warm smile.

Brigida invited him to the best parlor, where she knew he would be unaccustomed to sitting, then ordered Cook to prepare a platter of meat and cheese. Dagr arrived just in time to see the man staring out the window, rubbing his short beard. He kissed Brigida on the cheek she offered, then extended his hand.

"Welcome, Monsieur...?"

"Signor Lopez. It is my pleasure to meet you finally," he said with a thick Spanish accent. "I have heard much about you from our mutual friend, Earl Dumont."

"Indeed," Dagr shook his hand. "Please sit down." He poured the man a generous tumbler of wine and one for himself. Brigida took a small glass of wine herself, and sat beside Dagr, to the discomfiture of their guest.

"Will you do us the honor of sharing our evening meal, Signor Lopez?" Brigida asked.

Lopez's eyes darted quickly to Brigida then back to his host. "It is not necessary," he protested, then noticed the look in Dagr's eye and accepted graciously. "I have some river business to discuss," he continued, "perhaps the lady will be bored with such talk?"

"There is time for all that, Signor Lopez. For now, why not tell us a little about yourself?"

A few big gulps of wine later, Signor Lopez was a more relaxed version of himself and suddenly remembered he had some correspondence in his pocket, which he handed to Dagr. Brigida tried very hard to not rip the thing from him and sat fidgeting in her chair.

"There is not much to tell, I am afraid. I am the captain of the Earl's ship, the Lara." He said the name with a very pronounced roll.

Dagr fairly jumped out of his chair. "The *Lara*?" he asked, incredulous.

"It is the best ship in the sea!" Lopez pronounced. "It was the best ship when the Earl's father owned it. She is not so young, but she is beautiful. My father was the captain before me. I grew up with her. She is the mother I never had."

Brigida looked to Dagr, who was flushed and tense. She took his hand, but he got up and began to pace.

"Where is Hermine with that platter?" he barked, just as the door swung open and Cook came in with an array of smoked meats, cheeses, and a loaf of crusty bread. He poured more wine. Brigida declined, feeling swimmy in her head, partly from the wine and partly from her anxiety about Dagr's feelings. Surely, he was angry his mother's name was being sullied by Richard's mysterious business? She knew how Dagr revered her.

"Do you have a family?" she asked innocently, trying to steer the conversation away from the ship.

Signor Lopez guffawed into his wine. "Family? Oh no, my lady. I do not have time for a wife and children. My life is the sea."

"Well, then you may not have the chance for a home-cooked meal too often. I will make sure Cook makes one of her specialties. It is nice to have visitors."

Dagr smiled at Brigida's kindness. He was sure Signor Lopez was not usually entertained by any ladies of noble birth; he was too unsavory for such sensibilities. But Brigida was new to her role, and it was not in her nature to look down her nose at anyone in any case. He took the letter from his pocket and handed it to her. She took it, hoping to be excused.

"I look forward to seeing you soon, my lady? Perhaps some flowers for the table would be nice. And please speak to Cook about that pear tart. I should like some tonight."

Brigida smiled. He understood her so well. She stood. The men stood. She left.

In the envelope were two letters. One for Dagr. One for her. She tucked the letter to Dagr into her pocket. The other, addressed to her in Richard's handwriting she opened and stared at for a long moment. Her heart fluttered wildly beneath her breast. Slowly, to draw out the moments, she began to read;

My Lady,

Please accept my apologies. I am living with daily regret that when we last saw each other I behaved without honor.

A gentleman would have accepted the challenge before him with grace, and I, when faced with Dagr's request to care for your beloved, acted as a coward and questioned my assignment. I should have immediately given you confidence that I would and could care for Lady Arinn to the best of my ability. For this, I hope you can forgive me.

Rest assured that since the first day, although not without some resistance from her, I have provided your beloved with every possible convenience. She lacks for nothing as far as one can expect under the circumstances. Arinn has taken over Hannah's herbal practice and her head rests each night on a comfortable bed. Her table is well laden. I have personally seen to the outfitting of her quarters. We are slowly becoming friends again.

I wish to convict you of my ability to be forever the man you expect me to be, your faithful servant in this matter.

It is my hope that you and Dagr find the chateau to your liking. Whatever else is needed for your comfort and delight, can be attained through Signor Lopez, whom you will have met if this letter finds your hands. Try to overlook his appearance and know that he has been a trusted ally for many years, since my father's time. There is no shortage of resources where you and Dagr are concerned, and you do me a great favor to care for the property as it was intended to be looked after. When I come to visit, we will walk the estate and you can show me all the improvements. If I know Dagr, he will have it organized into something quite modern, and you..."

Brigida squinted hard to see what Richard had scratched over, and she thought she made out 'my love'.

The letter continued; *...will have surely made a wonderful garden and be furnishing every room with flowers and your kitchen with herbs.*

Will you teach your cook to bake the bread Hannah taught you, or will you bake it yourself, in a stillroom like the one you once apprenticed in? I am grateful for every day we spent in that room, because it is where I discovered that I could be decent. It was all because of you. I am overstepping here, and again I seek your and Dagr's forgiveness.

In the springtime, I will be making my journey to France. I, at once, ask permission and also do not expect it, I will come nonethe-

less. I am only a man, after all, and cannot, will not, live my life without my most treasured friends.

It is my most fervent desire to be accompanied by the Lady Arinn. I tell you now of her sadness not to increase yours, but there is truth in my words; she will not thrive with me, she desires only your and Dagr's love.

I pray for your happiness and safety every night, and although I know no Gods listen to me, I send my intentions on the wind. Any news you can write to me will be cherished.

In your eternal service,
Richard.

At the bottom of the page, there was another paragraph. Brigida gasped when she realized that the writing was different from Richard's. Arinn!

Beloved,
I write forever on my knees before you. I know I do not deserve to speak to you, nor to ask you for anything. For the rest of my days, I will regret my unspeakable actions. Please know that when I sought the fairies help, it was with the best of intentions for your healing, and I will always be sorrowful I had not listened to Dagr's council. I am caught in something now which I barely understand. My heart weeps for you and our beloved. Although I know I can never be with you again, I would give my life to reverse my actions. I would like only a few words from you to know that you have found happiness in your new life, and those I will treasure until I shed my mortal coil. It is not my place to say love words to you anymore, but just this one last time, I wish to say that I love you like the moon loves the dark sky.

The page was splattered with dried tears. Brigida's fell to meet them.

She lay under the tree she was sitting by, and there in the grass, she wept her heart empty. Clutching the letter to her, she fell asleep. And there Dagr found her, curled up against the evening damp.

"My lady," he shook her gently, kneeling beside her. She looked so fragile as she once had, and he felt a pang of fear.

"You must not allow yourself to lie on the damp ground!" he scolded but smiled. "Come, let us prepare for the evening meal. I have drawn you a warm bath."

Brigida gracefully accepted his hand up. Dagr had taken to drawing her bath himself now and then, a task he considered a great pleasure. Those waters always seemed the most healing to her.

She handed him his letter, and hers. There were no secrets between them, and she knew he would share his correspondence as well, perhaps not fairly to Richard, but it was their way.

"You should see the goods Signor Lopez has unloaded from his boat! You will have days of unpacking crates and dispersing the spoils. Richard has gone mad, I think, we already have everything we need, wouldn't you say?"

"Well, yes, my lord, we do." Brigida touched her belly protectively. "Except for one fair maiden, I'd say we were blessed beyond measure."

"You must give me time, my lady," Dagr winced.

Brigida stood on tiptoe to reach his lips. "It will be my constant request, my lord. Until you feel it safe to return her to us."

And they both knew this one thing between them could break their love, but neither of them would ever voice that thought out loud.

CHAPTER 25

My lord,

I would pretend at manners and decorum but know you do not expect it.

I hate the idea of years going by without contact or the pleasure of seeing you, and so have decided that neither of those things are to be tolerated. I am coming in the spring and that is as long a period away from you as I can muster.

I do take some pleasure in knowing that I have the right to visit you at the chateau and take it without remorse. We have been friends for far too long, and brothers, at that, for me to deny the ache in my heart.

I love you. That is all. I spent many a year grappling with the propriety of this, but now that we are embroiled in this ridiculous situation, I see no more reason to hide how I feel or what you mean to me. If I am to be miserable and alone for the rest of my life, as I do not see any way of finding happiness with anyone, I will at least drown myself in the knowledge that you have had my heart from the start. Beyond that—please forgive me, I simply must speak my truth. I miss the Lady Brigida with a desperation beyond measure. She is yours, and this I accept, but also accept that my love for her and her love for me brought out a man I had never met before, and he threatens to disappear if I at least do not keep the memory of those two years she was in my care.

What is to be, my lord? Shall I forever hold hostage your beloved golden lady? She is a creature too wild to keep locked in a cold, damp tower. She is well cared for, but she is broken with sorrow. What can I offer her that will assuage her grief? You must relent and allow her back into your arms. She has blossomed somewhat, but only because she has found her work rewarding. But this will not hold her for a lifetime. Should she be left to wither in her beauty, to have pleasure only at her own hand, to fade from a beautiful flower into a woebegone crone?

I am harsh to wake you from your ill-thought out plan to leave her with me. I could easily find comfort in her, had I such an intention. I could force her into a life with me, if you never came to your senses. Is this the plan you have for such a magical creature?

Take a hold of yourself, man, and forgive her transgressions.

She has wept her regret into my arms and if I know anything about women at all, it is that she herself cannot abide her sins. For the love of God melt your heart and set aside your fear.

If I know you, and I do my friend, you are angry and grinding your jaw at this moment, and permit me to say, I have always found that very attractive in you. But I digress.

Be angry, curse me, I provoke you with purpose. Lady Arinn is a fiery woman whose heart is given to you and Brigida. She belongs with you, not with me, even though I do already feel heavy emotions at her sight. I beg you to send for her.

I have written a small note to Brigida as you will most likely see. You have always had a curious habit of great openness with your lovers. If you would allow her to answer my letter, I would be most grateful.

All the goods sent to you in this shipment, with Signor Lopez, are my act of good faith, hoping you will not lack in anything, and offering you a position in the trade business begun by my father. Should you take the role, you will be lining your own coffers, as I know how much you despise being beholden to me. I trust you implicitly.

With kindness,
Richard

Dagr crushed the letter in his hand and threw it into the fire, regretting it immediately. But Richard was right, his jaw worked and he was filled with rage. How dare he? How dare he assume that sending for Arinn was something he put off due to some kind of inability to forgive? He could forgive, even forget, but he could not, would not, put Brigida and their child in danger. Dagr could not even fathom the desperation and melancholy that would beset his beloved should she lose another babe, from worry or, god forbid, any action Arinn would undertake.

It was not Arinn's own actions that he was afraid of anymore, because deep down he knew her horror and remorse. It was the agreement she had made with the Fey, and that was unbreakable.

There was a plan in place, one he did not understand. He would gladly pay whatever price in lieu of hers, but the Fey had already denied such a possibility. When could he relent? Not before the babe was born. Not while it was fragile and at Brigida's breast. No one could know when jealousy would rise again in Arinn's heart. Their once innocent love was spoiled forever.

He sat pondering until he remembered Brigida was waiting for him in her bath. He had promised to attend her. But an hour had passed, and she stood before him, fresh and flushed from the hot water. Dagr pulled her into his lap and sighed when she cradled her head against his neck.

"Well, sweeting? How was your bath? I have completely lost myself in my thoughts. Do forgive me?"

"There is nothing to forgive, my lord. I enjoy my time alone, and Agnes helped me to dress. How are you faring?"

"I have to admit that I have felt better. I burned his letter... I threw it into the fire before thinking it through." Dagr kissed her cheek, lingering his lips against her skin.

"Was it harsh, my lord?"

"How do you know?" Dagr asked, surprised.

"I know his way. He is brutally honest, to a fault."

"Yes, my lady, it was too honest for my liking. I feel trapped. I know what my heart wants, what we all want, but... to protect you, my lady, our babe..."

Brigida took his hand. She pressed it against her skirts. She waited a moment, lost in Dagr's eyes. His face was her addiction. "Soon, you will be able to feel our babe move, and then you will not be so afraid of curses or ill winds. All shall be well."

They sat by the fire, kissing. Silence surrounded them. Their thoughts were muddled with confusion. They should be sharing this with Arinn, making plans for a family to cheer their hearts. In these moments, Brigida absorbed the sinking feeling that Dagr would never relent and she would live out her life away from her beloved woman.

The door opened and Cook announced supper. Brigida stood, taking Dagr's hand.

"Come, my lord. We do not have to decide anything right now. Let us enjoy the next few months and when the babe is here, we will think again. There is time."

Dagr stood at her side and let her take his arm. "Wise words, my lady. We will think only about the babe for now, plan for his birth. And after..."

"His?" Brigida smiled, and their mood lightened.

"Who do you think it will be?"

"I have an idea, but I think it should be a surprise."

"Aaah. You do know!" Dagr smiled broadly. "But I am not like most men. I do not need a boy-child to find joy. Do not fret my lady, I am delighted for a girl just as much. One with dark curls and a pretty mouth like yours."

In fact, Dagr hoped for several daughters to spoil and devote himself to.

CHAPTER 26

"The principles of truth are seven; He who knows these, understandingly, possesses the magic key before whose touch all the doors of the temple fly open."
~ The Kyballion

The Seven Hermetic Laws

The Law of Mentalism—Everything that exists is in the mind of the All. The All is in everything that exists. All is Mind. The All is Spirit, unknowable and undefinable, but may be considered a Universal, Infinite and Living Mind.

The Law of Correspondence—As above, so below. As below, so above. As in Heaven, so in Earth, as in Earth, so in Heaven. Your body is the microcosm. The universe is the macrocosm. What occurs in the higher realms occurs down to the lower realms, and vice versa.

The Law of Vibration—Nothing rests; everything moves; everything vibrates. Everything is in motion. He who understands the Principle of Vibration, has grasped the Scepter of Power.

The Law of Polarity—Everything is Dual; everything has poles; everything has its pair of opposites; like and unlike are the same; opposites are identical in nature, but different in degree; extremes meet, all truths are but half-truths; all paradoxes may be reconciled.

The Law of Rhythm—Everything flows, out and in; everything has its tides; all things rise and fall; the pendulum-swing manifests in everything; the measure of the swing to the right is the measure of the swing to the left; rhythm compensates.

The Law of Cause and Effect—Every Cause has its Effect; every Effect has its Cause; everything happens according to Law; Chance is but a name for Law not recognized; there are many planes of causation, but nothing escapes the Law.

The Law of Gender—Gender is in everything; everything has its Masculine and Feminine Principles; Gender manifests on all planes. Everything and every person contain the two elements or principles. Male is will, or positive. Feminine is nurture, or negative. Together they are creation. Both forces must always come together to cause actions of success.

Arinn stared at the tiny script before her. She was trembling with cold. The fire in the hearth of the tower room had gone out long ago. She read the words and their extended meanings over and over, a strange rush of knowing coursing up and down her spine. The pile of papers sat spread over the desk, each mysterious page more confounding than the last. But she dared not remove herself from them; they held her with magnetic force.

The candle finally sputtered its death, and the room fell into semi-darkness. She sighed and was gathering everything into a neat pile when the door flew open. Richard stood in its place, dressed in the most extravagant outfit Arinn had seen thus far. She stood and curtsied.

"My lord?"

"Are you mad?" Richard seemed irritated.

"What is the matter?"

"You will catch your death of cold up here! How long have you been sitting here without a fire?"

"I... I do not know. I was about to return to my rooms," she lied. "Is there something you need from me my lord?"

"Oh, for the love of God Arinn! Dispense with the formalities. Call me Richard, so long as we are alone. And yes, I do need something. I need you to not catch a bad humor."

He almost added that he wanted her sound of skin and bone when he returned her to Dagr, but refrained.

Arinn nodded and clutched the papers to her chest. "Are you entertaining guests tonight?"

"No."

"Oh. I assumed... by your dress."

"I am dressed for the evening meal and would like you to join me."

He realized his invitation was rather abrupt, but he had been thinking about her all day and was now in a tumultuous emotional state. He had heard nothing from Dagr in many months, his letters remained unanswered. Each day he grew more and more despondent about the situation before him.

But she was not a situation, was she? She was a woman of flesh and blood, and the more time they spent together, the more he enjoyed her winsome ways. She had come to smile quite often now, even if the sadness in her eyes never faded. He had also noticed a curious ability to read her thoughts as they splayed across her face, which was very perplexing indeed. Right now, she grappled with how it would appear should she dine with the Earl at his table.

"I mean to share supper with you in my rooms," he explained.

Arinn's sharp look evoked his laughter.

"Do not fret, my lady. I mean no disrespect. It is simply so we can enjoy our meal without interruption and question."

"I have nothing to wear that will match your attire," Arinn replied.

"You will find something on your bed."

"Oh?" Arinn blushed.

"It is my pleasure to serve you, sweet lady." Richard bowed.

Arinn discreetly admired how his body suited such a gesture.

They stared at each other for a brief warm moment, and Arinn allowed herself to recall Richard as he'd served her on his knees that time they had all been together. Her blush deepened, but she did not turn away from the memory. She was tired of pushing Richard away. He had done nothing wrong, but tried every single day to please her in his own rough way.

"It would be my pleasure to join you."

"It is settled then. Come! Let us make our way. There is time for you to dress, but do not keep me waiting, I am quite hungry."

Neither of them were sure of the intent of this last statement, but they left it unexplored.

Richard's rooms were lavish to say the least. A great fire roared, and the room was lit with a plethora of candles. The table was dressed with an aromatic roast and an arrangement of bread, cheese, preserves and even a bowl of artichokes on a bed of wild greens. Arinn looked gratefully at the effort Richard had put into providing her with the vegetables. Hardly anyone ate the greens she so loved.

Richard poured two crystal glasses of wine.

"I think this robe suits you very well. I like the color green on you."

"It is Dagr's favorite color for me," she said without thinking.

Richard frowned. "I am sorry, I did not realize, I can send another."

She fingered the rich velvet fabric. "Thank you. No need to send another."

Richard admired the curve of her neck and the rise and fall of her breasts where they stood pressed up coquettishly. He invited her to sit.

"I wanted to tell you I have not received any correspondence from Dagr as yet, but that is not unusual. There is no way of predicting how long a letter may take from such a distance, or even if it was intercepted and waylaid somewhere."

Arinn gulped her wine. She had not expected to tread immediately into those waters.

"I do not wait for an answer. There is no need to protect me from the possibility that Dagr may never speak to me again."

Richard fixed her with a demonic stare. "He *will* answer! He is too well mannered not to."

"Ah. A polite answer. I should not want one such as that."

"I do not wish to talk about this all night, I simply wanted to get it out of the way. I would like to have an evening of food and wine and perhaps a game of cards or two, if you are so inclined."

"I do not know much about cards, but am willing to learn, my lord."

"Richard. Please."

"Richard."

They ate in silence for a moment before Arinn spoke again.

"I have just one question before we abandon the subject. What would you do with me, should we never hear?"

Richard's response shocked her, even though she presumed him to be jesting.

"I will tie you to my bed and ravage you nightly, shower you with every wish you harbor, give you children to gladden your heart, and love you until the day you die." He bristled with an intense energy, so much so that Arinn dropped her eyes.

"My lord! It is cruel to say such words to me, when I know you do not seek the company of a wife nor children, and that such things are impossible between us."

Richard grasped her hand and brought it to his lips. Arinn's skin seared.

"I tell you this, golden lady. I did not ask for what is before us, and although I have ever regarded you with great fondness, it has never been my intention to fall in love. I have already had my heart trampled once and it is more than enough for one lifetime. But I am only a man, and not a good one at that. I will not see you wither or marry some cabbage eating fool. Nor would I consider a wife were it not you or Bri... pardon me, I am a dishonorable wretch. Therefore, I *would* consider such a thing, and beg you to not think me cruel."

With that Richard downed his whole goblet of wine.

Arinn stared at him. "You have thought this through!"

"I have. Have you not?"

"No."

"Liar."

"I have not."

"Then I beg your pardon."

Arinn decided the best thing to do would be to serve Richard more of his meal and began to tear strips of meat from the platter. Richard played with his napkin.

"I should not have said that."

"I do not mind."

"You do not? How is that?"

"I also do not wish to marry a cabbage-eating fool, nor wither, nor sit here waiting for something to happen that I already know will not. I have spent months aching for Dagr's touch, for Brigida's kiss. I deserve to be left to the wolves, but so long as I have breath, it is not my way to live without anything to look forward to. If no one else can love us Richard... let us love each other."

Arin felt betrayal on her lips but the emptiness in her soul had spoken. She needed to be loved, to be cherished, to be touched with wild, savage fingers.

She was not prepared for the violence of Richard's movements... up from his seat in an instant, his chair scattered, and she wrenched from hers. The bodice of her dress was ripped in two, her breasts spilling out, traitorous nipples taut. Richard dragged her to his bed, where he did, indeed, bind her to a post. Her breath came short and quick. Her mouth opened as Richard brought her wine. She drank it obediently, some spilling on her chest. She gasped as Richard licked every drop and arched her body to accept his ardent attention.

"What do you want?" Richard's voice rumbled, stripping himself of his shirt. She had forgotten how chiseled he was, how brown and dangerous.

She fumbled for her words.

"If you want something, you must say it. Otherwise you will not get it."

"I want you to suck my nipples. Hard. Bite me. Here!" She stretched her neck.

"With pleasure my lady."

"Is this wrong?"

"I am sure of it, darling. I am sure of it."

Arinn cried out as he bit her neck while his hand searched under her skirt. She spread her legs willingly, already wet and tight with need. "Find my pleasure, my lord, find my pleasure!"

Richard groaned when his fingers found her cunt, sucking her nipples with his decadent mouth. "My God, you are wet!" He slid to his knees.

Arinn struggled against the ties on her wrists. She could not keep from calling his name. His tongue broke all barriers between them. It plunged and searched, tender then brutally rough. His fingers followed. Arinn came on his hand, her pleasure soaking the floor. Richard took her hair from its braid and spread it about her shoulders.

"Ahh, yes. I have worshipped you from afar."

He put his wet fingers in her mouth and insisted she lick them clean. She whimpered, unshed tears glistening in her eyes.

"You are thinking of them?"

"I am, my lord."

"Is it punishment you seek?"

Arinn could not answer, such was her agony and her desire, but he saw it in her eyes.

He untied her. She waited for his command

"On your knees."

She complied, down on the cold, hard floor. "I hate the cold floor," she complained, suspecting that Richard would not care. His stiff, elegant cock stood at attention before her.

She opened her mouth and stuck out her tongue. "Please, my lord," she begged.

He teased her with the tip, allowed her tongue to swipe him for some time then yanked her to her feet.

Laying her on his bed, he commanded her to present. She did as she was told, a trembling mess, wishing for his tongue again.

The first strike brought her flat again. He raised her by her hips.

"You are a whore, my lady, fucking every man who comes your way."

She nodded.

"Repeat what I said!" he roared.

"I am a dirty whore, fucking every man who comes my way!"

Richard melted at her words, her courage, her beauty, her pain. He wanted to engage in hours of wicked play, but he could see she needed him to save it for another day. Today was for release. Today was for letting her rise on a wave of forgetfulness.

"I wish to fuck you, sweet lady."

Arinn turned on her back, spread her legs and opened herself with her hands.

"Take this. But gaze at her a little first. Worship her."

Now who was commanding whom?

Richard bowed to her request. At first, he held her eyes, letting her fall into his. She never looked away, bravely facing their sin. His attention fell to her breasts, her long, peaked nipples... he licked his lips. What mouthwatering temptations!

Arinn pulled on them, on fire with anticipation, shoving her hips upward to hurry him along.

Slowly his whetted appetite fell to her blond mound, the pink of her flesh exposed, her clit a tender morsel hardened provocatively.

Richard's groan as she dared to play with herself in front of him was the encouragement she needed. He liked this; the fact that she was comfortable with her body and unashamed.

She closed her eyes. Richard's breath hovered over her calf, a tender hand stroking upward.

Why didn't she trust him? What intuition played with her heart, which fluttered fear like the wings of a captured dove? Anticipating pain, she was confounded by the sensation of fingers expertly kneading muscles—she began to relax. Where fingers abandoned flesh, kisses followed.

Aaah, so he was indeed capable of lovemaking after all. But it was all tinged with the promise of force, of being left without an ounce of control. Nothing too overt, just the promise!

Pleasure built itself in layers where hot words spilled from Richard's mouth. She practiced breathing like a deer when sensing the presence of a wolf. One soft, shallow inhale. One soft, inaudible exhale. She listened, waiting for each caress. He hadn't told her to keep her eyes closed but she understood she must. Richard had no need for words. His intention was the loudest thing in the room. She felt her wetness dripping. A moan escaped before she could stifle it. All she wanted in this moment was for him to fill the emptiness that consumed her.

Something startled her. A tear. On her breast. Richard whisked it away as quickly as it had fallen. And just as suddenly, he was inside her. He was hot, rough, determined... much too talented for a gentleman. The scent of his skin, the scrape of his short beard, the taste of his lips ripped her orgasm from somewhere abandoned these last months. And when she screamed, he encouraged her; gave her pleasure freedom. Then he turned her and took his own decadent delight. Her hips high, spreading her legs to expose her silken pussy, Richard came hot on her ass. Arinn savored the warmth of his seed on her skin. She cried out when his fingers explored her, rubbing it shamelessly inside her warmth.

Was he claiming her? This could easily produce a child, and then she would never be able to return to her beloveds? This thought was her undoing. Was she still so naïve as to harbor some hope? No. It would never be. She was sure of it. Sobbing silently, she welcomed Richard's embrace. He spoke endearments, but they did not soothe her. Eventually, she slept, unaware of Richard's agonized pacing, or his own cries of sorrow.

When Arinn opened her eyes, the fire was high once more, and a maid sat on a stool beside it. Sitting up, Arinn looked straight into the face of the nervous girl.

"Good morning, m'lady," the girl stood. "M'lord said you was to get in the bath he has drawn for you, and here are some sweetmeats to break your fast." She pointed at the table by the fire, where the evening had begun the night before.

Arinn blushed, remembering she was naked under the covers and that her dress would be useless to her, with the bodice ripped in half. The girl seemed unfazed by her lack of apparel... probably had seen many of the Earl's lovers in disrobe before.

"Are there any herbs brewed for tea?" she ventured a question.

"Herbs? No," sputtered the girl. "M'lord has sent mead." She offered to pour some.

Mead and sweetmeats. It was not how Dagr had taught her. An herb tisane and crusty bread, some preserves perhaps, but not mead and sweetmeats. But she was not with Dagr and she was not in the stillroom, where she could prepare her own sustenance.

"I will take the mead and sweetmeats, thank you." She was ravenous.

The girl looked up with surprise at being thanked and smiled shyly, then hurried to serve Arinn with her eyes glued to the floor.

"You do not have to stay, I can bathe and feed myself."

Surely the girl did not want to be here anymore than she wanted to be attended. She needed time to think, to organize her emotions. She wondered what indeed she would wear back down to her rooms. That's when she caught sight of the gown thrown over the desk chair. The servant followed her gaze.

"Would m'lady like to dress now?"

Arinn smiled warmly. "You do not need to address me as m'lady. Arinn will do."

"Oh no, m'lady! I could not! The Earl would thrash me within an inch of my life!"

"Oh, poppycock!" Arinn laughed. "Well, what is your name then?"

"Ann, m'lady.'

"Well, Ann, we would not want the Earl to thrash you, would we?"

"No, m'lady!"

"Then I shall take my bath now and be happy if you would assist me in getting dressed."

Ann beamed. Arinn sank into the copper tub in the corner of the chamber.

"Hot enough, m'lady?"

"Not quite so," Arinn confessed.

Ann ran to the door and opening it, commanded the boy sitting by the stairs to hurry his wretched legs to the kitchen for hot water, and to be quick about it.

Arinn grinned at the irony. The kitchen lad was clearly a rung or two beneath the lady's maid... or whatever she had been before Richard had promoted her to her current status.

"Will not be long now, m'lady." With that Ann began to vigorously scrub Arinn's back. Arinn asked her about her family. Ann chattered happily about how her mother would be pleased she was now a lady's maid. Arinn didn't want to disappoint her by telling her that by this afternoon she would be back in the stillroom, no longer a lady in the Earl's rooms. A sigh left her lips.

Scrubbed, dressed and with her hair combed until it shone, Arinn dismissed Ann, assuring her the Earl would not wish her to be disobeyed. Ann left with a curtsy and her cheeks glowing with accomplishment. Arinn sat down by the window to braid her hair. She wished for the simplicity of life in the forest. She wished to wake up from this dream where she and Richard were prisoners of their own misery. Her contemplation was interrupted by a knock. Richard.

He bowed. She wondered if he was mocking her. But she was glad to see him, and her woman's heart could not deny his exquisite charm.

"Good morning, my lady. I assume you have been sufficiently taken care of? Or is there something else I may provide you with?" He stood near, close enough she could tell he had been drinking and smoking all morning. She wrinkled her nose.

154

"Ah, the same reaction from Dagr once," he observed.

"You should abandon the habit."

"Should I now?" Richard rubbed his temples.

"I could brew you some herbs for that sore head of yours?" Arinn grinned, aware of her own insolence.

"Lead me to your witch's lair, my lady."

Richard was indeed mocking her, drunk and careless.

"Do not call me that, my lord," Arinn bristled. "You know the danger!" They locked eyes.

"My sincere apologies. I was merely jesting."

"Do not, my lord. It is not your life on the line, but mine."

Richard stood and held out his hand. "Come then. Take me and tell me what I must do to be good like your Dagr," he sneered.

"You are drunk, and I will not continue this conversation with you."

But she took him to the stillroom nonetheless and sat him down at her table. She built a good fire in the hearth and brewed a strong decoction of herbs to soothe Richard's head.

She set to making bread, working silently as he watched her, enjoying the quiet and seclusion of this end of the castle. He drank obediently and told her a story about Dagr's mother, in his opinion, a woman steeped in mysteries. Arinn realized that he could no less talk of Dagr and reminisce than she could still the pain wrenching her heart. So, she let him talk, until he was spent and then she led him to her cot, upon which he slept until evening fell.

And while he slept, Arinn made dark magic. A pallor had fallen over her, fed by the indescribable pain of her losses. She had tried to leave it behind, in prayers and poems and savage screams at the sky, but solace escaped her. She had tried peering into the future within dreams and those strange, marked stones Richard called runes. But all she could fathom were years of despair.

Gazing at Richard, as broken as she, Arinn began to knit her heart shut to the past. She wept, remembering Dagr's words forbidding her collusion with the Fey. He had known better. Now she wished she had listened. If only, if only!

Jealousy, so foreign to her then, now boiled fresh in her veins. She tried to reason with it, push it away, remind herself of the days when her heart had been innocent and open to love in its most pure form. But all that rose with consistency, was the agony of abandonment. She wept as it cocooned her soul. She wept thinking of Dagr and Brigida, in the life they had all imagined together, their sunny days in France. Did they think of her, or was she forgotten already?

Anguish became a bitter tonic for her heart. She threw a concoction of herbs, roots and berries into the fire, a stick figure bound with twine, and a ribbon cut in three. Another incantation and she recoiled with horror at her spell. Suddenly, she knew what she must do. With one last look at Richard, the man who would be her keeper, Arinn walked out into the pouring rain.

The aroma of the cooling bread woke Richard from his rest. The room was dark, with only the dying fire casting shadows on the walls. He thought perhaps Arinn had fallen asleep as well. But no, she was not in her chair by the hearth. He wondered the time. He touched the bread; still warm. Waiting rather impatiently, he finally cut into it, and left the stillroom. Perhaps she was in the main kitchen; although she usually shied away from the common areas of the castle. He had an idea about a way back to Dagr while waiting for her and was eager to share it.

But she was not in the kitchen, and no one had seen her. Puzzled now and beginning to worry, Richard took the steps to the secret room two at a time. Not there! He searched his own rooms, although she was not likely to have wandered there either. Finally, with a pang of fear, he had his horse saddled and brought from the stables.

Intuition nudged. He rode across the fields towards the woods, following the footpath from the castle garden. This was the way Brigida had, and now Arinn took, to the sanctity of the forest, where wild provisions were foraged. There was only a crescent moon to guide him. Richard's only idea of where to search was the small river by which they had shared a picnic weeks ago. Now the river would be rushing, and a sickening feeling overtook him. He should have paid more attention to her moods, he admonished himself. But surely, she, so full of life in kinder times, would never...

"My lady!" He called several times into the night. Then, more frantically... "Arinn! Arinn, answer me this instant!"

He would have ridden right over her, had a flash of light and a feeling in his gut not guided him to dismount. Arinn, sodden to the bone, lying half in, half out of the fast-flowing waters.

"My God, what have you done?" Richard threw his cape from his shoulders and bundled the blue-lipped Arinn as quickly as he could. He felt the presence of spirits and remembered Dagr had a way of communicating with them. Wishing he knew how, he held Arinn close to warm her. From the darkness, came that same light, now materializing into a solid form.

"I am Pan," the creature standing before him announced.

Richard stared.

"Dagr's guide from the Unseen Realm," Pan informed further.

"Yes. I remember now," Richard answered, grim and angry, placing Arinn on the back of his horse.

"There is no escaping what has been written," Pan came closer.

Richard felt peaceful suddenly. He tightened his arms around Arinn. His heart swelled with a surge of love. All he wanted was to get her home and sit her by a warm fire.

"Can you not speak to Dagr on her behalf? Can you not employ some form of magic to help them reconcile?"

Pan shook his magnificent horns. "It is written."

"I do not give a damn about what is written!" Richard roared. "What about forgiveness?"

"One can forgive, and even forget, but that does not change which way the winds blow."

"What the hell does that mean?" Richard barked.

"It means that you must live your life and Dagr must live his. What will be, will be."

"Do you call that wisdom? I know that damn well! Of course, I must live my life and he his…"

"Yes," Pan interrupted, coming closer, a hand on the reigns, "but how will you live it? With anger, resentment or will you accept your journey, seek a peaceful way to lay down your head at night?"

"I will live it as I damn well please. What do you know of me? Of my heart? You cannot understand what I have given up to, to…" Richard stared into the glow of Pan's eyes, softer now, empathetic. "Do you know what it is to live without love?" he asked, suddenly feeling quite defeated.

"The knowledge among us Fey is something that your kind rarely understand. You ARE love. Everything you need is within you, but humans continue to search for it outside of themselves, in each other, in possessions. Pan pointed to his heart. "Here is where all the secrets lie. Live from here, not from here," he said, now pointing to his head. "From here comes war, from your heart, comes peace. All you need to do is surrender to feeling, instead of thought."

"Will that save me? Save her?" Richard held Arinn tight in his arms, anxious to return her to the castle.

"You can save yourselves. Surrender to what is. That is all the riches you require while on this Earth."

Richard shook his head. "Do I know how to do that?"

"Decide. That is all." With that Pan dissolved into the night.

CHAPTER 27

Dagr paced the floor. It had been hours since Brigida had begun her labors, and although he had seen her through the early stages walking the gardens with her, holding her hand tight in his, she had finally taken to her bed and implored him to leave her be. Now he was wearing the floorboards thin outside her door. Her moans wrenched his heart. When she cried out, he burst into the room, only to be stopped in his tracks by the look of agony on her face. She did not even notice him.

"This is no place for a man," Cook admonished. The midwife had promised to hurry along from a difficult birth in the village, and for now they were left with Hermine's nervous administrations.

"Why does she not look at me?" Dagr asked, pushing past her.

"Ah, my lord, she is in such a state. There is no telling what happens to a woman while in her labors." She wrung her hands. "I have put a knife under the bed to cut the pain, you see..."

Dagr realized suddenly that Cook had no idea how to birth a child. Rolling up his sleeves, he strode to the fire. "Why is this fire so hot? She will suffocate in here! And there is neither light nor air! Open the drapes immediately."

"But my lord! I heard that the fairy spirits may take the babe if the drapes are open!" She began to mutter loudly in French, knowing full well that if a man were allowed in the room, all manner of things may go awry.

But Dagr ordered her to fetch more water and to brew the herbs Brigida had set aside for her birthing time. He pressed a cool cloth to Brigida's forehead. Her hands were clenched into fists. Dagr called to his Lady Mother.

"Help me, mother, help me. What am I to do?" He hardened his heart to the sudden cries and the way Brigida writhed on the bed, making gestures that could only be interpreted as her anxiousness to have the babe released from her body.

He whispered softly against Brigida's ear. "My darling, take some of this tea Cook has brewed for you. It will help."

Brigida turned her head, confused by his presence, eyes wild, fingers reaching for the bottom of her gown. He managed a few spoonsful of tea into her parched mouth; when she began, once more, to reach frantically toward the hem of her nightdress.

"What is it, my darling?"

Brigida became rigid suddenly, her chin thrust towards her chest, face red and uttering a terrifying howl.

By some miracle, Dagr knew what was required of him. He placed himself at the bottom of the bed and lifting her nightdress almost fell to the ground at the sight before him. Cook screamed that he must not! Brigida pushed with all her might. Dagr very gently massaged the inside of her thighs, having told Cook to keep up the cool cloths to Brigida's forehead. He encouraged his lady love with every soothing word he knew, and swore to himself he would never, ever create another child if this would be the pain bestowed upon his beloved.

The babe's head appeared in the impossibly tight channel from which it would have to escape. Cook sat down in the corner of the room, praying. Dagr, with a knowledge foreign to him, commanded her to bring him some oil, boil some cloths, and brew the herbs for after-birthing.

When the oil was brought, Cook asked him what he intended to do with it, exactly. But before she could warn him against any more strange proceedings, he was dipping his finger in the oil and gently massaging the birth opening. Cook succumbed to fits of hysteria. Dagr ordered her out.

"Come my darling, I know the pain is great, but we will birth this babe together."

Brigida nodded weakly. Dagr positioned her hands at the cloths tied to the bedframe.

"Now hold tight and scream if you need to. I am here, darling."

Tears streamed down his face. He was filled with wonder at the scene before him; anxious to meet his child, frustrated at his inability to help his love; besotted, already, with the tiny being struggling to emerge.

The babe's head slipped out, and after a brief moment of relief, Dagr realized the shoulders may be of greater worry. He placed his hands for the very first time on the precious face of his child, covered fully with a slippery, translucent film. What to do, remove it? When? Now? Or after she was birthed? He was sure it was a girl.

Frantic, he yelled loudly at Brigida to push, as she had, quite impossibly, fallen asleep! She came to and obeyed, calling to her child. The infant arrived with one more effort from Brigida's tired body. Dagr swiped his daughter's face quickly and put his face to her mouth. Her warm breath caressed his cheek. He tied the umbilical cord with string then cut it, swaddling the baby, offering his daughter to her mother. But Brigida was sleeping a deep sleep, and the look of her thus swept him with renewed fear.

He called Cook back in from the hallway then set her to tending Brigida while he cradled his child, a little too still, a little too shallow of breath. Should she not be crying as other babies did? In his heart he knew something was terribly wrong, but he had not the knowledge of a physician, and there was none to be summoned. Brigida refused to waken. He was horrified by the amount of blood in the bed. But instinct told him she would rally and return as she had once before.

So now, with a terrible ache in his heart, he held the babe until she took her last feeble breath with the tiniest of shudders. She had never opened her eyes, never looked into his; never seen the intense love her father held for her. He did not move for hours.

CHAPTER 28

"My lord?" Cook stirred the fire and came cautiously to Dagr's side. "We must bury the child."

Dagr's fierce eyes set her back a few steps. She gathered her courage. "It was the fairies, you know."

It took only one look and she was running from the room. The whole village waited the news of the birth, it would be best if she told it as it was. She knew what she knew, and the Fey had taken the babe. She ran down the hill, to the home of the widow, Marin, where she met a very curious sight. The midwife was bent over a basin, a knife in her hand, the tiniest naked infant cradled in her gnarled, old hand.

"Mon dieu!" she ran to the woman and snatched the babe, who proceeded to squall loudly. "What do you think you are doing, you old witch!"

"Look! She has six toes. The sign of the devil!" The midwife blessed herself and muttered a prayer.

Cook took the shawl from her head and wrapped the infant in it. "Six toes! Why not cut off the toe instead of slitting its throat? You old crow, where is your heart?"

"Pffft, heart! The mother is dead, as far as anyone would know, the babe died inside her. What are you doing here? Give me that child! Let me snuff out her miserable life." Suddenly, she remembered. "What of the manor child?"

"Dead. The fairies took her."

"Why would the fairies take her? What happened?"

"Never mind."

Cook stuck her finger in the child's mouth, who began to suckle immediately. "If you breathe a word of this to anyone I will kill you myself," she warned and ran out the door, knowing that the midwife would not. She was too old and too frail to ignore threats of any kind and was totally dependent on the kindnesses of others.

Hermine ran up the hill, the babe screaming at the top of her lungs. She ran through the dark even though she was terrified of whatever lived in the woods, and what God would do to her for stealing a child, lying, and threatening an old, old woman. But she loved her mistress and her lord. And even though he had intruded in the birth and caused the child's death, she could not bear the sadness in his eyes. She would make things right, if it meant she was going to hell. But perhaps the good Lord had made a way for everyone to be happy? She had completely forgotten she had meant to ask the midwife what should be done with the afterbirth. She had heard once that it should be buried under a tree planted in honor of the newborn.

She burst through the bedroom door. Dagr jumped to his feet. He looked as if he had aged by ten years.

"What is this? Whose child is this?" He peered at the impossibly tiny bundle.

"My lord, forgive me," Cook lowered her head, half expecting him to hit her. "The widow, Marin, is dead."

"What of family?"

"Since the day she arrived six months ago, already with child, there has been no mention of family, my lord. Of course there has been gossip, but as you know, her husband was killed in a riding accident and she came to grieve in solitude. Nothing else is known."

"I will look into it. Someone will have to pay for her burial." If no family was found, Dagr intended to make the arrangements. "How did you come to take the child from the midwife?"

"My lord, the midwife was about to..." Cook choked on her words, afraid to speak the words.

"About to what?"

"My lord, see the sixth toe, it is not unusual for the midwife to return the child to the devil." She pulled the tiny foot out of the shawl, exposing the offending toe.

"The devil?" Dagr roared. The baby screamed in fright. Both Dagr and Cook turned with surprise to look at Brigida who was sitting up with arms held out to the wailing child.

"Please give me my baby," she said. "I want my baby."

Dagr and Hermine exchanged glances. Had Brigida heard any of their conversation? They both understood what had to be done. Dagr took the baby from Cook and was struck by her vigor, her warmth. She stared up at him as if she knew the secret she was becoming part of. With two steps he was at Brigida's side, who opened her nightshirt and without any thought to propriety, began to nurse the famished child.

"Look, my love, what a beautiful girl we have. Finally, a child born to us. I wonder if she knew our others, if they had met before she was sent to us. I will ask the Fey." Brigida pondered.

Dagr's knees almost gave out. He was sick to his stomach for the lie he was perpetrating, but to tell Brigida that yet another child of hers had been taken was more than he could manage. He brewed tea and gave it in small sips to his beloved.

"You were so very brave my darling," he said. "I have never known anyone more brave."

He meant it. He did not know any man who would volunteer for such torture as giving birth.

"Lie down with us?" Brigida asked.

He looked at Cook, who was leaving the room with a large bundle of sheets. With the slightest nod of his head, he gave permission for his flesh and blood to be buried with a woman he hardly knew, in a cold grave, forever gone from his sight.

Brigida touched his hand. "You must be so very tired my love. Come lie with me and our daughter. She looks like me, does she not? Look at all this black hair!"

Dagr, to his amazement, had to agree the child did have hair the color of his lover. He had only twice seen such raven black hair. The other was Richard. She was the tiniest creature he had ever seen, but a very determined little bundle, much like his beloved.

"I do see, my love. She is perfect." He tucked himself in; they lay with the babe between them.

"Are you in pain my love?"

"Some, but it will soon pass. The powders I made will help me."

Dagr nodded, eyes closing.

"I know what you did," Brigida whispered.

Dagr's eyes flew open.

"Do not worry, I am not superstitious. Thank you for taking over from Cook. She probably would have killed me with all that heat and stuffy darkness."

Dagr sighed with relief. "She did her best. Somewhat frazzled, but she is devoted to you."

"Still, I am glad that you were here."

Dagr nodded. "I will never leave you in a time of such need. You have my word, my lady."

"I wish she was here. I need her." Brigida whispered.

"Who?" Dagr drifted toward sleep.

"Arinn. My heart aches for her so. I know she would be happy for me; for us."

A tear slipped from under Dagr's closed eyelids. He did not reply. He wondered now if Cook had been right; if the Fey had taken the child of his loins... the Fey and Arinn? Because he knew her magic was strong, and that jealousy once woken was a terrible enemy.

CHAPTER 29

"The bakery will have to close for a couple of days you know, when we create a bigger access to the new seating area," Aiden, Holly and Sahara surveyed the nearly completed renovation at the patisserie.

"It's beautiful, isn't it?" Holly admired the handsome fireplace and the bookshelves Aiden had built in surrounding it. "Just like being in a cozy living space at home. I'd like to fill those shelves with antique books and giftware for my customers. I've already ordered up a whole pile of beautiful things. I think it will add a nice touch. Richard is going to hook me up with an antiquarian book seller he knows."

"Richard? Were you talking to him?"

"Yes. We're planning something for Iona. For the baby. He's a bit anxious to not talk about it too much until he's confident the baby news is sure."

"Why, is there anything to worry about?" Sahara questioned.

"Well, no, I don't think so, but it's early, so I suppose they're being cautious?"

Aiden wondered how he felt about this new development in Holly and Richard's closeness. He suppressed a wry smile. It would be easier, he thought, if Richard were unpleasant looking. He pressed a kiss to Holly's cheek.

"I like the book idea, and I'm sure Richard will find you the best book seller on the planet."

"I have an idea about the closing of the café," Sahara interjected.

"What is it? I hate the idea of closing, FYI."

"You could make it an event of sorts. Have a big sale of what you have on the shelves now, and perhaps some of your frozen goods. Build some excitement about the new stock... people will be frothing at the mouth if you mention that opening day will have a new coffee blend, and maybe a special cake they've not tried before? We could also hire extra serving help and have them dress in black, with those proper little white aprons? So French! I'm pretty sure there will be a crowd, so we really should be prepared."

"Oooh, I like that! And wait till you see what I've ordered up for inventory. That's another thing Richard is helping me with—French suppliers. But I'll also have local wares. Pottery for the more rustic folk, and artisan cheese from the couple we met at the market last summer, remember?"

"Fantastic!" Aiden was impressed. "Good to support the local artisans. I love that. Not to mention that the labor for the reno is local, as is a lot of this reclaimed wood. Overall, this is something we can be proud of."

"Francois and I are also experimenting with cakes to sell by the slice. I meant to tell you, he has a dream of his own. He wants to bake cakes to order for special occasions. But I don't have enough ovens, nor time. His idea would be to apprentice another pastry chef, maybe from the school in Denver who would bunk with him upstairs, but the problem of an extra fridge and work space still remain. Not enough room, really, in the back."

"That's a brilliant idea darling!" Aiden had a flash of inspiration. "I think if we rearranged the back area, we could make better use of the space. There would be enough room for another oven if we got rid of the awkward little hallway and repurposed it. I think we can fit it all in."

"Really? Oh gosh! That would be amazing. Maybe we could tackle it next spring? It gives me a year to increase profits and save up."

"I will cover the cost of the renovation, since the increase in value to the building will be mine, and you can save up for the work tables, oven, and fridge. We should be able to find good used equipment online, which will be the biggest expense. But I'm sure we can work something out," Aiden winked, while Sahara poked him in the ribs.

"Pretty clever, mister," she teased, knowing he was walking a fine line of making things easier on Holly while giving her space to make her own way.

"I'll draw up a proper business plan," Holly said. "And don't even try to talk me out of it. You know it's important to me to have things organized."

Aiden laughed. "Sure thing. Don't worry, I've learned my lesson." He ran his hand through his hair.

"Anyway, I meant to tell you, I'm leaving for a week. I'm meeting with Richard's architect, visiting the building site and checking in with some of the trades involved in the early stages of the build."

"What?" Sahara protested. "You were supposed to be ours for another month!" She laughed when Holly pouted her displeasure.

"I'm not here for your exclusive use, ladies. A man has his work and his responsibilities," Aiden joked at their antics.

"Fine, but you'll have to pipe in a livestream communication from your hotel room so we can connect!" Sahara mused.

"Well, that will be impossible, wench, since I am bunking with Richard and Iona."

Holly and Sahara poked his ribs.

"Seriously?" Holly nipped his mouth with a loving bite. "What kind of plan is that?"

"Jealous?"

"Yes. For one, I can't go and you did promise me that hotel stay in Denver. And two, can you be trusted?" Holly's kiss deepened.

"You're joking of course? I know there was that one kiss..."

"Oh darling, don't be silly! Of course, I'm joking. But technically, there was that other kiss at Solstice too." Holly leaned in for a hug.

"For the record everyone was invited to Iona's."

"How far exactly is the build site from Denver anyway? Wait, let's talk all this over tonight. I gotta run... have stuff in the oven." Holly waved her hand and headed back to the bakery.

Sahara appraised the handsome man in front of her. They exchanged smiles.

"I'll miss you, of course, but am excited for this project. It will be your defining work Aiden. Life will change after that."

"I know. My once very insular lifestyle has taken a deliberate turn. I used think my life was pretty much set, then I met you. Nothing has been usual since."

"How we found each other... that was a beautiful synchronicity."

Aiden pulled Sahara in. He sighed into her hair. "I often think of the day we met on your porch."

Sahara felt a rush of emotion and sexual energy. She cuddled deeper into Aiden's embrace. "One of the best days of my life. The other was meeting Holly."

"This is what we were born to, darling; this impossible journey."

"Yes. I wonder what's ahead. I feel that what has been uncovered is just the tip of the iceberg."

"Soon we'll be leaving to meet with The Society. Holly will be without us both for the first time in months."

"I know. Do you have your airline tickets?"

"I do. I always book for the next year right after the gathering. Hey, I wanted to run something by you. Remember that day Richard and I went back to my place to get the yoga mats?"

"Hmmm, yes," Aiden grinned. "Not my finest moment. I think I may have been a bit possessive."

"Yeah, well, here's another thing. That day I asked Richard to look out for Holly when we're all away."

Aiden shut the lights to the room and closed the door behind them. They stood by the restroom doors. "I know. He told me. He said he would and that he wanted to, but he needed me to be comfortable with it. I don't think she'll need minding in any way of course, but just to know that if anything arises, she's got back up."

"This is the exact spot I met Holly," Sahara mused. "Anyway, I agree. She'll be driving back and forth, have this place, Willow and Ulfred to take care of..."

"And the Fey," Aiden interrupted.

"The Fey..." Sahara echoed. "Because now I feel something has been opened in that dimension for her and this would be the perfect time to lure her deeper."

Aiden scowled. "Ever wonder how our connection to the Fey does not protect us from their whims?"

"Or more precisely, the twists and turns of her own journey? This has really more to do with what her path is than ours. And you do trust Richard, right?"

"With her life, yes! He may want her on one level, and who could blame him considering our past lives and her resemblance to Arinn, but he's a gentleman through and through and devoted to Iona."

Sahara led the way out of the café. "But darling, we both know that Holly is attracted to Richard too. Not that she would ever act on it, she's wildly loyal, but under the right circumstances?"

"Under the right circumstances, you know I wouldn't stand in her way of exploring if she really wanted the experience. Not with any man, of course, but with Richard—considering the unconventionality of our group, it's not within the realm of impossibility."

"Wow, darling! I'm truly impressed. I thought you'd never."

"Well, I still think it would be difficult for me, but if she asked me, I would hardly be able to say no to her."

"What if Richard asked you?"

"No. It would have to be her desire."

They wandered into the green grocer, hand in hand.

"So, we will leave it as is," Sahara offered. "We'll find comfort in knowing should Holly need anything Richard will be available, and then, of course, they have their own plans, what with the antiquarian business."

Aiden had a sudden inspired thought. He suggested going to the wine store while Sahara shopped for food. Outside the grocer, he stopped to dial his phone.

"Richard? Hi. I wonder if you could do something for me."

He smiled when Richard asked him if the favor would involve changing all his house plans according to some builder's whim. "No," he answered, "something much harder to accomplish than that, actually."

CHAPTER 30

"So, you've got all your things packed? Won't you need more than this weekend bag?"

Holly looked dubiously at Aiden's leather travel bag. It was a very handsome bag to be sure, with some of the finest stitching she had ever seen, but it looked entirely too compact for a week away in the city. "What with meetings with architects and such, won't you need a wider range of clothing?"

"Darling, you're worrying about nothing!" Aiden kissed Holly's sweet mouth, amused by her concern. "I've done this before and my meeting with the architect is on site, where I will be meeting the tradesmen as well. We'll all be quite casual. It's the middle of winter and the most important thing will be a good coat and boots."

"But how are you meeting with the ground frozen and all... what can possibly be accomplished there?"

"Because, my love, we must all see the site and assess the scope of the project. It helps with visualizing the build and getting a feel for the design. It may seem as if nothing is happening but actually, this is a very important part of the process."

"Alright, but what about... umm... sleeping attire?"

Aiden laughed out loud. "Holly! I sleep in the nude, you know that. Whatever is the matter?"

"Nude! But you'll be staying with Iona and Richard. Sahara told me they only have one bedroom. Do you expect to sleep nude on the sofa?"

"Well now, I don't know exactly, I hadn't given it any thought. But I'm sure with all their combined resources, they will have some kind of copacetic arrangement figured out. Maybe they will sleep at Richard's and leave me at Iona's. All I know is they asked me to stay with them, and I trust I'll be comfortable."

"Alright," Holly grumbled.

Aiden pulled Holly down onto the bed. "Please tell me what's wrong? I never see you like this." He nuzzled along her neck, a strong grip around her waist.

"I'm sorry, I'm feeling a bit insecure with both of you going away soon and I've not stayed here on my own before. There's a powerful energy in this house and woods."

Aiden's grip tightened. "Darling you must tell me if you'll feel uncomfortable here by yourself. I figured that with Ulfred, it would be fine. And it's only five nights. I've got someone organized to keep our and Sahara's road plowed in case of bad weather." Now Aiden took to worrying.

"You know what? I'm being silly. If I felt really uncomfortable, or the weather turned I could pack up Willow and Ulfred and stay in town. Like you say, it's only a few nights."

"Ok, let's think on it. Sahara will be here soon; we'll have a cozy dinner and evening. You'll be staying at the cabin for the next bit, it'll be nice for the two of you to have some time alone again."

Holly stretched out across the big bed. "We'll have our long-awaited seed ordering weekend. We talked about it when we first met. I've been waiting for the magical winter day when we could sit by the fire and plan the garden and pour over seed catalogs. I'll bake something yummy and Sahara has bought snowshoes! We're planning a long adventure towards the mountains behind her cabin, with a proper winter picnic."

She grinned as Aiden began to unbutton her shirt, his large hands adept at unsnapping her bra without any visible effort.

"Mmmm. I love the feel of your hands on my skin."

Aiden removed his shirt then hers and pulled back the covers. "I just want to lie here and feel you against me."

"Yes please," Holly pulled her leggings down and tugged on Aiden's belt. "Off!"

Aiden kicked his jeans to the floor. His underwear did nothing to hide his erection. "Just ignore that," he said with a cheeky smile, pulling Holly into his arms.

"This is the best thing ever," Holly murmured.

"The best. Let's stay here for a bit."

"I'm not going anywhere. You?"

Aiden kissed along the top of Holly's back. "I love you. That is all."

CHAPTER 31

Don't wake the witches
From their impossible dreams
They're the keepers of wisdom
And the builders of new worlds

Sahara stood on her porch watching Aiden playing with Ulfred in the snow. He'd be leaving today, and she found it a strange turn of events—his staying at Iona's... somehow, she hadn't ever imagined that happening. It had been her territory except for that one time when Aiden and Iona had first met.

She knew it was because she'd been untrustworthy each time she'd stayed there; and she now wondered about possible transgressions. But she shrugged these thoughts off as quickly as they came. After all, neither she nor Aiden truly believed in monogamy in its usual sense; and they were all exceptionally secure within themselves.

Aiden looked up, giving Ulfred one last kiss on his third eye.

"Well," he sighed, "I guess I'd better be going."

He met Sahara on the porch and ran his hand over the plaque he'd given her as their commitment gift. *Hidden Hollow*. "Do you still love this?"

"Yes," Sahara stood on tiptoe to brush his lips with hers. "It's my daily reminder of your devotion and what we mean to each other."

"How do you feel about all this? My staying with Iona and Richard? Trust me?"

"Haha, more than I trust myself!" Sahara laughed.

"Wonderful," Aiden wrapped her in a big bear hug. "Now promise me your winter picnic will be within reasonable distance of home and you'll take the usual provisions when hiking—Swiss Army knife, flashlight, matches—you know the drill."

"Darling! It'll be daytime, nothing to worry about."

"Right, because mystics never get into any shenanigans with other realms or act on unreasonable whims," Aiden challenged.

"I promise. I won't lose myself nor Holly."

"I have to go."

"Go."

"Kiss me."

"You kiss me."

Aiden's blue eyes descended into a midnight hue. "Come here woman," he said, voice gruff, hands cupping Sahara's face. "My little witch."

His warm mouth coaxed hers to open, tongue meeting hers with hunger, the promise of future moments together fueling their passion. Sahara's body responded to his heat, the way he pressed into her, confident yet allowing for her response. She so very much loved this about him.

She took his hands and kissed them. "Darling, I send you with blessings for your journey. Be safe, be inspired! I know this new build will be the beginning of something powerful in your life. I'm so proud of you."

"Aaah, thank you my love," Aiden's heart surged with emotion for his beloved. "You understand."

"I do. Now go!" She let go, pulling her shawl tight around her body.

Aiden drove away with Sahara waving and Ulfred barking their goodbyes, until he turned the corner and couldn't be seen any more.

"Come Ulfred," Sahara called. "We have a picnic to prepare!"

When Holly arrived an hour later, Sahara had the snowshoes ready on the porch, one small backpack filled with extra socks, emergency supplies, tin cups, a thermos of coffee and a blanket tucked into the straps underneath.

"Wait till you see the food I brought us!" Holly exclaimed.

"Show me!"

"Ok. I have a variety of cheeses; baguette already sliced and some pate! Did you know the cheesemaker has expanded to making cured meats and sausages? Oh. My. Goodness. So, I brought some along with red pepper jelly, and a thermos of garlic/white bean soup. Will that be enough?"

"We could eat for two days on that. Goodness! Any dessert?"

"Yup. Francois made a mocha coffee cake. Perfect ending."

"Ok, I just have to bank the fire, pee and I'm ready. Can you bring Ulfred in?"

"What do you mean? Isn't he coming?"

"No. The snow will get too deep further out, and it'll be too difficult for him... too hard on his hips. Why? Do you feel unsafe without him?"

"Well, no, I guess I was thinking he'd have fun and I suppose a dog makes one feel a bit safer."

"There's nothing to be safe from anyway. Bears are sleeping, we'll be on open range, and cougars don't feed this time of day." She laughed at Holly's look of mock horror. "Plus, we'll be home way before dark. It's only nine a.m. woman and it's a beautiful, sunny day!"

"Right. Are we more pumped for the snowshoe or the picnic?"

"All of it. The adventure, the food, the coming home and fire, your sleeping over and another day of seed ordering. Two whole days with my lady love."

"Awww, sweetie," Holly purred. "This is going to be one of our best memories. Our great snowshoe adventure!"

<hr>

They left to Ulfred's plaintive howling at the back door.

"Aww, poor Ulfred," Holly sighed, looking back.

"The instinct to protect us at all times is strong. But as you can see, the snow is already deep," Sahara explained. "He'll be fine. And I've left him an especially yummy bone to gnaw on."

"Can you talk to him, I mean telepathically?"

"I do and have. I promise he'll settle down soon."

They walked a while in silence.

"Do you ever get tired of this view, Sahara? I mean those mountains, so grand and mysterious. I especially love when they're half covered in clouds. I get a feeling in my belly... it's like a call to my wild nature from a time when we were all wild on the planet."

"You remember. That's magic, being able to tap into that dimension."

"Do you think I'm becoming magical?" Holly puffed as they moved across the open field. "Wow, I didn't realize how hard trail blazing was! I'm sweating already."

"That's why I advised you to wear a wicking under-layer. Otherwise you'd freeze to death from your own sweat if you'd been wearing those cotton things you were planning on. And yes, you are very much magical. More and more each day."

174

"More I think since Aiden gave me my ring. It's a portal of sorts, he said."

"Speaking of... I didn't see it on you... please tell me you're wearing it on your chain? It's also your protection, your connection to the Fey if need be."

"I have it," Holly tapped her chest. "It was the last thing Aiden reminded me of when we said goodbye at the café. It's become a little tradition for us, him stopping by before he takes off for work. I'll never forget that day he first kissed me. I get a rush of excitement every time I think of it. That was the day my life changed."

"Must have been such a surprise, his kiss? I mean, he was taking a chance, thinking you'd probably reject him after telling him about Julie?"

"Has he talked about it?" Holly asked, her cheeks rosy from the wind.

"Yeah. About his fear and intense need to be close to you. He'd been in love with you for ages, and knew that if he didn't try he'd regret it for the rest of his life."

Sahara stopped and pointed towards the tree line. "Why don't we get a bit closer to there, the wind is picking up and I think it could get quite cold."

"Oh, ok." Holly steered to the right. "I find it so sexy he can talk about how vulnerable he was. I was so turned on by the confidence he showed despite his fear. His kiss overturned every notion I had about men. Identifying as a lesbian for so long, I hadn't explored that there was another possibility. Bi-sexuality wasn't an orientation I ever thought I'd relate to."

Sahara stopped for a water break. They stood staring into the distance for a few minutes, enjoying the silence except for the wind in the trees.

"So, here's what I think about sexuality," Sahara offered. "I believe we're all two-spirited, as the Indigenous Tribes speak of it; that heterosexuality, homosexuality, etc. are further expressions of our inherent bi-sexual nature. This is a spiritual philosophy, or maybe I should call it a spiritual law. Any messages I've received from spirit confirm that we're both genders in one. When we come into the world, we choose which expression we wish to embody—it could be lesbian, or bi, or queer, or hetero or non-binary, or whatever, on the scale of two-spiritedness. What do you think?"

Holly's eyes reflected her surprise at this wisdom. "Yeah! I've never ever heard that before. The usual comments about being bi are that we're greedy, or confused, or half gay. It's disrespectful and in-sensitive, *especially* when it comes from the LGBTQ community. I don't know why it bothers me more than from hetero folk."

"Because you expect misunderstanding from the hetero commu-nity but not from the gay community? You expect people who are al-ready facing the challenge of being discriminated against to support another orientation?" Sahara suggested.

"Right! I actually did a bunch of research on bi-sexuality when I began seeing Aiden. I know this sounds silly, but I wanted to under-stand myself... why I was feeling what I was feeling. Do you think that's a bit odd... to research one's own orientation?"

"Not at all, darling! Listen, we're programmed from birth about heterosexuality, told it's the 'norm', and we kinda just float along with the program until we begin to answer our internal knowing that we're just not like everyone else. I think pretty much everyone goes through some sort of searching process to understand their sexuality, where they fit, or don't fit. Anyway, I believe sexuality is fluid. We shouldn't have to expect ourselves to resonate with one orientation all our lives, we should just accept whatever pours out as it pours out."

"But we're expected to choose!"

"That's bullshit darling. We can't choose. Asking bi-folk to choose would be the same as telling a gay person to consider being something they're not. It's not us who have to change, lover, it's the world's understanding that has to shift. It's our spirituality. Our di-vine gift to come into the world as we do."

Holly sighed. "Yes! Our sexuality is our spirituality. I love that."

Sahara smiled. "There's no way to separate sexuality from spirit. Sexuality is a divine pathway. We've just been stripped of this knowledge and now we must find our way back." She pointed to a curve in the tree line. "We'll stop there for a sip of coffee?"

"Yes please. I'm ready for a break. And maybe a snack? Cheese!"

"Ok. Race ya!"

With that, Sahara took off laughing hysterically as Holly overtook her with her long-legged stride, then grabbing at Holly's coat and pulling her down into the snow.

"Come'ere wench! I want a kiss."

They fell to their knees, Sahara fisting her hand in Holly's hair, pulling her close. She took her lover's mouth with passion. Holly re-turned the heat with a warm tongue and determined lips, surprising Sahara with a string of bites along her neck.

"Fuck girl, you're making me wet. If it wasn't this cold, I'd rip your clothes off right here."

"You'd fuck me right here, in the snow?" Holly baited.

Sahara groaned and pushed Holly down. They sank into the snow. "I'd fuck you anywhere. Can't wait to get my lips on your cunt."

"Gah!" Holly struggled to her feet. "Into the woods, into the woods!"

CHAPTER 32

"Every tomorrow is determined by every today."
~ Yogananda

Aiden approached the very poised and elegantly dressed receptionist at the Montfort Gallery.

"Good morning," he greeted the smiling woman. "Aiden Halloran. Would you be so kind as to notify Richard that I'm here for our meeting?"

He kissed her hand, one she had extended for what he presumed was an ordinary handshaking experience. Richard's influence on even the lobby could be felt poignantly. Aiden smiled discreetly to himself, looking around the expansive, light-filled area with perfectly positioned art.

Simona returned with an apology. "Mr. Montfort will join you shortly. He's just finishing up in an earlier meeting. He apologizes for the delay."

Aiden didn't mind at all. It would give him time to relax after the long drive.

"I'll just take myself through the exhibit," he offered. "Perhaps you could let him know there's no need to hurry on my account."

The sparkle in Simona's eyes conveyed she understood the subtly sarcastic banter between two men, and that she found Aiden's disposition to her liking.

"May I interest you in a fresh cappuccino and a pastry? I promise they'll be excellent."

"You may, and I expect nothing less from Richard."

They shared a moment of quiet introspection—he at the emotions evoked by the space he was standing in, and she at the strength exuded by the man before her. Simona left to prepare the tray and Aiden wandered into the main gallery room.

Richard's taste in décor and art revealed an attention to detail, in architectural features, lighting and the furniture scattered throughout the room. Aiden noticed a love of classic French style, minimalism and muted shades of white with very reserved splashes of black and red to anchor the eye. He released a pleased breath feeling all tension leave his shoulders—tension of which he was previously unaware.

The coffee and pastry Simona brought were indeed superb. He relaxed in a chair she'd picked out for him.

"You'll be comfortable here," she'd said, and Aiden understood he'd been handled. No sitting on the rare antiques with food in hand. He thought this blend of coffee might be from Holly's patisserie. He'd ask. It tasted familiar. Allowing himself some time to release all thought, he sat in quite the meditative state until Richard's voice could be heard questioning Simona.

"You'll remember the flowers are coming before we open today, I'd like all the bouquets exchanged. Please make sure the florist remembers the back gallery room. Seven in total, as usual."

"Really, Richard. I think after all my time here, you'd remember you hired me for my memory and organizational skills. No need to worry about the details."

Richard laughed. "Apparently, I also hired you for your spectacular irreverence. Didn't we agree on Mr. Montfort?"

Simona returned his laugh. "Only when the gallery is open, Richard. I wouldn't want you to think you have that much power over me."

Aiden couldn't hear what Richard retorted. He greeted him with a sardonic grin.

"Women are impossible," Richard smiled.

"I can hear that. Looks like you have a fine handle on authority here."

"Bah! Authority is overrated. Simona runs a tight ship and I couldn't do without her. How's your coffee?"

"Excellent! Is this Holly's blend by the way?"

"It is. I couldn't resist it. I've had coffee all over the world and this, from a tiny corner of Colorado, is perfection on the palate."

"Hmmm," Aiden muttered, wondering if Richard was teasing him.

"Your gallery is quite the masterpiece, if you'll pardon the pun."

Richard accepted the compliment gracefully. "I'm happy you like it. It's a labor of love."

"What's the agenda then, for today?"

"If you're ready, we can leave in the next hour. I imagined you wouldn't want to drive any more today. My driver will pick us up. In the meantime, would you like to get a bit of air? Iona's isn't far, and we could sneak in a quick hello at her shop."

"Would love to. How's she feeling by the way?"

"Well," Richard led the way out the door, "she's feeling as obstinate as ever, busier than I'd like her to be. She doesn't listen to my pleas to take things easy until the first trimester is over."

"You know she knows what she's doing, right? She's not a fool. And did you expect any different?"

"Not really, but you know, I didn't think I'd ever be a father so now I'm a bit cautious. Plus, she'll be flying soon..."

Aiden understood completely. He knew this kind of vulnerability in love.

"Listen, I'll return the favor and promise to look out for Iona while we're away, just as you'll be available for Holly should she need you. You can count on me. And Sahara will do the same. She and Iona are sharing a room, so she'll have someone at night as well."

"What?" Richard asked, surprised. "Why aren't you and Sahara sharing a room? I don't understand."

"Well, they've always shared a suite while at the meetings, I hear. I'm just coming into it, so I didn't see any reason for them to change the plans they already had. I have a room next to theirs. Anything happens and I'm a knock on the door away. Stop worrying. We have very capable and strong women, I think it's you and I who are being paranoid and a bit ridiculous. Wouldn't you agree?"

They stopped in front of Iona's shop. Witchy energy poured out like a house on fire. Iona was definitely in.

Aiden's first impression as he stepped through the door was how the shop wrapped itself around him with its aroma of incense and herbs. Comforting, with a hint of mystery. He said he'd wait while Richard checked upstairs for his beloved. Strains of medieval music filtered through the speakers. Candles burned in antique holders on the counter, and strings of fairy lights lit up shelves of books and magic supplies.

There was just enough light so one could see the wares, but not so much that it ruined the experience. It could have been three hundred years earlier; the atmosphere was so highly evocative of an earlier time.

Aiden didn't notice the girl behind the counter, staring at him with disbelief. He turned when she made a clatter.

"Oh, hello. I'm sorry, I didn't notice you. Have you been there this whole time?" Aiden flashed a devastating smile in her direction, feeling rude at not addressing her earlier.

"Hello! Aiden?"

Aiden's eyebrows shot up. "Do we know each other?" He approached the counter with the array of herbal preparations on the shelves behind it, and an alluring fragrance of tea brewing.

"No, well... you don't know me. I'm Jessika. I know you through my aunt, Dianne?" She said the last bit with an odd inflection of a question, as if she wasn't sure whether Dianne was her aunt after all.

"Hello Jessika," Aiden held out his hand. She shook it, quite firmly, while still staring.

"Have we met at your aunt's?" He was sure they hadn't.

"No. But she has a picture of the two of you on her desk."

Aiden nodded. He knew the picture. Dianne had taken it one day while they were sitting in her garden having breakfast. Aiden had a rush of remembrance. The garden had just been installed, and he'd laughed that she must have spent a fortune on all those full grown trees. She had. The garden was a true sanctuary, with a view of the mountains, designed with several secret 'rooms'. It looked as if it had been there for years. They had made love the night before under the stars. Dianne, as always, a confident and exacting lover.

"What a small world," he said, reminiscence in his voice.

"My aunt said you built her house."

"Yes... I did." Aiden had the distinct impression Jessika knew he'd been more than the builder. How many people kept a photo of their builder on their desk? He hadn't ever seen it displayed.

"So, can I help you find anything? Is there something specific you're looking for?" Jessika came around the counter to offer her assistance.

"Thank you, no. I'm here with Richard. Just waiting for them to come down. But I did want to say the tea you have brewing smells amazing. So, on second thought, I will take a couple of bags, if you don't mind."

"Sure!" Jessika was happy to help. She looked like a girl who didn't know quite how to react to the male specimen before her. "Can you guess what's in it?"

"Guess?"

"Yeah, it's a game I play with customers."

Aiden grinned and pretended to think hard. "Let me see... rooibos, lavender, roses, and possibly lemon peel?"

"Oh. My. God! How did you do that?"

"He's an alchemist, an herbalist from way back," Iona's silvery voice filled the room.

Jessika laughed. Richard rolled his eyes. Aiden protested.

"No, really, he is," Iona insisted. "Jessika, meet Aiden Halloran, a man who could teach you a lot about the magic of herbs, and many other mysteries. He was my teacher once."

"You were?" Jessika drawled, completely spell bound. "I'm studying herbalism right now, under Iona. Well, I never!" She smiled shyly. "I'm much honored. My aunt never said..."

"We didn't get into it. I keep some things private."

He glared at Iona, who simply laughed and landed a kiss on Aiden's cheek, reaching up on her toes, balancing with one hand against his chest. He hadn't leaned down to accommodate her greeting.

"Oh, I won't say anything," Jessika blurted. "Iona has a strict code of confidence at the store." But her cheeks burned red, she had indeed been contemplating telling her aunt what she'd heard.

"Shall we go?" Richard suggested. "I've had the driver pick us up a basket lunch from the European deli to have at the site."

Aiden's discomfort was palpable.

"I'll meet you in the car," Aiden agreed, and walked out of the store.

The ride to the site sped through increasingly stunning scenery, with views of the Rockies and towards Arapaho National Forest. Aiden and Richard spent the next hour and a half talking over why Richard had chosen that particular area, heading west instead of south.

"We wanted forest, not dessert, trees were important when Iona and I discussed what atmosphere suited us best. Privacy. That was also important."

Aiden nodded, gazing out the window, his mood lifted by Colorado's indescribable beauty.

Richard continued. "I know you're angry with Iona, I won't make any excuses for her... well, except to say that if she said it, there was reason for it. She's not careless with her words—usually." He reached for a bottle of water and offered one to Aiden.

"She can explain herself later if she wants. I'm over it now," Aiden took the water. He was pleased it was a glass bottle, not plastic. "She caught me by surprise, that's all. And I can't imagine the necessity of Jessika knowing anything about it at all."

They left it at that, the driver making his way up a narrow, winding road to their final destination. They were the first to arrive.

The air was cool and fresh, fragranced by the evergreen forest. The views were breathtaking. The expanse of the outline for the foundation was immense.

Richard and Aiden exchanged looks. The energy of Richard's castle in that distant life couldn't possibly have any hold here, where the landscape was dramatically different, but somehow, both could feel the pounding of centuries rushing past.

"When I returned from England a few months ago," Richard explained, "I came up here and I don't know how, perhaps through longing, dragged something of those ruins here. Is it possible?"

"It is, intention is a powerful force; it's everything. My feeling is there has been an overlay of dimensions, and since all lifetimes happen simultaneously, this could be a portal between each experience."

182

"Is any one person so powerful, that they can create such a portal through sheer will?" Richard mused.

"It's not about power, but allowing, really. When we open to the possibility of something, imagine it, we create a physical something out of nothing. You lived very much through power that lifetime, you're much more expansive now... do you crave that time? I don't see you as a man who lingers in the past much, so this surprises me."

They stood at each corner of the proposed building, Aiden testing the energy.

"Well, good question. Until I met Sahara, and even though I knew something of Iona's and my past, I had no interest in poking around previous lifetimes. To me, done was done. Meeting Sahara and then, meeting Holly, remembering Arinn so visually through her, has opened a vortex of memories and even longing. Safe to say that I am not the man I was even two months ago."

"You should have Iona perform ceremony here, before you break ground, and then as you progress," Aiden said.

"She will. Are you going to reply to my last comment?"

Aiden sighed. "Do you mean the longing part?"

Richard nodded.

"I think it's best if we let things unfold as they will and not over think them." He paused. "And that you don't confuse Holly with Arinn."

"She's the catalyst though, isn't she? The spark that is drawing us into the past, unravelling this mystery, even though she wasn't part of us then."

"Yes. And I hate it. She's the purity that will alchemize our healing. I want to spare her, to offer her a simple and gratifying life. I know now that nothing between the five of us will ever be simple."

The sound of a car interrupted their discussion. Then another. The architect and engineers had arrived.

"Aiden?" Richard stopped Aiden before they reached the others.

"Yes?"

"This project, my home, is very important to me. We were meant to meet for many reasons, but this... this could not happen without you."

"I know. If I haven't told you, it's very important to me as well."

CHAPTER 33

"I could sit here and stare at those mountains forever. Funny thing is, the further we get, the more I realize how far away they really are. Do you know exactly where your property line is?" Holly sat on a tree stump, eating cheese and cucumber on a slice of baguette while Sahara poured cups of hot soup.

"I do. Easier to see in the summer. I can tell only because I have connected it in my mind to a spot in the tree line."

"How many acres?"

"Five hundred."

"Oh you land baroness, you!" Holly laughed.

"I'll deserve some proper respect tonight!" Sahara shot back. "I thought we'd go for another hour or so, then turn around. What do you think?"

"Ok. That will make it two hours out and two hours back, plus lunch, will put us back home by two-ish... with plenty of time to spare before dark. Plus, I'm tired! I thought I was in good shape, but now I don't know."

"We can have a snuggle this aft and rest up for later."

"What's later?"

"You and I is later," Sahara laughed.

"Seed ordering!"

"Noooo, you captive in my bed, woman."

"I can't wait. For all of it, darling."

"For the rest of our lives."

"That sounds perfect, my little witch," Holly blew a kiss. "The rest of our lives together."

With the plans spread out over the hood of the architect's car, five men poured over the details of a home that would stretch them all to excellence. The two engineers saw logistical nightmares, Andrew, the architect, mentioned the design had attracted his partner at the firm whom he thought could be brought on board. There was a buzz at his office about all this. It was quite the coup to be chosen for the work.

Richard, who had picked the engineers together with Andrew,

listened carefully to their suggestions. He would sack them without any qualms if they sounded unconfident. Their questions were well-founded, and Richard knew what the problem was... they didn't know Aiden and his particular set of skills.

"Gentlemen, if I may interject. Aiden understands the intricacies of building better than anyone I know. He also understands my vision implicitly, which is why he's the builder and not anyone else. I can confidently say whomever you have worked alongside with before..."

Aiden jumped in, hoping to stall Richard from waxing on any further. "It's safe to say we'll run into issues here and there, and I know coordinating trades will be one of our biggest challenges, but I'm putting together a crew who are used to unique designs and are a very dedicated bunch. With good communication, we can stay ahead of most problems. I'd say gaps in communication are almost always the reason things go awry. Other than that, it will be taking delivery of special materials that I see as problematic. The best thing for us to do, is to anticipate delays and not get too obsessed by them. It will come together in its own good time. A good build is only as successful as our ability to roll with the unexpected."

Richard smiled, knowing full well these men were used to seeing owner and builder clash, and rarely did owners care about their builder's opinion with such faith. Therefore, he was amused when the others exchanged surreptitious glances.

"In cases when I am unreachable," he insisted, "Aiden will be my second. All questions can be directed to him."

There were nods of agreement, hardy handshakes and then a bottle of scotch opened to seal the official opening of the project. Warmed by the alcohol and excitement, they feasted on a spectacular picnic, finishing it off with strong Turkish coffee from the thermos and baklava for dessert.

Once everyone had left, the two friends took a few moments to breath in cool mountain air.

"I want this place to be warm, Aiden. I know it's big and extravagant, but it has to be warm. Whatever touches you want to add, from your own vision, I know will suit us. Can you think of anything now that you're here and have had a couple of weeks to study the plans?"

"Well," Aiden reflected, "I think if you or I remember any details from your castle back in the day, and they mean anything to you, we should try to fit them in. They don't have to be exact but should evoke the essence of your life with Arinn. I know this is what you're trying to capture for yourself and Iona. For instance, I remember mullioned windows, stained glass, certain curves of handrails, a fireplace mantle; things like this that have stuck out for me in dreams."

"That's exactly what I'm talking about! Details that will give Iona a sense of home. As you come up with ideas, just shoot them over to me and we can incorporate as you see fit. I actually do have two areas I'd like to replicate as closely as possible. My rooms, and the still-room."

"I've already had that in my imagination. For your rooms, an open fireplace for which we'll source reclaimed oak. The mantel and surround will be quite large. I'd like to replicate two windows with stained glass. I have a blacksmith with whom we should place an order for candle sconces, door handles and other ironwork. I've already spoken to him, and he's willing to take on the work. The fireplace in the stillroom will be an important piece as well, as it will need a built-in oven. I saw the name of the master mason you have listed in your plans, and I agree, he's the man for the job. This project is... well, my creativity is fully engaged."

"I have one more request."

"What?"

"I'd like you to be the one to build our dining table. I've got the oak on order from England, reclaimed as well. To seat twenty. I want to sit at a table you've built."

Aiden felt a shiver along his spine. He could have sworn it was Richard in his past life speaking. He agreed, his hands tingling at the prospect of working with ancient wood.

Richard led the way back to the car. "By the way, that favor you called me about. I have it already," he grinned. There was no way Aiden would have expected it to show up this quickly and he was pleased to have been able to procure it.

"No! How?" Aiden exclaimed.

"There are no coincidences I suppose. The day you called me, I had been in touch with my source for another reason, and I called him back immediately. He happened to know in whose hands it was and I fully expected it to be somewhere in Europe, but it was with a collector in Oregon. And I have it."

"What do you mean you have it? How did you convince him to give it up? How much was it? I thought we were going to go over cost first?" Aiden felt the rush of excitement that comes with making a rare discovery.

"There are apparently three copies of this particular vintage. He had one. He's not well and is in the process of donating or selling his library. I took it right away because it would have been gone if I hadn't. I'm fairly certain you can afford it."

"How much?" Aiden grinned. "I can't thank you enough. It's the ultimate gift for Sahara and I want to give it to her in Europe, when we're done with the summit."

"It is the perfect gift for her," Richard's averted his eyes, a few steps from the car door.

Aiden stopped him. "I know you have a strong connection to Brigida, and, of course, Sahara. Many unresolved feelings from the past. I'm not jealous, I know you've loved her from that first meeting. Richard, I have come to accept our situation. You don't have to hide it from me. And besides, it's obvious."

Richard nodded, his handsome face tense. "Please know I'm careful to respect boundaries, and that I'm devoted to Iona, but I can't shake Sahara. And who could really? She's a force unto herself."

"I know all that. It is what it is. We'll navigate as we need to. But I would prefer if we were all upfront and honest about things, rather than pretend we don't feel the things we do."

Aiden had said, 'we', and Richard knew he was insinuating his own connection to Iona, but he left it at that.

"I'm looking forward to getting back to Iona's and sharing dinner." He got in the back of the car. The driver shut the glass divider.

"I am as well," Aiden replied. "I'm just wondering where I'll sleep? I really don't mind getting a room downtown."

"Don't be ridiculous," Richard retorted. "You'll stay with us, of course. We'll take the spare room, Iona has already prepared her room for you."

"The spare room is..."

"...has a perfectly comfortable accommodation. It won't be the first time we've slept in there."

CHAPTER 34

With the light fading much sooner than they had expected, Sahara and Holly turned towards home.

"This wind is terrible! It's blowing the clouds in so quickly... can't see the mountains at all now!" Holly shouted as they bent their bodies against the wind.

"For fuck's sake!" Sahara shouted back. "I was hoping for a longer snowshoe."

"It's ok. I'm tired anyway. Looking forward to sitting by the fire," Holly stopped and leaned in to kiss Sahara quickly. They laughed as snow covered their faces and got in their eyes.

"We better get going."

"I have my ring to guide us."

"I have a torch."

"Guess what?"

"What?"

"My ring must be activating, because it's becoming warm against my skin."

"Good, 'cause if this blowing keeps up we won't be able to see anything soon."

They kept on in silence each lost to her own thoughts, Holly thinking about what Aiden was doing, grateful for the ring which gently, she wasn't sure how, guided her steps. Sahara was busy calling on her guides and receiving intuitive knowledge they would make it home safely. They had been plodding for at least an hour, she estimated, but at a much slower pace than in going out. And so, they were both surprised when the cabin came into view, a dark shadow against the grey sky.

Sahara looked at Holly. "I think we just bent time."

Holly nodded. "I've never experienced anything like it! I wonder what time it is."

Ulfred's barking was a welcome sound. Sahara opened the front door and he came bounding out, running circles around them, yelping and nipping at their heels.

"Oh, you were worried, were you? Good boy. Go for a run!" Sahara flipped the light switch. "Damn. No power, darling."

"No worries. You get some candles lit and I'll restart the fire," Holly offered.

"I'll start the fire in the cook stove."

"It's hard to imagine it's only two in the afternoon. It's so dark." Holly sat at the counter peeling squash. The kettle whistled softly on the cook stove. "Get that, hon? What kind of tea will you make me?"

"Peppermint?"

"Sure."

"This is exactly how I pictured a seed ordering night." Sahara rummaged in the tea cupboard. "The two of us sequestered on a stormy day. We have the whole rest of the day and night and you better not be thinking about work."

"Aah, you've caught me. I was just thinking about what's happening at the café, it's hard not to worry. The power may be out there as well. Not having cell reception right now is a bit annoying."

"No matter what's happening, there's nothing we can do about it. Anyway, Francois and Lilith know what to do. That apprentice of yours has turned into an incredibly reliable assistant. And Lilith has always been pure gold."

"I know. This time last year I couldn't even have imagined the freedom having an apprentice would bring, and one who threw himself into his role so competently. And guess what? I gave Lilith the responsibility of hiring part-time servers and managing them. It's been wonderful to see her becoming more confident. The two of them have become more like partners than employees. They really do work the café as their own."

"I saw Francois checking Lilith out a few times," Sahara laughed. "I think he likes her. A lot. Do you?"

"I think so too. But she's being cool, not encouraging him."

"Why ever not?" Sahara passed the steaming cup of tea to Holly.

"Because she's a very serious girl and doesn't want to be played with, and she thinks he might be a player, being French and all."

"Oh my goodness! Seriously? But he's serious too. We must help them."

"Sahara!" Holly laughed. "Why you matchmaker, you! We're not going to help them. Let them figure it out on their own."

"Oh, don't say that. Can't I just have a little word with Lilith and guide her on a bit?"

"Absolutely not! Besides she's scared of you. She sees you as this dark witch who's thrown a spell over Aiden and me."

"What? But I've been friendly and..."

"...and you have an energy field the size of Manhattan that not everyone's comfortable with. Lilith still needs time to get used to you. She likes you, thinks you're amazing, but just isn't confident around women like you. And she had a fantasy Aiden and I would end up together, which happened of course, except for one little wrinkle." Holly smiled.

"Hmfff. I've never been referred to as a wrinkle before," Sahara mumbled but her eyes twinkled.

"That's ok, I'll straighten you out later," Holly replied and they burst into laughter.

"Hurry up with that squash, woman, I want to get started on this garden plan." Sahara poked the fire and arranged the seed catalogs into a pile on the floor.

"That's not how it's going to go," Holly said with a straight face.

"Oh no? Why not?" Sahara's nipples perked, hearing the hint in Holly's voice.

"We'll be having that nap first. Nekked." Holly dropped the knife she was using and stood up, pulling her sweater over her head. Her nipples strained through her bra. She removed her leggings. A scant, black g-string covered her mound.

"Take your clothes off," she commanded.

Sahara peeled her shirt quickly, pussy soaked, desire coursing. She tugged hard on her nipples.

Holly reached her hand to her g-string.

Sahara's sultry voice almost brought her to her knees. "Let me, darling. Come here."

Standing by the fire, they nipped none too gently at each other's necks and collar bones, kisses dropped on hungry lips, taking turns to lick and suck nipples to a painful hardness. Sahara slipped to the floor, teeth making pink marks on Holly's belly and hips, fingers hooking into lace, pulling down the only barrier between them.

"Jesus, fuck!" Holly moaned, spreading her legs, while Sahara nuzzled closer, breath on skin, tongue exploring.

Sahara's tongue plunged.

"Ohhh! Yes please."

Sahara's fingers dug sharply into Holly's ass cheeks, pain and pleasure, a blurred line. Her tongue pushed hard on her clit then licked softly in the folds of Holly's cunt, who rubbed herself against Sahara's face, begging for more.

Sahara looked up, mouth wet. "Fuck my face darling." She lay down on the floor, reaching her arms up. "Sit on my face, NOW, sweetness."

Holly did as she was instructed. The fire threw warm shadows on their bodies, illuminating their unencumbered lust.

"How hard can I fuck you?" Holly asked, lowering herself. She pushed against Sahara's mouth, pussy slick and swollen.

The only sounds were Sahara's muffled moans. Holly lifted and spread her lips. "Look!"

Sahara stared, hungry, then reached up and inserted her fingers. Holly fell backwards on the floor, her lover rising to meet her, spreading her legs wide.

"I love your pussy, it's fucking beautiful. I love how horny you are. I love making love to you."

"I love you."

"Want this?" Sahara positioned herself between Holly's legs, grinding clit on clit, mound on mound, rubbing slowly, wet cunt teasing wet cunt, juices running down their legs, patiently eliciting the ecstasy that rose between them.

"Oh my god... yes, keep doing that... darling, mmmm, fuck me."

"Your pussy against mine is heaven." Sahara ground harder, the pressure of their two clits colliding, building an irresistible desire to climax. Holly pulled Sahara lower. They kissed, bruising their lips. She pushed Sahara to the floor and took the top position, hips moving rhythmically with beautiful precision.

"I want to come. Make me come darling!" Sahara cried out. "Fuck me harder, bitch, harder!" She rose halfway and they held onto each other, plunging deep into the abyss of their own pleasure. Eyes closed, mouths open to fervent kisses; the movement of their hips brought a loud release. The cabin filled with their unrestrained voices, calling out to each other.

"More." Sahara breathed. "More."

Holly, eyes half crazed, clung to Sahara. "Oh. Where...?"

"Under here." Sahara reached under the sofa.

Holly lifted the lid from the box of sex toys. "This?" She pulled out the double-ended dildo.

"Yes!" Sahara almost shouted. "Let's do this."

Holly slowly slid one end of the dildo deep into Sahara's pussy. "Gorgeous," she said. "Mmmm, looks so good."

"You now."

Holly smiled. "I want to pretend that the two of us are fucking Aiden at once. This is his cock. Him filling us."

"Yaaaaaas!" Sahara began to move. They worked the dildo in unison, lifting up on their arms a little to give provide a harder thrust, tits bouncing, stopping for wet, sloppy kisses, their pussies tight after their first orgasm.

"I want to do this with Aiden when he gets back. Let him watch us." Holly bit out between moans.

"Keep talking dirty little whore. Tell me more."

"I want to tie him up and give him head but keep him from coming. Then I want to ride this with you for a bit. I want to lie down on the floor in front of him, and torture him with a slow show of my pussy and ass, tease him until he gets that dangerous look in his eye. I want to lick and finger you and let you come on my face. Then I want you to suck his cock, and finally, we'll untie him."

"You must want to be fucked by the devil," Sahara breathed against Holly's neck. "Because that's what you're going to unleash." Her hand tangled in Holly's hair, pulling her head back. She slid off the dildo and pushed Holly to the floor, lifting her ass.

Holly bucked her hips when Sahara's lips met her ass.

"Shhhh," Sahara warned. "Just one more bit of pleasure." A moment later she presented to Holly with a strap-on. "Open your mouth."

Holly complied.

"Say, please Mistress."

"Please Mistress."

"On your knees." Sahara waited until Holly gathered herself. "What are you going to do?"

"I'm going to suck your cock."

Sahara left a merciless slap on Holly's ass. Holly yelped, her pussy dripping down her legs.

"You mean, I'm going to suck your cock, *Mistress*."

Holly nodded. "Yes, Mistress. Please, Mistress, a tumbler of wine? I am so very thirsty."

Sahara let out a throaty laugh. "Oh, you are brave! Face down, slave. Kiss my feet and ask again."

Holly did as she was told, enduring with great anticipation Sahara's kindness or wickedness, she did not care which. She drank heartily then accepted without a whimper the spanking she received for not offering her Mistress the first sip. Her ass, tender and pink now, was further teased by a string of pearls inserted deftly by the hands of her lover.

Pleased with how Holly looked, Sahara resumed her position in front of her, and accepted the slow and decadent devotion she demanded. Further instructions had Holly finger fuck her until her come ran down Holly's arm. Deeply satisfied, Sahara granted Holly's last wish, to be fucked face down, her body shaking with orgasm while Sahara pulled the anal beads out one by one.

They lay curled up in front of the fire, hungry, thirsty and aching for the man they loved, dinner filling the room with savory aromas, the seed catalogs scattered all around them; no longer in a neat pile.

CHAPTER 35

"My messages aren't getting through," Aiden mentioned, sitting by the fire at Iona's. He was being carefully watched by the sorceress, a wine glass filled with soda and lime in her hand.

"The power and cell service must be out," he mused further. "They were going to go for a snowshoe towards the mountains."

"You're very attractive when you worry," Iona laughed.

Aiden smiled. "Tease. Do you have any sense of what's up with them? Usually I can tap in, at least to Sahara."

"They're safe," Iona replied and accepted the offer of more refreshment from Richard who had come into the room. "Fill Aiden's up too."

Richard gestured toward Aiden, who nodded agreement. "You're dwarfing that chair," Richard noted. "Want to change seats?"

"I'm fine, thanks. It's nice by the fire." Aiden put his phone down and focused his attention on his hosts. "Whatever you're cooking smells amazing and I'm starving!"

"Oh, damn!" Iona shot up from her place. "I've got appetizers. So sorry, I meant to put them out earlier."

"I'll get them, sit down." Richard kissed Iona's forehead. "You've been working too hard and I want you to sit here and let us serve you."

"An offer I can't refuse," Iona sat back down gratefully. It was true, she had been pushing herself, making preparations for her time away, organizing The Society's meeting as her last official act in the role of their leading alchemist. She had dark circles under her eyes which Richard had noticed but had carefully kept from alluding to.

"So, tell me a little about the dynamic of the group I'll be meeting. You've led them for several years and you'll know the personalities."

Aiden served Iona a small plate of savory phyllo pastries and some pickled vegetables.

"By the way, I haven't had a chance to mention it, but your attendance at the ceremony on New Year's was as much appreciated as it was unexpected. I didn't realize how far you had gone into your work with the Fey."

"Well, we don't know each other all that well... yet."

Iona settled deeper into the sofa, nibbling a little at her food. Aiden observed the dip of her collar bone, the way her lips pouted when she was deep in thought, and how strong her energy was despite her obvious tiredness.

He caught Richard's glance; they both knew Iona was struggling with the changes in her body. Somehow, she seemed as if she should be able to just produce a child from the void without the usual human process. He wondered if it was the lack of control she suddenly had on her physical environment that was her point of discomfort or something else. Other than that, it was difficult to ignore the swell of her breasts as her hormones surged toward motherhood.

"Hmmm, well, you'll be able to intuit who's who and what's what when you meet everyone. Everyone was chosen for their particular gifts. We're all men except for Sahara and I but there are two women in the queue who are replacements should anything happen to anyone. We need the specific number of twelve at all times. And for that reason, we have secured two more. They may not be called on for years and they know that."

"Who are they?"

"We'll meet them during the first meeting, they'll be present via web conference. One is a leader of a large coven, and the other is an apprentice to one of the men who's a geologist. She's quite young. Eighteen."

"Eighteen?" Aiden said with surprise.

"She is extraordinarily gifted in terms of understanding intergalactic connections between the Crystal Kingdom, our DNA and extraterrestrials. She's a walk-in."

"A what?" Richard asked, curious. He knew better than to pry into Society business but Iona always knew where to draw the line.

"A walk-in is a spirit that takes over another person's body per an agreement with the departing spirit, where the departing wishes to return to the spirit world and the walk-in wishes to experience human life. Usually a walk-in holds information key to the advancement of the planet, and this is a way for them to appear in the world," Iona explained.

"Christ!" Richard muttered. "I thought I'd heard it all from you by now."

"Darling, that time will never come," Iona purred.

They all laughed, for no truer words had ever been spoken.

"So, she's tethering the energy of the future for the group and channeling information which would help us join the world of Fey and humankind." Aiden knew of walk-ins but had yet to meet one.

"Exactly, Aiden. Her youth is the future manifested in our work and her knowledge surpasses all of us."

"I'm guessing everyone leaves their ego at the door then?"

"We all must. There is no room for ego. But having said that, prepare for a ceremony to honor your arrival. It has been highly anticipated. While no one is worshipped, the initiation and official appointing does come with a degree of respect and... well, you'll see."

"I have been prepared by the Fey, in some aspects, through dreams and visions. But obviously I had never anticipated this kind of development in my lifetime and there is a veil still. I have much to remember or learn."

"The initiation lifts the veil. Completely. There will be no doubt about your role after that. But you've read the documents and done your preparatory work?"

"Yes."

"And? Did you find yourself remembering as you read? The books on your shelves are clues you once knew the advanced workings of alchemy and magic, and if you pick them up now, I guarantee you will be fully cognizant of their meaning."

"That's already happened. Even reading Sahara's book... I felt as if I was being fed information intravenously. Aren't you going to eat?" Aiden looked skeptically at Iona's plate.

"I can't eat and talk at the same time. Will I now have the both of you badgering me?"

"Call it what you will, but you've got to finish your food. And if it takes two of us to make you do it, then so be it," Aiden grinned.

"I'm not one for taking orders."

"That's not what I heard."

Iona laughed heartily even as the blood rushed hotly through her body. "Oh Aiden, I'm so happy you're here. Richard and I rarely have company and it's nice to share this space."

"Nice to be had, my lady." Aiden allowed himself this one bit of whimsy. It was nice to spend time with Iona and Richard, they had come to the point in their friendship where trust had been measured and shared, and he had relaxed a little regarding Iona's intentions... yes, sitting here opposite her, he could see that although the sexual tension between them was very potent, they had developed a welcome ease.

They waited in silence for a while as Richard rustled about in the kitchen. Aiden sat with house plans strewn around him on the floor. Iona watched the fire. Every now and again their eyes connected; the early days of Dagr and Arinn's love remembered. There was sadness and joy in the memory—a whisper of longing for the finishing note.

Richard came upon them in one of those moments. To his surprise, the most pressing memory for him was Richard's obsession with Dagr as he contemplated what was passing between his beloved and the enigmatic builder. His throat dry, an ache in his heart for some unidentified emotion, Richard called them in to dinner.

"Come, my love," he held his hand out to Iona. "You've got to eat a proper meal."

Iona unfolded herself into his hands, her eyes lit with love. "I will eat, my darling, not to worry. This babe will be cared for with the utmost of diligence. I will protect him with my very life if need be."

Richard stared. "He? Do you know this to be true?"

Iona put a protective hand on her belly. "I know this to be true."

Richard dropped to one knee in front of her. He put his mouth to her body. "Hello sweet boy." He remained so for a moment, Iona's fingers in his hair. Aiden swept a kiss over Iona's cheek to congratulate her. She was flushed with joy and smelled of vanilla bean and lemon grass.

"Congratulations you two. Were you hoping for a boy?"

"No," Iona purred, touched deeply by Richard's tenderness. "Gender makes no difference to us... whomever wished to come through would have been perfect. But Richard had a dream we'd have a son... very real dream. Our son spoke to him in a language humans no longer understand. And while that is a gift in itself, the greater surprise was that Richard understood the language. It was the light language of the Pleiadeans."

"A star seed!"

"Yes! With a fully activated DNA. So, you see, this is something new for Richard, having this sort of intuition. And he has met our son already in his astral travels."

"And something incredible for the planet," Aiden added. "Sahara and Holly will be delighted to hear. May I tell them when I get home, or do you wish to call?"

"Of course, you may tell." Richard and Iona agreed.

"I worry though that the world will be a strange place for him." Richard stood.

"Ssshh," Iona reassured. "There's nothing to worry about, he will find his own way in the world. He will come with his own resources."

They sat to dinner. Iona's color had improved. Aiden poured water for them all while Richard served the meal. His thoughts turned to Brigida, and the last memory he had uncovered about the child she and Dagr had birthed.

CHAPTER 36

The kitchen garden turned out to be one of the very best of places for Brigida to sun herself and her babe. Truly she loved all of their estate, the green, cool forests, the vineyard, the fields by the river, the orchard with its orchestra of bees, the olive grove; but the potager was her favorite spot of all. It was quiet but for the sounds of the chickens, fragrant with herbs, secluded and serene.

Dagr had laid it out in the style of the monastery garden, granting her every wish and more. And now as she sat cooing to her daughter, she could feel almost complete happiness. Dagr, as she had fully expected, was a devoted father, taking every spare moment to spend time in the nursery or taking his daughter for strolls. It was not fashionable for a man to spend that much time with his child, but then, Dagr did not care much for fitting in. He delighted in his new role. Brigida fell in love all over again, seeing the tenderness in her lover's eyes when they lay together, baby tucked between them.

They had named her Leilah. *Born at night.*

She was a fighter right from the start. Tiny, but strong, eyes mysterious dark pools, with a stubborn wail.

"Are you disappointed she is not fair like you, my love?" Brigida had asked a smitten Dagr.

"No. She has your coloring, and that is just as well. Have you ever seen so much hair on a babe?" Dagr's hand covered the whole of Leilah's head, gently cradling, while she reached with stubby fingers to grasp his long hair. She pulled hard and jumped when Dagr called out in mock pain. But she did not cry, just stared deep into his eyes.

"She is a curious little creature, is she not?" Dagr had added.

"She is. Tenacious, I would say."

"Like you, my lady."

Brigida smiled at this memory, moving the basket that Leilah lay in. Cook had admonished her that she should not leave her in the sun, but each day, Brigida unswaddled her daughter and let the heat of the sun warm her little body. Just a little. She loved the sun and just knew in her bones it would make Leilah healthy. She put tiny sprigs of lavender in the basket among the cloths, so the aroma could soothe her sleep. And each evening, she massaged her baby with an oil steeped with calendula.

"How do you know what to do? I have not known any mother to massage her child as you do?" Dagr had asked.

"Instinct, I suppose, my lord. I do what feels natural and right. The village mothers have their own ideas, and I have mine."

"And do you tell them what your methods are?"

"I do. It is pleasant to visit with them, even though I feel they sometimes observe me with suspicion."

"Perhaps because it is not customary for the lady to keep company with the locals."

"But I have proven myself, over and over! I have come with healing potions and advice, shown I can be trusted. I do not feel above them..." Brigida cast down her eyes. "I am not. I am the daughter of a laboring man."

Dagr had winced. Still this matter of being a lady's maid stung at Brigida.

"Those things will not matter in the future, at least I pray so. You are my beloved, my wife," Dagr had soothed.

These were the thoughts that ran through Brigida's mind. She stood and stretched her back, patting her stomach which had shrunk quickly after childbirth. She missed the feeling of the baby's movements though. Perhaps she would have another.

The light was fading behind the olive grove. She wrapped Leilah and clasped her to her breast.

"There is just enough time, my darling girl. Let us hurry, so we can be back before Cook misses us!"

Leilah observed her with solemn eyes.

Brigida kissed her warm little cheek. "My heart, my love," she whispered and picked her way through the garden gate, a small bundle of flowers tucked into her apron pocket.

Hurrying now, Brigida turned down a forest path towards the village, towards the tiny churchyard with its assorted collection of graves.

CHAPTER 37

*"I seem to have loved you in numberless forms, numberless times, in
life after life, in age after age, forever."*
~ Rabindranath Tagore

"What is it?" Aiden sat up in bed, Iona's hand was pressed to his
chest. His heart was pounding hard, beads of sweat gathering on his
forehead.

"You were calling out in your sleep... having a nightmare."

"Mmm, yes... I was." He ran his hand through his hair, grasping
at quickly fading images from the dream.

"Can I get you some water?" Iona stepped back a little. Aiden
picked up the scent of rose and geranium on her skin.

"Please."

She was back shortly, tucking herself in at the end of the bed,
waiting for him to speak.

Aiden smiled at her; she was nothing if not presumptuous, assuming it was perfectly normal to sit in bed with one's guest. He
gulped the whole drink down at once. He had left the window open a
sliver and welcomed the wisp of night air filtering through.

"What time is it?"

"Close to three."

"You could hear me all the way from your dungeon... err, room?
I'm sorry to have woken you. Is Richard up as well?"

"No, he's asleep. I could feel your restlessness, and when I woke
up you were calling for Brigida."

"She knew."

"Knew what?"

"Oh, do you not know the whole history of Brigida and Dagr in
France? I assumed that you did."

"I know some. Because... well, I think I'll let you tell me what you
know. You should be able to explore for yourself, instead of me telling
you bits and pieces." She looked uncomfortable, shifting her body to
accommodate her back.

Aiden passed her a large pillow. "Put this behind you."

Iona did, leaning against one of the bed posts. She stretched out
her legs.

"Want some hot chocolate?" she asked.

"Chocolate? In the middle of the night? I'll never get back to sleep."

"Well? I mean just a demitasse. I have some Belgian chocolate that Richard bought for me. It's superbly smooth. Then you can tell me your dream."

Aiden grinned. "Alright. I haven't had hot chocolate in the middle of the night, possibly, ever."

"Stay here!" Iona said, delighted. "I won't be a minute. In the meantime, gather your thoughts."

She slid out of bed with the graceful ease of a gazelle, leaving her scent behind. Something about the fall of her nightdress reminded Aiden of a chemise that he, no, Dagr, had once brought back from France for Arinn. His chest knotted into a memory. Those early days at the manor, when Dagr and Arinn had been newlywed—those had been magical, heady times of love. Fleeting times, he thought sadly.

Iona arrived with a tray of water and hot chocolate in two espresso cups.

"That didn't take long did it?" she purred, taking a quick glance at Aiden's bare chest where he sat leaning against the headboard. "I didn't know you wore pajama bottoms to bed."

"Umm, I don't usually. They were a last-minute decision. And how would you know that kind of thing anyway?" Aiden laughed under his breath. "You're cheeky," he added. He took a sip of the chocolate. "Christ, this is good. I may have to do this at home."

Iona found her place at the end of the bed once more. She eyed him over her cup, his bare feet, the length of his legs, the curve of his arms, hair spilling over his shoulders.

"You've let your hair grow longer."

"Sahara's request."

They sat in silence for a while, savoring the chocolate and each other. Finally Aiden spoke.

"I'm not sure that telling you my dream will be good for you, Iona. I feel that it may make you sad, and in your present state..."

"But you will tell me?"

Aiden nodded, moonlight illuminating his body in the most attractive way.

Iona waited, breathless—he was splendidly masculine. Dagr's presence wasn't difficult to conjure.

"It's interesting that my dreams are fairly sequential. I don't seem to skip around much, except for the odd time. So far, I've remembered the chateau Richard bought for Dagr's use and the restoration Dagr undertook of the estate. Also, Brigida's pregnancy. This, the third..."

Here Iona's face registered sorrow.

"I'm sorry, I told you this would be a sensitive memory."

"Go on, please."

"Ok. As I was saying, this pregnancy was a joy for Brigida, except for the painful realization that Dagr wasn't going to bring Arinn to France so long as she was with child. It created a distance between them it seems, until the night of the birth. I must have been astral traveling because the birth is very poignant in my mind still. The midwife wasn't available, so they had to rely on the cook, who had no experience with birthing whatsoever." Aiden sighed. "To make this shorter, Dagr decided on contravening all convention and opened windows, let light in; essentially delivered the baby himself."

Iona's eyes filled with tears. Aiden couldn't be sure she was telling the truth about not knowing this part of Dagr's life.

He continued. "The baby died shortly after delivery."

Iona gasped, laying a protective hand over her belly.

"In the meantime," Aiden continued, "the cook had run down to the village to see about the midwife, who had just delivered an infant to a woman who'd passed in childbirth. She ran the baby to the chateau and she and Dagr devised a plan to simply pretend this new child was to the manor born. When Brigida woke up, Leilah was presented to her as her own."

"Leilah. *Born at night,*" Iona whispered.

"Yes."

"And Dagr never confessed?"

"As far as I know, he did not. But he thought she hadn't heard any of his conversation with the cook. In this dream, Brigida was placing flowers on the grave of her daughter, where she was buried with Leilah's mother. So, she knew. And I wonder now, how long before she said anything to Dagr, if ever? I also was thinking while you were preparing the chocolate, what became of Leilah's lineage, and whether I could trace it to where they are now. Iona?"

"I'm alright."

"You don't look alright." Aiden gestured for her to come closer. "Come sit by me."

She climbed closer and snuggled under the covers next to him. He got under as well, offering his body heat, Iona's small, delicate hand in his. The fire that erupted between them wore centuries of un-requited passion, as did their inherent friendship.

"You don't have to keep beating yourself up over the past. We've been over this countless times." Aiden's voice was firm but empathetic. "All we can do now is live our best life possible. I want you to promise me you won't carry this sorrow while you're pregnant. Please."

Iona nodded. "I'm working my way through it."

"Promise."

"I promise. Tell me, has Sahara spoken ever of wanting children?"

"The truth is, Sahara has assumed she would never be a mother in this lifetime. I want to propose adoption to her. There are so many children who need a home. When we get back from Europe and have had a minute to breathe, I will spend a few days alone with her and bring the subject up. In the end, it will be as she wishes. I won't meddle with her natural instincts. The first step is sharing with her what tonight's dream brought. That will be hurdle enough."

They sat listening to the whistle of the wind past the window. Iona rested her head on Aiden's shoulder. He put his arm around her in as natural an instinct as could be imagined, the two of them lost to their own contemplations. She was warm against his body, and little by little there was no separation between this lifetime and the one before. Aiden controlled the fire between them with a softly spoken incantation for wisdom, for healing, for truth.

"You should go back to your bed. Richard will be looking for you, and we've already crossed too many boundaries."

Turning slightly, he stared down at the woman beside him, devastating mouth parted slightly, breasts draped by thin fabric... she slept. Aiden's breath caught somewhere between his heart and his throat. She was splendid, almost appearing innocent as she lay where he'd released her to the bed. He fought the desire that swept his body. It was no stretch of his imagination what they could engage in, and was his integrity not on the line he would have already shredded the nightdress and surrendered his mouth at her altar. His lips burned for the pleasure even as he heard Richard's voice in the doorway, who lifted his hand to shush him.

"Don't. I'm not in need of any explanations." He held two glasses of scotch in his other hand.

"She's sound asleep," Aiden whispered, reaching for his glass. "Apparently this is a night for drinking and no rest."

"Come sit by the fire? Leave her there."

"Sure," Aiden agreed and they wandered into the living room.

Nothing was said for moments that turned into half an hour. They drank, they warmed by the fire, each of them knowing the truth of the matter between them. Iona could well never get past her mad attraction to Aiden, or her longing for their past life together. Richard knew it with absolute clarity. Aiden argued with his own thoughts. More than once they caught each other's eye. Richard, though having come later to the realization, could not deny he wanted Sahara with the same intensity that Iona craved the man before him.

They were all too emotionally intelligent to ignore the fact that at least four of them wanted to explore the sexual tension between them. Richard and Iona had never said so out loud, but they had fantasized a group ménage, while Aiden and Sahara didn't need to, it was an unspoken wickedness. At one time, Aiden had pushed Iona away with a vengeance, wishing her gone from his life and the complications that arose with that. But now, having come to know her heart, having spent time seeing her power as a magic worker, having revisited the past together, he could no longer wished her absent. His body was wired from chocolate, unrequited animal instincts and alcohol.

"I know you need to sleep, but I wonder if you'd indulge me in something," Richard asked.

"Well, I doubt I could sleep now anyway. What is it?" Aiden had to admire Richard's dark handsomeness, accentuated by his acceptance of Iona's foibles. Richard of old had also begun to show his mark on the present-day man, Aiden could almost feel their ancient camaraderie. Their comfort with each other had grown immensely. If they wanted to, they could easily conjure a drink shared in a castle room.

Richard got up to pull a canister roll from the book case. "I have these old maps I procured in Europe. I'm interested in creating a piece we could frame, one for each of us." He spread the maps on the coffee table.

"We could use antique stamps to mark Richard's castle, Dagr's old demesne, the Oracle Wood, Dark Pool... road to the coast? What do you think? I think it could be quite artistic and unique?"

Aiden ran his hand over the maps, gaging their energy. "I love this idea. These maps are exquisite and in great shape. Where do you get these things?"

Richard laughed. "I have my ways. You know, I love old things. Maps are a favorite of mine."

"Yes, I thought so. I saw the antique ones you have hanging in your office. This could be a nice way to unite our households, each of us with one of these. As much as I want to move past our soul wounds from back then, I also am intrigued with and miss those days in some ways. Let's do some research. You were at the castle ruins not long ago, that's a start."

"I was. The ruins are loud with ghosts and impressions of those times. It was quite the thing, being there."

"What would you say was most memorable?"

"Richard's connection with Arinn, but that was mainly an impression, no details. Also, his friendship with Dagr."

Richard touched the tattoo of Dagr's name and met Aiden's eyes, which held the inevitable question. He shook his head in disbelief.

"I know this will sound strange, but feeling what Richard felt for Dagr gave me new insight into gender. For the first time, I understood what it meant to love a human being for their own essence, gender aside. And yes, it did make me more curious about desire as it relates to any human being. I could see that question on your face," Richard laughed. "You're pretty transparent."

"Am I?" Aiden shared in Richard's laughter. "And?"

"And it shifted my impression of you, to be honest. I saw you as less of an enemy, I could feel the bond between them. I don't know if you'd agree, but love between men, as brothers, can be quite a force. Add to it a romantic interest, and I think it would make for a powerful energy. Transformative... if more people loved with such ferocity."

Aiden sat back by the fire. "I have to admit, I thought you would find that part unsavory. I mean, you can hardly blame me, you *are* the picture of heterosexuality," he grinned.

"Right," Richard returned the grin. "Let's just say I had never entertained any thoughts of guy on guy. I have interactions with gay men all the time in my business, bi men too. There have been propositions..."

"No doubt," Aiden interrupted.

"As I was saying, there have been opportunities, but I'm just not inclined that way. Still, it doesn't stop me from appreciating the love between Dagr and Richard. It adds another dimension to the memories."

Aiden closed his eyes, a thought on his mind, grateful Richard wasn't telepathic because the question he had would cross boundaries. A smile flickered on his lips though, and Richard guffawed.

"Your mind is in the gutter I can tell," Richard accused. "No, Iona and I have not had a ménage with another man. Not that she hasn't wanted it."

Aiden opened his eyes. They met glances honestly. He decided to leave it there. In that moment, Iona slipped in quietly to sit by Richard, pulling a soft blanket over her shivering body.

Richard held her close. "You're freezing darling!"

"What are the two of you thick-as-thieves about?" She accepted Richard's kiss on her forehead with a sigh of love.

"Richard was just telling me how he has a new appreciation for Dagr and Richard's relationship."

"Oh really?" Iona's eyes lit up with interest. "Do tell. Richard Dumont was a bit of an enigma. Arinn certainly had her hands full."

They laughed at the pun just as the sun cast its first rays through the tall loft windows.

CHAPTER 38

"I don't want you to go," Brigida stood with fists curled tight. "We've only just begun our life here, and... anything could happen!"

Dagr paced the floor with Leilah in his arms, holding her head against his chest as she wailed. She had been doing so for the last hour, and nothing would soothe her.

"Darling, I must go, and it will not be for long. It is simply a short voyage to meet some of Richard's contacts. It is barely far, I will be back in two short weeks. Before I can take on a longer voyage, I need to get the feel of the ship. We knew this day would come, I have an agreement with Richard."

"I know but you had said next summer when Leilah was a little older!"

"Look, I cannot change what I cannot change!" Dagr's voice rose and so did Leilah's. He handed her to Brigida. "I hoped for next summer as well, but Richard's letter brought different news. You will be safe, your brother is more than capable of looking after the estate and you."

"And who will look after you, my love?" Brigida whispered, tears rolling down her face.

"There is nothing to worry about, I say. Nothing."

Brigida shook her head. "I shall never forgive Richard if anything happens. Nor you!" She stomped her foot for good measure.

Dagr's eyes flashed a hint of pain. "Well you can add it to the other things I am not to be forgiven for!"

"My lord! You are cruel." With that Brigida left the room.

Dagr reached for the decanter of wine. A quiet knock brought Cook bobbing up and down.

"Your dinner is served," she announced, with a look in her eye that told Dagr she had heard the whole fight.

"Please serve it in the orchard. We will eat there."

"It is already laid..."

"In the orchard Hermine!" Dagr commanded and stormed out after Brigida.

He found her with Leilah sprawled on the grass, gripping it tightly with her tiny hands as she attempted to roll over. Brigida looked up at him, following the surge of love she felt whenever she saw him. He towered over her, his face remorseful.

"We will eat in the orchard tonight."

Brigida put her hand up to him, beckoning him to the ground.

"I cannot bear to argue with you," she admitted.

Dagr laid down in the grass, his head in her lap.

"I am sorry for raising my voice, my darling. I wish I could avoid this rotten business of Richard's, you must know it is not my wish to engage in it."

"I know. And I know you have to go. We have gone through so much already, I just want a peaceful, quiet life."

Dagr sighed. "As do I. As do I."

Leilah gurgled as Dagr lifted her high over his head then brought her down for a kiss.

"I will miss you both."

"And we you."

"Is there anything I can do for you before I leave, darling?"

"Yes. Make love to me... every single night."

CHAPTER 39

"How was your trip?" Holly opened the bakery door, letting Aiden through. He grinned, catching her around the waist. It was still dark, with a determined wind slamming the screen door shut after him. The aroma of baking bread filled the café.

"I'll tell you all about it." He kissed her hands and then her mouth, deliberately soft, intentionally teasing. He laughed as she pretended to swoon. "Are you alone?"

"Nope." Holly handed Aiden a coffee. He settled into one of the counter stools.

"Mmmm. So good."

"We missed you."

"I bet you did."

"You're cheeky."

"Breakfast?"

"Oh, and demanding."

Aiden closed his eyes as Holly leaned over the counter to kiss them. "You know what I missed most darling?" he asked.

"What?"

"This. The feeling I have right now. Complete peace."

"Awww, sweet man!" Holly came around and sank into Aiden's embrace. "I can't believe you're leaving in a few days... I don't know why, but I feel so very protective over you..." Holly shook her head to hide her misted eyes.

"Darling! What's this about?"

"I'm not sure. Maybe because you're going far away, it's not my way to get in the way of your plans, you know that."

"I do, but if you're feeling this way, let's try to get underneath it. Are you worried something might happen?"

"I'm not entirely sure, but you'll be doing this big initiation and I don't know, I mean, I read somewhere that alchemy can be dangerous?"

"Oh sweetheart, there's no danger."

"No?"

"No," Aiden lied.

"Is that all there is?"

Holly couldn't avoid Aiden's scrutiny as he was holding her face up by her chin, staring her down with his clear, blue eyes.

"I know this will sound like jealousy, and I don't mean it that way, but what about other, mmm, rituals? Maybe I've been reading too much about alchemy and coven practices."

Aiden sat Holly down in the chair next to him. He took her hands between his. "Darling, are you asking me if there will be any sacred sexuality rituals? Just be plain, I want you to be comfortable with my going away."

"Well, yes? What goes on in the transfer of power?"

"As you know, I haven't attended before, and in everything I have been prepared for..."

Holly interrupted. "You know what? I don't even know why I'm worried or asking. I'm sorry, this is so not like me. I know this work is important on levels I can't even begin to comprehend. I trust that whatever transpires will be as it should be. No matter what."

"Mmmm, I think we need to address this more. Because I do know your heart, this tells me something has triggered it, you wouldn't ask just to stir up things that weren't there. I have an idea. Why don't we go out to dinner tonight, where we went on our first date, and there'll be plenty of time on the drive over to talk things through?"

"Yes! Perfect darling. I'd like that very much. I'll wear something pretty."

Aiden pulled her closer to whisper in her ear. "I'm so fucking into you."

He drove home after picking up a book he had ordered at the post office, his mind racing through Holly's questions. Of all the things he had imagined might happen at the alchemist's summit, this one possibility had never crossed his mind. He knew that what was contained in his briefing notes wasn't everything; certain elements were left to spontaneous ceremony, but this! Surely Sahara or Iona would have mentioned? He wanted to reassure Holly and leave knowing she was comfortable in their union. But he knew now the life he had been born to was anything but conventional. He arrived home greatly anticipating the evening alone with her.

A note stuck to his door put a smile on his face.

"Hey stranger. Come to my place. I may have missed your face."

He loved that Sahara still left real notes. A quick shower and he headed to the path through the Aspen wood. He remembered the first night he had crossed into the opening between their homes, the sight of Sahara dancing naked around her fire, and how his heart had so quickly fallen for the solitary witch. He marveled at how much had happened since then. He had spent the first thirty-five years of his life preparing for the surprising events before him. And he wouldn't change a thing.

CHAPTER 40

"See you later?" Holly messaged Sahara.

"See you tomorrow, lover."

"Tomorrow? Won't you come over at all?"

"No. I've too much to do before I go away and left it all too late."

"Oh. Ok."

"I saw Aiden this aft. I think the two of you need some time alone, yes?"

"Yes! Thank you".

"Love you, Sweet Pea."

"Love you... did Aiden tell you about our conversation this morning?"

"No?"

"I was being Miss Jealous Pants."

"No, you weren't! I don't believe that..."

"I was. I asked him about the ritual. Sacred sexuality to be exact."

"I see."

"You see what?"

"It's a logical question, considering our lifestyle, what I gave you to read and all."

"Yup. But I think I came off as being clingy."

"Never."

"Truly."

"Well, how did Aiden take it?"

"He asked me to dinner, the silly man."

"To relax you and give you a chance to talk it through."

"Exactly! He knows me. Are you sure he didn't tell you?"

"Sure. Would I lie, haha?"

"Yup."

"Oh, I'm hurt."

"Well you would, if you were protecting me."

"Right."

"Love you."

"Love you."

"See you tomorrow. Let's have dinner at the cabin? Like a date with me and Aiden?"

"Yes, please."

"One week isn't all that long."

"It'll be over in a flash, then we'll be back. I want to plan chickens and honey bees with you for the spring, and Aiden said he's got someone to build your herb beds."

"Kisses!"

"Kisses darling."

CHAPTER 41

"Are you hungry?" Holly called to Aiden from the bedroom.

"Loaded question darling."

"Ready already?"

"Yes ma'am. I'll warm up the truck. Be right back."

"K."

Holly took one last look in the bathroom mirror. She had picked something Aiden hadn't seen yet, it wasn't anything new, but a favorite of hers she hadn't had the chance to wear much; a sleek, long-sleeved jumpsuit, with an elegant V-neck in the palest shade of pink. The slim fit of the bodice with wide-legged pants over stilettos gave her legs even more drama, a Celtic cross pendant hung daringly between her breasts. She tousled her hair into a messy bun and moistened her lips with a sheer pink gloss. Satisfied with her look, she closed all the upstairs lights, and turned to head down the stairs.

She hadn't heard him come up. The warmth of his mouth on her neck and the strength of his hands around her waist surprised her. Her breath let out as her body surrendered to their familiar heat.

"Aiden!" She said his name, as was her custom, to express her love.

"Don't move."

Aiden's kisses continued down the nape of her neck, unzipping the jumpsuit, and leaving a hungry trail down her back. He stopped short of her bottom, and getting up from his knees, slipped the jumpsuit below her breasts. It would have fallen to the floor was he not pressed against her. Her nipples ached for his touch. He took them without any apology for his roughness. Holly's back arched, she gripped his arms. Suddenly, he let go. He helped her with her zipper in silence, but his eyes spoke everything he wanted to say.

"I'm so looking forward to this evening with you," Holly stood trembling before him.

He took her hand firmly. "Let's go."

So often they didn't need words. With her hand in his, they fell into new layers of love. Aiden had reserved their table by the fire. Tucked into the corner, a bottle of prosecco initiating their dinner, they found it easy to ignore the usual stares and cacophony of the restaurant.

Holly dabbled at her food, feeling suddenly shy before this man who commanded her love with such force. He leaned in, taking her hand to his lips.

"Still shy my love?" His eyes twinkled.

"There's just so much of you."

How she loved that growl of his. She shivered with anticipation of his nakedness upon her. She wanted to be underneath him, to feel his weight and his devotion.

"I wanted to explain about this morning. Where my feelings were coming from."

"You can tell me anything, you know that."

Holly took a sip of her drink, watching him over her glass. She simply would never get used to that easy handsomeness.

"I was actually feeling guilty."

She felt his curiosity peak, although his face did not betray it.

"Guilty? For what darling?"

There was that tension! The possibility of being disrobed for his pleasure. She wasn't sure how he summoned it, but he was skilled at it.

"Well," she whispered, which only brought him closer, "I've had a few fantasies." Her pussy soaked wet anticipating her confession.

Aiden leaned back now, signaled the waiter for wine, and allowed the space between them to fill with unsaid words.

She waited for the wine to arrive, for him to fill her glass, for her courage to rise.

Aiden sat patiently.

"I think my worries were... well, they were... born of my recent fantasies as I said. They happened quite innocently in a dream. At first that is."

"Do tell," Aiden's voice rumbled toward her.

"Ok. Do you remember the storm, when we were stuck at Sahara's, and—what I asked you for?"

"I do. I remember forbidding it."

So, the game began... his dominance, her submission.

"And because you forbid it, I have been dreaming of it."

They each imagined the price for her dreams.

"And because I've been dreaming it, my mind went to imagining what could possibly happen in Europe between you and Sahara, and... Iona."

"And what do you imagine would happen?"

"You'll laugh at me."

"I assure you I will not."

"I imagined them naked in hooded cloaks, of ritualistic submission, of your taking your role from Iona, not being given it." Her hands gripped the table edge, Aiden's eyes full of raw desire.

"Are you picturing it now?"

She nodded, eyes cast down.

"And this guilt, where does that come in? So far it is I who is compromising our fidelity to each other?"

"I've been afraid of you wanting to go back to Iona, or Arinn, as it were... maybe in one of your journeys to the past, you'd want to stay, or at least in this lifetime, find it impossible to resist Iona."

"And?"

"And it proceeded to re-awaken in me the desire for that thing I asked you for."

"Say it." Aiden pulled her chair closer so they could speak in complete privacy. Oblivious now to anyone else in the room, he pressed his mouth to her ear. "Tell me everything."

She complied. "I remembered my desire to be taken by all of you. At once."

He moved back. Her clit sang suddenly into release. He watched her face intently while she orgasmed, the only clue visible her eyes closing to hide her pleasure.

"But there's more, am I right?"

"Yes."

"I'm getting tired of having to draw this out of you. Tell me."

Oh, the sweet anticipation of his ripping her from her clothes, and splaying her for a lashing with his tongue, adopting every position he demanded, of his pressing her to her knees... hoping for his hand on her ass, and of having to beg for it.

"I dreamt of making you watch while Richard fucked me. That you had tied me for his pleasure." These last words landed with precision on Aiden's possessiveness of her. Her clit hardened once more. She wasn't sure now what she saw in his eyes. It could have been passion, but it could have been rage. Or it could have been both.

She drank her glass of water in one gulp, mouth dry, heart racing. Later, she remembered nothing of the rest of dinner, nothing of their ride home, but clearly recalled how he bent her over a chair and pulled her panties to her knees. How he spanked her until she gushed to the floor. How he tied her with legs wide open, teased her clit into a frenzy, then commanded her to tell him what she wanted Richard to do to her... gave in to her every wish. She wept in his arms from the crushing love in her heart, from the freedom she had to explore herself.

Aiden lay spent and consumed by the honesty between them. He would give her everything, anything, and even though he had once thought it impossible, share her with another man if she craved it. Because their love was born of impossibility, he would honor the widest manifestation of it. Sex was nothing to him if it didn't include honesty, and their sex was everything he could want.

CHAPTER 42

"Hey Richard."

"You're leaving today?"

"I am. Has Iona left already?"

"Yesterday."

"I know we've talked about this, but I wanted to make sure you'll be available to Holly if she needs anything. I'm sure everything will be as it should be, but just in case."

"You're being very cautious, I'm sure she won't need me for any-thing in a week's time."

"I'm not being overly cautious. Alchemy is not without its very real dangers and I'll be with Iona and Sahara, so anything goes."

"I'm teasing you. And I know the dangers of alchemy. Iona promised... ah well, I see your point. Rest assured I'll be there if Hol-ly needs anything at all."

Aiden thought back to Holly's fantasies. *Anything at all...*

"I appreciate it. I'll do the same for Iona. How's she been feeling the last week?"

"She's still got those dark circles under her eyes, doing too much as usual, but surprisingly has had a lot of energy."

"Perhaps the energy she's raising for the group is feeding that."

"Perhaps."

"Sooo, don't worry. I'll be there for her."

"I know. Thank you. And, I was going to call you today any-way. I have some news for you."

"What news?"

"I sent an inquiry to a business acquaintance who researches family lineage. About Leilah. We had talked about that remember?"

"I remember. And? Anything for us to work with?"

"Are you sitting down?"

CHAPTER 43

"Lovers don't finally meet somewhere. They're in each other all along."
~ Mawlana Jalal-al-Din Rumi

Two weeks went by and Brigida took to standing by the river bank.

There had been much to occupy her within that time. Dagr had hired a renovation of the rest of the chateau rooms. There were details to oversee, workmen to corral, even though they balked at taking instructions from a woman. She knew enough of the language now to know they were making lewd remarks about her. But in the end, they did as she bid them.

Mark was in his usual form; running the estate while Dagr was away took all his days, even with help. Somehow, though, he had found time to court a young woman with hair burnished golden by the summer sun. She had spirited green eyes, a joyous laugh and a lithe, girlish figure.

It did not take Brigida long to figure out what the attraction was, and it only made her ache for Arinn more. In these two weeks she had let her mind wander back to the past. Her body remembered all too well the passion they had shared and the love they had vowed.

With Leilah strapped to her body, she made the rounds of the village women, sometimes bringing medicine, sometimes song, sometimes a helping hand with a birth. She fell into bed each night exhausted and knew it wasn't from the work. It was from her anxiety about Dagr. She could not, would not, live without him.

Mark found her one day in the potager, digging up potatoes.

"You don't have to do that. Let me call the kitchen lad."

"I want to."

"Dagr will be back."

"I know."

"It has only been three weeks. There is no way of accurately estimating any sea voyage."

"Have there been any letters? Any word from that Spaniard?"

"You would have been the first to know if there had been. Come, I will have Cook make us a tray of tea."

Brigida looked up at him. "Thank you, brother. I can always count on you."

"Yes, you can... until my dying breath."

"Tell me about your young woman."

They strolled through the orchard, after a quick stop in the kitchen.

"Annabelle. Is that not a pretty name?" Mark beamed.

"Ah, I see this is serious! Tell me about her."

"She is a fine woman. Perhaps too young for me, but I find her so kind of heart and sweet of soul it would take a hundred horses to keep me from courting her."

"She resembles someone."

"Yes. I suppose you knew all along that I had my eye on Arinn... that is to say, before Dagr made his intentions known."

"I did. Dagr too."

"You talked about it?" Mark questioned with some alarm.

"We did. And we knew you did not approve of our strange little life. And that when you tried to discourage me from Arinn it was because you had genuine concerns. But tell me more about your plans with Annabelle?"

Mark laughed. "You are relentless! I plan to ask for her hand in marriage. She has only her father. Mother is long gone. I am hoping you will be friends; and welcome her as my beloved."

"Why of course we would! Oh, I am so very happy for you both! We will be a full home with the two of you and maybe, some little ones? Some cousins for Leilah?"

They laughed at the thought and hugged.

"I still have to speak to Dagr about the marriage, and I do not expect us to live in the main house. We can live in one of the unused cottages on the estate."

"Never! You will take some of the renovated rooms. There is too much house for the three of us. Now do not argue with me, I will have my way."

"I suppose you will, my darling sister," Mark smiled his gratitude.

He did not give it away when from the corner of his eye he saw Dagr approaching from across the orchard. How did the man walk so lightly? He continued talking until Dagr's hands were over Brigida's eyes.

"Guess who, my lady!"

Brigida lept to her feet, swirled in the air by the jubilant Dagr.

"Oh, I have never been so happy to see anyone! And oh how you smell of ocean life! Off to the bath, my lord."

They left Mark in the orchard. The bath was drawn and Brigida set her stool by the metal tub.

"Allow me, my lord."

"I am sorry it took so long. There were delays in delivering our cargo. I knew you would worry."

Brigida's hands worked their way through Dagr's hair. She washed and rinsed and washed and finally worked fragrant rosemary oil through it. He relaxed as she brushed it then worked the knots in his shoulders and arms.

"You are heaven sent, woman!"

"Use this soap. Smell it! I made it myself, with calendula, honey and goat's milk."

Dagr sniffed the soap and closed his eyes. "Luxury, my darling. Pure luxury. Here, let me. You go look at that parcel on the bed." He grinned when Brigida squealed her delight.

"These stockings! And this chemise!"

"I also have material for dresses. There are some chests to open downstairs. I found some crockery to adorn your table as well, my love."

"Ooooh, you spoil me. So, you would consider your trip a success?"

"I would. Though not my choice of professions, I am surprised by how much I enjoyed the business end of it."

Brigida caught the exaggeration. She would not press for details about the cargo or the process. She was grateful for his return, and that was all that mattered at the moment.

"I have news too, darling."

"Oh? What could you have gotten into while I was away?" Dagr stepped out of the tub.

"You expect me to be able to remember anything with you looking like that?"

Dagr had quite obviously been working hard, his body toned and tan.

"Do you do the work yourself? I do swear, my lord, you have grown in these three weeks."

"Never mind. What is the news?" Dagr chuckled.

"Oh, fine! About Mark. Let him tell you himself, but, he has a lady love! The only reason I am telling you anything is because he has this crazy idea about making his marriage home in one of the cottages. I want you to insist he live in the house. I do not want it any other way. Those rooms will be ready soon enough. And I would like to plan a wedding supper, if you allow my lord."

"Allow? My lady, do as you will, and I will most certainly insist they live in the house. Is it that serious then?"

"It is. Do you know of a girl named Annabelle in the village?"

"Annabelle!" Dagr hooted.

"You do know her then!"

"A good choice, I must say."

Brigida laughed. "I see she has not escaped your notice."

"She works for Comte de Beauchene."

"I am happy for him. He has been lonely for a lover."

"I am as well. And more family for us."

"Yes." Brigida turned her back to hide her tears.

Dagr wrapped himself around her. "Darling. I have been thinking while I was at sea."

She did not dare to assume, but her heart leapt anyway. She turned toward him. Could it be possible that he would finally relent?

Dagr continued. "I do not often think about my mortality, even though I have been in enough life and death situations, but while I was away, I thought about you being left alone should anything happen. I have wanted to control everything so you would be safe. I have so much remorse, my love, for breaking your and Arinn's heart. Watching your pain these last months has been near to unbearable."

"Shush, my lord. I understand."

"I know you understand, my lady, but you also ache for Arinn every waking moment."

"Do you not? Have you forgotten your love for her?"

"My God, Brigida, how could I? She... ah, I cannot bear to open that wound, what she has been to me, her essence, her enchantment of my soul."

"And so, my lord... what have you concluded while at sea? Dare I have hope?"

"I wanted to speak to you about writing a letter to Richard. I dreamed of spending an evening with our supper by the fire, writing our letters and discussing the future. Would that suit you my love?"

Tears streamed down Brigida's face. She buried herself against him, sobbing into his chest.

"Oh how I have dreamed of hearing you say that your love for our beloved was not dead! How I have longed for her body against mine. My darling! How can I thank you for this change of heart?"

"By promising me that you will be vigilant about your own safety. I know I have been wrong to dictate your and Arinn's life. You must be sovereign, my love. Three weeks is not a long time but long enough for me to lay awake at night and search my heart and motivations. I beg your forgiveness, and I will beg Arinn's."

"And Richard? He has suffered."

"It has been the darkest night of my soul thinking of what I have done because of fear." Dagr admitted. "I do not know if I could have done any different in the moment, but perhaps could have relented sooner. But my worries about the babe—I just could not be sure."

"Sure of what?"

"Sure of, well..." Dagr stumbled over his words. This lie between them! How he hated not baring his heart. "Just sure of your safety while carrying a little one."

"Of course, my darling, if I know of anything it is of your devotion for me. I can forgive what has passed between us, your heart is always bent on my happiness. But let us bring our family together again! If there is one thing I could ever want from you, it is this."

Dagr's intuition and warrior instincts grappled with Brigida's words. His guilt over Leilah tore his very soul. If he should confess, it should be now... or did she know, her words of forgiveness seemed to speak of it? Every bit of honor in his bones rebelled against his lie. And yet, he could not bring himself to tear her heart if she did not know... she *did not* know! He would believe that.

She was on the bed, undressing, ripping at her garments, turning around so he could help her. Dagr matched her urgency. He did as she commanded, untied her stays, released her breasts into his hands. Breasts that had soaked her tunic with mother's milk, and that now dripped wet through his fingers.

Her whole body shook as he tasted, nipples seeking his teeth.

"I want you to take me like you took us once... remember?"

Before Dagr could respond, she was on hands and widely-placed knees, pussy wet and swollen, her scent rising to his nose. His mouth was on her before she could ask for it, her voice rang loud in the room. He did not bother to silence her, nor did he reign in his lust. She called Arinn's name and Richard's. She demanded his fingers. Harder! Harder! She bore the ferocity of Dagr's thrusts. He wore the mark of her handprints on his face, and the pain of her bites on his arms. All that had been broken between them came to the surface. It was violent and sacred. It was the agony of these long months away from the ones they loved. Theirs was a complicated life. Dagr sucked her clit, rolling it with his sensual lips until she screamed her release. "Fuck me, fuck me!" she yelled with her whole being. "Fingers inside me!" as she gushed over his tongue. He did all that and more, until the wee hours of the morning, their supper lying cold on a tray outside their door.

CHAPTER 44

"Bone by bone, hair by hair, Wild Woman comes back. Through night dreams, through events half understood and half remembered"
~ Clarissa Pinkola Estes

Arinn walked the gardens at dawn clutching a basket and knife. A heavy fog covered the landscape; she was wrapped in a heavy shawl, yet her shivering would not stop. She had woken from a dream so real that she had been sure Dagr was in the bed with her. She thought she had heard him calling out to her. Nothing could have been more disappointing than waking and finding herself alone.

Richard had been away for weeks and she was lonely for his voice and his touch. He had been the most ardent lover and teacher of the erotic arts. She had grown accustomed to his fierceness, had come to crave it. And, she had found his heart generous. He hid it under a gruff exterior, but when he loved, oh, how he loved! She had been sheltered by his tenderness. Sheltered and allowed her grief. She had been nurtured as much as she would allow. But as much as he had become her lover and her heart, the sacred connection with Dagr never waned.

She had come out with the intention of gathering herbs for a savory breakfast pie, but now that she was here, inside this dense cloud which sat upon the Earth, all she could think about was how to find her way back to Dagr and Brigida.

Her longing for a woman's touch was so fervent that she spent many a moment conjuring the feelings of Brigida's mouth on hers, and finding pleasure at her own hand.

Richard had come to love watching her in this kind of play, and she had demanded it in return, asking his compliance while thinking of Dagr. Now, with this dream so evocative of years past, she walked in circles around the garden beds without picking a single thing.

Somehow her presence at the castle had been accepted. She was Richard's playmate... which was what everyone thought; even though she was every bit the herbalist who had taken over old Hannah's work. She had every freedom, every need tended to by Richard. The luxuries she was afforded were what gave her away as his lover. She was dressed in whatever finery he felt she should be adorned with.

While she worked, she wore plain things, as was her pleasure, but later, she dressed for him. Not that she minded. It reminded her of those early days at the demesne with Dagr. Richard's admiration of her in French silks gave a woman great confidence. Still, she was that strange creature roaming the halls as either the seductress or the baker of his favorite bread. Either way, she was his sustenance.

Frustrated, she climbed the stairs to her secret chamber. She opened the doors and breathed the air of alchemical fires. Here she was in her element. She had the only key to this room, and thus far, no one had ever followed here. She took great care to be most invisible when finding her way up. It was part of the castle that did not interest anyone, far from the kitchens and public rooms.

She touched her tools and lit a fire. She had to carry all her own wood plus other supplies. No one could be asked to assist her. When her teacher, that old wizard, came to attend to her lessons, he was whisked in under the cover of night. And here, she studied the movements of the moon and the planets. Here they poured over old scrolls of magical spells. Here they stocked shelves of ingredients for boiling in special crocks. The danger of what they did was ever-present. She knew that with every alchemical process came the possibility of death. But now she was adept at calling in spirits who came from the Underworld to help her understand the properties of the many elements they worked with. Even the old wizard did not have such assistance; and gave way when she summoned them.

This dark, musty room, along with the kitchen garden and herbalist's kitchen was her home now. But here she was in her power. She knew the fullness of what she was born to. She was a witch and a sorceress, and she remembered things that others had never known.

She cast her spells according to what the skies foretold. In a few short months, she had become masterful in her practice. Because she honored the world of the Fey and carried on the work given to Woman in the beginning of earthly time, she was granted knowledge of many dimensions. She became a keeper of stories. They were all on her lips the moment she wished to voice them... stories of the Earth, stories of the spirits which lived within every tree and blade of grass. She would keep these for the ages, until mankind woke up again and remembered how to live peacefully.

What had been awoken in her could not be extinguished. She was no longer a girl searching for a safe place to reveal her unconventional soul as she had once been with Dagr. For now, everything she knew would remain hidden. There would be other centuries when she would not be burned for her wisdom—other places. Even Richard could not know that she had felt the beginnings of being able to shape-shift. A raven had visited her many a time in her dreams, and she knew that one of these days, her wings would grow from mysterious places, and she would fly. When she did, she would seek the guidance of the winds and search for the lovers who had abandoned her.

A river of tears wet her face as she thought of them now. She stared into the fire, looking for signs of the future. But this was one thing she had been denied... any divining of the rest of her life. The flames hissed and leapt as she spit into them in anger. All she wanted was a word, one word of hope. This was the debt she carried. The debt of jealousy. With what could she pay to erase this scar on her soul?

"My lady, shush... it is I." Richard smoothed the hair from Arinn's face. She lay sleeping in her chair by the bread oven.

She opened her eyes and smiled into his. "You are returned, my lord. Let me serve you some bread. I have a fine butter churned." She attempted to stand but he put a warm, insistent hand on her shoulder.

"No. I will make the tea and serve the bread. Stay where you are."

She watched in silence as he prepared the herbs for their drink. He laid their cups by the hearth, and a plate of bread and preserves. Finally, he sat by her side and took her hand. Arinn felt a certain excitement under his skin. He must have missed her, and she admitted readily to herself that it made her happy to know this.

"I have missed you, my lady, all your impertinence and fire. Let me hold you, touch your lips with mine." They embraced and kissed, savoring the moment, imagining the night ahead.

"And how was it for you my lady, during my time away? What have you been doing with yourself?" Richard drawled.

"Oh, nothing much. Slaying dragons and the like."

Richard laughed. "I would not be in the least surprised my lady!"

"How was it for you?"

"Court life is for fools. The King no longer has my loyalty, although one has to do what one can to appear loyal. Unpleasant business, all of it."

"I suppose the women fawned all over you?"

Richard guffawed. "How did I know you would say that? Of course, they did. I am as yet unmarried, and no one understands why. There is talk I prefer the company of men..."

Arinn raised an eyebrow and smiled. "I should think your sizeable reputation would erase all such speculations? On the other hand, have there been...?"

"Shush woman! Never mind all that." Richard leaned in. "I do have something to share with you." Richard's eyes gave away his complete happiness. "I rode day and night to bring you this news."

"What is it?" Arinn straightened her spine.

"I have a letter." He pulled a neatly folded paper from a small pocket inside the waist of his riding leathers.

"No!" Arinn paled. "Is it?"

"It is. Miraculously. I had lost all hope, my lady. But upon meeting with my man who runs messages for my import business, I was handed a parcel with the supplies you asked for—wait, let me tell you all of it!"

Arinn was clutching for the paper in his hand.

"Tell me! Hurry!"

"As I was saying, the parcel... the letter was tucked into the packet. The whole thing was addressed in Dagr's hand. I told you he would eventually help me with shipping and purveying of goods, yes?"

"Yes! My lord, stop dallying. Read me the letter for the love of God! And all of heaven and earth help you if you are pretending good news." She wanted to believe it, but her heart had been broken one too many times to trust anything altogether.

"Come darling. Do not doubt me. I am not that cruel." Richard pulled her chair closer to his, and began to read.

"How can I begin, a letter that must at once beg forgiveness and ask a favor?"

"Who is it addressed to?" Arinn demanded.

"No one, they are being careful."

"They?"

"Just listen!"

"In the last few months, I have come to realize I have wronged you both greatly. My fear and anger were the agents for a decision I now regret from the depths of my heart.

Perhaps it is too late to ask for reconciliation?

Perhaps I have done irreparable damage?

But if not, I beg you consider joining us here. We are four now in our household. I eagerly await your response and will accept whatever reply you see fit to send."

She could not believe it! Was she awake? Her dream had been an oracle after all.

"He is asking *our* forgiveness? After what *I* did?" Arinn sobbed into Richard's arms.

"There is more, my love."

Suddenly, they became aware of the irony of their situation. Now, it would be she, like Brigida, going home with a heart full of two very enigmatic men.

"My darlings," the letter continued, in another familiar hand, *"Come home to me. As I sit here and write this, it is the happiest day of my life. We are well, and hope you are also. My heart is full of love and I want to share this beautiful place with you. We will be making ready for your arrival. Make haste, my loves."*

They sat with hands clasped together. Words were unnecessary as they shared an embrace after long moments staring into each other's eyes. So many unknowns ahead. What would become of their combined love?

Richard hid his greatest fear; that after their reunion, he would be returning home alone.

Arinn faced hers. Was the price she had paid for Brigida's healing at the Dark Pool finished with? Could she trust herself? Perhaps the spell she had cast some months past had been powerless? Now there were four. Richard had told her about Mark joining Dagr and Brigida. The fourth... a child? She would summon Pan, perhaps travel to the Underworld and seek the favor of the King of the Fey. She would do all she could. But she would have to ask Richard to bring her to the Dark Pool, to the Oracle Wood. And in that, there was danger. Richard did not know who was watching him and who was not. She would find a way. She had to, or she would not make the trip to France.

CHAPTER 45

The hotel was tucked into a scrap of cobbled street in Paris. An exclusive, boutique establishment which catered to a particular clientele, as it had for the last two-hundred years. It was appointed with an ambiance of mystery and magic, every luxury catered to, fireplaces for warmth, hidden rooms and secret passageways. The sign always read, *Complet*. Full.

Each one of The Society's members arrived to a room picked to their particular taste, fire lit, bed turned down; Belgian chocolate and a vase of flowers dressing the table; their favorite wine or spirits, along with a delectable room service menu.

Aiden's room adjoined Sahara and Iona's via a wall of bookcases—the portal accessed by three random books removed from a shelf. It was up to the occupant to use his intuition to divine which books were the keys.

Aiden unpacked his belongings. His was a suite with a spacious sitting room and a balcony to suit. He thought he had seen luxury but this had an entirely different flavor. He would have hazarded a guess as to the cost of their collective stay but a knock on the door interrupted his thoughts.

Sahara stood in the hallway, smiling from ear to ear.

"Why are you standing out there?" Aiden pulled her into the room. "Why not use the passageway?"

"I thought it would be more fun to visit you this way. What do you think?" She laughed and fell into one of the comfy chairs.

"Bloody luxury, that's what!" Aiden grinned. "How much..."

"Ah, ah! We don't concern ourselves with the mundane while here. It's all arranged by Sophia, our accountant."

"I see. And so, do we...?"

"No, we do not. It's all taken care of. Now stop meddling in these affairs!"

"I'm just saying. I can't imagine."

"Well don't."

"Don't I get to know any of this? What happened to being the Grand Poobah and all?"

Sahara broke into peals of laughter. "Grand Poobah indeed! All will be revealed after the initiation. Now, shower up, my love, we will be meeting in the dining room in a few short hours."

"And Iona? I heard she left a day before you and me?"

"She's somewhere in this place."

"Getting answers around here is like pulling chicken's teeth."

"Ok, well, I'll see you then." Sahara got up to leave.

"What? Just like that? Stay with me."

"No darling. Later, perhaps." She stood with her hand on the door. "I've ordered you something to nibble on. Shower, nap. The dress for tonight's dinner is formal, but I'm sure you've received the itinerary."

Aiden smiled his devastating smile and Sahara weakened in the knees. "I'll see you then," he said, removing his shirt.

She couldn't help herself, the sight of his naked chest called her toward him. "One hug," she whispered.

"One hug, my love," he replied.

In the dimly lit dining room, a group of powerfully gifted people sat to dinner together. Although the dress was formal, the mood was light. It was an evening to commune with the forces of each other's personalities, to be nothing more than human. Through the act of literally breaking bread, each person tearing a piece from the loaf then passing on to the next, they grounded and observed the abundance of the Goddess.

Iona sat at the head of the table. She had called upon the spirits to join them in their meal, blessed the food and the days ahead. Aiden had never seen her more joyful. This was clearly where she belonged, among these brilliant minds. Among her tribe. He sat to her right, Sahara to her left.

There was an air of expectation among them, an excitement to begin. But as they ate, everything seemed to slow down, they were transported into layers of timelessness. Introductions were made. Aiden was warmly welcomed into the fold. He had the sense that after tonight there would be none of this informality, none of this pretense. They were to here to shift Consciousness by virtue of sacred ceremony.

He thought of Holly often, as he listened to the conversations around him—missing her calm touch. She was his grounding, every time. He was grateful for her words as she had seen him off on his journey.

"All that is and all that will be is right between us. Go with my love, darling."

He cherished those words and they were permanently etched on his heart. Holly's gentle soul kept him centered on what mattered most.

Watching Iona and Sahara spread their laughter and essence around the table also brought him peace. Effervescent, that's what he would call them. He saw, just under the surface, how they brimmed with mysticism. It was difficult to contain, their centuries of living their purpose, of embodying the Divine Feminine. They were stunning side by side. And he knew they felt his admiration. Their eyes flashed when they addressed him. No doubt everyone could sense the electricity between them.

Their meal was decadently simple. All the flavors of haute cuisine but contained in five mini courses. Quantity was reserved, whereas quality was heightened. No one would leave the table stuffed, but they would leave supremely nourished. Before them; one delicate squash blossom flash-fried to perfect crispness on a bed of tender arugula. A delicate cupful of vichyssoise, baguette crisps accompanying, fragrant with Spanish olive oil and sprinkled with fresh thyme. Tender morsels of lamb with roasted parsnip mash. A bite of brie and camembert with warmed walnuts. Bourbon-baked pear with a lashing of fresh cream.

Three high candelabras sat atop the long table dressed in antique white linens; iron wall sconces with white candles splattering shadows on old stone walls. Baroque music filled the spaces between words. Every detail added to a perfectly curated atmosphere. The world fell away. Muscles relaxed with each sip of a drink that defied description. Aiden took to scrutinizing the glass in his hand... what was this?

They moved to the sofas scattered around the two massive fireplaces after several hours of indulgence.

Aiden had never felt so responsive to outside stimuli. He could feel every person in the room on his skin. This heightened awareness allowed him to completely integrate with the others, to almost hear all their thoughts at once, and none of it jumbled. Indeed, he felt infinite, as if every cell of his body had boundless territory. Sahara came to sit by his side. She took his hand. He felt her deep in his bones. It was as if her hand melded with his, her bones became his bones.

"And so, my love? How fare you?" Aiden heard the distinct voice of Brigida, the lilt of her accent, the smoothness of her youthful tone. Sahara closed her mouth over his. A dainty kiss which immediately unraveled him.

"Ahhh, darling. A perfect evening. So much more than I expected."

"And what did you expect?"

"To be honest, I had no idea what to think or expect. One always has thoughts about what might be, but truly I could not have imagined this. What, pray tell, is in that delicious drink we've been sipping?" Thinking back, it had been served almost in thimblefuls, the tiniest of crystal sherry glasses. "A most potent drink," he observed.

Sahara laughed. "Darling, I have asked that question myself. But suffice it to say it has been brewed by our own Iona, and she never shares her alchemical secrets."

"I should have known. Well then, let us just enjoy. Are you feeling as expansive as I am?"

"Yes. We will be traveling the stars tonight. Feeling into the mystery of all creation. I did hear the Fey had brought Iona the ingredients for the cordial."

"Cordial?" Aiden laughed. "Is that what we're calling it?"

Sahara joined him in his laughter. "Enjoy, sweetness." And she was gone. Iona took her place.

"My lord," Arinn's voice broke through the veils of centuries past. For moments she shapeshifted and Arinn sat beside him, innocent and trusting, in that way she had been when they had first been together, a warrior and a maiden too young to know life could be savage and cruel.

He sat upright, every inch of his being responding to the girl before him. Remembering. He hadn't known how much he had craved to feel her next to him. To know the beautiful simplicity of love between a man already too scarred by war and a girl whose purity could remind him of his.

"Is it you?" Aiden asked, reaching for her.

"It is I, my love."

They sat in silence for what seemed like hours. Filling up on lost moments, on lost years and lost opportunity.

"We lost each other, didn't we, my lady?"

"But not without purpose, my lord."

"I mourn those days."

"As do I. But there is a way back. And if you can trust me just one more time, we can heal the wound of our past. We must. Do you desire it?"

"I do. And I do trust you. I may have said otherwise even a few days back, but in this moment, I can feel the true intention of the vow you made at the Dark Pool. I trust you only wanted healing for the one you loved. I trust there has been purpose for this lesson—this dark period between us."

"This darkness has almost destroyed me my lord. It has torn at my soul for centuries. It has almost swayed me from my sacred work. But we meet again this lifetime for a conclusion to that ancient vow. And now we must step into the Underworld together. You, I and Brigida. And when we return, all will be washed with the healing balm of new understanding."

"Tonight?" Aiden's head felt heavy. He sorely wished for sleep.

"Not tonight. Tonight is for dreaming, my lord."

CHAPTER 46

"Will you take me my lord?" Arinn pleaded. "Please say that you will!" Her voice reached a frantic crescendo.

"I cannot." Richard flatly refused once more. "I would give you anything, you know that. Except for this. It is simply asking for every danger that could befall us. I have done my best to keep your identity secret, and we have been lucky, taking as many liberties as we have. But I cannot and will not take you to the Oracle Wood. Surely, you can summon your beasts and Underworld creatures from anywhere? I have seen you work your magic. Why does it have to be in that wretched place?"

Arinn shook her head. "I do not know why but feel it must be so."

"Well can you not ask?" Richard paced his room as Arinn fell to her knees before him. He hated seeing this strong, willful creature in such despair and he unable to help her.

"I need not ask!" she barked. "I just know it has to be this way, the same portal. I do not need to know why to obey the laws of the Fey."

"Please get up. Let us leave this for tonight."

"Tomorrow will bring the same answer from you, I fear, my lord." Bitter tears streamed from Arinn's eyes. "If you will not bring me, I cannot travel to France. Both of us know this."

"But I will be there, Dagr, too. You will be with us at all times. I do not see the danger."

The look Arinn fixed on him left Richard with a cold shiver up his spine.

"I think we both know my magic is not bound to any physical laws."

He knew it. She could cast a spell with a single thought. He sat down. She came to him and laid her head on his knee.

"Do you know what it is like to fear oneself, my lord?"

Richard felt such a surge of love, such intense emotion, that he found his fist gripping her hair and pulling her up towards him. She came willingly. They embraced with the question hanging between them. Heart to heart, they sat watching the fire, only moving when a knock on the chamber door signaled the evening meal.

CHAPTER 47

They had to hire more help. With the excitement of Arinn and Richard's arrival spurring uncommon activity at the chateau, there were not enough hands to do the work.

Now that all the rooms were renovated, there was furniture and linens to buy. The kitchen needed more supplies. The gardener was given a crew of young lads to help with the grooming of the orchard and gardens. The olives were ready for picking and brining. Summer mushrooms were pickled or dried, and jams cooked from the overabundance of blackberries in the hedgerows.

Cook was forever in a mad rush to organize the pantry into abundance. Dagr had sourced delicious charcuterie and cheese to be delivered to their cold storage. Brigida teased him that one would think the King was coming. Dagr replied with a growl that should the King be coming, he would have stocked up on rotten cabbages.

She stood on the doorstep of their home with the wind blowing her hair, the view of the olive-treed avenue leading to their front door—a soul satisfying sight. The light was at its most glorious—golden shadows cast between the deep green branches of the trees.

Her heart was full and several times each day she pinched herself to see if it was all real. Arinn and Richard were coming! They were coming! The long draught of being without her loves was coming to an end and all it had taken was one short journey to sea for Dagr to give in to his heart.

About to turn in, Brigida caught something in the corner of her eye. Hand to brow, she squinted down the long drive. Someone approached. Now who could be coming at this time and unannounced? She removed her apron and smoothed her hair into its unruly bun. She had time to run to the stables and ask Mark to receive them. She would come down if needed but right now she wanted to check on Leilah, asleep in her cot.

But she could not find Mark in the stables, and by the time she was back to check on the progress of the visitor, she was surprised to find them disappeared from the lane. Sighing, she stepped into the cool of the library. A lone tendril of her dark hair slipped disobediently across her face. She was flushed with running to and fro.

Looking up, Brigida cried out at the impossible sight before her. Gripping the corner of a chair, her knees buckled and was caught in the arms of the dark horse, the Earl Richard Dumont.

Disbelief flooded her brain. But he was early, and where was Arinn? Oh how she had missed his dark, dangerous eyes. He held her firmly in his arms. They stood listening to each other's breathing—the pounding of each other's hearts.

And in those moments, Arinn stepped into the room. She was holding a tray of tea, with Cook in a displeased mood right behind her.

They began to emote sounds of their separation, in virtual hysterics. Arinn laid down the tray and ran to Brigida. Cook was ushered out by Richard who assured her she was not needed and requesting Mark's presence. But Mark, Hermine said, was down by the river tending to a dispute between two tenants. No matter, Richard assured her, she should leave them to their reunion.

Among the tears and the embraces, Brigida managed to choke out a few words. Her eyes could barely believe what they were seeing. Arinn, her beloved, was changed. She was, if possible, more stunning, more in her power. This was not the girl she had left behind. Her heart burst with love and an unexpected shyness.

"But you are early. Months early!" She wished she was in the dress Dagr had bought for her, not with her hair in a mess and in her garden clothes.

They nodded at her words.

"Dagr is not due to return from his voyage until four weeks from now! You have caught us with so much to do still, and I look a mess. Darlings, are you really here?"

Richard was down on one knee before her, handsome in his tailored travel clothes. Arinn sat next to her holding her hands. Tea had been poured but forgotten.

What was this chill she felt in her heart and bones? Why was Richard so few of words, staring into her eyes with such sadness in his? In the end, it was Arinn who spoke.

"My love, I have missed you so. We have missed you so."

"And we you. I have prayed for this day. I knew that one day, we would all be reunited. I just knew in my heart life could not possibly be so cruel as to separate us forever. And here you are." Brigida steeled herself against the sight of Arinn's quivering mouth.

Arinn hung her head.

"What is it my darling? Are you still thinking I would not forgive you? Because I have. Everything that happened was due to a big misunderstanding. I know you only wanted my healing. All is forgotten, sweetness."

"Oh, but you will never forgive me!" Arinn cried out. "Not with the news I bring." And she collapsed into Brigida's lap.

Brigida looked to Richard. "What will I not forgive her? Tell me this instant if you know." She was cold now. She wanted to run to her rooms, to hear Leilah's cry.

Richard broke down into great heaving sobs, his hands crushing hers. She began to cry also. To scream. She wrenched herself away from him and tried to run from the room, to climb the stairs to Leilah. But he caught her and held her fiercely.

"Let me go! Let me go!" she yelled at the top of her agonized lungs.

Richard choked out words that shook her foundation. Strange words that landed like sharp knives on her ears. She knew it was a lie. And she hated them both for bringing it to her door.

"My love, my darling. There is no way to say this. I have no way of preparing you," Richard uttered, completely forlorn. Suddenly he stiffened. "My lady, I regret to tell you that your... our, Dagr, is feared dead... is perished at sea."

The room was spinning and Brigida was retching on the floor. Her lungs collapsed in her chest and she fought for breath.

"No. He is not." She announced flatly. "He is away to sea and will be returning in a month's time. He has been to sea and it is not dangerous as I thought. He will return. You will see."

They pulled her to the sofa where she sat with a challenging look in her eye. She dared them to say those ugly words again. To her horror, they did.

"If he were to return he would have by now," Richard began all over again. "There was an accident and the whole ship went aflame. No bodies have surfaced. I have conducted as thorough a search as I could. There are no survivors. I am very sorry, my lady."

"When? When?" Brigida grasped at hope. Perhaps not enough time had passed. Perhaps he was out there, waiting to be rescued?

"It has been a month," Arinn whispered, paler than a winter cloud. "It happened at the beginning of the voyage. Richard received word and immediately began the search." Her face was stained with tears and pain.

"But I imagine he could have floated somewhere you have yet to look? Surely, there are many places he could have landed? The sea may have carried him as far as Spain?"

"Dagr is gone. He is the most capable man I have ever known and if he survived we would have known by now." Richard sat down, defeated.

She looked at the two of them and suddenly realized they had been living with this pain for weeks. They had had to find the courage to tell her, and she knew their grief. Somehow that solitary thought gave her strength. She gathered them up in her arms. Allowing them to cry their sorrow, she clung on to them with determination.

"I will find him. I will go to sea and find him. Richard you must get me a ship. Dagr is not lost. He has a daughter to raise." She looked up. That was it! They would all feel better if they saw Leilah. She called to Cook.

"Oh, you must see our babe! She is Dagr's pride and joy." She cackled a strange laugh and clapped her hands.

Richard and Arinn exchanged looks. Brigida was in shock. But to be honest, they could not wait to meet Leilah. It was the one ray of sunshine they had to look forward to in all this miserable time. The last month had been one soulless day after another, receiving word of the fire, the frantic waiting for news of Dagr, the realization of his disappearance, and finally, knowing their reunion with Brigida would be to share the horrible news. They had forgotten all worry about Arinn's dilemma, their only task each day was to get through their heart-wrenching grief. How many days had they laid in each other's arms, their hearts in unbearable agony? No one wanted to believe it. It was an unspeakable ending for a man so full of life and vigor. Deep down, they each held hope. Perhaps...

Leilah was brought to the library. She stared at Arinn and Richard solemnly. Her tiny hand gripped Arinn's finger. And in that moment, Arinn's heart shattered into too many pieces to gather. This was not Dagr's child. She had hoped for a little piece of him to have saved them all. But this child, so serious and precious, so wise of soul, was not the one Brigida had birthed. She realized that her spell months ago in her herbalist's kitchen had worked and she had once again betrayed Dagr and Brigida's love. She cursed herself and the little stick figure she had hurtled into the fire. She wept and wept. Another secret to burn her into forever.

Richard thought she was overcome by the sight of Dagr's blue eyes in the child's face. He held them all in the warmth of his embrace. He kissed Brigida's cheek and congratulated her on her babe. His heart was already bursting with love for the tiny girl held between them. At least they had this.

But Arinn wished she was at the bottom of the sea with Dagr. Anywhere but here, facing her truth.

CHAPTER 48

"So, it's true, when all is said and done, grief is the price we pay for love."
~ *E.A. Bucchianer*

Mark returned to find them sitting by a raging fire in the library even though the evening was warm. He laughed at their curious tea huddle, extending his hand to Richard.

"My lord! What a great surprise," he bowed. "Lady Arinn," he greeted the woman who had occupied so many of his thoughts after that fateful day in England, not comprehending the depth of sadness in her eyes.

"Mark," Brigida said, taking his arm. "I think you should sit down."

"What is the matter?" he asked with alarm.

Richard stood, facing the hearth. "There was a fire at sea. Dagr is feared dead."

Silence—the kind that is full of denial. Mark paced the floor.

"When?"

"A month ago. At the beginning of the journey," Brigida whispered. She was rocking the cradle Cook had brought down for Leilah.

"Ah!" Mark cried out. He sat down. He stood up. He contemplated his sister and scanned the faces of the two people whom Dagr had confessed he could not wait to see once more. Dagr, whom he had loved like a brother and friend for many years. Whom he had protected and would have died for. "Ah!" he said again, then allowed tears to flow.

"Is there any hope?" he asked, finally.

"We think not. The search was thorough," Richard said.

"Perhaps we should search again? Dagr has survived many things we thought impossible," Mark offered.

Richard shrugged his shoulders. "If you wish me to resume the search, I will."

But they all knew Richard would only have ended it because of overwhelming evidence to support his suspicion that Dagr had perished. After all, they had been friends since boyhood.

Brigida left to advise Cook about dinner. She could not imagine eating but engaging in the everyday routine seemed somehow to call up Dagr's presence.

Oh, my lord! her heart cried out. *Come back to me. I once came back to you.*

Why could she not feel him? Her mind had wandered a few times to ghastly images of the ship burning. Surely he had escaped? Surely, with all his warrior wits about him, he would have abandoned a ship in flames? But then, she knew him, he would have tried to save every soul on board.

"Come home to me, my love," she whispered as she had a bath drawn. Her bones ached with cold, no amount of fire could warm her. Mark had shown Richard and Arinn to their rooms and sent for their trunks left at the river's edge. She had not the strength to rejoice in their arrival. If she could shut her eyes and retrace the day to an earlier time, she could erase the last few hours and begin again. She could still be waiting for her beloveds to return and anticipate their foursome as it had once been. It was all so strange. She could barely make sense of any of it. Perhaps it was a dream.

She closed her eyes to remember the last time they'd all been together. Those cabin days had been a constant struggle for survival and yet... so full of everything she had needed. She recalled the love and irreverence of their nights. She allowed herself to remember Dagr's touch. His voice. His strength and his love. She did not realize that she was howling out loud, her agony echoing through the chateau, shaking its very timbers.

A calming hand smoothed her hair. A silvery voice sang a meditative chant. Brigida opened her eyes to find Arinn sitting beside her.

"Shhh, my darling! Let me help you out of this cold bath. You will catch your death sitting here any longer."

Brigida offered a wan smile. She allowed herself to be helped from the tub. She stood obediently as Arinn dried her. And still that chant of mysterious origin. A cup of warm tea was passed to her lips. It was sweet and pleasant. Her mind calmed with each garment added to her shivering body.

She observed Arinn curiously. She had bathed and brushed her waist long hair to a shimmering gold. Dressed in a simple but stunning gown; she was the picture of a goddess. Had they ever been apart? This woman standing before her felt as familiar as did her own skin, her own breath. If anything could heal her, Arinn's magic could. Her heart warmed with love. An excruciating love which spoke of so many trials, so many beautiful moments, so much exploration of the human spirit.

They touched hands to faces. At last.

Arinn brushed Brigida's hair and braided it into the familiar way she had of wearing it in days past. She tied it with a ribbon and helped Brigida step into an elegant gown of midnight blue with silver embroidery.

"Come, my love. You must eat. Even if just a little."

"I do not think I can."

"But you will. Just a little," Arinn insisted.

It felt good to have someone else make this decision. The numbness she felt encompassed every thought. Would she ever be able to feel different than this? She thought not. She imagined this melancholy would be her constant companion for years to come.

"Leilah?"

"With Richard in the library. She woke for a while but is back to sleep again. Cook fed her some porridge and that seemed to settle her."

"Dagr had a way of settling her to sleep," Brigida recalled.

"Did he? Will you tell me about it?"

Brigida brightened. "You will see, when he returns. It is the way he swaddles her. Oh, I know she is too big for swaddling now but he would wrap her in a blanket, tightly, and hold her close to kiss her face. He would croon the most ridiculous songs... songs about rabbits and birds and sheep in the fields. And she would save her biggest smiles for him. You will see."

"I imagine she fit so safely in his big hands, did she not my darling?"

"Oh yes! She did. He always knew just what to do with her. Not common I should say for a man, would you agree? Most men leave that to their wives."

"There was nothing common about Dagr. I agree."

"Is nothing common!" Brigida insisted.

"Is," Arinn corrected herself. "Ah here we are. Richard, will you please seat Brigida at the table? I will check on the meal."

Mark and Richard stood as they entered. Richard gave his arm to Brigida. She took it gratefully, noticing the cut of his suit, the ribbon in his hair. She had forgotten some of the nuances of his face. How fierce his countenance. How much fire he held in his body and soul.

"My lord, are you rested from your journey?"

"That I am, my lady. Your hospitality has been my respite."

He sat her down to the right of the head of the table. Arinn appeared and he sat her next to Brigida. Mark sat opposite. Richard sat opposite Arinn.

The empty chair at the head of the table tore at Brigida's soul. She looked to Mark who shook his head. Richard made the decision. He sat in Dagr's seat. Mark moved over to his left. So positioned, they ate their meal with few words spoken.

By now, the whole household had heard the news and spread it to the village. Richard had brought bottles of wine to the service quarters and ordered them all to drink. No one thought to question him when he had Cook lay out a platter of their best cheese and cold meat for their meal. Everyone understood this man would not be disobeyed. Their downtrodden hearts were grateful for his generosity in a time such as this. They mourned together the man who had brought prosperity to their village, who had ended the hunger of the most poor, and who had seen to the longevity of the estate. But what would be from now on?

CHAPTER 49

Aiden woke up in a sweat. He checked the clock. Two-thirty a.m.

He pressed his hands to his temples. His head pounded, and he realized he had been emoting in his sleep. His face was wet with tears. It was bizarre hearing of Dagr's death as he had in this journey to the past.

Getting up, he poured a glass of water and sat down in the chair by the fire. It had burned down to a few remaining embers. He stirred them and added a few pieces of wood to the hearth. He wondered if Sahara or Iona had joined him in his dream travels. Reticent to wake them if not; he decided to wait till morning to investigate further.

An overwhelming feeling of compassion burned in his heart for Iona. His fervent desire was to do the soul work required for Iona to reach multi-centurial self-forgiveness. He knew this was the perfect time and place for Sahara to do her womb work as well. Brigida's scars of miscarriage and the loss of a child at birth had carried forward to this lifetime. He knew that the guilt he felt in his soul, right now, for Dagr leaving his loved ones in such devastating pain had to be moved out as well.

It was also soul work to begin the healing of the collective womb space of every woman who had ever faced such deep loss.

It was work to heal the womb of the Great Mother, to find pathways for restoring what had been ravaged on the planet and within the Divine Feminine archetype. Aiden felt it all deeply in his soul. Healing of such magnitude would require the raising of sacred, magical energy, and there was no more powerful gathering than this for such work.

A cacophony of questions crowded his mind. His dreams came with as much information as he needed to continue his immediate soul growth. But it was frustrating as hell!

The fire kicked up and he stretched his legs out towards it. Fire sprites danced before his eyes. He tried to see into the past, but visions eluded him. He had never been good with divining anyway.

If sleep would not come he decided to write in his journal. Perhaps hot chocolate like Iona had made for him not long ago would soothe him? He rang room service but doubted anyone would answer at this time of night. Surprisingly, someone did, and soon enough, a delicious pot of creamy *chocolat chaud* arrived at his door—the perfect antidote to visioning into his past lives.

They were to meet in a few short hours before sunrise to perform their opening ceremony. The chocolate did the trick in soothing his emotions, and while he hardly had expected it, it offered a soporific effect. When he woke up, it was to a sweet kiss on his shoulder from Sahara. She had slipped into his bed, naked, warm and tucked against his back.

"Good morning darling," she purred.

He turned into her arms. "Mmm. This is the best surprise ever."

"Did you sleep well?"

"Umm, yes and no. I dreamed of Dagr." He waited to see if Sahara would add anything to this, not sure how to tell her if she hadn't. "I got up after that and had some hot chocolate. Room service never closes here, apparently. It did the trick, I slept soundly after that." He felt surprised by how awake he was only three hours later.

"Tell me the dream? We have a bit of time."

"Oh. Well, I thought you may have had the same recollections."

"No. I had a dreamless sleep. Was it something I would find upsetting? You did know we would be traveling back this week, did you not? Through dreams or regressions, or time travel?"

"I anticipated only Society business, to be honest."

"In this powerful energy, it will be easy to access other dimensions and our shadows. I think we should take advantage."

Aiden pulled her on top of him.

"I love your weight on me."

Sahara sank into him.

"So, what happened? Tell me."

Aiden kissed her neck. She still had the cloak of Brigida's energy clinging. He closed his eyes. "Dagr was proclaimed missing... or effectively, dead, by Richard and Arinn when they came to visit Bigida. It was heart wrenching."

Sahara kissed his eyes. "Ahhh," she sighed with sadness. "Don't tell me anymore, darling. Let's leave it for our evening together."

"What are you feeling?"

"A tightness in my chest. A feeling of tearing away, of grief. Brigida had faced such unbearable loss already, this would have been... well, I don't know, too much in her young life."

"In my dream I could feel her pain, and my guilt over leaving her, having already created the situation we were in by leaving Arinn in England with Richard."

"Darling, you keep slipping into identifying Dagr as yourself, and while you are his reincarnation, all new lives are sovereign."

"I understand. But the work is before me, to journey into the past and release the karmic cords. I need to feel the release in all my chakras and bodies, especially my heart and etheric body. I feel this stretching into my aura, and it will affect everyone I come into contact with."

"Especially us as lovers. We're meshing what's within our energetic bodies, our DNA, and will affect whomever we create with our bodies." She smiled at the surprise in his eyes.

"What are you saying?"

"I'm saying, my love, that when we leave here, after our healing work, I would like to make a baby with you!" She grinned. Aiden sat up on his elbow.

"I was going to talk to you about this when we got home. Actually, about adoption. But yes! Very much yes!" He hugged her so tight that she yelped.

"I am ready to face my scars and emotional wounds from lives past and this one. I had even pushed away the pain of my parent's death. I've never spoken of it, really. And yes, to adoption. Even if I do get pregnant, let's adopt. I want it all. I want to heal this womb space that has been weeping for a child for so long. I just had never admitted it to myself."

"Sahara, darling! You could not have given me a better gift to begin this week. I am very, very ready for children. Some free-range bohemian ones!"

They laughed, cried, and forgot what time it was until Iona slipped in through the secret passageway with a tray of coffee, croissants and soft-boiled eggs.

"And what is this? Have you forgotten we have all the world's problems to fix?"

They laughed, love flowing freely between them, all the centuries colliding.

"So, tell me," she insisted as they relished the first exquisite sips of coffee and tender, flaky pastry.

"We're talking babies," Sahara offered between bites on croissants on par with Holly's.

"You are? Now that makes my day." Iona kissed them both on the mouth, leaving a trail of electricity on their lips.

"You're a brat," Sahara laughed.

"Well, we already knew that," Iona smiled. "Tell me more about babies." She patted her belly affectionately.

Aiden mentioned his dream. They agreed the time was perfect

for journeying into their shadows and wounds. Sahara spoke of her parents, wrapped now in a blanket and Iona's arms. She cried as she talked of her ache for a little one and how it was tied to Brigida's incarnation. Her healing work had begun. This was the first step.

Aiden allowed a warm satisfaction to wrap his heart space. His life would transform dramatically after this week, he gathered. Life would take on a new flavor and ascend to new dimensions. He got out of bed and took the tray to the table.

"I think we'd better get ready. I'm getting in the shower," he said, as if he wasn't spectacularly naked.

It was Iona's first look at him fully, unabashedly nude. He was divine. His masculinity was arresting. His smile teasing. The sculpted muscle at his hips and abdomen drew her eye and lust. Her hand tightened around Sahara's. They shared a memory. Dagr stripping to meet their needs at the Oracle Wood cabin. A warrior on his knees. For a few sacred moments, they embraced the love that had bound them, and it was enough. Enough to carry them into the day's occult rituals.

CHAPTER 50

Everywhere he went, Richard saw evidence of Dagr.

It was in the way the villagers spoke of him; it was the sorrow in the faces of the tenant farmers. It was in the way the estate had been organized into prosperity. He saw Dagr's touch with the way the fields were fertilized, planted or left fallow to renew. Dagr had always been one for caring for the land. Mark had taken him through all the estate accounts; not a franc out of place. The yields from the crops would be handsome at harvest time.

"Are you able to continue on in the same fashion?" he asked Mark.

Mark looked out over the horizon. "I don't have his touch, or his exact way of commanding respect, but I have been with him for long enough over the years to run things fairly smoothly."

"Are you willing to stay on, and run this estate?"

"If I do not, where would Brigida go? She cannot return with you, can she now, my lord?"

"No. She cannot. She would be remembered and now that Arinn has taken over the herbalists work... well, it would be quite the conundrum how to organize who was who."

Richard remembered all too poignantly the day Dagr had asked him to look after his lady loves should anything happen to him. He winced as his heart broke all over again.

Damn you! He cursed. Through all the years they had fought together in battles waged by the King, he had felt this fear of losing Dagr to war. Of course, he had known there would also be dangers at sea. They had talked about all the ways the venture could run into trouble, who to watch for, who to avoid. But never had he expected Dagr to really ever be gone. The suddenness had him reeling with shock still. He seemed so invincible, so much the conqueror, never the conquered. Death was always sudden, even if one expected it.

Where did one go when they passed? Richard did not believe in what the priests called 'heaven'. He had a vague instinct about spirits and the continuum of life from Dagr's pagan concepts.

When the pain of it all was too much to bear, he wished to be wherever Dagr was now. He wished to smell the scent of forest in his hair and skin. He wished to see that flash of genuine smile; to watch those powerful hands as they saddled a horse. All those things he loved about Dagr, that he had fallen for years ago, now haunted him.

Realizing he had been lost in thought, Richard turned back to Mark.

"I do not think Arinn would go back with me anyway. And I would not ask her to. She belongs with Brigida."

They stood silent for a moment.

"You are in love with her," Mark observed, taking the liberty of frankness.

"I am," Richard admitted. "Before you judge my character too harshly, we had been sure Dagr would never relent about Arinn, until a few months ago, and a woman like her... well, she was silently wishing herself dead. I am not her first choice by any means, but somehow, we found solace in..."

"My lord, no need to go on." Mark felt the pain of the man before him. He knew about challenges of the heart, but he was, after all, a hired hand, not anyone that Richard owed any explanations to.

"Of course, pardon me, I digress."

"I am to be married," Mark stated flatly.

"Brigida mentioned. Congratulations. When is the date?"

"In a month's time."

"We shall still be here. Perhaps that will lift everyone's spirits?"

Mark's gaze remained on the ground where he was kicking some dirt around. "Dagr was planning a celebration, but I do not expect that now. I have enough saved for a simple wedding. Brigida will argue differently, but I think this is for the best." He cleared the pain in his throat.

"Ah, is that so? Dagr would want you to go on with the plans. There is plenty in the estate purse to afford it and I think this is exactly what we all need; to continue something Dagr was planning already. To honor his kindness."

They parted with a bow.

Richard wandered the olive grove. Fragrant and sunny, it reminded him of what he loved most about this part of France—the bone-warming heat. He loved the green of England with his whole heart, but the chill and the moisture could certainly make a man wish for warmer climes. The sound of bees and lavender breeze soothed him somewhat. No, he did not regret purchasing this estate. Here, at least, Brigida and Arinn could live in peace. He remembered the cottage Dagr had struggled to keep warm in the Oracle Wood and was glad for the opportunity to provide them with a softer life.

He closed his mind to the impossibility of leaving Arinn here, of his heart's dilemma. How did this happen? This strange reality of falling in love with not one but both of Dagr's women? What kind of life was this, where one would lose the comfort of their arms and their affection? What kind of cruelty took all of whom he cherished? Was this the punishment for the life he had lived? For the way he had treated women until one opened his heart?

He was stripped of all hope for the future, because there would be no partner in life who would understand him like Brigida or Arinn. Now he knew what he had once chided Dagr for—the love that blooms between souls breaking all convention. He had once felt scorn for such indulgence; or what he had considered foolishness. What Dagr had sought had been doomed to fail, he had known it from the start. But, had it not been the most wondrous time of his life? Surely, would all the rest of life be a torture he could not imagine himself enduring?

Despondent, he lay down in the grass and stared up at the sky. It occurred to him he had never done this, just taken moments to enjoy such simplicity. He recalled Dagr's smile, the way he had of connecting with all creatures and the land he lived on. Perhaps he would take this up? Adopt some of Dagr's pagan ways. It would keep him close. He allowed himself a stream of memories. The times they had sparred as boys; times during battle when Dagr had saved his life, his brute strength when he needed to call it up; his gentleness with a lover. Dagr had taught him many things by being true to his character. That perhaps had been his greatest gift; his fearless authenticity.

I will search again, he decided.

His mind refused the finality of Dagr's death. He would need to see him perished with his own eyes. Yes, he would tell them, Brigida and Arinn and Mark! The search was on again.

He sat up, hopeful. His heart raced with possibility. He would arrange it all tomorrow. He sprang up and walked quickly toward the house. Meandering through the orchard, and passing through the potager gate, he paused on the narrow pathway to the stillroom. A familiar aroma greeted him. Bread. He followed the scent.

The door to the stillroom was open to the light and air. He stooped to cross the threshold and was welcomed in. Witches! These women were by any description something one encountered in stories of ageless mystics who captured the hearts of men and dragged them to their underground caves. There they speared their hearts with an arrow of a love so exquisite, the captured never would desire to leave.

He sat down as he was bid and took the plate of bread and butter with gratitude. It was followed by a platter of cold-cured meat, and a flagon of wine. They did not speak much, except to accept Richard's compliment on the meal.

He watched as they continued their chores of crushing herbs for stuffing into pillows and steeping in the olive oil that would soon be filling the larder. They worked as one. As if time had not passed and they had never parted. As if no ill will had ever broken them apart. As if by the touch of hand to hand they shared ancient knowledge. Wise women practicing a sacred art—wild women who had stolen his imagination and devotion. He wished never to leave this room.

"Are you satisfied, my lord?" Brigida brushed his arm picking up his plate. She refilled his cup with wine.

Richard's skin responded to her touch. He bowed his head and thanked her.

"Now which one of you baked this? I swear it would be difficult to judge which one of you put their hand to it."

"Hannah was a gifted teacher," Arinn smiled. "We made it together, taking turns to knead, and following her exact receipt."

"Ah, so you seek to trick me!" he laughed, and they joined in.

"No trickery. Just something we both find pleasure in," Brigida put her arm around Arinn's waist. "Thank you, my lord, for taking such good care of my beloved. She has been telling me of her stay with you."

Richard felt his face grow warm. He wondered how much had been shared but could not tell by either of their expressions. "It was my honor, my lady."

Arinn returned to the pounding of herbs and seeds. Brigida took a moment to sit by Richard's side. His whole body ached to hold her.

"My lord, I know this may not be the right time to beg your favor, but my heart is too broken, and I am too anxious with worry to care about propriety. What will become of me, of us... she gestured toward Arinn... now that Dagr is no longer?"

Richard stared her down so fiercely she lowered her eyes. She was not sure if he was angry or grief stricken or both, but the gruffness of his voice stirred her memories and her eyes filled with tears. She had missed this rough, irreverent man.

"My lady! Do not for a moment think you are both not free to make your own decisions!" He stood to make his point. "You are free to choose your future, as Dagr would have wanted, and indeed, as I want. I will not be making any demands on either of you. This is your home, and I will be writing the deed as such."

Brigida fell into his arms. "You will not be separating us, my lord? Taking Arinn back home then?"

Richard steeled himself against the fire in his blood. Surely, he should not be feeling the desire that coursed his veins. Not now.

"My lady. As I live and breathe I vow never to separate you, nor to ask anything of you that would cause you pain or grief. No. The days of you living in fear or absent from each other are done. I give you my word."

They embraced him and stood on tiptoe to kiss his mouth. For a few seconds they experienced joy unlaced with sorrow. For a few moments they fell into the rawness of the moment. Soft, full mouths searching for his, receiving his fervent response.

He broke away. "Forgive me."

"For what, my lord?" Arinn asked, soothing his hand in hers.

"For taking this liberty," puzzled, Richard pulled away.

"Liberty? With women you love and who love you? My lord, you are confused by grief."

"Do we not dishonor Dagr? Do we not?" Richard grasped for words.

"By honoring what is already between us? By honoring your promise to Dagr to look to our welfare? What other man in this situation would offer us sovereignty and not take advantage of us? My lord, although our grief drowns us, we are right to love each other. What else do we have, if not this? How else will we survive our beloved's passing?" Arinn looked with tenderness into Richard's tear-clouded eyes.

"Please be plain with me, my lady, I beg you. I cannot bear to guess at the meaning behind your words. Do give me some hope." Richard sat down heavily.

"So be it then, my lord. Let me speak plainly. We have already discussed this and come to agreement. If you will agree as well, we choose to love you as we have loved you. It is our desire that you may, when your duties allow you to be in France, be our lord, in body and in soul."

Richard stood and scattered the chair behind him. He then bent on one knee before them. And as they had done once for Dagr, they blessed him as their beloved, their incantations foreign to his ears but familiar to his soul.

They sat to seal their vows with a shared tumbler of wine passed between them.

"How will it be, then, my lord?" Brigida asked. The prospect of living a secret life once more was too difficult to contemplate.

"Before we make any decisions," Richard explained, "I wanted to tell you I have decided to open the search for Dagr once more. Mark is right, Dagr has survived many things. Perhaps, he sought shelter on some remote island, or on some passing ship. We should not give up! Brigida where are you going?" Richard called after her.

"To have Cook make us a celebratory dinner," she yelled back. "Dagr may well be alive. Thank you, my lord!"

Richard and Arinn embraced.

"We must protect her for as long as we can, my lord." Arinn said. "She seems strong but underneath her suffering is deep. And I cannot bear it. I know you cannot as well. Do you really think Dagr may be alive?"

Richard kissed her face tenderly before taking his leave. "I do believe so. I had given up but have new hope."

Arinn knew then she would have to be the strength for them all, because this man would grasp at anything to believe.

Speak to me, my darling. Speak to me! Show me the way to you, wherever you are. Spare me this agony of guessing Arinn called upon the spirit of Dagr. She would summon the King of the Fey whatever the cost, but she had to know for sure; would he ever return? The heart of her heart, her soul's flame. She fell to weeping on the floor. Her grief felt like skin being ripped from bone. Like an eternal fire singeing her feet.

Why would she find such love if it was to be ripped from her so soon? Her mind raced back to those early days, those heady days of discovering Dagr's love and desire. That first kiss when he confessed his love for her. The way her body has responded. The pain in her heart twisted and turned. Why when he had just allowed their reunion? She tried to will that fateful letter away, to scratch that day from reality. She told herself it was a dream and that soon she would wake and hear his voice once more. But all that remained once her tears were spent was the desire to close her eyes and sleep. Sleep until she heard his footsteps again and if not, to sleep forever.

A determined hand swept the hair from her face. Her heart leapt. The smell of masculine skin. She held it to her cheek. She heard his voice from far away. *"Come, my love. No more tears. I am here."*

She knew better but allowed herself a second of pretense. She held it close. She made love to the possibility in her heart. But then, she had to let go of the dream. It was Richard's arms which held her.

CHAPTER 51

Today I see you
As the magic beneath your skin
As the shadows behind the moon
As the depths of the seven seas
I travel your heart
Whose landscape has bewitched me

Down a narrow, stone staircase, descending below the Earth, his fingers brushing an iron banister worn smooth by years of use, Aiden left the world above him. Each step he took led further into a gathering of spirits known and unknown. The Underworld was manifesting before him in layers of timelessness and altered consciousness. He had expected the Fey, but the others were a surprise. He felt them through his third eye before he saw them. They were a community of souls all intent on the advancement of humanity and the preservation of the planet they called Gaia, the Mother.

He entered the cavernous room lit by dozens of candles and fragranced by a familiar incense. It took a few moments for his eyes to adjust to the dim lighting. He was met at the door by Sahara and led to his place at a round table. He glanced around, greeting and being greeted silently. A large scroll lay at the center of the table. Each place setting held an inkwell and a fountain pen, a sizable rose quartz crystal and a white candle, while his and Iona's had also an athame, a clear quartz point, an exquisite silver chalice, and a bell.

Surrounding them, at the edges of the room, Pan, with a host of Fey of every description and skill. Spirit guides and beings representing Lemuria, Atlantis, Mount Shasta, Sirius and other star nations, as well. Among them was a luminous woman whose appearance shimmered between that of a maiden and a dolphin. She represented the oceans. An ancient Tree Crone represented the Standing Ones—grounding the gathering. The Aspen King and his Queen. Aiden fell into the warmth of his Lady Mother's eyes.

"Welcome my beloved son. Blessings on your duties here. May your ancestral wisdom serve you well, and your soul's call be answered"

Aiden received her message with love. She held a tender spot in his heart, and he would ever be the loyal son she had birthed once upon a time. Her blessing was the portal for the knowledge which would pour through the centuries as he needed it during these next two days.

Iona stood. A deep silence preceded her words. She bowed her head in reverence to the beings who had journeyed to assist them with their work. She held Aiden's attention and infused him with a telepathic intention of the heart.

"May we bring to our work an open heart, a clear soul and the wisdom of the Creatress."

He answered, *"May Her will be done and may we serve with honor, humility and truth."*

The whole room resounded with a hum of agreement.

Iona asked Aiden to stand.

"Let us greet him who has awoken to his sacred purpose. In times past, he was the keeper of the ancient ways, and we all know him as trustworthy in the work of an Earthbuilder. We are gathered here today to raise energy for the healing and support of Gaia, with his leadership and wisdom. He has been entrusted with the codes of transformation for the planet and humanity. We shall unlock these codes with the assistance of our most benevolent friends from the star nations."

She sat down while a murmur of greeting rang around the room. From the sound of their voices, rose one most clear in song and blessing. The Dolphin Maiden sang in the Language of Light. No time and all time passed. Waves upon waves of remembering fell upon them all; from when the Earth was first born and the intention for humanity's existence had been spoken into word. And when she was done, she led them into the sound that had begun it all. Aum. And they became it; the sound of creation. They went back to the One, no longer having bodies or thoughts, personalities or interpretations of what it meant to be human. And as effortlessly as it happened, they returned to their incarnated selves.

The scroll lay unfurled before Aiden. He picked up the pen before him, dipped it into the ink well and signed his name to the opening invocation in symbols that depicted his purpose.

How empowering, he thought, to sign one's name with such symbols; to be called daily by one's purpose! But to receive these symbols, one would have to pass through the veil, to awaken from life and enter the realms of all knowledge. He would discuss this with the others. He was anxious to bring this teaching back to the world. 'Remembering', he knew, was the birthright of every man and woman.

His symbols read 'Earthbuilder'; his chosen profession of home builder was a clue to his greater purpose. His given name of Aiden, meaning *little fire*, alluded to the fire of the eternal soul flame, and his reincarnation of the warrior Dagr, whose name meant a *new day*. His purpose as an Earthbuilder was to help open the portals for the new Earth. Five letters in his name, signaled the 5th dimension. Each clue to be uncovered as he gained consciousness in an awakened state of dreamtime.

He laid down his pen and passed the scroll to his left. Everyone would now sign with their purpose. There was no more powerful way to seal their intention. While the signing was proceeding, Iona cast a circle to contain their work. A witch fully awoken, a shaman and an alchemist, she called in the old language of the Wise Ones to the four directions—East, South, North and West, to the Green Man and Goddess. She invoked the powers of the four elements—Fire, Water, Earth and Air. She called in the ancestors and all powers aligned with the restoration of the planet.

Gaia, a living, breathing entity, had once been stripped of her power through the stripping away of woman's sovereignty. She had been raped and left powerless through centuries of fear. Fear of her intuition and her chaos. But she was ready to rise, and rise she would.

The room filled with the sound of ancestral drumming. A pipe with sacred herb was passed around the table. One inhale and connection was made with the natural world, Pan and the Fey. All were of one mind, one thought. The table top lowered before them aligning with the floor, their crystals and candles part of the central altar. Iona held her hand out to Aiden. He joined her and received the kiss of the Priestess. All fell away. They began a familiar dance.

The room and everyone in it began to sway to the heartbeat of the Earth. Where the drumming was coming from, Aiden could not say, but as the spiral dance continued, they became part of the Great Mother. One with her purpose, which had long been forgotten. Their ecstatic dance and the sound of their voices, as they followed the song of the light beings, vanished the walls around them. No longer in the confines of a room in the bowels of France, they were transported to the forever lands of Avalon. The others fell away into the mists of this magical and sacred place. All but Iona, and, emerging from the distance, Dagr.

257

"And so, your initiation, my love," Iona whispered.

"But how is it so?" Aiden wondered, feeling the curious experience of seeing his former self advancing towards him. The warrior he had once been, the towering, muscled knight, long, fair hair knotted into a waist long braid, unscarred, glowing with health and vitality stood before him. He, a tall, strong man himself, felt dwarfed beside this Viking-like apparition. Dagr smiled at him through striking blue eyes, one hand placed over Aiden's heart, the other over his own.

"Welcome."

This simple greeting was all that was needed between them as dimensions merged.

"I want to understand," Aiden found himself asking.

"What we think is life," Dagr offered as they walked, *"is as the ancient tribes of Earth speak. The Indigenous know we exist in a dream, an illusion. All time is an illusion. Consciousness is a hologram, a reality projected into linear time. Here, within this matrix, we come to learn the mystery of this hologram we call life lies within grids of sacred geometry and the processes of alchemy. All is brought to the physical plane for you to experience through electromagnetic frequency. As your frequency, so your experience, how and what you create on this plane. Consciousness is brought into an awareness of itself through your experience. Listen to the ancient tribes. This is the message you must bring back. Listen to the ancients. They remember."*

Aiden was then allowed to view the depth of the indigenous tribes suffering, entering into their hologram and merging with their wisdom.

"So, you see," Dagr continued, *"this wisdom was eradicated as ego outgrew its intended purpose and became a system which governs the Earth. But there is a way from this. And the way is simple. As the Divine Feminine rises, she brings back the memories, the stories. She is a bone-gatherer. All ancient wisdom is stored in the bones of the Earth, in human bones, within your DNA. It is within the crystals and rocks, within the trees and the shells. Help Her rise. Protect Her ways. Protect the tribes."*

Aiden sank to his knees as Dagr reached for the sword in its scabbard. His heart was full of tears and hope. Humbled, he lowered his head. The sound of steel on steel cascaded centuries of memories to his ears. For Dagr, the sword had been the symbol of war and oppression, but for Aiden it would become the symbol of change through the element of Air—where spirit met the mundane. For the Divine Masculine, this was a profound shift. Action through intellect, to marry with the creative emotions of the Divine Feminine.

258

"With this sword, I knight you into your purpose as the leader of the Earthbuilders, for the return of the Goddess and the restoration of Her sacred cauldron, the cosmic womb, along with all those who would work alongside of you. Do you accept the journey before you?"

"I accept."

"So mote it be. Your path lies before you. May you journey with strength, grace, humility, and wisdom."

Dagr touched the sword to Aiden's shoulder. He took Iona's hand and asked Aiden to stand. They continued on their walk through a labyrinth to seal the initiation. Iona led the way.

"Years ago," Dagr began, *"a brave young woman came to the Dark Pool with a clear heart. Her wish was to find healing for her beloved, and for this gift she was willing to pay any price. The gift was granted, with an existential life lesson attached.*

Love seeks to honor authenticity. It seeks freedom and joy. Love seeks to exist unconditionally. Love does not ask to be validated by another, it values itself. Love seeks only to walk along beside its beloved, taking joy in their existence.

When love becomes an addiction, it asks the beloved to change, to prove itself. It no longer exists as itself; it begins to feed on the beloved. Therefore, it is no longer Love. Love gives wings because it is free. Addiction, so often called love by humans, asks to be possessed, and to possess.

The journey of the clear, bright heart of my beloved Arinn, so long ago, has served humanity and Consciousness well. She willingly carried the collective pain of many generations who have confused addiction with love. Her wisdom now is the collective wisdom. She offers it freely to the next generation carried within her. Do you remember her, the beloved who once carried your child?"

Iona turned to Aiden.

Aiden, greatly perplexed by this last statement, took her hands in his. Her eyes filled with tears. They stood, the love they had once known searing their souls.

"When did you carry Dagr's child?" It was all so strange, hopping centuries, shifting lifetimes.

Iona lowered her eyes. "When you left her with Richard... she was with child."

Aiden's heart twisted with a horrible intuition. "What happened to the child?"

"She... she got rid of it." She broke down into a torrent of tears.

Between sobs, she uttered, "She could not, could not keep it. To have a child after what she had done to Brigida and to Dagr, to their union... she did not feel she deserved it."

"Did Richard know? Did he nurse her afterward?" Aiden's mind reeled with the pain Arinn and Iona had endured over the centuries, the unresolved karmic bonds.

"She told no one. She found the herbs to heal herself in Brigida's old garden. Forgive her! Forgive me!"

"All is forgiven, my darling. There is only love."

In that moment, within those simple yet profound words, something magical occurred.

Aiden and Dagr merged, centuries collapsed into the present moment, Iona and Arinn became one. A portal to the overlapping dimensions opened. Karmic cords were cut. Arinn and Iona were released from the spell of the Fey.

They saw each other again as they once had, in the field on Dagr's great horse, when Dagr's love had been fervent and hopeful and Arinn's awareness had been opened to his lust. Once more they stood heart to heart, Dagr with his hands on Arinn's face, staring deep into her eyes as they searched his for courage. He kissed her with the force of all his young years, in her eyes the man whom she could always trust. He waited for her response, the heat of her tongue on his, the moan that gave consent.

And then they were on the ground. He had waited so long. Years. She was yet a girl, and he a seasoned warrior, she had only just discovered the kiss of a woman and confessed her sexuality. And here he was pulling himself out of his shirt, Arinn's fingers digging into his flesh. Amid her cries of surprise at herself and her lips on his skin, tasting around the hard muscle of his belly, Dagr managed to remove her dress. She lay panting, wild-eyed, nipples pushing hard against her chemise. His hands slid beneath it. Her hips thrust up.

"Rip it!" she managed words between breaths.

She called out when he did, exposing her shamelessly in the sunlit meadow. For a few moments, he could do nothing but stare. Nipples peaked upon maiden breasts, her belly heaving as her face turned pink with shyness. He stared at the soft of her blond mound, wet with desire.

"Look at me. Do not turn away." He held her captive, hands above her head.

"I will not turn away, my lord," she promised.

No one heard her moans when he ravaged her neck, speaking the unspeakable into her ears. No one heard her when he sucked her nipples with a hungry mouth or kissed the tenderness of her breasts on his way down her body.

He ignored her pleas for mercy when he bit along her hip bones and slipped his lips toward her inner thighs. His long hair teased her skin and she grasped it madly when his hand parted her innocent lips. He was determined to look.

"Oh, my lord. Please!" she pleaded, half out of her mind.

She was helpless when he gripped her legs apart and lowered his face. She began to shake, tears rolled down her face. It was almost unbearable, this sensation of love that ripped her chest in two and had her pushing her pussy against him. She was not sure what overtook her. Eyes rolled back, hips in the air with Dagr's hands holding her secure, she let go as he lashed her with his tongue. It was more than she had ever experienced, a tremor in her body, a rise of heat up her spine, a gush of wet against his face. She knew nothing of what happened between women and men, and she certainly had no knowledge of Dagr's intent.

He wiped his mouth on his shoulder and raised a teasing eyebrow as she grew curious about the contours of his leathers. He kissed her tenderly but it was a ruse.

"I love you, my lady," he said seconds before he threw her onto her stomach. Kisses hot as fire landed on her back. Her hips lifted to meet his. He let her feel the weight of his body between bites of her skin. When he got to the round of her ass, he stopped. She tensed. She remained silent when he licked the length of her pussy from her clit to her ass with a wide, insistent tongue.

She was swollen and soaked. When he explored her opening with his fingers, softly teasing, gently filling her with one then two fingers, she remained quiet still. Observant. Listening to the sensations in her body. When she began to move and beg for hard thrusts, when she was drenching him while he finger fucked her, he knew she was ready.

He covered her once, kissed the back of her neck and whispered she was beautiful to his eyes. Wild and wicked, Arinn begged for his manhood. And he gave it, hard, unrelenting, the front of his thighs wet with her cum. He relished every thrust inside her, the sight of her swallowing him and the sound of her moans. She had not moved away on the first pain of her maidenhead taken, nor when his cock massaged her into another loud orgasm.

Later, she lay on top of him, listening to his heart beat. She would never forget the smell of his skin nor the feel of his lips in her hair.

And here they slept in the afternoon sun, history and the future rewritten.

They awoke, a little disoriented and stirred in each other's arms.

"Are you well, my lady?" he asked

"I am well, my lord," she answered.

The scent of lovemaking and passion still lingered on their skin and lips.

They smiled, then laughed. And their laughter filled the air perfumed with apples and the nectar of bees.

Aiden stood and offered his hand to Iona. He kissed her third eye. She kissed his.

All that had been broken between them was healed. All that had been forbidden had been explored. Peace was restored to the centuries of discord between them. They could carry on with the purpose of their days; Twin flames reunited under the skies of Avalon.

CHAPTER 52

"We must go back. The others will be waiting," Iona took Aiden's hand. "This evening will be a time for celebration. Tomorrow we do the work."

They sat down under an ancient oak and closed their eyes. When they opened them again, they were being summoned by the sound of a bell. Iona was calling the end of a meditation, where as one, all who were gathered in the room ceased their chanting.

Closing their circle as they had begun it, with the sound of Aum; those who were human remained in the space while the others returned to their dimensions.

Sahara passed crystal glassware with a refreshing cordial and dishes of dried apricots, chocolate truffles and roasted almonds. Grounding into the present, they agreed to meet again for their evening meal. Only Aiden, Iona and Sahara remained in the room.

"Come with me," Sahara beckoned.

They followed her to yet another underground room; a grotto lit with flaming torches and fragrant beeswax candles. Their footsteps echoed as they followed her to a dark pool. It was silent but for the sound of an underground brook which fed the pool with mineral waters.

"We are given this time to return to the past," Sahara whispered, "if you wish." She let her dress slip from her shoulders and stood naked before them. "We may return to any period of our previous life together. We must choose only one moment, the one we think will benefit our soul journey most, of one mind and one intention."

Iona stepped out of her gown.

Aiden fell under an age-old enchantment. He was drowned to Sahara's sensuality, the boldness of her nipples, the curve of her smile. She and Iona radiated with the ancient illumination of the Goddess, the call of her wisdom.

Iona's nakedness was the beauty of a million maidens who had held the secrets of the universe within their womb, her belly round with child. It was a potent elixir for a man who craved to immerse himself in the alchemy of woman. He closed his eyes. There was only one reason why he would refuse their journey. Holly. If he refused for himself he refused for them all. They went together or not at all.

Reaching into the quiet, intuitive knowing of his higher self, he asked for guidance. A man need follow his soul quest above all else, or he could not present to his beloved in his full truth. He cherished the trust that existed between himself and Holly. He also knew intimately the fear he felt of losing her. But she was not his to keep, nor should the idea of loss govern their love. One question remained. Would he, should Holly embark on a part of her soul path, stand in her way; let jealousy or ego stop her? Although he had slayed that dragon already, there were remnants of the urge to possess her. But no, he would not keep her bound to his insecurities.

He nodded his agreement. Virile, naked masculinity met the witch's elemental beauty; Iona, flame-haired, willowy, Fey featured and glowing; Sahara, a dark, petite creature, mystery lighting her eyes.

"What shall it be, beloveds?" Aiden stood at the edge and they followed suit. The Dark Pool stirred, awoken. The King of the Fey sat closer to the edge of his throne, intrigued. What would be? What would these humans learn on their journey to the Underworld?

One memory claimed their hearts. One moment could have changed the course of time, their past and their future. Of one intent, hands held fast and hearts beating wildly, they slipped beneath the waters.

"Just checking in. How's everything on the home front?" Richard put his phone down, not expecting an answer. It was high noon. He figured Holly would be busy at the bakery. Still, she had been on his mind all morning and he chose to ignore it no longer. To his surprise, a response came right away.

"All good here. Busy! How are you?"

"I'm well. Thank you. No problems with snow or bad weather? You know to call right away if you need anything, yes?"

"I do. Oh, you're just like Aiden. Worrying too much about us damsels!"

Richard scowled. Shit, he hadn't meant to come across as if she was incapable. *"Damn! And here I thought I was being all gentlemanly."* He added a cross-eyed smiley face.

"I'm teasing. The weather's good and I haven't had a minute to think about anything because it's brought in bus-loads of tourists.

I'm busier than a mosquito at a nudist colony!"

Richard laughed out loud. *"I'm getting the visual."*

Holly sent her favorite laughing emoji. She thought she had hidden her nervousness very well. After finding boys and men mostly less than interesting her whole life; she had had to meet the two who made her bashful and tingly all at the same time. *"Have you heard anything from those wayward lovers of ours?*

"Nothing. That's good news. Iona's not one to message much unless there's something urgent. So, I'm assuming it's business as usual for the group."

"I think so, too." Except, she was thinking, Aiden *was* one to message.

Richard felt something in that response. *"I don't mind coming out if you need anything. I can easily get a room at the hotel."*

Holly stared at the phone. *"Aren't you busy running the universe over there?"*

"Are you being obstreperous?"

"Yes, but no! I don't want you coming here for nothing." Holly opened the door to the back of the bakery and stood in the frigid winter air.

"Aren't you looking after the store and your place and Sahara's as well?"

"Yup."

"I'm going to come out for a couple. I can work from my laptop. I'll book a room and be out tomorrow morning."

Richard wondered if he was actually going insane. The woman had said she didn't need anything. She would have asked him to come if she wanted him to. Still, something in her message made him think otherwise.

Holly took a deep breath. Her fingers were numb from the cold. *"Don't be ridiculous,"* she typed, *"you can stay at Aiden's. Our house. He wouldn't want it any other way."*

Richard smiled. He understood women and understood she was being brave. He wanted to put her at ease, to make her feel safe. *"Is there anything I can bring you from Denver? Anything from Iona's store maybe? Ask while I'm being generous."*

Holly relaxed. She recognized his playfulness as the sanctuary he was offering. He was a gentleman through and through. It would be good to see him. She decided that she was being silly. *"Perhaps some of those soaps Iona sells. I could use some here at the bakery."*

"Done. See you tomorrow. I'll come grab keys from you around noon and check on Sahara's. And don't worry about dinner. We can go out when you're done working. Okay?"

"Oh, let's stay in. I'm so tired of people right now."

"Okay. But I'll bring the food. Please don't argue."

"K. See you tomorrow."

"Cheers."

CHAPTER 53

She knew he was there because she heard the shift in conversation when he came in. Holly was pretty sensitive to the energy of the patisserie. Right now, the women were staring him down. She giggled. Wiping her hands on her apron and giving one last check to the ovens, she went out to greet him.

He took the hands she held out and kissed her on both cheeks. He was, as always, the epitome of class and good looks. Holly showed him to a quiet table near the window and sat down with him. They exchanged bemused looks.

"Small towns are fishbowls," Holly offered.

"I see. How inconvenient," Richard laughed. "Is it always like this?"

"Well, I'm not exactly in a conventional relationship, you know."

"Right. So, want to give me the keys to Sahara's? I'll go check on things."

"Hold up one moment, cowboy. First coffee and something to eat. What will you have?"

Holly couldn't help but fall into the dark of Richard's enigmatic eyes.

"I'll have whatever you recommend," he answered. "I'll admit, it smells amazing in here!"

"Coffee coming right up," Holly got up and winked. "Trust me to guess how you like it?"

"I'm quite sure it'll be perfect," he smiled with a flash of perfect, white teeth.

She went away, and Richard did his best to calm himself. How, on God's green earth, could someone incarnate to so closely resemble Iona's past? How could he ever get used to seeing the image of Arinn in such surreal circumstances? Holly's long, blond hair caught in a braid brought a rush of emotions for his long-ago lover.

He placed his coat, scarf and driving gloves on the back of his chair and picked up the local paper. Running a hand over his three-day old beard, he almost knocked the coffee out of Holly's hand with his elbow.

"Christ! Sorry." He stood.

"Oh geez. Relax." She ran a hand over his shoulder. "Try this."

He took a sip and groaned. "God, that's good."

"Lost in thought?"

"Hmm? Oh yeah. You know me, a million things on my mind."

"See, that's why I feel bad I pulled you away from your work!"

"You didn't. I insisted, remember?"

Lilith came with roasted red pepper soup and a baguette piled with rocket, taleggio and prosciutto. A bowl of warmed olives accompanied.

Richard grinned at Lilith and thanked her.

She rolled her eyes at Holly and left.

"She thinks good-looking men aren't to be trusted," Holly explained. That's what she told me when I started out with Aiden." She blushed at calling attention to Richard's handsomeness.

"Ah," Richard nodded. "Good advice, perhaps. Does she approve of you and him now?"

"Oh yes. She's very loyal to me. I don't mind her little quirks. She just didn't understand how I could love him and Sahara; and then there was talk of Aiden and someone he was dating before. So, she was worried I'd be hurt."

Richard finished his coffee. He set his cup down. "Dianne, right?"

Holly sat down and removed her apron. "Dianne, yes. Aiden's told you about her? Sahara and I have met her. She's beautiful. She comes in now and then and we've become friends. I don't see any reason why we shouldn't. She's lovely, and I hear she's seeing someone now."

"Oh?" Richard bit into the baguette.

"Funny thing, when I see her it reminds me of you because she has jet-black hair like yours. She's French-Canadian. I guess that's where she gets it."

Richard looked up. "French-Canadian? Here in Riverbend? I wonder what brought her here. Interesting how we get around, isn't it?"

"I know! Look at me. From the Midwest, via France. One never knows where they'll end up. It's just a matter of being open to where life takes us."

"Indeed," Richard sat back and observed Holly with an intense stare. She squirmed in her seat and looked down.

"You're staring," she said.

"I'm sorry," Richard said with a start. "Thinking. Forgive me, I'm being rude."

"Do I make you go back in time? Is that it? Because I've made my peace with all that. I understand that seeing me will bring up memories now and again for all of you. I want you to know I feel very secure in my love with Aiden and Sahara. I may not know the purpose of it all... yet, but... you know, Richard, I'm stronger than I look," Holly whispered, leaning in. They were definitely being watched now, curious eyes glued to her back.

"Oh darling, truly, please forgive me!" Richard said, remorsefully. He squeezed her hand. "Listen, before I met Iona, my life was quite mundane. I did my work, things I loved... a privileged life, I'll admit, but fairly normal. I've done my best to acclimatize to the... erm, unusual events, let's say, that meeting all of you has presented; but I'm still caught unawares by my feelings now and again." He smiled a consolatory smile.

Holly, undone by his honesty and ineffable charm, looked him straight in the eye. It was Richard's blood that rushed hot to his face. She was not trying to charm him, but the innocence and integrity in her clear blue eyes, the purse of determined lips and the heat of her hands as she gripped his, made his pirate heart skip a beat.

"Richard, please know we are all in this together, and I trust everything will be as it should be. I don't know what you think of me, but let me tell you that I am deeply, deeply committed to this crazy life we have concocted! I may look innocent, but I'm learning quickly what it means to love Aiden and Sahara. And I do love you and Iona with my whole heart. I had never imagined I'd have such relationships, or friendships, and I'm not about to give any of it up. And if you look at me and see Arinn, and emotions or memories come up, I'm not going to be upset with you."

Richard decided to leave certain things unsaid. He did indeed have strong recollections of Arinn, but that was not all. He had not been able, from the beginning, to erase his fondness for Holly herself and he knew, beyond a shadow of a doubt, she had spoken of him to Aiden. Richard was no magician, but he did know when a woman felt something when she met him. And knowing her and Aiden's relationship, she would have revealed those feelings. He wasn't about to do anything about it. But he felt bad for being here and putting Holly in this situation where she knew that he knew. It was all over her face.

He stood. "I'll go check on Sahara's. Perhaps, after all, it will be less trouble if I do check in at the hotel."

Holly handed him his gloves and scarf. "I'll never forgive you if you do, Richard. I want us to be real and honest. Aiden would agree.

I'm looking forward to the dinner you promised to make me. Here's the keys you'll need."

She placed a warm kiss on his cheek and grinned. He grinned back. She knew why Sahara had not been able to resist him. It was so much more than his looks or the way he carried himself. It was that ancientness she could not tap into yet. If she was jealous of anything ever, it was that she had not been part of their magical world from the start.

CHAPTER 54

"You carry away with you a reflection of me, a part of me. I dreamed you; I wished for your existence. You will always be a part of my life. If I love you, it must be because we shared, at some moment, the same imaginings, the same madness."
~ Anais Nin

If a cabin could smell of a woman, this one did. Richard stepped through the door to Sahara's. There was hint of warmth from the backup heaters. The fireplace was prepared for the next fire. Appreciating the lingering aroma of previous fires, Richard recollected the days they had all spent here waiting out a winter storm. Those had been the days which had bound them together in friendship.

He ran the taps to make sure nothing had frozen and looked for Willow. She must have taken him to Aiden's because the cat, he was sure, would have greeted him on entry. He sent a quick message to Holly to ask. Next, he cleared the front porch of snow and ice, and made a pathway to the car.

He stood with his hands resting on the shovel handle. This was an exceptional property—Sahara's energy was stamped all over the land. The undulating hills to the larger mountains, the forest and fields, the sound of the aspens—peaceful and enchanted. There was privacy for miles and essence of the Fey. He knew it all had to do with how Aiden and Sahara treated the land and the plans they had for the future. Aiden had told him of Sahara's plan for a garden and chickens; their intention to grow things communally for their tables and the café.

A small wind turbine and solar panels would, not only, create power for the cabin but the excess would feed back into the grid. Self-sustainability was important to Sahara and Aiden, and Holly was happy to learn from the two of them.

Aiden had convinced him to also take advantage of the high hilltop position of his own new house. Plans were underway for wind and solar options. Sahara was drawing up ideas for an extensive potager for Iona. They were calling on the memories of a garden they had both cherished once. And he was determined to give his beloved every pleasure. He smiled thinking of Iona and their little one in the garden sometime in the future. His heart swelled with love and excitement for the years ahead.

The sound of his phone jarred him from daydreaming. Holly confirmed Willow was at Aiden's with the dog, and to tell him snow was on its way. *"Best get to our place before Sahara's driveway gets blown over,"* she said.

"Drive safe," he cautioned.

He locked up. He was looking forward to a relaxed evening and cooking dinner for Holly. Usually, his mind was churning with business details, but tonight he promised himself he would put it all aside and dedicate the time to deepening his friendship with her. He sent a few messages to the gallery and his personal assistant while the car warmed up, then wound his way around the long drive to Aiden's.

Maybe he should write to Aiden to tell him he was here and that all was fine at Sahara's. Yes, he'd do that.

"How are you? Everything's fine here, I'm up to your place for a couple of days. Just checked on Sahara's to give Holly a break. Making her dinner. Offered to take her out but she's had enough of people. Shoot me a message if you want."

He put his phone in his pocket and got out of the car, calling out to Ulfred who was barking and pawing the door. He felt a satisfying comfort in his bones looking at Aiden's home. It was like a safe, dark cave where one could rest their bones and feel supported in their soul. Richard was not much for escaping to places for solace because he felt very much at home in his own skin, but if he were to, he would come here.

Ulfred greeted him with a short howl then bounded around the car while Richard unloaded his bag and the food. It was early in the afternoon, but he decided on a glass of the scotch he had brought along. He made a roaring fire then sat down to enjoy his drink. The sky was darkening quickly with the snow, so he lit some candles just in case of a power out.

The bookcase pulled him in. He liked the idea of living with books. There was something very grounding about it; to be surrounded by knowledge. Books and libraries were one of his passions and he considered funding libraries an investment in humanity. Ulfred's barking outside and the sound of a car surprised him. Holly walked through the door.

"Do you have the appies ready?" she joked. "What?" Richard took her coat. He looked at his watch. "Here already! And no."

Holly laughed. "Don't worry, I brought stuff from the café. I was told to go home by Francois and Lilith. The snow scared customers away and they didn't want me driving in it. So here I am!"

"I see. That's just fine. Just makes for a longer, relaxed evening. By the way, I messaged Aiden to tell him I'm here."

"Well that just blows our secret rendezvous, doesn't it?" She broke into peals of laughter.

"Very funny, little lady."

"Just give me a few minutes to change. Pour me some of that and I'll come down to make us a tray of nibbles to cozy up with by the fire." She ran up the stairs, leaving Richard staring after her. She was a lot more relaxed than she had ever been with him and he was glad of it. It meant she trusted him.

"I didn't know you drank scotch," he said, half to himself.

"I heard that! Aiden got me into it. What's for dinner anyway?"

"I brought some tenderloin to wrap in puff pastry. Glazed parsnips and carrots. Good for a winter night?"

"Oh God, I love that. As if you know how to make beef Wellington!"

Holly came down in a pair of torn jeans and a navy cardigan, top buttons undone to an almost respectable place. Both hugged her curves with something of a vengeance. She had brushed her hair out and tied it in a loose pony at the base of her neck.

Richard smiled and handed her a drink. "Well, many years of bachelorhood can make one quite proficient in the kitchen."

"I'll just sit for a bit by the fire if you don't mind, then I'll put our tray together."

"I'll make it, we have plenty of time. Sit."

He threw another log on the fire and joined her on the sofa.

"Cheers!" He leaned over for a toast.

"Cheers!" Holly took a long sip. "Mmm. Fire in my belly."

Richard pressed his lips together, savoring the whisky. "One of the good things about winter, you know?" He noticed Holly staring at his tattoos.

"Tell me about that," she said, pointing at the one that read *Dagr*. "Must have been so bizarre finding out about the person behind it; meeting Aiden?"

"It was. One of those things that serendipitously arrives in life and that you have no inkling of where it will lead you. Each of my tattoos were chosen by instinct."

"I'm thinking of getting one myself. I'm the only one out of the five of us who doesn't have one. Maybe I should join the clan?"

Richard peered over his glass. "Really? What of, pray tell? And you are part of the clan. Is there any question anymore that the five of us are meant to have met?"

"Nooo, no question anymore, I suppose. I just keep feeling I'm the odd woman out, as it were."

"Ridiculous."

Richard refilled Holly's glass. "Don't get drunk. Apparently, I will answer for anything that happens to you."

"Now that's ridiculous! Did those two put you up to being responsible for me? Sahara even said I'm not to go out into the woods alone. I feel like Little Red Riding Hood for the love of God. I may meet the big bad wolf," Holly laughed.

Richard's eyes flashed. The big bad wolf was sitting in her house. Dark and dangerous, should he choose to be. This wolf was keeping his cards close to his heart. Holly blushed.

Richard stretched his legs out to the fire. He took a measured sip of his drink. A gentleman, he chose not to comment on her last statement.

"Tell me about your tattoo idea," he drawled.

CHAPTER 55

History Re-written

In the quiet of the early morning, thick fog hanging on ancient oaks and the path ahead, three lovers wound their way to their favorite sunrise spot.

Dagr looked back to where Brigida was straggling along. She was singing in that way she had since losing her voice, a few syllables of broken sound here and there. The plaintive resonance broke his heart. He would gladly trade places with her, take her affliction away. Frustrated, when she slipped into the fog and out of sight, he called out.

"Come along my lady!"

He loved her unrestrained joy, the way she had of making them all see the brighter side of life, no matter what was happening or how much she longed to speak to them as before.

Arinn took his hand. "This is my favorite part of the day, my lord. When we leave our troubles behind and set off to watch the sunrise. There is so much hope in such a simple act. One day, perhaps, we will live freely again?" After a few moments of silence, she broached a subject she had been reticent to discuss. "Darling, I have decided on something."

"Hmm? You have?" Dagr stopped to give Brigida a chance to catch up.

"Yes. I have decided to go to the Dark Pool."

Dagr turned sharply. "For what?"

Arinn, surprised by his sudden ire, straightened her spine in determination.

"For to seek healing for our beloved, of course!"

"To go to the Dark Pool is to seek a magic you have no knowledge of," Dagr hissed. "It is dangerous to play with the Fey. There is no healing or favor given without a price."

"I do not believe you! The Fey would not ask me, their ally, to pay a price too high."

Dagr took her by the chin, angry and gruff. "Promise me you will not, my lady. I forbid it. You clearly do not understand how the Fey do their work and how convincing they can be to entrap one into something they will later regret."

Arinn pulled away. "You dare to forbid me, my lord? I think we have established once before that I am willfully sovereign. I shall make up my own mind!"

Brigida came within earshot and observed them with curiosity. She wondered about the scowl on Dagr's face, instantly recognizing Arinn's stubborn stance.

Dagr checked himself and kissed Brigida's cheek as she passed.

He hung behind the two women, now arm in arm, Arinn humming sweetly. They approached the edge of the cliff where they would break their fast. He spread his cloak for them to sit on and started a small fire. Brigida laid out the bread and the bits of cold, roast rabbit. Arinn added herbs and roots to the pot in which they would brew their tea. He wanted to make peace with Arinn, to tell her he did value her judgement, and that his anxiety about it all was purely because he had experience with the way of the Fey.

Friends or not, they did not concern themselves with human problems and did as they felt best for the evolution of the planet. Besides, they were especially potent now, having had to hide away from human eyes since the Druids had been largely eradicated. Being cast away had only made them more determined and an energy to approach respectfully—eyes wide open.

He sat with his arms around his knees, his hair loose around his shoulders, muscular body ripped to the bone. There was nothing to get fat on when living in the woods and plenty of work to keep him toned. He knew the hunger pangs he had felt of late would have been felt by his lovers too; their once supple figures were now as toned and lean as his. He knew also that when the sun came out and shone high over the rocks on which they perched, they would all strip their clothes and let the heat warm their bones. Oh how he longed for the fields they had once roamed, the long grass and the orchards that had fed them. He would kill for a dinner of eggs and roasted potatoes. As skilled as they all were at foraging, they missed the bounty of the gardens and barn yard. They had to make a change. He did not want this for his beloveds, this scratching for a meager existence.

He took the cup of brew Arinn offered. She pressed her lips to his.

"Look, how beautiful the sun in the sky! Another hour and it will be high enough to truly warm us."

Dagr smiled. "Yes, my lady."

"Are you angry with me?"

"Not angry, worried your impulsiveness may lead you down a regrettable path."

"Do you trust me?"

"It is not a matter of trust. You know that. I simply want you to know all is not always as it appears in the world of Fey."

Brigida sat beside them. She shrugged her shoulders. It was her way of asking what was happening.

Arinn leaned against the rock face behind her and motioned Brigida to lay in her arms. She was sorry she had said anything to Dagr. She wished she had kept it to herself. Now she would have to tell Brigida and she would have two of them against it. She kissed Brigida's head.

"Darling, Dagr disagrees with me, and you may also, but it is the only way, I believe. I wish to go to the Dark Pool to ask healing for you from the Fey."

Brigida shook her head vehemently. "No..." she mouthed. "No!" She took hold of Dagr's hand, seeking solidarity.

"But darling!" Arinn protested. "How else will we heal you? We have tried every herb, every spell!"

Brigida pulled on Dagr's sleeve.

"I agree, my lady," he replied to her anxiety. "I want more than anything to hear you speak, but this idea is fraught with danger. The Fey will ask for something in return, and under their enchantment, Arinn will agree to anything. Therefore, I cannot allow it."

It would be easy to want to please him, but in her heart, Arinn had already decided.

Nothing more was said of it that day. They lay naked in the sun, letting it brown their skin. Dagr had often said the sun was, if used wisely, a tonic for the body. As it rose higher and higher in the sky, it witnessed the eroticism of their love. Alone with the elements, they could explore and seek pleasure. It was shameless and bold.

The whole universe rejoiced in their lust, after all, the universe itself was ecstatic by nature.

In time, they packed their small picnic and began the trek down the escarpment, deep into the woods and back to the cabin for their evening meal. Their routine was always the same. Dagr would bring a rabbit or sometimes a partridge for their table. Brigida would bake some hard, unleavened bread while Arinn prepared any greens or roots available. Mushrooms, wild herbs and berries, when in season, would flavor their stew.

Any supplies brought by Richard were rationed and divided with care. Sometimes they had preserves, sometimes salt and honey, but most often, it was a bag of cabbages, onions and apples. Any grease left from roasting game was kept, as preciously as gold, to flavor their often-bland diet. Still, they made each meal with love asking the spirits to bless their health. Together, they made the best of what had turned into a life of living on the bare essentials.

Arinn appreciated the way Dagr had become part of their meal-making. He kept them alive with what he hunted, but he also helped them by setting the table, pouring their tea, and always, serving his lovers first. Often, he left the smallest portion for himself though they protested vehemently.

Today, they waited for his return from the hunt. He had taught himself to set traps near rabbit burrows. There were days when he returned empty-handed. On those days, they boiled the bones from the night before for a gray, murky soup. Every part of the rabbit was used, the organs being the most nourishing. Intestines were washed and saved for use as binding. Fur was stuffed into shoes or sewn into slippers. Nothing was wasted.

Brigida looked to the woods from where Dagr would surely arrive shortly. The sun was soon to set and dark would fall quickly in the thick of the trees. She stirred the broth they had been boiling for several hours. It was fragrant with wild onions she had found on the edges of the stream.

When dark fell, she and Arinn sat by the hearth and stared into the flames.

"He must be bringing us something quite wonderful, if it is taking this long," Arinn said.

Brigida nodded but kept her eyes to her work.

"Perhaps a buck, or a wild boar has delayed his return," Arinn continued. She regretted it as soon as she said it... a wild boar could have speared Dagr and left him dead and gored. "Oh, but he is fine!" she insisted at Brigida's alarmed look. "He always comes back."

And in that moment, a loud thump alerted their attention. Dagr burst through the door, his clothes covered with blood.

They jumped from their seats.

"Are you hurt my lord?" Arinn ran to his side and lifted his shirt to see from where he was bleeding. But he had not a scratch on his body, though he stank from the sweet, coagulated blood drenching his sleeves.

He laughed. "Not hurt my darlings! But look what I have brought for you." He pointed to the young boar crumpled on the porch steps.

"Oh! We were so worried, my lord. So very worried!"

But Dagr only smiled and requested a pot of water to be boiled so he could wash himself. "I smell too badly to be let into the house," he said.

They rushed around heating the water and pouring him a cup of soup while he gutted the boar and prepared a sturdy pole to hang it on. They would have to work hard and fast to dress and roast the pig before flies, maggots and wolves arrived to take their share. With a long night ahead of tending the fire, dizzy with joy their lord had not been lost to them, Arinn and Brigida did not notice the secret behind his eyes.

They took turns napping and turning the wild pig on the spit for the next twelve hours. By daybreak, they were feasting on crisp, fatty belly and the choicest pieces of meat. The nights were cold enough now, that roasted meat would keep for a few days. Perhaps Richard would happen by to share in their good fortune, they wished out loud. Warm, full stomachs made for much merriment and dancing around the fire.

Finally, Dagr fell into bed with Arinn and Brigida curled up around him. They barely fit in the alcove all together, but he wanted them close. They fretted when he shivered with cold... perhaps the hunt had worn him out and he was taking ill? But sleep took over them eventually, full and happy in his arms while Dagr lay awake, staring at the ceiling.

He could not help but struggle to recall the details of the journey he had been on the day before. Under the guise of the hunt, he had ridden to the only place where he could protect Arinn from falling under the spell of the Fey. The Dark Pool had received him as if it had known he was coming. He was to be escorted to the Underworld by his old, trusted friend, Pan.

"You know you cannot interfere with Arinn's quest?" Pan had cautioned when Dagr informed him of his reasons for being there. "You can only petition for yourself."

"I know," Dagr had replied. They hurried along the path.

"Leave your horse here," Pan pointed to a Rowan tree. The Dark Pool was already stirring, the Fey in a circle around it, shimmering lights lighting a stairway beneath the water Dagr had never seen before. When beckoned by a water sprite he left his clothes at the edge of the pool and ventured to the top step. The next second, he was somewhere else, in a field of wild flowers and a path leading into the distance.

Pan had left him somewhere along the way. His clothes now were of the finest cut and fit, as much befitting a lord as he could imagine. He ran his hands over the sleeve of his shirt, stark white and embroidered with gold thread, trimmed with black at the wrist. Ah, he had, after all, missed the finer things in life. But enough of reminiscing, the Fey were playing their flutes and it was time for him to meet with their King.

Everything was happening in the split of a second. Before he knew it, he was at the gate to the Great Hall, and the cacophony of the waiting Fey was resounding. But when he opened the gate, silence fell, and he stood before a thousand curious eyes.

Not unaccustomed to being received by the King, Dagr, nonetheless, felt a sense of anxiety. He was coming to ask for a favor and though he was always well received, he knew instinctively, this time, he would be interfering with the King's business, should Arinn come to call. And she would. He was sure of it. He could not stop her though he wished to. He did not know when she would go, and that made him furious. She had her own magic, she could slip away at any time. So, all that was left for him was to come beforehand and try to entice the King into an exchange of his own.

Kneeling on one knee before the throne, he noticed the hunting outfit of the King, his crown of stag horns and the bow and arrow at his feet. Dagr was familiar enough with the Fey to know this signaled some part of the day's events. The Fey were always three steps ahead of humans. The King had been waiting for him with purpose and intent.

"What favor do you seek Dagr? Ask quickly! I am impatient to take you on the hunt. Did you not leave your fair maidens on the excuse of providing for your table?" Before Dagr could answer, the King answered for him. "You did, and we shall be off as soon as you make your request. What shall it be?" he thundered.

Dagr stood. "My request, my lord, is to offer myself in the stead of my lady, Arinn. She has a favor to ask and it comes from the heart. She only wishes to find healing for our lady love, Brigida. May I bear the price for her request, should she come to you?"

"You may not!" the King rose to his full height. He stood twice as tall as Dagr. He shook his crown and the roomful of Fey lowered their eyes in reverence. Dagr stood his ground. This fearsome creature was his ally. They were not enemies, this was a friendly if dangerous meeting. Still, Dagr understood he must tread respectfully.

"If I may not, then what can I do to protect her?"

"Ah, but you cannot protect her from the path she chooses!"

"There is something we can arrange. I have not yet used all the favors allotted me."

The King eyed him with all seriousness. "You have been a trusted ally, this is true and I will honor your friendship. Come, let us hunt. We will discuss along the way."

And then he was off, with Dagr at his heels. They stopped some time later at the edge of a wood. The King handed Dagr the bow and arrow.

"What will you give for the protection you seek? Did you once not follow a code of chivalry, of bravery, courtesy and honor? Would you not have given your life for some worthy cause?" The King laughed out loud. "Only humans would seek honor through killing." He shook his head. "So, what is it you will offer?"

So... he would have to choose his own price. Was that it?

Dagr lifted his head to the easterly wind. He sought wisdom. But in the end, he would give anything to protect his beloveds, and he knew that the King knew it also.

"What I wish, is whatever price Arinn agrees to, whatever lesson you set before her, may it not last a lifetime. She is tender and young, and I cannot bear to have her suffer for the rest of her days. I will give anything. Anything."

The King's eyes glittered. "I see your love is pure and I know hers to be. What we ask, is that she bring her wisdom to the world above, but wisdom is not knowledge, wisdom is earned, not learned. And so, she will, according to the laws of the Fey, and the favor you redeem now, earn her wisdom until the time comes for us to collect on your offering. Then and only then, will she have the opportunity to carry this wisdom onwards to future generations and future lifetimes. Should you choose to meet again in another century, you will all be awoken to the full release of the spell, through all dimensions. Do you agree?"

"What am I agreeing to?" Dagr asked, puzzled.

"Anything, as you said," the King replied.

Dagr paled but kept his word. "Anything."

The King softened. "You cannot see all that can be, with your human eyes. You see only what is before you, cursing what was before and fearing what is ahead of you. All shall be well, even when it is not. What will be will be, even when it is not. The tapestry of time and space continues, and what is born must die but will be born again."

He went on, speaking in riddles and rhymes, weaving a story

which left Dagr accepting his role in the workings of consciousness. As magic would have it, he forgot the conversation but remembered one was had. Life would go on. He had done the right thing, he was sure of it.

He found himself at the edge of the Dark Pool, the fresh carcass of a young boar lying beside him. Hoisting it up on his horse, blood staining his shirt sleeves and chest, he rode home to his beloveds.

CHAPTER 56

"I was born in the middle of a storm
You won't find me under the sun
My feet are chaos
I belong to the wild things."
~ Evy Michaels

Aiden ran to his suite. Somewhere along the way of their time travel, he had parted company with Sahara and Iona. He felt the nausea of fear pounding in his chest. They had crossed the dimensions of time to break a spell and find healing for them all. He knew time existed only in the third dimension; that all lifetimes existed simultaneously; and portals could be traversed to exist in any of those lifetimes. They had entered the same portal on entry and exit. So where was Sahara and Iona? He felt absolutely sick when he thought of Richard and Holly.

He was not a man to crumble under pressure, but his hands shook when he attempted to use the key to his door. The silence of his rooms told him they weren't there. He pushed through the secret passageway to Iona's bedroom. Empty.

Where are you? He contemplated going back in time but knew this was the last resort, and one which could end with all of them not returning.

All he could do was return to the grotto and hope.

———— ❈ ————

A gentle knock on the spare room door woke Richard from a heavy sleep.

"Come in!" He sat up in bed and reached for a t-shirt. The clock read five a.m. Holly poked her head through the door.

"Hey. Sooo sorry! Keep sleeping. I've got to go to the bakery for an hour or so. I'll be back for breakfast."

Richard got out of bed. "I'll drive you."

"No, no! Get back in there. I'll be back at eight at the latest."

Richard looked doubtful. "You'll get caught up in work. I thought you had the day off?"

"I do. But Francois called and has a problem with one of the ovens and I need to be there. We may have to improvise today. Anyway, don't worry, as soon as I have this worked out, I'll be back with fresh goodies."

A knock on the front door surprised them both.

"Are you expecting someone?" Richard got back out of bed.

"I have no idea who it could be!"

"Okay if I answer it?"

"Yes, of course. Thank you." Holly followed behind him.

The door opened to a rather frazzled Francois. They ushered him in from the cold.

"Are you ok? I was just on my way in." Holly brushed the snow from Francois' coat. She introduced Richard.

"Everything is fine, I just felt so bad calling you out in bad weather, I thought I'd come get you. I'll bring you back."

"Did you leave the other oven on?" Holly asked with some alarm and annoyed she was being shuttled around. Could no one trust she could drive herself anywhere?

Francois shuffled his feet. "Lilith is there," he said, his accent elongating certain vowels.

"Lilith? What... oh!" Realization dawned. "I see." Holly pulled her coat on.

"We were going to tell you soon." Francois shrugged his shoulders. "Are you happy? You're not upset about us?"

"I am happy! I was wondering what was taking you two so long."

Francois gawked past Holly at the painting of the French chateau.

"What is that?" he pointed, pushing through to take a closer look.

Was everyone going mad today? Holly wondered. The Francois she knew would never have brushed past her like that.

"That's a painting Richard bought for Aiden in France. Why?" She looked at Richard. He too was looking strangely unsettled.

Francois turned to her. "That's a painting of my ancestral home."

"What? Are you sure?"

Francois reached for his wallet. "Absolutely." He pulled out a business card and showed it to Holly.

"See? The identical chateau. It's an inn now. My mother runs the business. That's how I got my start with baking, following my grandmere around the kitchen. It's been in my family since the fifteenth century. We have a very beautiful tapestry in the main reception room

284

with our family tree, beginning with the Vicomte Montagne. There are a few legends in the village about how to do you say, *les sorcierres...* witches in our family!" He scratched his head. "I don't believe it. What a coincidence."

"I have to sit down," Holly leaned against the sofa.

"What's wrong?" Francois asked.

"The answer to that," Richard explained, "is quite complicated, but the short of it is, François, you are the descendent of who Aiden and Sahara once were."

"Pardon?"

"Do you believe in past lives?"

"Yes. My grand-mere talked about it. My parents said it was nonsense, but I believed it. But explain to me, please, this thing about Aiden and Sahara? They are related to me?"

"Not exactly related. They are the reincarnation of your Vicomte Montagne and his wife, Brigitte. They remember that lifetime and could tell you quite a bit about where the family tree began. I recently made an inquiry with a genealogist about the descendants of their daughter, Leilah."

"Did you know about this, Richard? About Francois?" Holly asked, incredulous.

Richard offered a wan smile. "Yes, my dear. I only just received the information and was waiting for the others to come back to tell you. I did send a message to Aiden. He couldn't get into it before they went away, just not enough time. And he wanted us all to be together to dig deeper."

She nodded. "I understand." She got her coat. "Let's go," she gathered Francois.

Francois took another look at the painting. *"Incroyable,"* he muttered and walked out to the car.

Richard wrapped a scarf around Holly's neck. "Are you upset with me? For not saying anything before? Aiden thought it best if he told you. I haven't had a chance to give him all the details yet, anyway."

"I'm very surprised, or maybe I should say shocked, but no, not upset," she replied. "Can you believe the synchronicity though? About Francois I mean?"

Richard's deep timber laugh resonated through her bones. "Nothing surprises me anymore about the five of us." He took her hands in his. "Where are your gloves? It's freezing out there."

"In my bag. I've got to go." She walked out the door, cheeks flaming.

There was a fierceness beneath his gentle manner. A familiar fierceness. One she had felt at Aiden's hands. She turned back to wave. He was leaning against the frame of the door and smiling at her with his rakish eyes. Funny to see him in this setting, in her beloved's home. Somewhat like seeing a panther in the lair of a lion.

CHAPTER 57

*"Do not make the mistake of supposing that the little world you see
around you—the Earth, which is a mere grain of dust in the universe—is the universe itself. There are millions upon millions of such
worlds, and greater. And there are millions of millions of such uni-
verses in existence within the Infinite Mind of THE ALL"*
~ Three Initiates, The Kyballion

In the silence of the grotto, a glimmer of light began to form. Aiden
leapt to his feet. Was this them?

A lone figure materialized. Aiden greeted the woman he had noticed the night before while in ceremony. It was the maiden from the
dolphin tribe. He felt soothed just to have her sit by his side.

"What worries you, traveler?" she asked telepathically.

Aiden searched her eyes. They were clear pools of ocean blue. In
them, Aiden found the calm that was eluding him.

"For once, I do not know what to do." He felt there was no need
to explain anything. She knew.

"There is nothing to do. You are living your life, they are living
theirs. You have your journey, they must each find their own way."

"But are they safe? Will they return?"

"I cannot answer. You must have faith in the order of things."

"But I cannot return home without them!" Aiden cried out. "You
don't understand. I must return and so must they."

"Everything is evolving as it should. There is a wisdom to the
universe, a chaos which defies order and an order which defies chaos.
Anything that should be, is. And anything that should not, is not. You
must trust."

"Iona is pregnant. I must return her. And Sahara..." The pain in
his heart choked all thought. He stared into the dark pool of the grotto.

"You must come with me now. The time has come for you to join
the others. They are waiting for you, and the work must be done."

Aiden stared in disbelief. "That's tomorrow!"

"You must lead us today, traveler. Come!"

"Impossible!"

"Will you lead us? You accepted this role."

Aiden closed his eyes. Every cell in his body rebelled against the idea of leaving the grotto. Every sinew and every bone rebelled against the idea of not keeping his word to The Society. He had to choose. And this choice seemed impossible. He thought his brain would explode. How would he lead with purpose when worry consumed him?

But somehow, he found himself following the ethereal creature up the stairs and to the sanctuary. Somehow, he donned the cloak of the alchemist, and the responsibility of his position. Somehow, he oversaw the processes of transformation, transmutation and creation while the room hummed with sacred chants. Somehow, he called on each member and oversaw their contributions to the work. Somehow, he raised the energy of the room and cast a spell for the healing of the Mother energy and the rise of the Divine Feminine to her fullest intention.

In certain moments he thought he felt Iona beside him, lending her energy and wisdom. At times, he felt the cool hand of Sahara on his arm, encouraging him. Once he thought he heard their voices raised in song.

When the room stopped spinning, and all had been cast into the cauldron; when he had burned soul deep and shed his old mantle; when he had understood he had been alone in the room all along, mastering himself, he finally saw them.

He fell to his knees, surrendered. Finally, he understood that all a man could do to create a better world was to burn away his base nature and reveal the gold of his soul. He had to commit his whole being to this purpose, and realize his purpose was sacred. If he could commit to the sacredness, then he could offer his love to his beloved fully and without compromise.

Grateful for their presence and safety, Aiden returned to his work. The others appeared once more, filing into the room, each with a gift for the Great Mother. The ceremony to end the gathering could now begin.

———————✵———————

Sahara, my love,

I thought of all the different ways that I could present you with this gift, and all of them, in the end, seemed to focus on me rather than you.

And that is why you will find this token of my love to be opened in your own timing and within the energy of the solitude you so deeply crave.

I think it will be the perfect addition to your cabin home and the life you have carved for yourself in the wilds of Colorado.

With much devotion,

Your Aiden

Sahara untied the white satin ribbon and removed the lid from the gift box. She had no idea what Aiden had thought to give her but knowing his heart, he would have put a lot of thought into what would please her.

Her heart skipped a beat and she mouthed a silent *ooooh*.

In the box, an early and rare copy of Hildegard de Bingen's *Physica*.

She was breathless with excitement. The medieval nun's work as a mystic and healer had been some of Sahara's earliest immersions into herbalism. Her philosophy regarding the patterns of Four—the four elements; the four seasons; the four humors; the four zones of the Earth and the four major winds had long fascinated this modern witch's mind. She, like Hildegard, believed in the relationship between the microcosm of mankind and the macrocosm of the universe. To hold this work was to tap into the wisdom of centuries past and the incredible achievements of a medieval woman ahead of her time.

She held the book with reverence. It would indeed, be a sacred addition to her cabin's bookshelf. It must have cost Aiden a pretty penny. Gratitude washed over her; for her good fortune and the lover who knew her soul.

Thank you, darling Aiden! Thank you!

She closed her eyes, book clutched to her breast. A perfect ending to a week that would shift all their futures.

CHAPTER 58

*"You were an unexpected surprise, the defining moment. The colli-
sion of stars that slammed into me hard and sent my neat little
world plummeting into the ocean. I never expected it to be you, you
know? But it is you. It's all you. And now there's no looking back."*
~ Beau Taplin

He found her alone in the new lounge room of the café, sorting
books and placing them on the shelves surrounding the open fireplace. She was humming to the music piping in through the sound
system, a golden maiden lost to her thoughts. She didn't notice
him right away and he took those few moments to fall deeper in
love. He had missed her acutely. It never changed, this desire to
know her at her core, to love her and cherish her. He vowed he
would never get used to the rush of longing which overtook his
body when he saw her.

She looked up presently. A surprised gasp left her mouth. They
stood absorbing each other for a moment before Aiden met her in
three long strides. His hands cupped her face. His eyes said all he
wanted to say. He kissed her, a delicious, fervent greeting, hot mouth
on her lips.

Holly pressed her head to his chest. She listened to his heart.
"You were gone forever," she said.

Aiden's kisses followed the curve of her neck. Her body formed to
his. "Did you miss me?" she asked.

"Shall we get married, my love? I am done with waiting," he answered.

They had agreed to put it off until the time was right, until they
weren't so busy, but now, that seemed a ridiculous idea. The shine in
her eyes was the answer he had hoped for.

"I never really wanted to wait," she confessed.

"When, then?"

"In the spring. A hand-fasting. Sahara will marry us in her sacred
grove."

"Have you and Sahara already conspired about this?" Aiden
laughed.

"We have. And we have it all planned out. Just Richard and Iona to stand up for us, our parents, and the Fey."

"And after? Where shall we go?"

"Take me to France, Aiden. Take me to where Dagr once walked this Earth. I know my love for France is no coincidence. Will you take me?"

In the warmth of their embrace all words became unnecessary. Standing so silently, their love flowed as invisible energy between them. Eyes closed, Aiden's mouth pressed to Holly's hair, her hands wound tightly around his waist, they knew the abundance of a life well lived and a love unconditionally shared.

⁂

Sahara put her pen down and closed her journal. She stared into the fire. Her heart was at peace. Funny, how she had left the work of healing over the death of her parents until now. She had stuffed it into the deepest corner, and layered it upon the ancient wounds from centuries past. Loss had been her journey. First Brigida's babies, and then the two people who had given her life. She had given up on ever birthing her own children. But now, she felt her womb responding to the deep, magical work she had undertaken while with Aiden and Iona in France. She had called upon the Great Mother while in ceremony and cried the many tears which had lodged themselves into her sacred birthing space. She had released the torment of children lost and the ache of Dagr's disappearance. On their last afternoon together at the hotel, the three of them had cast powerful spells to cut the cords that had bound them all to misfortune, jealousy and death.

Their past lives would no longer carry anything forward but the fruits of the lessons they had learned. The bond between them all could never be broken; they were by choice, committed to each other's life paths.

Since she had come home, Sahara had been mainly reclusive, save for an erotic reunion with Holly. They had bonded in a way that could only have happened after their time apart. Sahara had shared everything which had been hers to share and left the rest to Aiden. Their urgency to bare all of their honest thoughts had spurred a deep discussion about Holly's role as the catalyst for their collective healing which ended with Holly's confessions of her most secret desires. And so, they had explored each other with renewed passion. Holly could no more be the outsider of the foursome's love than could they keep her from joining them. In all honesty and integrity of their soul's purpose, they recognized that to resist what existed between them was folly.

Iona was no longer the sorceress trapped in a web of jealousy and longing for a man she had once lost to the turbulent sea. Fully in her power, she was, as had been revealed, Aiden's twin flame. They all now understood the force between the two of them, and why they led The Society in the healing work of the Great Mother. While they partnered with others in this lifetime, their connection could never be extinguished.

Not lost on Sahara was the significance and symbolism of their fivesome. The universe operated through synchronicity at all times, never by coincidence. Five represented the Divine Feminine, Spirit plus the Four Elements, the five points of the pentagram, freedom, sensuality and visionary action. Holly had brought to their original dynamic, cohesion and the energy needed for manifestation of their purpose on Earth. No more perfect of an empathetic person could have been added to the fold.

She got up and stirred the fire. She thought of the man who would soon be joining her for an evening of conscious co-creation. Tonight, on a bed surrounded by a grid of crystals and other objects sacred to the two of them, they would make love and stir the cauldron which birthed souls into the physical world. They would call their child's name.

Aiden's footsteps on her porch broke her reverie and set her heart to racing. He was the one. The one man who could hold all her vastness. He understood her, inside and out, the child, the woman, the witch, the future crone. He was worthy of her surrender. He opened the door and stepped inside. He smiled, his same charming, seductive smile which had only a few months before, woken her from her centuries-old sleep.

She walked into his arms. He smelled of forest and magic. He was strong and tall, like the Vikings from which Dagr's father originated. He pulled all those centuries forth with the touch of his hands on her waist. Her body responded with a searing fire. She moaned her consent and surrendered to his kiss.

Wet, anticipating his tongue and mouth on her sacred places, she asked to be his. She wrapped her legs around his waist when he lifted her up to carry her up the stairs. Their breath warmed the space between them. Aiden's hands close to her swollen sex were an impossible torture. She squirmed to bring his fingers closer, but he was determined to have her wait.

"Mine," he said, a fierce look in his eye that told her all she needed to know about the night ahead.

"Yours," she agreed, and slipped into his hand a paper folded in
four.

"What's this, my love?"

"I promised you once I would tell you the name given to me by
my parents," Sahara answered, complete in her love for the man who
evoked her honesty.

EPILOGUE

"Everything before us or behind us is nothing compared to that
which is within us"
~ Sulamith Wulfing

The first glimpse of trouble was a ship's mast appearing on the horizon. It was by instinct Dagr knew to prepare for battle. He had never fought on water and could not know the ferocity of the attack about to follow.

As evening fell and the ship, bearing a flag depicting the colors of what he could only assume were raiding pirates, closed in on his. He had already assembled his crew and set his plan in motion. He thought of Brigida and Leilah. Adrenaline rushed through his veins. He would return to them! Killing was in his blood. He could do this one more time because he had to, because he had never run from battle. He was trained for survival.

The first men who boarded his vessel reminded him of the Moroccans he had met once when in Spain. These swarthy men, with eyes full of anticipated glory and riches, were the first of his victims. He hated the look that stole away their confidence.

They soon succumbed to regret and death. Surely the slaughter would end before long. Surely, they would stop climbing over the ropes and into their gruesome demise. But while he was busy with the horrors of killing; of shouting orders and reorganizing their defense; he did not notice the plume of smoke rising from the stern. And when he finally smelled it over the stench of blood, it was too late to do anything but face the frigid waters.

Shouting to the young boy who hung on for dear life to the main mast, he turned around only to be met by a man swinging a thick piece of timber to his forehead.

He heard the sickening thud, then darkness enclosed.

———————✳———————

"Open your eyes," a slurring accent reached deep into Dagr's subconscious.

He struggled to do so. He lifted a hand to his head. It pounded with an excruciating pain. His fingers smoothed over a wound crusted with blood.

"Do not get up!" the same voice admonished.

Dagr heard the slap-slap of water and his stomach churned from the motion of the boat. The dingy he was in reeked with the overwhelming stench of fish.

"Who are you?" he asked in English.

"Who are *you*?" came back the same question.

"Where am I?"

"What you remember?" came the question in broken English.

Dagr, irritated and thirsty beyond belief, sat up suddenly then fell back down as agony speared his head.

"Aha! You must not get up!"

Dagr groaned, "water."

Water was provided, then wrenched away. "Not too much"

The accent was unrecognizable. The man smelled of garlic and rotten teeth.

After a long silence, the man returned to his labored speech. Dagr made out that he had been found clinging to a piece of splintered timber. He fell back to sleep.

A cacophony of voices woke him just before he was hoisted roughly from the boat by several men. He did not know the language. The heat was oppressive. Someone swabbed his eyes with a wet cloth and hummed a soothing song while doing so. He thought it was a woman but was not sure. The hands were gentle.

He fought very hard to remember anything which could give him a clue as to where he was or why. He opened one eye, then the other. The sun was blindingly painful.

A woman sat by his side wrapped in a long, loose dress. It covered everything except her eyes. She offered him a plate of food. He noticed that her hands were smooth and brown. The aroma of the food reminded him of something vaguely familiar, but he could not grasp what. He picked a little using his fingers. Strong spices cleared his nostrils. After a few bites, the plate was taken away. The woman smiled encouragement with her eyes. She handed him a cup of hot mint tea then got up to leave.

"Wait!" he said, but she left without a word.

Fear was a bitter enemy. He lay staring at the ceiling of a hut built from stone. At least it was cooler in here. Soon, he was sure, when this wretched pain left him, he would remember something. Anything.

He searched to the very corners of his mind, but nothing appeared. He looked at his clothes, but they offered no clues.

He turned his eyes to the wall, as blank as his memory.

Sleep found him once more. When he woke, he recalled a dream and a twisting longing in his heart. What hope could be found in the face of a man with raven hair and a fierce, determined countenance? What could be made of his saying to a creature belonging in a fairy tale, "I'd give anything..."?

The End

ABOUT THE AUTHOR

photoworks by Sara Deyell

Wild Woman, Witch, Rebel, Monika lives for the moments where words meet spirit. A daughter of change, she is a seeker who lives on the magical shores of Vancouver Island, B.C. guiding kindred spirits on their sacred journey through life, sexuality and relationships.

You may find her at times in the company of the Fey, or soaking her feet in the salty sea, but most often you'll find her with stories spilling from her fingertips. This Scorpio loves nothing more than to wander the Underworld unraveling ancient mysteries, or casting spells under a full moon.

Born in Poland, Monika is inspired to challenge social norms. Close to her heart as a queer, poly woman, is her life's work, 'Re-Wilding the Soul Through Fearless Authenticity'.

Monika is published in print and on-line magazines on a variety of topics, including relationships, intimacy, spirituality, self-empowerment and the environment.

Contributing columnist @   www.elephantjournal.com
                                             www.urbanhowl.com

Blog, Tarot Readings and Coaching for The Wild Soul
@ monikacarless.com
Instagram: @monikacarless
FB: The Raven and The Mystic

Made in the USA
Middletown, DE
19 February 2019